CAMERON SCOTT PATTERSON

~

THE NEED TO KNOW

A Novel

The Need to Know
Copyright © 2021 Cam Patterson

The characters, places, incidents, and events in this book are a work of fiction. Any resemblance or similarities to actual persons, living or dead, or actual events is coincidental and not intended by the author.

All rights reserved. No part of this book may be reproduced in any form without permission in writing from the publisher, except by reviewers, who may quote brief passages in a review.

Published by SoGo Books, Inc.

Cover art design
by
Jennette Heinrichs & Ty Rogers

Library and Archives Canada Cataloguing in Publication

Patterson, Cam

The Need to Know – 1st edition

ISBN 978-1-7777942-0-0

To Mom & Dad
Because they loved me as their own
And to Elie
The reason I'm here at all

THE NEED TO KNOW

Prologue
thirty-seven years ago...

CHAPTER 1

The Killings

The black Lincoln Continental had been parked in front of the quaint house on First and Yew for the last fifteen minutes. The engine idling, front wheels turned into the curb. Bing Crosby's White Christmas played on the radio. The driver watched the silhouettes of a little boy and girl frolicking around a Christmas tree beyond the drawn front window. He gripped the wheel, squeezed his eyes. He could feel a blackness smothering all that was good and decent and honourable in him. But regardless of regret, there was no turning back now. He made his choice. He glanced at the rear-view mirror. The man in the backseat possessed the stillness of a seasoned killer, his face shadowed under an expensive fedora. The burly one beside him took a long pull of good Russian vodka. "Turn that shit off," he sneered at the driver.

The driver complied and Bing was gone. The silence was awkward and still. He had never killed before, not even in the line of duty, but what happened to Murphy Henderson only an hour ago out at Jericho Beach wasn't just killing, it was brutal murder. The driver was helpless to watch the burly one drag Murphy through the slush to the water, force him to his knees, hands tied behind his back, blood oozing from pistol-whipped gashes. Murphy shivered in the cold for ten minutes before the man in the backseat climbed out of the Lincoln. Alec Garva buttoned up his trench coat, adjusted that expensive fedora, and took a moment to admire the Vancouver skyline twinkling across English Bay. He waved for the driver sitting behind the wheel of the Lincoln to join them. The driver obeyed. He knew he had to follow through or he would feel the whip of the revolver for himself. Once among them, Garva finally looked at Murphy slumped at his feet.

"So, this is where you took your pictures," Garva said, sounding more disappointed than angry. "Isn't that right, Mr. Henderson."

Murphy held his head high in the Lincoln's searing headlight glare, eyes swollen, nose broken, coughing wafts of freezing air while he teetered on his knees, staring at the driver who was too ashamed to return his gaze.

A terse nod from Garva was all the burly one needed to snap a violent kick to Murphy's ribs that sent him tobogganing a good couple feet, the barrel of the .45 digging into a nasty gash. "I hate you fucking watchers," Jake Munroe hissed. "Where are the others?"

"Fuck you," Murphy mumbled only to get another round of pistol whips across the face. Munroe was a man who knew how to inflict pain but with a mere touch of Garva's hand on his shoulder, he stepped off without question; a disciplined soldier.

Garva looked down at Murphy crumpled in the slush. "Mr. Henderson, the time for bravery is over. Where are the pictures and the tapes from your wiretaps? Does this Larry Hicks have them? Perhaps MacMillan maybe?"

Murphy struggled back to his knees, managed a triumphant smirk.

Garva sighed. "Good bye, Mr. Henderson," he said with another nod to Munroe that could not be misinterpreted.

The driver couldn't watch Munroe force the .45 into Murphy's mouth, breaking teeth to get it done. Murphy gagged, his tongue pushing against the barrel, against dying, writhing and kicking in the slush. The gun fired. The driver flinched when the report bounced across English Bay, ricocheting off the tankers that chugged for the Juan de Fuca.

Munroe stepped off his victim, the adrenaline that goes with killing seen in his eyes and felt in his breathing. He held the hot barrel of his smoking .45 right up to the driver's face and smiled. "Where is this fucking house?"

The driver told them because he had too. He was one of them now.

Garva and Munroe climbed back into the Lincoln, leaving the driver standing in the cold December wind off Jericho beach, regretting the brutally murdered Murphy Henderson. He staggered a few paces from the mess of blood and slush, buckled to his knees and puked until nothing but bile soured his throat and stung his nostrils.

And so an hour later the driver glanced down at a crumpled list on the front seat of the Lincoln; a list with large black margins, and labeled "Operation Scarlet." There were only three names written on it; Larry Hicks, Roger McMillan, and Murphy Henderson; the latter crossed out. The paper was handed to him during a clandestine rendezvous with a corrupt cabinet minister somewhere along the Rideau Canal last week. It was snowing that night and the view of the Parliament Buildings in the distance would have stirred patriotic pride on any other night for the driver, but not that night. That was the moment he had crossed the line; the proverbial point of no return.

The driver looked through the frosted windows of the Lincoln at the quaint house on First and Yew, the silhouettes of the little boy and girl still frolicking around the Christmas tree beyond the drawn front window sickened him.

What's Christmas without murdering children?

Jake Munroe eyed the driver with a look that seemed to suggest he get his shit together. One command from Garva and Munroe obediently climbed out of the backseat and fetched a couple of rifles out of the trunk.

The driver knew the answer before he asked. "All of them?"

Alec Garva watched the children with no flicker of remorse in his seasoned face shadowed under the fedora. He looked up until his cold eyes found the driver in the rear-view mirror. A nod was all that was needed.

The driver gripped the wheel and braced himself for hell.

CHAPTER 2

The Tape

Roger McMillan's wife was trying to get the children to bed, unaware of the Lincoln parked out front of their rented house on First and Yew. They said good night to dad – getting more hugs than usual because after all it was Christmas Eve - then mom herded them upstairs. Roger, sitting at the roller top desk where he had spent the majority of his time over the past three months, returned to his J Section partner on the phone. The tape rolls on a mini reel-to-reel recorder were turning, still recording; a procedure the team practiced since starting the operation back in September in case the old political soft shoe left them in the cold.

Fucking politicians!

That was a common motto in the trade craft world they were now a part of since being recruited right out of the academy only six months ago.

"So," the partner on the other end said. "Is Murphy back yet?"

"No." Roger glanced at the new, shiny Timex on his wrist; the present the kids insisted he open since mom allowed one gift for each of them to open every Christmas Eve. Roger was concerned the third member of their elite unit hadn't checked in yet. "The ferry docked over an hour ago."

"Well, maybe the ferries are bit off schedule. It is Christmas Eve."

"Yeah, maybe."

Roger's wife leaned over the banister half way up the stairs, her voice bright and giddy. She was young and beautiful and Roger was still hopelessly in love with her from the moment he had met her back in college, only six short years ago. "Tell Evelyn I miss her already, Larry," she said.

Roger shook his head with that typical chuckle. "Women and babies," he said over the phone to Larry Hicks. "How's Evelyn doing anyway?"

"You know her," Larry replied. "She's always fine."

"Flight was okay?"

"Yeah. I forgot how cold it is here though."

"It's Winter-peg," Roger said with a quip.

"Yeah, yeah. Listen, we're heading out for a Christmas party. Ev's sister and husband insist we go."

"Good, supposed to be festive, remember. It's Christmas."

"I'm a bit concerned, Roger. It's not like Murphy to not report in."

"I'm sure he's –." Roger noticed the reel-to-reel still recording. "Oh damn, guess you're on record, Larry," he quipped. He almost flicked it off but the children were at the top of the stairs, begging for him to come tuck them in. "Must've forgot to turn it off after Phillip phoned," he said as he blew kisses they caught then giggled. The wife rolled her eyes as if he wasn't helping.

"Lehman can be trusted?" Larry asked.

"Yeah," Roger said, shooing the kids to get a move on. "I trust my brother-in-law and if he and my sister say Lehman is okay then he's okay." He reached for the reel-to-reel again. "By the way, Larry, we expect a call to let us know if it's a boy or girl the instant the baby is--." He heard something, eyed the front door.

What was that?

Roger glanced up at his wife. The worried look on her face told him she heard it. He eased out of his chair, his breathing slow and deep.

"Roger, what's going on?" Larry beckoned over the phone, anxiousness in his voice.

Mom quieted the kids. Roger was frozen on the door, listening.

"Roger?" Larry begged.

The doorknob turned slowly. Roger's eyes ripped wide. And before he could make it to his family up the stairs, the front door to the quaint little house on First and Yew exploded open and a hail of gunfire forever changed Larry Hicks's life.

And the reel to reel was recording.

CHAPTER 3

The Birth

It was cold as hell, colder than he remembered the winters in Winnipeg, and the view out of the hospital window was disheartening. A thick bed of fresh snow blanketed the gateway city that sprawled in an illuminated maze of streetlights and high-rises, the auroras dissolving high into the winter sky. But the numbing weather was inconsequential for Larry Hicks. He was too exhausted, too worried and preoccupied while his baby was being born just down the hall. The murders of Murphy Henderson and Roger McMillan were a week ago.

It was nearly midnight and the hospital was quiet. The waiting room, decorated with 'Happy New Year' streamers and balloons, felt more like a tomb. The nurse's chatter trickled up the hall over the constant din of pinging elevators and jostling medicine carts.

A young man who had earlier introduced himself as Roberts was sitting on the couch, dressed in a plaid sport coat and white slacks with shiny black wingtips; a little too over dressed Larry had thought. He was suspicious of any new faces. Roberts flipped through the morning edition of the Winnipeg Free Press, acknowledging Larry every now and then. Larry returned with a nervous grin. The waiting was hell.

"So," Roberts finally said. "Hoping for a girl or a boy?"

"Doesn't matter," Larry said, uncomfortable with any questions from a total stranger.

Who is he?

"My wife and I are hoping for a girl," Roberts proclaimed, flopping the paper back on the coffee table. "Or rather my wife is hoping. I wouldn't mind a boy," he quipped then followed Larry's empty gaze at the front page. "Damn shame," he remarked with a frown. "A real damn shame." Two photos of Roger and Murphy in red serge uniforms and signature hats dominated the front page.

Larry remembered the very moment those pictures were taken on their Graduation Day from the Royal Canadian Mounted Police Academy in Regina. The headline read;

SLAIN OFFICERS HONORED

"Yep. A damn shame," Roberts said.
"Officers..."
"Excuse me."
"They were RCMP officers." The elite of the Security Service's J-Section Larry wanted to say in Murphy and Roger's honour, but saying more could be tantamount to issuing death sentences for Evelyn, her sister and husband, and most importantly his child being born down the hall. They all had to stick to the plan; reticence was now paramount to survival. He needed to change the subject. "So you're hoping for a girl?" Larry asked.

"Well, if I had my way, a boy," Roberts said with a chuckle. "But if I want the wife happy, I'm okay with a girl. I mean, it's why we work as hard as we do, isn't it. For them, right? I mean, what's that saying; a happy wife is a happy life. Boy they sure got that right."

The guy named Roberts wouldn't shut up. Larry returned to the window. He'd have to be more focused if he was going to keep them alive; could not let anger and fear lower his guard.

Roberts sensed something wrong - not at all uncommon in a delivery room. "Your first one too, huh?" he said and joined Larry at the window.

He could be a watcher, Larry thought, glancing at Robert's plaid sport coat for any bulges that would suggest concealed guns. "Yeah, our first one."

Roberts put a friendly hand on Larry's shoulder; fathers-to-be waiting it out together while they looked out over the cold view. "City sure is growing," Roberts remarked like he had a hand in it. "Heck of a housing boom this year don't you think?"

"We're not from Winnipeg."
"Oh really, just moved here?"
"Yeah, you could say so."
"Well, if you're in the market for a house, give me a call." Roberts flashed a realtor card. "I'll give you a hell of a deal."

Larry smirked at the irony. Plaid coat, shiny wingtips, it all made sense now. The guy was not a killer but a harmless salesman with a child about to be born. Larry was suddenly envious of this gaudy dressed man who didn't have to do what he was about to do. A man who didn't have to put the woman he loved through an unimaginable nightmare. How was Evelyn ever going to forgive him? How would she ever be normal or happy again? And all because of his naive decision to sign on to an operation six months ago, straight out of the academy, because he wanted to be in the Security Service, he wanted to make a difference, he wanted to serve and protect his country. But they all betrayed him, sought him out as a criminal now. The only person he could trust was an FBI agent in San Diego, someone he didn't initially trust when he, Murphy and Roger joined Operation Scarlet. Hindsight now was screaming that he was in over his head from the moment he signed on with J Section and raised his hand and pledged the oath. And for what? To be condemned a mole and traitor by the force he dreamed of serving his whole life, and hunted by the very criminals he pledged to defeat. Now he was stripped of any honour, living like a fugitive and forced to run and hide and surrender his baby.

Fucking politicians!

A nurse entered the waiting room, her loafers biting the sanitized tile just in time to cut off Robert's sales pitch.

"Mr. Roberts?" she said perfunctorily.

"Yes." Roberts said, grin widening.

"Congratulations, you have a healthy baby girl." Roberts kissed the nurse full on the lips. She was one of those older, married a long time ago ones and was definitely miffed. "Mr. Roberts!" she huffed and turned her red face for the door.

Larry forced a smile but it wasn't easy. There would be no celebration for Evelyn and him; just pain and regret and anger.

"I'll be damned!" Roberts snatched Larry's hand, shaking exuberantly. "I don't even know your name," he said as he reached in his breast pocket and pulled out an It's a Girl! cigar. "You wanna believe that, I'm a salesman and I forgot to ask you your name. Can you believe it!"

"Your wife must be waiting," Larry diverted, reluctantly taking the cigar.

"Holly shit my wife!" Robert's said like he just remembered she was all a part of the joyous occasion. He grabbed a fistful of It's a boy! cigars from his other pocket and pushed them into Larry's hand. "I won't need these," he sang with a wink and a smile and a slap to Larry's shoulder. "Maybe you will," he said then scurried for the doorway, stopping to say, "Remember to call me about that house."

The moment was killing Larry. Robert's elated voice trailed off and he slipped the cigars in his pocket and slumped to the couch. He stared at that front page. Murphy and Roger's pictures stared back at him – his guilt digging deep. He thought of Murphy drifting in the tide with his face shot off. The last call with Roger replayed over and over, always ending with the kids dancing around the Christmas tree - the very tree he and Murphy helped Roger set up the week before - their innocent giggles haunting him. Then the gunfire jolted him as if the memory was so vivid the killings had just happened right in front of him in the waiting room; the screaming over the phone, the popping gunfire, and Roger's wife and her gut-wrenching screams. Larry could see her crawling across the bloodied floor to their murdered little bodies while Christmas music played from the record player. A couple more pops silenced her. It was a nightmare that wouldn't go away, that wouldn't stop playing. Larry knew it would never go away.

~

A pretty brunette stepped into the quiet waiting room. Larry rose off the couch and hugged his sister-in-law. Maggie Gunthier hugged back. "Any time now," she said.

Larry wanted to ask about Evelyn but knew Maggie couldn't bring about an answer. He visibly saw the change in her over the last week; a bright and happy woman reduced to despair. But she had to stick to the plan regardless and that meant he had to say what really needed to be said. "You understand what's going to happen now, right Maggie?"

She wiped her wet eyes. "She's my sister, Larry."

He ached for her. "I know. I'm sorry."

"This can't be the only way. We could all go, we could all leave and I'll quit my job and we'll all go!" Larry held her shoulders firm and she knew no amount of begging was going to change their fate now. She tipped into his shoulder, crying into her hands.

Larry eased her onto the couch and returned to the window, to that dismal scene. "You've made the arrangements?" he asked, a quiver squeaking through his voice.

Maggie forced a nod, dug in her handbag for a tissue. "Damn them to hell!" she cursed.

~

A doctor with a face mask dangling around his neck shuffled into the waiting room and sat beside Maggie. He kissed her, their hands groping together. Larry watched from the window, twisting one of those cigars Roberts had given him earlier between his fingers. It took everything for Dr. Carl Friesen to simply say, "It's a boy."

Larry returned to the cold window, the tragedy of it all crushing the cigar in his fist. The tears welled up in his blue eyes and trickled down his cheeks. He had a son.

Damn them to hell!

CHAPTER 4

The Lie

A half hour later a city ambulance sped over the Norwood Bridge, gaping the frozen Red River, then under the Canadian National Railroad overpass and onto Main Street. Carl and Maggie followed in a new '81 candy apple red Corvette convertible, both wrapped in heavy winter coats and thick scarves because the Vette was designed for sun-drenched California and not the sub-zero climate north of the 49th parallel. The heater barely thawed the iced-up windshield, never mind actually spewing heat. But Maggie could care less. Her eyes were swollen and red and she couldn't say a word.

Carl turned onto Broadway. The headlights glistened off the ambulance ahead. There were no sirens or flashing lights. "Are you going to be okay, honey?" he asked between glancing and driving.

Maggie was utterly numb now. Christmas had come and gone virtually uncelebrated and now fate dictated that she would never see Evelyn again. For sisters as close as they had been growing up, this was insufferable. Their parents had died years before and it had been the two of them against the world until Evelyn met Larry and Maggie, in turn, fell in love with Carl. But now she would never be able to spoil the nephew that she had dreamed about countless times since Evelyn first called with news that she was pregnant. Maggie and Evelyn had cried endlessly in these last few days before her water broke and the time had come to follow through with the unthinkable.

Carl was worried about her, keeping the Vette on the road with one hand, and holding Maggie's clenched hands with the other. Minutes later the Corvette came to an abrupt stop while the ambulance proceeded for the Grace Hospital emergency carport. The brake lights flashed in the distance and a paramedic jumped out of the rear door into the cold, running through the exhaust cloud swirling under carport lights with a wrapped bundle in his arms.

"It's not fair, Carl!" Maggie spat, her eyes wet with one more defiant outburst.

Carl kissed her cheek then leaned across her lap and unlatched her door. "I know."

Fucking Politicians!!

~

A plump and perky admitting nurse was half way through a quiet nightshift when Carl led Maggie through the front doors of the Grace Hospital. The nurse recognized them right off. "Good evening, Dr. Friesen. Hello Maggie."

Maggie simply nodded. It was the best she could.

"Happy New Year, Elma," Carl said, better at feigning all was normal.

"Same to you, doctor. And where is the infant?" Elma inquired, curious as to Maggie's state.

"Paramedics took the child straight up to pediatrics," he said and kissed Maggie then continued on for the elevators. "Apgar was a ten, Elma, and he's stabilized."

There was nothing unusual about that so Elma reached for the shelf of copious forms behind her. "Are you going to admit the child under Children's Aid or the mother's name, Maggie?" She fed the form into the typewriter.

Maggie couldn't respond. She watched Carl step into the elevator. It was bitter irony knowing the instant the doors closed she would never see her sister's child again, would never see Evelyn again. She rubbed her wet eyes.

"Maggie, are you alright?" Elma asked.

"Yes, of course," Maggie said as professionally as she could muster. "The child is a ward of CAS, Elma."

Elma started typing. "St. James division, right?"

"Yeah, that's right."

"Lily Atkinson is your supervisor, right?"

"Yes."

"And the mother of the child?" There was no answer. Maggie was struggling. "I need her name, Maggie."

"Hanis," Maggie lied. Her jaw clenched, reconciling her promise to stick to Larry's plan. Fuck him. "Susan Hanis." Elma typed the name then waited. Maggie bit her lip. There was no turning back now.

"Deceased," she finally said.

CHAPTER 5

The Loose End

It was particularly sunny on that February morning when Canada's youngest ever Minister of Justice stood naked at his patio window, staring beyond the 12th floor balcony of his upscale apartment at the Parliament Buildings three blocks away, the Peace Tower erect and proud. Usually the view offered a good dose of patriotism but on this record cold morning it was all but lost on Francis Lavelle.

He had come a long way from that pudgy kid from Penticton, British Columbia to an honorable Member of Parliament in Pierre Trudeau's caucus. It had been a great ride since Trudeaumania hit its stride in '68 and the writing was on the wall. Lavelle knew deep in his bones that Trudeau could take them all the way to Ottawa, could unseat the Conservative strong hold in the House of Commons and that was of particular importance to Francis Lavelle; he had suffered long enough from the narrow minded, prejudice of a conservative minded Canada.

Nonetheless, he was driven as a result, graduating from UBC with degrees in both political sciences and economics. But something truly amazing happened to young Francis during those hedonistic days so common to university; he came out of the proverbial closet and for the first time in his life experienced acceptance and not ridicule for his sexuality. By the time he was tossing his graduation cap in the air he had newfound confidence, determination and success he never dreamed. He truly believed he could make a difference in the political arena by the time Trudeau was firing up the nation during that '68 federal election. Lavelle's ticket to ride all the way to the Hill had presented itself and the young candidate was not going to sit on the sidelines. He cast his bid to run and surprising everyone - most of all his bully father and complacent mother he left in Penticton - and won the Okanagan-Coquihalla riding. Lavelle rode the victory all the way to his plush apartment in Ottawa, blocks from the

Rideau Canal.

What he didn't see coming was his cabinet appointment on the heels of Bill C-84, abolishing the death penalty forever. Whatever it was that Trudeau saw in the young politician, Lavelle could never have predicted he would be appointed the Minister of Justice shortly after. That was the moment Francis Lavelle knew he was going to change policy and tolerance so young boys like him would never have to hide in closets ever again.

It was all going to be an amazing political ride but that all changed for Lavelle. It would be a warm September night when he would become the target of Mario Morelatto, the west coast tycoon with questionable ties to the Montreal mob. Morelatto was feeling the pressure from Ottawa and the Mounties who suspected his Northern Scarlet ships sailing between Vancouver and Cuba, were loaded with drugs and guns and immigrants.

Morelatto's top enforcer, Alec Garva, knew Lavelle had a weakness for the rugged Greek Adonis types who forced his willing mouth to their groins underneath the Pretoria Bridge along the Rideau Canal. It was all on 16mm film. The Justice Minister found himself back in that closet, prepared to do anything to save his privileged life.

And now he stood naked in his apartment, facing his political demise. He knew by the end of the day the headlines would hit the streets, and his beloved Canada was going to know exactly what he was, and what he had done. That Canada's Justice Minister had the blood of those murdered children in that quaint house on First and Yew all over his hands.

But fate had a different plan that cold morning in February.

He picked out his finest suit, polished his shoes, and groomed for a legal affairs committee hearing that was going to feel more like a public stoning. Twenty minutes later he was easing his new Cadillac off Wellington on to Kent Street, past the Justice Building to Vittoria Street. The titular Supreme Court of Canada building was directly across the street; an omen to the judgment coming.

A horn honked behind him. It looked like a government car so common to the parliamentary district this time of day. He released the brake and the Cadillac proceeded along the lane until a free spot presented itself in the parking circle behind the Justice Building, properly overlooking the Ottawa River.

He sat there a moment, staring at the Peace Tower looming in the distance. It filled him with guilt. He turned off the keys, the engine ticking under the massive hood, building his courage to even get out of the car. He grabbed the door latch, eyes squeezed tight, because he knew this was his moment of reckoning. But because his eyes were closed in that instant, and it was eight in the morning on such a cold February morning, not he or anyone else would see the killer approach the Cadillac with a Browning 9mm complete with silencer. The assassin fired two quick shots through the driver's side window and continued on for the government sedan idling two parking stalls over. A driver was behind the wheel. The sedan eased off the parking circle with no urgency.

Lavelle laid splayed out on the front seat of his Cadillac, eyes wide and dead, blood staining the fine white leather upholstery. It would be an hour before some young woman would happen by and notice the shattered driver's window. By the end of the day the killing would be front page news across Canada, and that was the moment that Operation Scarlet would be out of the bag, and the Mounties would find out their precious Security Service had been hunting for their missing agent now labeled the mole responsible for the murders of Roger McMillan and Murphy Henderson. The name Larry Hicks would shudder the corridors of power for years to come.

CHAPTER 6

The Adoption

Maggie Gunthier sat behind her desk in her dingy grey office on the second floor of the turn of the century government services building on Portage Avenue, more terrified than she had been in the past three months since Christmas. The front page of the Winnipeg Free Press shook her to the core and she couldn't look away from the photo of the murdered justice minister, Francis Lavelle, shot to death in broad daylight, in his fancy new Cadillac in Ottawa. She knew about Operation Scarlet. She knew more than she wanted too. But for the first time since Larry whisked Evelyn out of her life, she now believed he was absolutely right; they would come.

She opened the Children's Aid file before her and forced herself to double check the pertinent, albeit false, information. The baby of the deceased Susan Hanis weighed in at six pounds, two ounces, blue eyes, the apgar was a healthy ten, but a complication had arisen over the past month. The foster parents reported the kid was puking milk with enough intensity to hit the wall. Pyloric Stenosis, Carl diagnosed. One of the few truths contained in the file. Nonetheless the surgery went well, performed of course by Carl. He said he was a cute little tyke. Maggie didn't want to hear it. She would not let herself cry anymore.

Satisfied the lie read true she closed the file and braced herself for the final step. She hated herself for what she had to do. At this point she pretty much hated everybody and everything; even Carl if it suited her but definitely Larry most of all. A bottle was stashed in her lower drawer. She had a couple quick pulls before she heard her name.

"Maggie Gunthier?"

A thirty something woman stood in the doorway. She was a pretty blonde and Maggie figured her to be an ex-cheer leader – didn't like her right off. She had an overcoat draped over her arm and a brief case in her other hand.

"Julie Grossman?" Maggie asked with her hand extended over her desk. Julie Grossman was another Children's Aid worker from the North Winnipeg division.

Damn her!

Grossman set her brief case down. "Am I late? The traffic was terrible. I think there was a stalled car at every light."

"No not at all." Maggie hung Grossman's coat on the rack just inside the door.

Grossman sat down. "I hate this time of year," she said.

"Don't we all," Maggie said thinking whatever.

"I don't even know what the wind chill is. My car barely even started."

"I know what you mean." Maggie assumed her desk. "My fiancé's car barely started this morning. Not much of a winter car I'm afraid."

"Sports car, right?" Grossman guessed, nuzzling herself in close to the desk. "My husband has one too. He just drives it with the darn radio blaring and those big tires on the back." She pulled a file out of her brief case. "I think it's some kind of arrested adolescence. You know, men and their toys thing."

Grossman laughed and Maggie tried her best at faking. She got right down to business. She just wanted to get this over and done with and get this cheerleader wannabe out of her office and out of her life so she could go on hating everyone. God she hated Larry.

"Well, Mrs. Grossman, I understand you have a couple for our little infant," Maggie said and opened her file. Grossman followed and forty minutes later was placing her signature on a guardianship transfer, thus changing onus of responsibility for baby Hanis to her North Winnipeg office. The two women said good-bye and Maggie watched Julie Grossman leave through the bustling Children's Aid Society office. An office that had no inkling of the subterfuge that had just transpired right under their noses. Maggie had never felt as alone as she did at that moment sitting in her dingy grey office. She hoped the Spencers' would be loving parents.

Office supervisor Lily Atkinson stuck her head in Maggie's door. "How did it go?" She asked. Lily was one of the few bright spots to working in the CAS office now, always fashionable, hair just so, and an infectious smile. Maggie hadn't smiled since the office Christmas party, punch drunk and introducing her pregnant sister with the chant, "I'm going to be an auntie!" There wasn't a lot of acting involved when Maggie said she was hurt and angry over the past few months; she was. Lily Atkinson was keeping a close eye on her of late.

"Fine," Maggie said. Lying was getting easier.

"Good," Lily said. "Archie and I want you and Carl to come for dinner tonight. What do you say? Like a double date."

"That would be nice," Maggie said with a forced smile. She was numb again. Acting normal was key to keeping Evelyn alive and Lily's little questions at bay.

"Okay. About seven," Lily said, flashed that undeniable smile and dissolved back into the hectic environment she commanded so effortlessly.

Maggie slipped open the bottom drawer of her desk and retrieved another file similar to the one that Grossman had just taken. She opened the real file on Larry and Evelyn, covertly removing a slip of paper with a phone number and the name "Sam Mitchell" scribbled below. She knew the number was in San Diego. The paper found its way into her purse.

She made it unnoticed to the boiler room in the basement, approached one of the four large boilers that heated the turn of the century building. She opened the steel furnace door and stepped back from the oil stoked fire blazing within the boilers belly. It mesmerized her and for a brief moment she considered not doing it because this was it, the last task expected of her to complete the lie and keep Evelyn out of her life forever. The warmth washed over her but she felt cold, betrayed and angry. She tossed the file inside and watched it boil and bend to black as the fire swallowed it up.

It was done.

Part One
thirty-seven years later...

CHAPTER 7

The Adoptee

Michael Spencer was more preoccupied than usual the past two weeks. Even his evening jog down the paved footpath that hugged the Red River couldn't keep his thoughts focused. Usually it did. Michael was an avid runner, ever since the glory days of his track and field championship victories right up to the daily jog along Churchill Drive. His wife, Jasmine, preferred the evening shift at the hospital, and Katie was anything but a little girl anymore, so 6:00 pm was go time for Michael. It was his time. He sorted out the little hardships the rest of the free world called life while he jogged along the banks of their quaint wooded neighborhood. These past two weeks were anything but typical in the life of Michael Spencer, so he jogged more.

He waved to the occasional neighbor enjoying the evening from their front porch. Everyone along the jogging route knew Michael Spencer. His column in the Winnipeg Free Press turned him into something of a celebrity over the last four years. But his popularity of late had dropped; a point his editor John Lund took every opportunity to tell him. But Michael couldn't help it. He had his opinion on the current Prime Minister aiming for his second term, and his biting satire wasn't exactly winning popularity contests with the country caught up in a fairly divisive election campaign.

But falling out of favour was nothing new for Michael. Over the years he'd even had the odd fist shook from a disgruntled neighbor who didn't like what they read in the evening edition. One lady even threw her shoe at him as he ran past once, but that was the worst of it. For Michael, impassioned reaction was always confirmation they were reading. Everyone is not going to agree with you, but they are going to get the truth, and that is what people should expect from their newspapers; the motto his University of Manitoba English professor hammered into him.

He married Jasmine in their second year at U of M; she was on her way to a career in nursing. They fell in love and, shortly after, she got a nursing job at the Victoria Hospital so he could finish his degree and support them with a Free Press salary. He was going to need it. Jasmine dragged him through a plethora of viewings and open houses until they finally walked into the Churchill Drive bungalow they would call home. Jasmine had her palace with to-die-for kitchen island, gleaming hardwood floors, bay windows and walk-in closets. Michael got the home he had always wanted on the river, and enough garage that he could buy that speed boat of his dreams; he did. He carried his bride across the threshold then carried Katie through the same door a year later. He was twenty-six that year.

Now nearing his fortieth birthday this coming New Years Eve, and despite a headstrong daughter racing for sixteen, and a Great Dane the size of a horse that he could have done without, Michael Spencer was leading a pretty good life. If his mom had not died unexpectedly last fall from a rare form of Leukemia that took her within two months of the diagnosis, one could say his life was perfect. His dad moved to Oahu six months after the funeral; the retirement his parents had always dreamed. Michael and his dad have a catch up call every Friday evening; the last one to tell him he went ahead with the adoption search after all. Dad knew it was the right thing to do. Besides it was Mom's dying wish that her son find his birth mother; she even wrote a letter to her. So Michael did what his mother asked. And now he was waiting for Jessica Ingham's call to tell him she had found the mysterious woman who had given him up. He didn't want to admit it but the reasons as to why mattered; he had a good childhood and just couldn't understand why the possibility of a birth mother's rejection would even cross his mind. Nonetheless, the waiting had a lot to do with his need to run more than usual.

So he jogged the last leg for home, kicking the pace up a notch. The Federal election campaign had finally made it to Winnipeg and Michael only had an hour before the press conference. It would be his first time coming face to face with Prime Minister Petersen. And considering that Michael had been focusing his column on the Coastal Holding scandal that had been plaguing the campaign, this conference in particular could be the highlight of Michael's career or the end of it. He knew Petersen's press secretary, Allison McKay, from their days together at U of M, so she had promised to get Michael a front row seat.

It was going to be an interesting twenty minutes.

CHAPTER 8

The Prime Minister

    The limousine broke through an intersection under repair and sped like a freed animal for an open lane. An Oscar Peterson tune soothed Prime Minister Seth Peterson while he admired his press secretary, Allison McKay, as she dozed beside him; a pastime he secretly indulged from time to time. She wore below the knee dresses and over sized frame glasses with her auburn hair spun tightly into a ball; her moderate fashion was a pointless endeavor as far as he was concerned. Allison McKay was one of those women with an allure that cannot be camouflaged by overt professionalism. The Prime Minister knew there was no chance of ever sleeping with her. But what the hell, he rationalized, it had been a long shitty week so far, and her wisp of exposed cleavage pleased him. That only led to craving a cigarette something awful, bad enough he figured it was worth the risk sneaking one. Why not. He was down in the polls and the Conservatives were setting their campaign hounds on him so what harm was smoking going to do to his image now.
    Fucking Graham!
    He had a stash of smokes in his personal attaché, but before he could reach for it Allison stirred from an overzealous speed bump as the limousine descended into the underground parking lot of the Westin Hotel. She adjusted her glasses on her perfect little nose. "Sorry," she said.
    The Prime Minister quipped like he hadn't noticed, knowing full well the guilt she would inflict upon herself. "You've earned a cat nap, Allison," he said.
    And she had. They arrived in Winnipeg four days ago amid a media blitz and Allison was up before dawn, planning a ridiculous itinerary while simultaneously directing PR operations back in the Prime Minister's Ottawa Office, otherwise referred to as the PMO, via her iPad. She was your typical type 'A' and placed trust in no one, especially when a fall

election loomed.

Premier Roy Graham's mess in British Columbia wasn't helping either – hence the shitty week. It was supposed to be spun as a simple conflict of interest scandal over a misappropriated slot of land in the Jervis Inlet near Stillwater, BC. Graham's Coastal Holding firm was caught red-handed trying to purchase an old government fishery site before the actual sale went public. They were acting on behalf of Westfor International, a lumber conglomerate that unfortunately the Prime Minister held a boardroom chair in and a sizable share of the stocks climbing the TSX, NASDAQ and NYSE. He had underestimated the opposition capitalizing on that little tidbit.

To make Allison's job even harder, rumor mills were churning up more and more romps of licentious behavior; the political death knell. Allison had her hands full and she was fighting to save her career just as much as she was to keep her Prime Minister out of any more scandals. She didn't like it when he sneaked cigarettes in the limousine either. She eyed him as if she knew exactly what was going on in his head; it was the way his fingers twitched when the cravings hit.

"You should hide them better," she said, adjusting herself for a public appearance as a squad of RCMP rushed strategically to their points around the limo. Prime Minister Seth Peterson sighed and climbed out. The force huddled him straight into the elevator.

Allison's iPhone buzzed. She quickly glanced the text message while keeping up with the entourage. She suddenly dropped back; something about the text was concerning. She replied then hustled for the elevator, the Prime Minister's bodyguards holding the doors for her. Allison McKay didn't have a good feeling about this press conference. Her intuition was going to fall short. It was going to be disastrous.

CHAPTER 9

The Beginning of the End

The double doors to the right of the podium flung open and two RCMP sentries rigidly assumed a stance on either side of the main banquet room entrance. An instant later the Prime Minister entered, flanked by six security officers and Allison McKay, who found a good center spot giving her a direct eye line with the podium among the crowd of hungry media. The casual din was suddenly serious as countless reporters clamored forward, ENG cameras hoisted to shoulders and diffused light bleached the room white. Flashbulbs popped from all corners, microphones and iPhones pointing.

The Prime Minister usually loved the media, but the constant probing into the Graham scandal was wearing on his nerves. He opened with his trademark sense of humor. "Well, ladies and gentlemen, I would like to apologize for my tardiness. I know it's a tad warm to wait in here. You might be amused to know the caucus fell a little behind today. All those educated people in one room and no one knew how to turn on the air conditioning." The assembly conjured a tolerated laugh. He checked Allison among them. She was smiling, as usual at his misguided sense of humor and hubris. The faces of the RCMP remained in disciplined stone, their eyes combing the crowd.

"I'm sure that after four days of meetings you all have your share of questions. I will try to do my best to answer most of them. However, I would just like to add at this moment that I am very pleased with the outcome of the conference, and feel we have made headway with some of the issues facing our Federal/Provincial assembly." He checked Allison. Five fingers flashed twice. "We have only ten or so minutes to field your questions, so we may as well get started."

A barrage of raised hands begged for selection. He pointed out a vivacious reporter whom he knew to be Tabitha Reynolds, BCTV. She was one of his favorites.

"Good morning, Tabitha," he said.

"Morning, Mr. Prime Minister. Can you tell us what the general atmosphere of the conference is in the wake of several of your ministers suddenly resigning over some questionable party politics?"

He smiled. He always wanted her. But the question pissed him off. "Well, Tabitha, no one seemed to bring the subject up. The Premiers seemed more concerned with Medicare and other federal subsidies." He quickly pointed to another reporter.

A gruff looking guy rose above the crowd. "Ralph Forbes from the Sun, Mr. Prime Minister. I was curious if you had anything to add on the softwood trade problem. Since Premier Graham isn't attending this conference from BC we're wondering if any headway is being gained to deal with the US tariffs?"

The Prime Minister eyed the reporter. He looked like he just rolled out of bed with his suit on and couldn't find his razor in the bathroom cabinet; clearly not a distinguished member of the press. "Well the issue is more federal and hasn't been discussed." He searched a hand more deserving.

Forbes was about to push another question when a rival reporter in the first row cut him off.

"Michael Spencer, Mr. Prime Minister, Winnipeg Free Press."

The name seemed familiar to the Prime Minister, and the confident smile all but disappeared. For reasons he would never understand at that moment behind the podium, the name Spencer made him nervous. And there was something about the face, the blue eyes; it was something disturbingly unfamiliar to feel from a complete stranger. The Prime Minister could never have foreseen what was coming. "Good morning," he said; the greeting was more to disarm then an actual courtesy.

Michael Spencer was an old school reporter with pad and pencil, something out of the ordinary these days. He zeroed in on the Prime Minister. "It's obvious the softwood issue has kept the Coastal Holding situation front and center, but you've yet to comment on Premier Graham's acquisition attempt, Mr. Prime Minster."

The Prime Minister held his composure. He could easily read Allison's nervousness from the middle of the room. Regardless, he forced that politician's smile from ear to ear. What is it about this guy? "Premier Graham is not in attendance, Mr. Spencer. I think that says enough, doesn't it?"

"Yes sir," Michael said. "Was it suggested he not attend?"

The press noticed the Prime Minster tense up. "Excuse me?"

"Were you aware of the purchase, Mr. Prime Minister?"

"I've already addressed this."

"Actually you've danced around it," Michael countered. Allison was uncomfortable now, edging her way to the podium.

"The Coastal Holding affair is completely a BC provincial matter, Mr. Spencer," the Prime Minister deflected.

"Is it?"

"Yes, it is."

"Was SeaCorp involved in the bid as well?"

"SeaCorp?" the Prime Minister said – he didn't trust this Spencer guy at all.

"They are the parent corporation over Westfor, the company that made you a millionaire."

The room was dead silent. The Prime Minister felt his back tighten. The sweat tickling under his collar was throwing him off his game. "Well SeaCorp is in the business of transporting lumber. Why wouldn't they be involved," he said with his hands raised, suggesting 'why even ask the question you moron.' He could see Allison inching closer out of the corner of his eye.

Spencer eyed him the way reporters do when they smell blood. "The Canadian Securities Commission is suspicious enough to bring a case against SeaCorp CEO Mario Morelatto not to mention the RCMP investigating him on criminal charges, all in the wake of Coastal Holding's impropriety__."

"Supposed impropriety."

"Mr. Prime Minister, with all this and your position on the board of Westfor International, and your business dealings with Mario Morelatto, don't you think that just a little suspect?"

"Excuse me." It was the way Michael Spencer looked at him, like he was about to go for the jugular; the final lunge for the kill. "I think you're reaching Mr. Spencer."

"I don't think so. You orchestrated the sale for Morelatto and turned Premier Graham into the patsy, didn't you?"

"What!"

The RCMP guards focused on the reporter from the Free Press now. Allison McKay hurried for the podium to save her Prime Minister while the congregation erupted and flashes began popping again. The microphones pushed closer. They all smelled the blood now.

Michael Spencer persisted. "Premier Graham just as much as insinuated last week that Westfor, which you are a major shareholder, initiated the move to bid on the Jervis Inlet property at the behest of SeaCorp; in other words under orders from Mario Morelatto - a known Vancouver mobster and your biggest campaign financier."

The Prime Minister eyed Spencer as a cameraman zoomed to get both of them in frame. It was not personal, he reminded himself. This insignificant shit knows nothing. He flashed a disarming smile. "Well, I am not aware of Mr. Graham's disclosures Mr. Spencer, but these questions are not very relevant to the issues of today's conference."

Another reporter from the back rows chimed in over the din of hungry media. "Did that include discussion of the $450,000 of tax money spent on 24 Sussex Drive since your occupation of office three years ago?"

Allison was nearly to the front row, entering the cameraman's frame. Flash bulbs were popping like radical strobe lights as she reached her man in Ottawa. She went to ease him away from the mic, but the Prime Minister held firm, his hand raised. A moment later the din settled. The Prime Minister gripped the podium, eyed the reporter from the Free Press. This insignificant shit knows nothing, he reminded himself. And that thought alone brought the smirk back and awakened the fighter in him.

"Mr. Spencer," the Prime Minister said evenly. "Do you honestly think I'm that stupid? Do you think I'd throw away my career, my distinguished office, this country's respect, for such malfeasance? Or do you think I'm just a stockholder, who - I might add - relinquished my voting seat on the board once I was elected, and was simply not told until after the events transpired. I assure you I'm a little smarter than that."

Amused chortles sprang up through the room. Spencer noticed the camera lens rotating for a close up of him. And then Allison's hard glare that screamed 'Fuck you, Michael'. "That's all the time we have, ladies and gentlemen," she said into the mic. "Thank you."

The Prime Minister was well aware of the cameras fixed on him. With a final wave he and Allison stepped into the huddled bodyguards and were gone. The popping cameras and television lights dowsed. Television crews scurried out to edit their copy for the six o'clock broadcasts. Cell phones were already speed dialing producers.

Michael just stood there and sighed. He spotted Ralph Forbes stern gaze from across the room.

CHAPTER 10

Micheal Spencer's Mentor

The media scrum emptied out of the hotel banquet room. In the midst of the exodus many were glancing at Michael. He caught Tabitha Reynolds's grin from the other side of the room; he hadn't seen her in years. She waved then headed for the doors. Michael joined the flow out of the banquet room. The instant he made in the lobby a hand grabbed him into a corner. "Something on your mind, Ralph?"

Ralph Forbes was 55 but showed the hard facial lines of a 65-year-old. His tie undone with the top button unlatched; little about him was professional to the eye. And yet, lackluster appearance notwithstanding, the irony of the man was he had the reputation for being a hard-nosed reporter, but somewhere along the way the gritty world he reported became more obsession than career. Any semblance of a normal life - wife and kids and white picket fences – had all but faded away. "What was that bullshit in there?" he scoffed with a squeeze of Michael's arm.

Michael pulled his elbow free. "It's called reporting, Ralph."

Forbes leaned in. "You got an angle on the Coastal Holding deal. Who's your source, Michael?"

Michael smiled that off. "Are you deluded?"

Again with the elbow. "Cut the song and dance crap. They're gonna stamp the Official Secrets Act all over your head after that little show in there, Michael. Wouldn't be the first time I've had to help your ass out of a shit hole would it?"

Michael sighed. "What do you want, Ralph?"

Forbes led him down the hall, further away from the crowded foyer. Once they were safely out of earshot he said, "You can't dig up this story by yourself."

Michael smirked. "We're not on the same team anymore, Ralph."

And there was the irony. Forbes was fired from the Free Press when he did a story on a court judge caught in a homosexual tryst involving minors. He fed the story without confirmation from his sources and refused to name the RCMP officer who gave him the story. The paper had to let Forbes go or face the Justice Minister's office. Forbes was a bitter man. But a collaborative story on the Coastal Holding scandal involving the Prime Minister could put his reputation back in place. The Sun didn't pay as well and he was up to his armpits with alimony payments to his ex-wife who left him when his career went south.

"You're gonna need my help," Forbes said, "and you know it."

Michael eased back. He had more respect for his mentor than he ever let on and a lot of Michael's reluctance came from Forbes drinking more than anything else. The same went for his editor, John Lund, who was far less forgiving of Forbes smearing the Free Press than Michael. "Lund would eat me alive if I shared a by-line with you. You know that."

Forbes could only throw off his hands and turn for the crowded foyer. "You know where to find me if this thing is too big."

"Smileys is not my style, Ralph."

"Neither is being a buffoon on the six o'clock news," Forbes said then strolled out of the hotel lobby.

Chapter 11

The Free Press

"Are you out of your mind!" John Lund, the executive editor of the Winnipeg Free Press, was a round, stumpy man with a big bald head, sweaty underarms, and a temper currently aimed at Michael. He marched around his desk, whipped open his door. "Neuwerth, get in here!" He yelled over the newsroom chatter.

Lance Nuewerth was a timid, shy kid of twenty-three years with short red hair and black-rimmed glasses that constantly slid down the skinny bridge of his nose. "Yes, Mr. Lund?"

"I don't see any coffee on my desk, Nuewerth!" he said loud enough so every one of his staff could feel his wrath. "A reporter who doesn't want to write the obits for the rest of his days would be on top of those things, huh Nuewerth."

"Yes, sir. I di__." The door slammed, the impact slapping through the newsroom.

Lund zeroed back on Michael without missing a beat. "So it's nearly five o'clock and it's been one helluva day. It's my wife's bingo night tonight, so I get to sit at home by myself, watch whatever I want on TV, maybe even have a cold beer. I enjoy my Wednesday nights, Michael. But this one is ruined. Know why?"

This wasn't the first time Michael had to endure Lund's tantrums. "Okay, I'll bite. Why?"

"I get a call from a friend of mine who was at the press conference this afternoon. Guess what he tells me, Michael?"

"I'm going to be on the six o'clock news," Michael guessed.

"He even commented on your profile. Said, 'that guy should be doing television'. And now I find out that all this free publicity was for a shot in the dark assumption that the goddamn Prime Minister of Canada may be, and I emphasize - may be - involved in the Coastal Holding scandal."

"He is."

"Okay, well then," Lund said, his volume pitching, "tell me who this mysterious yet reliable source is who is going to corroborate your accusations in a fucking conflict of interest scandal!"

"C'mon, John. You sound like you never followed your hunches."

"Hunches." Lund said with a dramatic throw of the arms. "If I had Pulitzer for every time one my reporters went off on a___."

Nuewerth knocked and entered, the newsroom suddenly alive in the office again. Lund glared at his clerk with a well-practiced scowl as he sank into his chair that cried out under the stress. Nuewerth set the coffee on the desk and quickly left.

"Thought you had to relax more at work or something," Michael prodded.

Lund rubbed at a headache, rifled through his drawer for Advil. "Don't push my button, Michael." Another drawer; still no pills. "Shit."

"Top drawer," Michael smirked.

"Fuck off." Lund popped a couple Advils, slammed the drawer. "Don't make us look like a bunch of assholes from the Sun." Lund grabbed his coffee. "Think you can manage that?"

"I can try," Michael said.

That stopped Lund's coffee cup at mid lift. "Thin ice, Mike. Thin ice."

"Can I go now?" Michael was done.

"Yeah, just bring me something on the conference I can print tomorrow." Lund gulped his coffee, his scalding hot coffee that burnt his mouth and stained his shirt. "Shit," he cursed. "Nuewerth!"

Michael headed for his desk grinning with slight pleasure. A few staff scoffed secretly to their computers. Lance, the wannabe reporter, cowered in his cubical, muttering something derogatory under his breath while Lund cursed until his office door slammed - again.

Michael flipped through a stack of fan mail – most of it hate letters of late - fired up his computer. He checked his iPhone again; a few messages, one email from Forbes that he didn't need to read, and a couple texts from Jasmine.

Maybe we should go out for my birthday, what do you think? Just a thought. I'll pick Katie up from Milt's so don't worry about that. And Sabe needs more food btw, pick up on the way home. Jessica texted, she's trying to get a hold of you. *Fyi, I took a shift tonight. Luv u.*

"Dammit," he muttered just as his iPhone rang. Lance shuffled past with a fresh cup for the boss. "Hang in there, Lance."

"I'm trying," Lance said, pushing those big glasses up his nose.

The kid should get some contacts, Michael thought as he answered.

"Hello, Michael Spencer."

"Hi, Michael." A familiar voice.

"Jessica." He perked up. "Any news?"

"Yeah," Jessica Ingham said. "I didn't get the file till late today."

Michael checked the little digital clock Katie gave him for Father's Day back when she was six and cute and loved her daddy forever; she was sixteen now and resented everything about him. Jasmine, Katie and Sabe's pictures were inset in the face of the clock. Jasmine was a brunette back then and Sabe was just a puppy; the dog was now a monster Great Dane eating them out of house and home as far as Michael was concerned. It was 4:30 pm.

"I think you should come by my office," Jessica said. There was something about the way she said it.

"Bad news?"

"My office, Michael."

"Did you talk to her?"

"Michael..."

"She didn't want to meet me did she?"

"Just get here as soon as you can."

There was only one reason that made sense why Child and Family Services counselor, Jessica Ingham, would ask him to stop by her office; to give him news she didn't want to say over the phone. His hopes were about to be defeated by a single question.

"Is she dead?"

CHAPTER 12

The Friend at CFS

Evening's dusk glistened off the ultramodern Child and Family Services building on Portage Avenue. The mirrored, three-story building was an impressive architectural landmark commonly referred to as 'the big ice cube.' Michael skipped up the front steps, walking briskly for the mirrored doors. As promised, Jessica Ingham waited for him in the main foyer.

"Hi, Mike," Jessica greeted with her usual smile.

"Hi, Jess," he said, wiping his sweaty brow. "Hot one, huh."

"Yeah." She pressed the elevator button. "Jasmine told me you were covering the Prime Minister's press conference today. How'd it go?"

Michael watched the elevator light skip from number to number. "Well, it went," he said with a quip.

The doors opened. "How's the birthday plans coming?" she asked.

"Good," he said. "Jas doesn't know what Milt and I are planning, does she?"

"Not by me," she said.

He smirked. "It's going to be awesome."

"With you and Milt behind it, I have no doubt," she said as the doors closed.

They entered the adoption department on the third floor that looked like an impenetrable maze of ubiquitous cubicles. Michael followed Jessica through the prefabricated hallways. She was Michael's favorite of Jasmine's friends from college. She was outgoing, beautiful, and single; a mystery Michael could never figure out.

He sat down. A yellow file lay on her desk, the corners bent and creased and soiled, stained from an eternity in some forgotten file cabinet. "She's dead isn't she?" he asked.

Jessica smiled the way someone does when they have to let a friend down easy. "This file says she died during childbirth." Before Michael could react to the news, she added, "but I'm not so sure."

"What? What do you mean?"

Jessica sighed and said, "Michael, your case is just…weird."

"Weird, how?"

"As in not making sense. Just weird."

"Weird isn't telling me anything, Jess."

"I don't know what else to say. I've never had a search like this. I went through all of it several times, spent a day combing through every file we have on your case, and a lot of it still doesn't add up."

"Like what?"

"Okay, well, let's start with your name. You knew your birth name was Hanis, right?"

"Right."

"You knew the counselor for your parents was Julie Grossman, right?"

"Yeah. Did you get a hold of her?"

"No. She passed away in '84. Her and her husband perished in a small plane crash." She opened the file. "And that's where it got weird."

"Because..?"

"Because the trail ended with Julie Grossman." Jessica smiled sympathetically before she said, "I don't think your name was Hanis."

Michael's jaw dropped. "What? How'd you come to that?"

"Well, hear me out. Everything about you is in your parent's files just like you told me." Jessica counted fingers with each instance. "You were born New Year's Eve '81. You weighed six pounds, two ounces, blue eyes, healthy apgar, and pyloric stenosis a month later. It's all there."

"Okay. And…?"

"And…when I searched through the CFS archives there was no record of a Hanis in '81. Not one. No listing, nothing."

"How's that possible?"

"It's not. That's the problem," she said as she slipped a form from the file labeled *Guardianship transfer*. "Look at this."

"What's this?"

"This form authorizes guardianship of the baby – you - from your birth mother, supposedly Hanis, to the counsellor, Julie Grossman, on behalf of your adoptive parents - your mom and dad." Jessica pointed to a signature at the bottom. "Normally a birth counselor signs it."

"Lily Atkinson," Michael read.

"Right, but when I looked her up in the system she was a supervisor not a counselor. She's been retired for years now."

"Not sure I'm getting the problem here, Jess."

"Your birth mother would've had a counsellor, and that's what our system would've let me search on to find your birth mother's records, to cross reference her to your birth mother, but without the counselor listed, well, it's like you were never born - on paper anyway."

He noticed the letterhead. *Children's Aid Society*. The name of the agency had been changed to Child and Family Services (CFS) in '91, right at the height of computers replacing typewriters and file cabinets. "Is it possible that when CFS was digitizing old Children's Aid files some got messed up...maybe..?"

"I've never seen that before, Michael," she said, easing another paper out of the file for him to read. "Her name was Susan. At least that's what the file says."

Michael choked up a little. "It says here she was only eighteen." That hit him. "Wow, eighteen in '81 and having a baby. That's rough. This woman was a kid when she died." The tragedy of her death sunk in.

"And that's the other thing that is just plain weird. There is no death certificate, Michael," Jessica said with a sigh. "None of the hospitals here show a deceased woman who perished during child birth on New Year's Eve in 1981. Not one. I even searched Vital Statistics."

"Wouldn't this Grossman woman have checked on this?"

"What reasons would she have? She had your parents ready to adopt." Jessica leaned back, arms folded, truly baffled. "I think someone made a terrible error in your file."

Michael eyed her. "An error?"

"Honestly, I'm just guessing," she said. "But then there's this." She pointed further down the form Michael was reading, right where it said paternal father/sponsor. There was no name. "Usually the father's name went here, and if he was out of the picture, then a sponsor, typically a parent – more specifically, either your grandmother or grandfather, but at the very least a family member. Someone's name has to go in there, and it's blank. That is unusual."

"You mean *also* unusual."

"Exactly."

Michael perused further down till he saw "Pyloric Stenosis" and a name he didn't recall – Dr. Carl Friesen. "What about this Dr. Friesen? He performed the surgery. Maybe he's still kicking."

"Yeah, but –."

"What the..." Something in the file stood out. "Says here, he admitted me into the Grace Hospital. If I was admitted then where in the hell was I born? I was told I was born at the Grace."

She eased the file closed. "That's what I'm talking about. We need the counselor's name, Michael." She stood.

Michael was thinking like a reporter now. "If I could find this Atkinson woman then maybe..."

"Do you know what the chances of her even remotely remembering your adoption are? It's one isolated case out of thousands. And that's if she's alive."

"Hey, can't hurt to ask," he said. "I'll see about this Dr. Friesen as well. There's always a way to get to the bottom of every story." His optimism was cute and it made her feel better. "It's okay, Jess."

"I just wanted you to be able to give her that letter, that's all."

"Yeah, me too." He checked his watch. "I gotta go."

"Okay. Jas working tonight?"

"Yeah, late shift. You're coming to the party though, right?"

"Are you kidding," she said with a coy smirk. "I'm not missing whatever you and Milt have dreamed up this time."

CHAPTER 13

The Assassin

The Javelin stood under the camouflage netting deep in Australia's Red Center, watching the private jet approach the make shift runway with landing lights searing the blackness enveloping the outback. Right on time, he thought, glancing at his watch with a terse look to the stars above. They had fifteen minutes before being vulnerable to NSA's reconnaissance satellites spying from the heavens. The weather was brisk, but actually quite good for June.

The jet banked slightly and steadied for touchdown. The Javelin wondered if the pilot had ever negotiated such a runway before. The temporary airstrip was not exactly FAA standard. Few even knew of it's existence since it was cultivated out of the red desert dune 25kms due west of Ayers Rock and directly south of the Olgas by Australia's elite Black Teams; the clandestine units run by the CIA into Vietnam. The location was not chosen out of happenstance either. The Olgas conglomerates afforded stealth landings for covert aircraft from the probing radar of Connellan Airport roughly 30kms to the north-east. When it came to covert operations, the Javelin was more informed than the CIA would've liked.

The jet touched down with reverse thrusters kicking in the moment the wheels connected loose sand, a thick cloud fan-tailing behind, barely visible in the moonlight. The Javelin stepped out from under the netting, pulling a small pocket-sized flashlight from his overcoat. He waited until the jet came to a stop a few hundred feet from the camouflage meshing before raising the flashlight at the plane and clicking twice. Three clicks would've meant abort, but that was not necessary. He had taken the precaution of arriving an hour earlier to secure the deserted camp.

He walked to the edge of the airstrip as the jet's turbofan motors powered down, the whine carrying forever. A man dressed in a dark coat emerged from the plane. He walked with a tired stride and his hand over his mouth to prevent breathing windswept sand.

The two men came together in the middle of the runway, in the middle of Australia's Red Center. A package was handed to the Javelin. He knew the contents would be pictures of an estate in San Diego.

"The money?" he asked.

A seventy-year-old Alec Garva nodded and said, "All taken care of as you requested." His eyes hadn't changed over the years.

The Javelin handed over a piece of paper. "Here's the account."

"I trust this can be done within the week, no?" Garva asked. The Javelin's grin said everything. "Good. The White Knight will meet you as planned."

Alec Garva turned for the waiting plane without bidding good-bye to the Javelin, who in turn headed back for the camouflage meshing. Five minutes later the private jet was back in the air.

The Javelin glanced at his watch then to the stars above. Perfect. Three minutes left. He climbed into his Land Rover parked under the netting and sped away, heading south for Docker River Road. Alice Springs was four hours drive.

CHAPTER 14

The Letter

Michael finally pulled into his driveway at about 6:30 pm. He heard Sabe's bark explode from inside the house. The Great Dane stood four and half feet from the floor to his head. He was a giant and ate like one too.

"Sabe down!" Michael commanded as he tried to push his way through the backdoor into the kitchen with a ten-pound bag of Dog Chow in his arms. His supper was waiting for him on a cellophane wrapped plate on the island counter. Michael could hear the television in the living room. "Hey, I'm home."

"Hi, honey." Jasmine answered from the living room. "I left a plate for you."

Michael unwrapped his supper while Sabe watched with his chin resting on the counter, his big eyes begging. "Forget it." Sabe responded with a grunt.

"You're on TV, babe," Jasmine said over the television.

Michael strolled into the living room just as the anchorwoman was delivering an update on the Coastal Holding situation in British Columbia. A flattering picture of Premier Graham and his lawyer, Coleman Dresher, filled in behind her. Apparently the Premier refused to comment on his absence at the Federal/Provincial conference in Winnipeg when cornered on the pier in Horseshoe Bay, attempting to board his yacht *Rachel's Dream*. The mere sight of Premier Roy Graham made Michael's senses tingle. He knew there was a connection between the Premier and the Prime Minister; all he had to do was dig deeper for it. John Lund's lecture echoed like a bad headache.

Jasmine pushed off the couch and wrapped her arms around his waist and kissed him as if they hadn't seen each other all week. He never grew tired of her kisses, and after seventeen years of marriage couldn't imagine living without them. She was a beauty with long, flowing brunette hair, glistening green eyes, and petite figure. As far as Michael was concerned she was even more beautiful than the day he married her.

"Nice profile, honey," she teased.

"Got a lot of compliments on that today."

"I bet." She smiled, kissed him fully.

"And hello to you," he said. She definitely got his full attention.

"You're in store for more of that if I'm satisfied with my birthday present."

He kissed her back. "Oh, you'll be satisfied."

"Michael," she said, a dead serious look. "Tell me you and Milt aren't doing a surprise party."

He acted as best he could. "Of course not."

"Michael..."

Time to change the subject. "Kat in her bedroom?"

"Michael, I'm serious."

"I know. Where is she?"

"She's out with Danny." Danny was the first boyfriend so naturally Michael despised him. "And don't say it."

"I don't like that kid."

"He's a nice boy. And you're ruining this moment. I'm working on foreplay here." She kissed him hard again, this time reading that look in his eyes; the one she was hoping to get. "You're going to have to wait up for me."

"Can't promise anything," he joked and sat.

"Wanna bet," she said, flopping on the couch beside him, resting her chin on his shoulder.

He knew that look. "What?"

"Are you gonna tell me how it went with Jessica?"

He could read her to a tee. "You already know, don't you?"

"It's just fun to ask," she said, kissed his cheek and headed off down the hall. "You can tell me later."

Michael didn't want to think about the adoption search. He watched himself on TV; the moment from the press conference where he went for the Prime Minister's jugular. For whatever reason, beyond just his gut instinct, he really had no use for Prime Minister Seth Petersen. He was about to eat his chicken when he noticed Sabe sitting just inside the living room, his rump firmly placed on the polished hardwoods, big puppy dog eyes fixed on Michael. "What do you think, Sabe? Think he's crooked?" A bark. "Me too."

~

The evening jog along the river was a little more like a sprint. It bothered Michael more than he anticipated to find out the woman that bore him had died doing it. The fact he knew so little, or worse was completely oblivious to the simple fact she was a teenager who lost her life so he could have his, filled him with a deep guilt. He wasn't sure what to expect when he first started the search, but this displaced sense of obligation was dominating his thoughts. It also bothered him that as of only a couple of hours ago he didn't even know the minor detail of his birth name. If he wasn't a *Hanis* at the time of his birth, in who knows what hospital, who in the hell is he? If there was one thing Michael had always been absolutely sure of, it was he was Michael Spencer, the son of his mom and dad, a reporter with a good life with Jas and Katie, and yeah, even Sabe. But now it felt like the very foundation of him was dislodged somehow. And the running wasn't doing the trick. He needed to know, at the very least, who she was and why she died undocumented, like some Jane Doe that didn't matter in the world.

The setting sun spurred Michael on along the riverbank path, kicking it up a notch. He burned the last leg home, right up to the front yard, just in time to see Katie and Danny Gregory getting out of Danny's high performance street racer and kiss.

Danny had all the ear markings of a boy a father should distrust in a first boyfriend. The white boy rapper thing was going on with baseball cap cranked at an angle, clean tee shirt and over-sized jeans. Michael did his best to tolerate the kid.

"Hey, Mr. S. How's it going?" Danny was always pleasant – the father he had to impress.

Michael forced a smile. "Hi Danny." He slouched over, hands on his knees, getting his breath back. "Mom's working." It was all he could think of to say to Katie. It was always awkward when he saw his little girl kissing a boy.

"I know, dad." She said it like he should dismiss himself while her and Danny were saying goodbye.

"Right." He hated when she looked at him like that. "See ya, Danny."

"See ya, Mr. S."

Michael slipped inside. He wasn't sure what bothered him more, the fact she was growing up, or feeling like he wasn't allowed to be a part of it. At least Jasmine was. She was the glue more than Michael wanted to admit. He stepped inside to Sabe guarding the landing as usual, his big snout pressed to the window with a slight growl. Sabe didn't like Danny either.

Michael's iPhone rang on the island. "Hello?" He watched Katie and Danny kissing through the living room window.

Do they have to do it right there?

"Hi, Mike." It was Jessica.

"Hey, Jess. What do we know?"

"Well, I got a hold of Lily Atkinson."

"Great."

"Ah, yeah, but you're not going to believe this."

"What"

"She lives right across the river from you on Kingston Row."

"What!" Michael said, peering across the river at the row of exquisite houses with fancy docks and decks. "You're kidding."

"Talk about weird," Jessica said, some guilt still in her voice.

Michael rapped the window. Enough was enough already. The young lovers broke apart. "So is she okay meeting with us?" he asked, watching Danny climb into his street racer. Katie burned her best glare through the window at him.

"She's excited actually. How's tomorrow morning?" Jessica suggested.

"Good."

"Okay, I'll pop around and we can go over."

"Yeah, sounds good."

He hung up when Katie came in the back door, her usual chiding for Sabe to get out of her way; he used to be her best friend. She just eyed Michael as if he embarrassed her yet again and went straight for her bedroom. The hip-hop music flared up at full volume an instant later. Michael marched for her door – it was still his house dammit. It wasn't a pleasant knocking. "Kat!"

Katie snapped open her door with that teenager's look of privacy violated. "What, dad?"

"Human level. Please."

Another eye roll as the door shut. Michael just stood there, dejected as usual with Sabe sitting with his butt on the hardwood, his big puppy eyes seemingly saying, "our little girl is all grown up."

"Shut up," Michael said. He needed a shower.

~

It was just after eleven when Michael flicked off the bedroom TV. He had no interest to hear more one-sided news anchors prattle on about his defeat at the press conference. He opened his laptop and checked his emails. There was one from Milt telling Michael he got Jasmine's cake for the party, and that he booked their favourite court for racquetball this Friday; underlined the sentence telling Michael he better not blow it off again this week.

There was one more from Dad. There always was at the end of the day, sometimes iPhone video attached, or a Skype request to catch up. But this time the email only had a picture of Dad in a flashy pink Hawaiian shirt with his retirement buddies down at the local bar called the Hula Hut. Michael missed him. And then at the bottom of the email was added a P.S. that gave Michael pause.

How's the search going?

Michael had told his dad he was going to initiate the search before he called Jessica two weeks ago. Olie Spencer thought it was a good idea, besides it was his mom's dying wish. Michael couldn't email back the news his teenaged birth mother was dead.

He shoved the laptop aside; wasn't going to get anything done anyway. He opened the nightstand drawer, slipped out an envelope. He hadn't read the handwritten letter in over two weeks, but now that he knew he'd never be able to honor the wish his mom had written, why not read it and torture himself some more.

Dear Michael,

The diagnosis came back today. They're going to send me for a mammogram and do all that they can, but I feel it won't change what's coming. I don't want you to worry, please. But I do want to tell you how proud I am of you, and Jasmine and Katie. Jasmine has been the daughter I always wanted and Katie is so full of life, growing up so fast and is so much like you, dear. But you'll see that soon enough. Anyway, the reason I'm writing this note is because I have a request of you. There is something I want you to do for me and I hope you understand why this is important to me. Before you came, your dad and I were sure we would not be able to have a family. But God smiled on us and gave us you. I don't know anything about your birth-mother, Michael, but since you're such a good reporter, I'd like to think that you could find her. If I had the chance I would've liked to have met her, and told her the child she surrendered was loved and made us a family. I can't help but think this would be good for you to, sweetheart. I want you to thank her for me, Michael, thank her for giving me you for a son. Please try.

I Love you. Mom.

Michael took a deep breath, wiped the tear forming in the corner of his eye. He had never let Mom down while she was alive, and now he felt he just had. He put the letter back in the drawer and gently slid it shut. "Sorry, mom," he said underbreath.

~

Jasmine loved her work on the ER ward of the Victoria Hospital but could have done without the night shifts. She waved good night to security as she passed through the ER entrance doors. Twenty minutes later she was inserting her key in the back door lock of their Churchill Drive home. Sabe, her trusted sentry was still on duty, as usual, stretched out on the kitchen floor waiting for her. She patted his belly then tiptoed to the front foyer to reset the Compsec alarm pad then slipped into the master bedroom and undressed as quietly as possible. Her hair hung freely, caressing over her shoulders and spilling around her breasts. Her nipples were dark and voluptuous, and her smooth, supple curves soft in the moonlight that filtered the room with translucent white.

Michael had been watching. Without a word she climbed into bed and they made love.

~

An hour later Jasmine cranked the air up a few notches and slipped back into bed. Michael was wide-awake, lost in thought.

"What's up, honey?"

"I can't stop thinking about what Jessica told me today," he said.

"Yeah, she told me about your birth mother's file. Sorry, babe." She cuddled into him. "I wish I could help."

"Actually, you might be able to. There has to be some records somewhere in the old Grace hospital...so...I thought maybe my unbelievably sexy, gorgeous, and charismatic wife who just happens to be a nurse could__."

"You forgot expensive. You're gonna owe me for this. I want a trip to some place tropical this year."

"Done."

They kissed goodnight and Jasmine nodded off quickly. Michael, however, couldn't fall asleep. He was staring at the lines painted on the wall by the moonlight streaming in through the blinds, going over in his mind what he was going to ask Lily Atkinson in the morning.

CHAPTER 15

The Atkinsons

Michael's SUV clipped over the Osborne Street Bridge then swung onto the off ramp that eventually merged into Kingston Row. The Row was a park like community. The houses were exquisite, each one unique in character and design. The lower end of the Row rested on a peninsula, giving most of the homes a backyard that bordered the Red River.

"It should be that one there," Jessica said, pointing to an old white colonial with black trim.

She stood pensively beside Michael on the front step as the door chimes hymned inside. A moment later the large front door swung open to reveal a vibrant and remarkably young looking Lily Atkinson, her infectious smile a welcoming invitation to enter. They stepped into the foyer. It offered a pleasant coolness from the heat. Lily took Jessica's hand. "You must be Jessica?"

"Yes." Jessica smiled. "It's nice to meet you, ma'__,"

"Ah,ah," Lily teased, her wrinkled hand raised. "No ma'am stuff. I'm not ready for the casket yet. And I'm sure as hell not from the south." She aimed her smile at Michael, took his hand in both of hers. "And this must be Michael." The old girl's grip was firm yet nimble, gentle. "It's very nice to meet you."

"Nice to meet you," he said. He liked her.

Lily leaned into him. "I'll bet you're as curious as hell, aren't you?" she said with a mischievous grin.

Archie Atkinson entered the foyer dressed in white shorts and a bright orange Hawaiian shirt. Michael smiled, stepped forward to shake the outstretched hand. He couldn't help picturing his dad playing checkers at the Hula Hut in that hot pink Hawaiian shirt Katie picked out for him when they visited last Christmas.

Formalities over, Jessica and Michael followed Archie through the house to the back porch overlooking the Red River. The porch had been built just past a second floor mezzanine and was under full attack of the sun. They all sat around an oval picnic table with an overhead umbrella that Archie said he had made. Michael couldn't put his finger on it, but there was something off putting about Archie Atkinson; he seemed tense and uncomfortable sitting at the table with them.

Lily arrived on the porch carrying a tray with a pitcher of iced tea and four tall, frosted glass tumblers. She poured and recruited Jessica to pass glasses around.

"So any trouble finding the place?" Archie said. Even Jessica sensed his uneasiness.

"No, I had no trouble at all," Michael answered after a long sip. "I live just across the river."

"Really?" Lily said surprisingly.

"Yeah." Michael twisted in his chair and pointed out his house. "See that white bungalow directly across."

"Well, how's that for a small world," Lily said. "Isn't it, Archie?" Archie nodded and sipped his tea.

Michael had had enough small talk. "Mrs. Atkinson," he said, "I can't tell you how surprised we were to know you remembered my adoption when Jessica called."

Lily tapped her head. "Sharp as a tack."

Archie huffed. "When she wants to be."

"Oh hush." Lily patted Michael's hand. "Why don't you tell me what you know and I'll see if I can help."

Michael recited a brief synopsis of his history and what they had found out so far. Jessica nodded in agreement when Lily occasionally looked to her for confirmation. He told them of Jasmine and Jessica's friendship since high school and when Jessica got her job at CFS years ago that the idea of finding his birth parents came up. He talked about his dad retiring to Hawaii last spring after a thirty-year career at the CBC as a newsroom producer. His mother was a stay at home mom who freelanced for *Homemaker and Reader's Digest* magazines. But sadly they lost her a year ago and it was her dying letter that ultimately compelled him to find his birth mother named Hanis. Jessica chimed in, telling Lily about their disappointment to discover Michael's birthmother was dead. Lily and Archie exchanged a glance that had Michael and Jessica wondering. By the time Michael got around to the missing death certificate and the fact there was no counselor assigned to the case – on paper anyway - Lily was shaking her head and tapping the table with her nimble little finger.

"The name is wrong," Lily cut in.

"Excuse me," Michael said.

"Her name wasn't Hanis." She was tapping her forehead, frustrated with her poor recall. "I don't remember her last name, it was so long ago, but I know that's not it. Maggie told me, but after Carl died, she___."

"Died?" Michael said. "Recently?"

"No, dear. He died in '81."

"How?" Jessica asked.

"Car accident. Remember, Archie," Lily said and Archie barely nodded. "It was on the Main Street Bridge. They had to cut his body out of the car. Very tragic. It tore Maggie something fierce. She was so sad. And then she...left. No good-bye or anything."

Michael glanced between Lily and Archie, the reporter in him sensing something pertinent. "Why do you think she left so suddenly?"

Lily looked to Archie; there was definitely something secret between the Atkinsons. Michael and Jessica shared a look – they felt it.

"You have to understand," Lily finally said, "I've never talked about this since."

Michael leaned into the table. "Anything you can remember would be helpful."

Lily rubbed her hands, that cheery smile fading, as if memories were coming back. "Maggie came to me shortly after Christmas that year and said her sister had decided she wanted to put her baby up for adoption. It was a shock to say the least because...well, because they seemed to be so excited. Her sister and her husband were at our office Christmas party that year and well..," she glanced at Archie again who simply remained stone faced, "...they seemed very close and very happy about the baby." She touched Archie's hand. "That was the night I met my Archie." Archie managed a forced smile. Michael's senses were in high gear, noticing every subtle sign of Archie's growing discomfort. "Anyway, Maggie said something had happened between them, and that her sister suddenly wanted to have a quick and quiet adoption. Of course they all were very back door back then, but I sensed there was something more dire about it all. I had only just met them but it...well...was so secretive and so tragic and seemed so..," she searched for the right words, "...out of character for them. She told me her sister had a history of instability and that she had been warned a pregnancy could be dangerous for her to carry full term. Between you and me, it sounded pretty thin, but I didn't say that to Maggie. I didn't want to upset her more than she already was."

Lily took a sip of ice tea. Jessica glanced at Michael, feeling that guilt again.

"Anyway," Lily continued, "her sister had her baby New Year's Day.

Maggie was really depressed about it all. She didn't want to talk about it, wouldn't talk about it actually. She wouldn't even go to that foster home and you know that poor baby was throwing up all the time. They called it___." Lily tapped the table as if that would jar her memory.

"Pyloric Stenosis," Michael said.

Lily looked right at him, fully realizing the man at her table was the same baby from all those years ago. Archie just twisted his tea tumbler.

Lily rubbed Michael's hand and said, "I only met your mother that one time. But I know her name was not Hanis and I know for a fact she didn't die during childbirth. I even remember asking Maggie when you were placed if your mother was okay and she told me she was fine. No one handled that case but Maggie, and she was thorough. I don't know how that information got all___."

"She lied," Michael said. "The question is why?"

"That's not like Maggie," Lily defended.

"Do you know how I can get a hold of her?" Michael asked.

"I wish I did. I'm sorry. It was like she disappeared," Lily said regrettably. Archie just forced another one of his thin smiles.

Michael sighed. It was just an adoption search, a last request from his mom. But now it was turning into something bizarre he wasn't sure he wanted to pursue any further.

Lily's face tensed. "You know I just remembered...when Jessica told me on the phone that you had my name on a hospital admittance form, I found that very odd. And the fact you were admitted at the Old Grace doesn't add up either."

"Why?" Michael asked.

"Carl Friesen was on staff at the St. Boniface hospital. That's the hospital you would've been born in had he delivered you."

"Are you sure?"

"Very sure," she said with no second thought whatsoever. "Go to the St. Boniface and get your record of birth from them," Lily suggested while patting Michael's hand.

Michael smiled. It all felt like a dead end. "I will. Thank you."

"Oh you're welcome."

Michael shot Jessica a look that implied leaving.

"Thanks for the ice tea, it was very refreshing," Jessica said graciously.

"Oh, you're welcome, dear," Lily said as if there was no need to even mention it. "Archie and I like the visits." The old girl rolled her eyes over Archie's stone face. "Of course I like them a bit more."

Michael stood. A question was nagging at him. "Can you tell me anything about my birthfather, something that might help?"

"Yes, I remember meeting him just that once at the Christmas party," Lily said. "He was tall, like you. But, I don't remember his name. I'm so sorry." The lapse bothered her. They were back in the cool foyer when Lily slapped her nimble hands together and interrupted Michael and Archie bidding an awkward good-bye. "Wait. That's right, I do remember."

"What?" Michael asked as Archie opened the big white door with a huge sigh hard to miss.

"His name was Larry," Lily said proudly. Her infectious smile radiated. "He was a policeman."

CHAPTER 16

The First Clue

The Patient Relations Officer of the St. Boniface Hospital was paged to the front reception area. She was taken aback by the fact that Michael was the man she saw on the six o'clock news last night. Michael's iPhone buzzed in his pocket. He dug it out. It was Lund. He sighed and told Jessica he had to take the call, stepped out of earshot and answered.

"Hi, John"

"Michael, nice of you to let me know you weren't coming in today." Michael heard the familiar squeak from Lund's chair. "So where the hell are you?"

"St. Boniface Hospital."

"Don't remember sending you there."

"It's personal, John."

"I don't care. I want that press conference covered."

"I'm not going to make it."

"Yes you are."

"Send someone else."

"It's at two, Michael. Be there or start writing obits!" And Lund was gone.

~

The Public Relations Officer led Michael and Jessica to the Health Records Department of the St. Boniface Hospital. She explained to yet another receptionist that Michael was from the Free Press and required some records of birth from 1981. The receptionist buzzed her boss, and the Medical Secretary appeared moments later. She was a lean woman, with straight blonde hair and stoic expression; clearly been working the St. B for far too long. "Can I help you?" she asked while the receptionist blatantly eavesdropped.

Michael produced his press badge. "Hi. Michael Spencer from the Free Press. This is Jessica Ingham of CFS, St. James division." The Secretary seemed rather unimpressed. "We would like to view birth records from January 1/1981."

"Which records?" She was polite but stiff.

"Mine. It's in regards to an adoption search."

"No problem, Mr. Spencer. There is a twenty-five dollar fee to view the archives for one hour and it's fifty cents a page for photocopies."

"Okay." Michael paused. Now came the big question. "We also need to see all the births that night."

The Secretary's back went up. "I'm sorry, Mr. Spencer, but we can't reveal records of other people to you. Unless of course you have a court order or written permissions to that effect."

Jessica stood silent. There was nothing she could do.

"You don't understand," Michael said. "We're not sure what my last name was, therefore we need to see records of all the children born under Dr. Carl Friesen. I had pyloric stenosis so it shouldn't be too hard to___."

"They wouldn't have that on any birth record, Mr. Spencer," the Secretary said with a know-it-all tone. "Pyloric stenosis is not usually detected at birth. How familiar are you with the condition?"

Jessica touched Michael's elbow - easy. "She's right."

Michael could see this woman was not going to budge. Reporters have their tricks for just such a situation, and Michael had a big one in the medical field. He excused himself, made a quick call to the Provincial Health Minister's office and after a few exchanges with aids and secretaries got through to the Minister's direct line. They conversed briefly, the Minister asking how Michael's family was, how his racquetball game was going lately. All Jessica could do was smile when the Medical Secretary figured out what was going on. Within a few minutes they had the unlimited access they needed and Michael and Jessica followed the Secretary through the congested Health Records Department to a spare workstation. She showed them the password codes then left them to their search. Her nose was definitely out of joint and Michael figured she was going to torment the department for the rest of the day. He didn't care. Even though he was conflicted at this point, the reporter in him was curious as to what happened with his adoption.

He punched in the password and found the records folder for 1981 then a sub folder labeled January. He looked at Jessica with a wink. "Moment of truth."

They searched for a birthmother they hoped was still alive.

CHAPTER 17

The Watcher

Archie Atkinson stood at his window, peering across the Red River, watching the white bungalow he had been keeping an eye on ever since Michael Spencer had bought the place. He had watched them come home the day of their wedding, smiled when all his friends and family threw confetti and celebrated. He watched that Great Dane of theirs grow from a pup to a monster, and he had watched Michael jog the path along the riverbank more times than he could count. There were many moments for Archie where he had wished he could have told Lily, could have let her share in the moments that were milestones in Michael Spencer's life. The day they brought home baby Katie being one of them. But he couldn't. He couldn't risk Lily talking to someone, much like she had just done a mere hour ago on the deck.

Archie eased the bedroom door shut. Lily was resting. She needed it. He worried they were out on the deck too long, that the heat and sun would flair into another migraine. It had only been two weeks since her MRI and their appointment next week with the oncologist was scaring the hell out of him. In some ways it was both a blessing and a disaster that Michael ended up at their front door. It would do Lily a world of good knowing the nephew of her good friend Maggie Gunthier was okay. What Lily could never know was how intricately and paralleled her life had been to Larry and Evelyn Hicks' son.

Archie grabbed the wireless handset on his way back to the window just as that Danny kid's street racer pulled up in front of the Spencer home. In some small way a part of Archie felt parental over young Katie, and right at that moment, peering across the river through his binoculars, he worried she was going to get herself into the kind of trouble teenage girls shouldn't get themselves into. He thought Danny Gregory was a nice enough kid whose father was an executive at the Grain Exchange, and his mother taught grade eleven math at Churchill High. But boys will be boys, and right then, with the Spencer house empty, Danny was about to do wrong with young Katie Spencer. Archie could make a call to Compsec home security and make-up some bogus emergency as he had done in the past when he had spotted burglars casing the Spencer house when they were in Hawaii visiting his dad. But now there was a bigger problem than keeping sixteen-year-old Katie away from her boyfriend. If Michael kept digging into the adoption any further, the Spencer's lives would be doomed.

Archie was going to miss them. He glanced down at the wireless handset in his hand. The call he was about to make was one he never had to do since making the promise to his Security Service brother, Larry Hicks, back in '81. That was the night he went to the St. Boniface Hospital with Lily, whom he had just started dating, and stood with Larry when he put his newborn son into Maggie Gunthier's arms. Evelyn was hysterically screaming to hold her baby, begging Larry not do this. But Larry pushed a sobbing Maggie into the arms of her doctor lover, yelling at them to go, and dropped to his knees, the anguish of it all incomprehensible.

Archie had no idea where Larry whisked Evelyn to and didn't want to know. It was better that way and was all part of the plan Larry had sworn them all to carry out days after their Security Service brethren, Murphy Henderson and Roger MacMillan, were murdered. Archie knew Roger's wife and their kids. He knew why Larry's choice to outrun Mario Morelatto and his killers was necessary. What he or anyone connected to Operation Scarlett didn't know was how the undercover operation was blown. Who in the force or in Ottawa had traded names for money? This was the real reason for surrendering their child and hiding.

Two other Security Service members were there as well that night. Archie lost contact with them after Larry and Evelyn disappeared. He had been told Floyd Webber had left the agency, crossed the hall back in '84 when the Mounties lost the Security Service to Ottawa and renamed it CSIS. Archie had heard rumours Webber was now running a special team for the CSE – the most secretive of Canada's intelligence apparatus. Mac Loewen had left the force after his investment in some small computer start up in California had gone onto to rule the world as Apple. Last Archie knew Mac Loewen had bought himself a fancy lake house in Kenora, Ontario, overlooking the Lake of the Woods.

As for Archie, he had been living in the Kingston Row house bought for him by the man he was about to call in San Diego, specifically to honor the promise he had made that night in the hospital. He didn't need to read the number from a piece of paper. He knew it by heart. What he didn't know was if the contact who represented the FBI's interest in Operation Scarlet back in '81, was in fact still living in southern California, or if he was even still alive. For that matter he had no way of knowing if Larry was even still alive. But of one thing he was certain; the moment he made the call his clandestine life would end up in the hands of the investigative reporter he had been watching for the past thirty-seven years.

He dialed. Sam Mitchell answered and he was concerned Archie Atkinson was calling.

CHAPTER 18

The Call

    Michael got home to the usual routine. His afternoon spent again tolerating another rant from Lund and then the drive home through five o'clock congestion made all the more worse with the unrelenting heat wave. It should have all felt different; he had new hope that his birth mother may be alive. There was nothing in the St. Boniface Hospital records to suggest he should be thinking otherwise. There had only been four babies born New Years Eve 1981 at the St. B. He ventured to the Grace Hospital earlier in the day and found the admittance form that Maggie Gunthier had signed and that some EMS receptionist named Elma had typed out. His curiosity was definitely piqued all over again by the time he dropped Jessica back at The Big Ice Cube on Portage Avenue. So much so that he could barely concentrate on his column once back at his newsroom desk. Ralph Forbes shared what little he had gleaned from Prime Minister Seth Petersen's final press conference before heading back to Ottawa. Lund, in true form, responded "over my dead body" when Michael informed him he was sharing the by-line with Forbes. John Lund really hated Ralph Forbes.

    By the time Michael rolled the SUV into the garage, fed Sabe, and sprawled out on the couch, Jessica had already called with a number for Maggie Gunthier in Toronto. She had found her through a CFS friend who lived in Toronto's Liberty Village. He told Jessica to stop apologizing; none of it was her fault. Jasmine was working the late shift again. Sabe was laid out at the back door for another shift of sentry duty. And Katie was out, as usual, with Danny.

~

    Michael eyed his iPhone, thought what the hell, and dialed Maggie Gunther's number. He just as quickly hung up. The idea of actually talking to someone who could be his natural aunt gave him a pause of courage he couldn't fully understand.

~

When Michael got back from his daily jog he dialed Maggie's number again. It rang enough times that Michael second-guessed whether this was a good idea; what if this call really did lead to meeting his birth mother. Hope had lingered back into his search.

"Hello." The lady who answered didn't sound that old. He could hear background talking coming from a television and Michael instantly recognized Orson Wells as Citizen Kane; one of his favorites.

"Hello," Michael said. "Is this Maggie Gunthier?"

"Yes, it is." She seemed a bit guarded; no doubt wondering why someone would call at this time of night. "One second," she said. Michael heard Wells's dying voice calling out for Rosebud lower in the background. A small dog barked from a far off room. Maggie Gunthier told 'Fefe' to be quiet. A rocking chair squeak followed and she was back on the phone. "Who is calling?"

"Sorry to call so late. My name is Michael Spencer, Mrs. Gunthier."

"Yes..?" she said cautiously.

"I'm phoning in regards to my adoption search and your name was on the admittance form I found at the Grace Hospital."
Michael could feel the anxiousness in her breathing.

"What was your birth name Mr. Spencer?"

He took a breath of his own, knowing the moment he said his name it was going to go either one way or the other. "Hicks."

The receiver slammed in his ear.

~

Jasmine was asleep the second her head hit the pillow, but not Michael. He was staring at the moonlight coming through the blinds for the second night in a row. Suddenly his iPhone beside the bed rang. Jasmine startled as he quickly snapped it out of the charging dock. The caller id was *Unknown*.

"Hello," he answered. There was a long silence. "Hello?"

Jasmine rolled over. Prank calls in the middle of the night went along with being married to an investigative reporter. He walked the phone into the living room to let her sleep.

"Hello," Michael said once more.

"Is this Michael Spencer?" A woman's voice asked quietly, as if trying to hide the call.

A sensation swept through him. Oh my God. "Yes, this is Michael Spencer."

"Did you phone Maggie Gunthier?" The question came slowly, as if hinging on the outcome of the answer.

He felt his breath catch in his throat. "I did," he said.

The woman sobbed as quietly as she could. A full minute passed. He prayed he wouldn't have another hang up - not now.

"I thought I'd never hear your voice," she whispered through gasps and sobs. She was a little louder now, maybe not so conscious of hiding the call - emotion overriding caution.

"Are you___?"

"No, you can't ask any questions." She said, her sobbing quickly under control. "Just listen to me. I can't talk long. You can't phone Maggie again. She is very scared. Everything was done to protect you. You must believe that." She sobbed again, then regained. "I only hoped that your life would be good and that you were loved. But you must let this go. Enough people have died."

"People died?" Michael asked, struggling with latent emotions he didn't even understand.

The woman wept some more then said, "There are dangerous people, very dangerous." She said dangerous as if she couldn't emphasize it enough. Then a man called from somewhere in the background of the call - calling for Evelyn.

Her name is Evelyn!!

Michael would never be able to explain it, but tears rolled down his cheek the instant he heard her name. She talked faster now, rushing to finish what she had wanted to say.

"I love you...I'm sorry___," she choked out the last words. "I love you very much. Whatever you think of me and what we did, always remember that I love you. Always remem___."

Click!

Michael stared at his iPhone, commingled disbelief and shock.

Did this just happen?

~

"Baby, what is it?" Jasmine asked when he came back into the room and sat on the edge of the bed. His tears moved her to wrap her arms around him.

"I don't know what this is all about, Jas."

He told her everything.

~

What Michael and Jasmine could never have suspected was someone sitting in a black GMC suburban parked just down the street from the bungalow, cloaked in the shadows of overhanging Oak trees, a wire dangling from his ear.

CHAPTER 19

Larry and Evelyn

The fire cracked and popped, the flames leaping up, lashing the overhanging palm trees with flickering orange and red. It was a little late for a fire but this was Larry Hicks's ritual for the past thirty-seven years, laying in his hammock overlooking the tiny village of Governor's Harbor on the Caribbean side of Elethuera Island, Bahamas, and waiting. Usually it was New Year's Eve when he'd drink a bottle of Rum, watch the fire and wrestle his own demons until Evelyn would return from her ritual sojourn up the beach to cry in his arms and mourn the child they surrendered all those years ago. The guilt was still deep for Larry. But he had not seen Evelyn this distraught since that cold night in '81; the eve she last held the baby boy they were going to name Justin. And now he was Michael, Maggie had just told them a little over three hours ago.

Larry called Maggie immediately after Sam Mitchell's call from San Diego, who called him right after Archie Atkinson had called from Winnipeg. But Evelyn closing the bedroom door and calling Michael Spencer was not supposed to happen. It was all unraveling very fast and Larry would have no choice now that his natural son found Maggie. That meant he uncovered his true name and that would prove fatal for all of them – their sacrifice would've been for nothing.

Larry wandered back into their beachfront villa and walked straight to the phone on a wicker end table, situated beside a purple beanbag chair; a chair he had yet to sit in, for obvious posterior reasons, since Evelyn lugged the stupid thing home from the Goombay Festival last year.

He dialed the number. Sam Mitchell was waiting for his decision. Larry was all too aware of the Coastal Holding scandal and the irony was just too close for comfort. He would make a second call to an old friend. An ex-security service officer from Operation Scarlet he had not spoken to since that fateful Christmas in the hospital back in '81. He wondered if

Mac Loewen had ever married. He knew he wouldn't be able to get Floyd Webber's number in Winnipeg and calling Archie was just too risky.

As the phone rang in Sam Mitchell's San Diego home, Evelyn stepped wearily through the patio doors, the pain seeping from her very soul.

CHAPTER 20

Beware the Covert World

Cindy Greene worked the Bureau of Police Records, Administration Division for the Winnipeg Police Service and was rather excited by Milt Smith's impromptu visit to her small office on the main floor of the city hall complex. She waved when he and Michael entered through the frosted glass doors.

At six-foot-six and tipping the scales at just over two hundred and thirty pounds of lean muscle, Milt Smith was a giant next to Michael. Yet what always struck someone like Cindy Greene upon seeing them together was the similarities between them; mannerisms they seemed to have picked up from each other over the years; much the same way you can tell brothers just by a glance. And that would be the way to best describe Michael and Milt Smith; brothers without being blood.

They had met during one of the worst serial murder cases to terrorize Winnipeg. The case was tagged the Tattletale Killer – a pen name created by Ralph Forbes who was the lead reporter for the Free Press at the time. The rampage galvanized the city with a string of teenaged girl murders. Michael was working under Forbes, dreaming of his own column at the Free Press, and Milt was a constable aiming to join SWAT. They were inseparable friends almost immediately.

So, naturally, when Milt and his wife, Claudette, were at the house after Michael's mother's funeral, Michael led Milt into the garage where a beer fridge was always stocked, and let Milt read the letter. Milt, as expected, pledged to help however he could. That help would come after Lily Atkinson recalled Michael's birthfather being a policeman. Michael's next call was to Milt who knew exactly who to call. Cindy Greene.

"If he's worn the blues, Cindy can find him," Milt proclaimed as they climbed out of the SUV and stepped through the doors of city hall, then into the WPS HQ wing, and down the long marble corridor that eventually led to the frosted glass doors into the bureau of police records where Cindy wheeled herself through the large office to the front desk, always smiling when Milt paid her a visit.

"Hi, gorgeous." Milt said, stepping around the front counter and bending down to hug her in her wheelchair. Michael knew Greene suffered from Muscular Dystrophy, having met her once before at one of the many fundraisers he and Jasmine helped organize. Milt and Claudette's young son Wyatt suffered from the disease.

"Gorgeous, well, well, you must really need something from me pretty badly," Cindy joked as she took the hug.

"Not me. Michael here needs your special talents." Michael and Cindy reacquainted then Milt nodded to the back of the office. "Can we talk?"

"Sure, follow me." Cindy spun around and led them through the heart of the office to her cubicle. Five large monitors were set up around a single ergonomic keyboard on a semi-circular desk. Underneath a series of computer towers and a massive RAID 5 SAN hummed effortlessly. Cindy Greene was a hacker, Michael concluded - another Lance Neuwerth. What was missing were chairs.

"Oh, sorry guys. Just wheel a couple in," she said, pointing to a couple of unoccupied desks. "Cut backs," she offered with usual civic duty distain.

Milt explained Michael's search and the mysterious call last night.

"And this Hicks was a cop?" she asked as her fingers flew across the keyboard, nimbly assigning commands as quickly as she was thinking them; definitely a hacker.

"Yeah," Michael said.

"Where?" she asked.

"I think Edmonton."

Milt winked at Michael – *here we go*.

"First name?" Cindy asked, bouncing from one user-interface to another.

"Don't know."

She eyed Milt. "You do know it's Friday, right?" Milt threw his best 'pretty please' smile. "Okay," she said with a quip. "This could take a bit." She turned to Michael. "Do you at least know if he was municipal or RCMP?"

"No."

~

NSID (National Security Investigations Directorate) - RCMP headquarters – Ottawa

The Corporal watched the computer screen intently. It was the second time in ten minutes the Winnipeg Police Service tried to access a restricted file from the RCMP personnel database. He was too young to have known why L. Hicks and three other names of 'K' division were so highly confidential, but that was beside the point. His surveillance computers screened all communications over the RCMP's CPIC system as well as intranets, LAN's, the web, email, text, chat rooms and blog hits - government or otherwise.

Suddenly there was a ping. His tracer highlighted a login from the same WPS terminal to an RCMP personnel terminal in Ottawa while the CPIC user access codes were still open. A few moments later that someone from personnel attempted the same restricted file. His screen mirrored the user ID he was spying on, thus looking at the same, blinking message box Cindy Greene was seeing in her cubical in Winnipeg.

ACCESS DENIED!

The pinging silenced, indicating the connection terminated. The Corporal logged the time. It was 11:05am in Ottawa. In Winnipeg it would be 10:05am.

He pressed a button and an instant later his Sergeant entered the security screening room. The office was inconspicuously hidden within the RCMP's Alta Vista Drive headquarters, occupying the former space of the long ago disbanded Security Service's E-Special unit.

The Sergeant read the restricted names on the computer screen. "Better give me a copy of this, Corporal. Where did the inquiry originate?"

"Winnipeg Police Service, sir, their bureau of records section, according to the access code clearance." The corporal clicked the printer icon on his task bar.

The Sergeant studied the screen and said, "Why are they trying to get into restricted Security Service personnel files? This stuff is nearly forty-years-old."

"Don't know. Personnel here in Ottawa also tried to access."

"Alright," the Sergeant said. "Trace them. Let's hope it's no one we know." The Sergeant turned to leave.

"Sir," the corporal said.

"Yeah."

"What the hell was 'op' SC?"
"I have no idea, Corporal."

~

Winnipeg-Bureau of Police Records

Cindy's hacking abruptly stopped. Her computer screen displayed a long column of names with a large, blinking message;

ACCESS DENIED!

Cindy looked at them with a grimace. "This is very weird."
"What's up?" Milt said. Michael sighed.
"Okay," Cindy said. "This is what we got. There was no Hicks in any municipal employment files for Edmonton. There was one in Calgary however, but he was killed WOD in '83."
"While on duty," Milt clarified for Michael. Michael knew what it meant; Milt tended to play big brother.
She looked right at Michael. "Was your guy from Alberta?" Michael didn't know. "You guys aren't making this easy" she quipped. "Anyway, I tried to access personnel records from the RCMP's database."
"You can do that?" Michael asked.
"Comes along with the CPIC clearance, and the fact I have a contact in Ottawa. She's in their Personnel Department. Trust me, that's always helpful."
"I told you," Milt said, nudging Michael's shoulder. "Cindy's the best."
Michael knew CPIC was the acronym for the RCMP's Canadian Police Information Center network. Any police department in the world from Interpol to Scotland Yard to the FBI could access its databases for fingerprints, crime index, firearms registration, parole lists, international felons, known terrorists, etc.
"It's not that big of a deal usually," Cindy explained. "We do joint investigations with the Mounties all the time and it's never been a problem getting that information before, so long as they were just regular service, you know, CIB, Customs and Excise, the public sector, so on and so forth. So I tagged my contact..." Cindy tapped the screen with that blinking alert. "And we found him. He was listed under 'K' division in 1981. That's Alberta. All the other names are listed in alphabetical order, except for four of them. These four are indexed differently and I'm not sure why. One of them is your guy, L. Hicks, and the other three are; R. McMillan; S. Henderson and M. Loewen. These names mean anything?" Michael and Milt

both nodded no. "Okay, well when I went to access I got this." She tapped the alert message on her monitor the way hackers do when they can't figure out how to crack their way in.

"Access denied," Milt said. "Why?"

"That's what I'd like to know. Read this," Cindy said, running her finger along a line of fine print near the bottom border of the box. "This is pretty archaic code, definitely Cobol from the old mainframe systems."

>>>PER/REST.'OP'SC-SS-C-DG//<<<

"So, what the hell does this mean?" Michael asked curiously.

"Security Service," Cindy said in hushed tones. Michael and Milt glanced at each other.

Shit!

"Well, that's enough to spook the hell outta of me," Milt quipped.

"Yeah, it freaked out my contact too," Cindy said. She popped open a secure chat window. "She sent this translation to me. PER/REST-means personnel restricted-'OP'-is for operation-SC-is the code for that operation, but I haven't got a clue what that would be, SS-for Security Service and-C-represents classified or confidential and -DG- is the Director-General's office." She looked at Michael. "These were four serious Security Service guys. Probably E-Specials. I'm sorry but unfortunately this all means___."

"I'm never going to know," Michael said. He leaned back, defeated. "Dammit."

Milt slapped his knee with that never-give-up enthusiasm of his. "Maybe Nolan can help us out."

CHAPTER 21

CSIS & the Mountie

Liaison Officer Chris Kominski breezed past the secretary and walked directly into the office of the Deputy Director of Operations on the third floor of the CSIS building. He stepped right up to the desk and placed a printout down. "I think you should see this," he said urgently.

Sixty-eight-year old Braden MacDuff was standing at his window, as he did every morning, looking east down Metcalfe Street at the Center Block's Peace Tower – that iconic center point of Parliament Hill. MacDuff was regarded in the agency as a hell of a patriot and a true intelligence man with decades of field training and covert operations to his credit. Many who toiled under him came to fear his legendary stare of unblinking stone, perfected over decades serving in the RCMP's Security Service before it's demise in 1984.

MacDuff sat down, slipped on his glasses and read the printout. "Do you know anything about this particular operation?" he asked dryly.

"No."

"You should find out who made this inquiry."

"I believe it was the Winnipeg Police Service," Kominski said. "Their bureau of records department."

The Deputy Director's eye slits were narrow and it was pretty much impossible to tell the color of his eyes. The eyebrows were red. So was the military crop back in the day. Now it was pure grey. "You want us to follow this up?" he said while Kominski sat with a pompous air that did nothing to cloak the intimidation he suffered in the Deputy Director's presence. MacDuff barely tolerated him at the best of times. As far as he was concerned Chris Kominski was just another lawyer on his way to the Hill with too many double-breasted suits; a politician at heart.

"Yes," Kominski said. "Deputy Commissioner Klassen made it very clear that I was to move on this now. He said to see Director McIvor."

"Interesting." The eye slits tightened on the politician. "So you just thought you'd override protocol?"

Kominski adjusted in his seat, cautious to not offend the relic. "Protocol dictates I see you. However, he seemed to suggest Director McIvor would move on this right away."

"Fine, I'll check with him this afternoon." MacDuff waved his hand at the door. "Now if you don't mind, Mr. Kominski, I have matters that need my attention."

"Certainly. The Israelis visit?"

"That's classified," MacDuff said with zero tolerance.

"Thank you for your time." Forced courtesies; a talent Kominski had become smoothly adept. He adjusted his suit and left the unremarkable office just as he had entered; quickly.

Normally, MacDuff would mutter some derogatory comment to himself whenever the Liaison Officer left his office, but this time when the door closed he remained focused on the memo, held by the names just below an Access Denied box. *Son of a bitch.*

L. Hicks/R. McMillan/S. Henderson/M. Loewen

He pressed the intercom button on his phone. Sheila, his secretary for what seemed to be forever, responded promptly.

"Yes, sir?"

"Get me the Director on the phone."

"Yes, sir." Sheila broke off for a quick minute then returned with a buzz. MacDuff hit the button. There were no lines holding. "Director McIvor is out of his office until around noon. I left a message for him to call immediately upon his return."

"Thank you, Sheila."

"Yes, sir."

Braden MacDuff rose thoughtfully and stood at his window, staring at the Peace Tower and remembering his former Security Service brethren. He knew he'd have to make a quick call to the two other agents of Operation Scarlet, Archie Atkinson and Floyd Webber.

"Shit," he said at the window.

~

Headingley Detachment

RCMP Corporal Nolan Grant was at home when his racquetball partner and friend, Milt Smith, phoned from city hall. Earlier in the week

Milt had booked them a court at the Winnipeg Racquetball Club for 11:30am this coming Friday. Well it was Friday and in a very unusual move Milt cancelled the match. "Meet me at your detachment," he had said. Grant asked what it was all about but the question met with a very irritating, "I'll tell you when I get there." Nolan Grant knew nothing short of little Wyatt could keep Milt off a racquetball court; he assumed this was pretty important.

Nolan swung his Virago motorcycle into the parking lot beside a black SUV, noticing the laminated Winnipeg Free Press card with pocket clip wedged between the windshield and dash. A few hours in this heat and that will be melted but good, he thought as he skipped up the steps and bounded through the main entrance of his detachment.

~

"There he is!" Milt said when Nolan stepped inside, draping his arm around his neck and rubbing his brush cut. "Man, I could light this whole building with the electricity coming off your head."

The rest of the Mounties that made up Headingley detachment all laughed until the Superintendent in Charge stepped out of his office. "What is the meaning of this!" he scorned. Michael was taken aback when the entire office froze at attention and even Milt knew it was wise not to answer. There was something eerie about that kind of authority. "I'm waiting for an answer, Smith," the Superintendent snapped. Then his face began to crack with a grin that exploded into a raucous laugh and slap to Milt's shoulder.

Milt just shook his head when Grant shoulder checked him. "Got ya, Milt."

"Yeah, yeah, yuk it up but I know where all of you live," Milt said as he flopped into an empty desk chair.

The Superintendent in Charge offered his hand and a friendly smile and introduced himself to Michael. "Sam Eastman."

"Michael Spencer." Michael shook the offered hand.

Eastman pointed at Milt. "Nice to meet you, Michael, but how do you know this bum?"

"Michael was the reporter I worked with on the Tattletale case," Milt said proudly.

The chortling quelled and the officers looked at the reporter as if they had just noticed him in the room for the first time. Superintendent Eastman was no longer smiling. He was sincere. "That was damn good work, son." The compliment was genuine.

Nolan reached his hand over to Michael. "Nice to finally meet you, Mike."

"Same here, Nolan." He felt accepted momentarily for his heroism years ago, and damn it felt good.

"Yeah," Milt added with an impish grin, "but Michael was speeding on the way over."

Suddenly there was moaning and waving fingers. Eastman twisted a scowl and pointed at the floor. "Get down and give me twenty."

~

"So you think your birth father might still be with the force?" Eastman asked after Michael provided a quick synopsis of the search thus far. They were sitting in Eastman's office where a picture of the famed RCMP musical ride hung behind the Superintendent. Nolan was leaning just inside the open door.

"Maybe," Milt said and Michael nodded.

"Well, that shouldn't be hard to find," Eastman said. "They have an association for retired members of the force."

Michael slipped the piece of paper from his pocket. "Maybe you could help us with this, sir," he said as he handed it across the desk.

Eastman took the paper. It was the 'K' Division posting list with the Access Denied window. The Superintendent of 'D' division, Headingly detachment stood with a grave countenance that restored Michael's uneasiness. "Corporal, I'd like a few words in private with Milt and Michael," he said to Nolan. It was not a request, but an order. Even though he was confused, Nolan Grant did not dispute an order. Eastman closed the door behind him. Michael and Milt glanced at each other, both wondering what the hell was going on.

"Here," Eastman said and handed the printout back. "You boys would do better by going to divisional headquarters."

Michael's succinct tongue could no longer hold itself. "You sent your corporal out of your office to tell us that?"

Milt nudged Michael to cool it. "Mike."

"No, I sent him out of the room so I could explain a top secret code to you so you'd understand why I can't help you, Mr. Spencer," Eastman said like a Superintendent.

"It's just a name," Michael countered.

"I can appreciate that," Eastman offered.

"I just need his whereabouts. I can do the rest."

Eastman sighed. He was going to have to be more direct. "I'm sure you could. But as for the matter of your inquiry, I am not the person you should be talking with. I'd like to help but I can't." He looked sincerely at Michael. "I'm sorry, Michael. I hope you understand."

Michael leaned back in his chair, clearly frustrated.

"Can you tell us what operation this was?" Milt asked.

"I don't know, Milt," Eastman said. "But I can phone the Officer Commanding and you can speak with him."

"Thanks, Sam." Milt stood along with Michael.

"I am truly sorry." Eastman opened the door to reveal a curious Nolan sitting at his desk. Eastman snapped up Milt's hand. "Don't be such a stranger, Milt."

"I'll try, sir."

It was an awkward moment and Eastman escaped it by closing himself in his office. After the chorus of good-byes and so-longs, Milt and Michael filed out of the detachment with Nolan in tow. As soon as they cleared the main doors, the corporal asked his question. "So what's this all about?"

They walked between the SUV and the Virago. Michael handed him the printout. "I need to know about L. Hicks and what operation-SC was." Michael slipped the paper back in his jeans.

"That's Security Service." Nolan said, donning his helmet and straddling the Virago. "I'll see what I can do. But I'm not going to violate any orders or anything. Okay."

Milt shot him a thumbs-up then climbed into the SUV when Nolan sped off. Michael pulled out of the parking lot and onto the Trans Canada and tromped the gas back for the city.

"You know", Milt said as they passed under the Perimeter Highway overpass. "Don't get your hopes up. I think it's a long shot the Officer Commanding is going to give us anything on E-Specials."

"What makes you think they were E-Specials? Cindy?"

"No," Milt said with a look of real concern. "The look on Eastman's face."

CHAPTER 22

The Decision

Chris Kominski's secretary entered Braden MacDuff's third floor office. The Deputy Director was on the phone but Sheila instructed her to go right on in anyway. She placed a thick attaché file on his desk and waited patiently for him to complete his call, which from the poignancy of the conversation seemed rather important. The Deputy Director spat something about Residency Analysis and how it was a waste of time. "We should have more manpower for the Israeli Prime Minister's visit next week. The Prime Minister is a prime terrorism target, goddammit!" But the cold war was long over, and with it the need for an overabundance of agents in the counter-intelligence unit; that has been the political agenda Braden MacDuff had taken issue with since getting his appointment overlooking Metcalfe street. "There should be more manpower in the counter-terrorism unit," he argued but as usual met on deaf ears. He slammed the receiver without a goodbye and grabbed for the attaché file. The poor secretary was nervous.

"Thanks," he huffed.

"You're welcome." And she was gone.

The attaché was about two inches thick. MacDuff slid his hand under the confidential seal, tore it off and pulled out five separate files. He dropped the attaché beside his desk as if it was an annoyance. It was. It wouldn't be long before the files before him were to become a superior pain in the ass. He opened the first one. All the pages were black striped on the right margin, tantamount to all top-secret files from those once glorious Security Service days. The header read;

OPERATION SCARLET
Top Secret - Highest Clearance
Security Service: E-Special

MacDuff pushed the button for Sheila.

"Yes, sir?"

"Director McIvor in yet?"

"He's been delayed, sir. Apparently he's in a meeting with Paul Young this morning."

Paul Young was the Privy Council Security and Intelligence Coordinator, and he always had a lot of questions - especially so when a federal election loomed only a few months away. He was the mandarin responsible to keep that government leash tight and, like all intelligence agencies, CSIS was knee deep in a lot of cases at present, some hot, some cold. Nonetheless, they all had to be scrutinized by the Security Intelligence Review Committee (SIRC), and the more covert ones had to be kept quiet, of course. MacDuff knew Director McIvor's meeting could take a while. "Let me know when he's back."

"Yes, sir." Sheila was a good secretary.

MacDuff stepped to his window - the patriot's view. A decision had to be made. He had built a career on following his gut instinct and here he was once again about to put his career on the line. He glanced at the first page of the open file on his desk. 1981 was a long time ago. But Larry Hicks and Operation Scarlet were far from forgotten at RCMP HQ and especially along the corridors of power in Parliament; not to mention the timing of an election was ridiculous. He also had to consider the Prime Minister's position, and Braden MacDuff knew that would be like walking barefoot over broken glass.

Dammit!

The decision made, he snapped up his phone and dialed SSET Chief Floyd Webber's direct number in Winnipeg. It was a number he recalled by memory. SSET numbers were not to be written down.

CHAPTER 23

The Soft Shoe

"Hello, gentlemen. Follow me, please," the constable greeted. He had been waiting for Michael and Milt in the front lobby of RCMP 'D' division headquarters since Superintendent Sam Eastman's call. "Assistant Commissioner Jefkins is expecting you," he said, pushing the elevator button for the second floor. Michael watched the elevator light until it blinked on and a few minutes later he and Milt were standing in front of Assistant Commissioner Hubert Jefkins.

Jefkins merely glanced at his constable, who spun on his heels and retreated from the office. In contrast to his higher rank, Jefkins was shorter and older than Michael would have imagined. He walked directly to his large chair behind his massive, mahogany desk and sat as if he had unfinished work that demanded his immediate attention.

"Well now," Jefkins said, barely giving them a second glance. "Which one is Michael Spencer?"

"I am, sir," Michael said. Milt nudged him, pointing out the crowned badge plaque of the RCMP hanging on the wall behind Jefkins. The words *"Maintiens Le Droit"* under the buffalo head seemed poignant. Milt knew those words. Nolan Grant lived religiously by those words.

Jefkins finished signing what he needed to sign and finally said, "I understand you are requiring some information on a former RCMP officer, Mr. Spencer."

"Yes I am." Michael didn't like Jefkin's air and Milt's stolid stare told him his intuition was right on the money.

Jefkins glanced at Milt as if evaluating. "Sam Eastman speaks highly of you, Sergeant Smith."

"Good to know, sir."

Jefkins returned to Michael, everything about him thoughtful and deliberate. "I'm sorry but the names you are asking about are all restricted access."

Jefkins lacked sincerity and Michael responded accordingly. "Even if they're Security Service and the records are close to forty years old?"

"Especially if they're Security Service. Regardless of how old case files are, we honor those restrictions in order to protect those officers and their families. I am sorry."

"Perhaps I should contact the Commissioner directly then."

Jefkins calmly folded his hands; empty threats were pointless here. "I'm well aware of your reputation, Mr. Spencer, not to mention that impressive press conference the other day." Michael shrugged that off. "But there is no story here, nothing to uncover. We simply can't provide what you're asking, regardless of how far up the chain of command you threaten to go."

"All I'm asking for is some information about my birth father. Honestly, this is just a little more than ridiculous."

Jefkins rose, suggesting the door. "I truly wish I could help. But, I assure you, there is nothing I can do."

"So you refuse to give me any information on my birth father?"

"If his file was restricted by the Security Service at the time he left the Force, then I am bound and cannot disclose anything." Again he suggested the door. "Now if you don't mind, I have an appointment with the Prime Minister before he departs for Ottawa today."

"Say hi for me," Michael said with just enough snide to make Milt wince as they filed out of Hubert Jefkin's office.

~

Minutes later they were back in the SUV. Neither Michael nor Milt, who was fiddling with the air-conditioning, noticed a light brown Chevy pick-up tailing three cars behind them.

CHAPTER 24

The Past is Alive

A buzz.

"Sir. Director McIvor is on line one," Sheila informed over the intercom.

Braden MacDuff was flipping through the Operation Scarlet files. The reading was like déjà vu from his old days, combing over the black margin reports and copious memos from FBI and US Naval Intelligence urging the RCMP's Security Service investigate the Northern Scarlet fleet operating out of Vancouver. But there were no surveillance photos of the targets at all. This seemed a little strange. But what disturbed Braden MacDuff most was the operational authorization signed by Justice Minister Francis Lavelle and then Attorney-General of British Columbia, Seth Petersen, who would go on to become the Prime Minister of Canada. Peterson's signature on a thirty-seven year old E-Special document left MacDuff unsettled; what patriot wouldn't feel a small tug in his gut.

He depressed the blinking line one button. "Clifton."

"Braden." The Director's voice was smooth, with a deepness that suggested authority and confidence. "What's all the urgency? Sheila has been calling my office every hour."

"Something has come to my attention that could pose a serious threat." MacDuff lifted out of his unremarkable chair. It was easier to discuss such matters with the Peace Tower in view.

"How serious?"

"National Security."

"Well that's pretty serious. What's going on, Braden?"

MacDuff hoped the Director, a former military man himself, would comply with his gut instincts. "How much do you remember about Operation Scarlet, Clifton?"

"Scarlet. Jesus. I remember enough," the Director said, his voice tentative. "So, why are we talking about this today?"

"NSID monitored an inquiry this morning. Someone tried to access the restricted files."

"As concerning as that is, that doesn't sound like a reason to ring the national security bell, Braden?"

MacDuff slid back into his chair. "They were after one personnel record in particular." He slipped a picture of a young, sandy blonde haired, steel blue-eyed Security Service officer from the documents. "Larry Hicks."

The Director's breathing carried over the intercom, indicating he had just leaned very close to his own speaker. "Who made the inquiry?"

"A Michael Spencer. He's a reporter from the Winnipeg Free Press." MacDuff closed the file, those bushy red eyebrows lifting over the irony. "It's an adoption search, Clifton. Spencer is Hicks's son."

The intercom was silent.

~

It was 5:20 pm on a Friday afternoon when Braden stepped off the elevator, relieved to find the fifth floor of the CSIS building all but deserted. Civil staff had already abandoned their desks for home. No one was loitering in any of the conference rooms or executive lounge. At the end of the hall was the Liaison office. MacDuff hoped Chris Kominski wasn't working overtime, planning his ascent to Parliament Hill; to his relief he was not. MacDuff knocked and stepped into Clifton McIvor's office.

The Director of the Canadian Security Intelligence Service was sitting on one of two leather sofas with an oval coffee table in between. He was a large, slightly rounded man, reclined with his elbow perched on the sofa's arm, his face scrunched into the palm of his hand, his tan suit unfastened and his tie loosened with the collar button open. The Director had had an arduous day so far. It was supposed to be over. He should have been heading across the Ottawa River for home - home was in Hull, Quebec – but instead his second in command stepped across his expansive office, set an attaché on the coffee table, and sat on the sofa opposite, his red brow creased.

"So what do we know about this Michael Spencer?" McIvor asked like it was the last thing he needed to deal with on a Friday. Braden MacDuff did not get nervous but he did have the habit of rubbing his thumb and forefinger together when he was apprehensive. McIvor noticed the rubbing. "Braden?"

"I called Floyd Webber," MacDuff said as if he could predict the sigh from McIvor that would follow.

"Jesus." The director stared into the pale yellow sun setting beyond his floor to ceiling windows; his day was not getting any easier. "You can't authorize SSET surveillance without TARC approval, Braden, SIRC is going to have a field day with this."

To engage an SSET unit in any level of surveillance without TARC authorization was a direct violation of the protocols set up to protect against the misuse of CSE eavesdropping technology. The SSET units, of which there are only three, are CSE and CSIS's defense against domestic counter-intelligence espionage, and TARC was the watchdog. The Target Approval Review Committee was made up of handpicked officials and a few ministers who scrutinized CSE and CSIS investigations. Of course the bulk of this burden was shouldered by the Inspector General, the minister directly responsible to the Solicitor General of Canada for domestic and foreign intelligence actions, and since shit always rolls down the proverbial hill, that meant the heat ostensibly fell to the CSE or CSIS directors. On this occasion it would be CSIS and Clifton McIvor. It was not the first time MacDuff, the intelligence soldier, had put McIvor in the hot seat, but the director put a lot of stock in his Deputy Director's gut instincts.

"Okay," McIvor said, reconciling himself to what was done was done. "What do we know?"

MacDuff opened the attaché and handed McIvor a surveillance photo of Michael and Milt leaving division D head quarters in Winnipeg. "He's the shorter one. This was taken today as they were leaving Jefkins office."

"You're worried, Braden. Why?"

"This is the same guy who broke the Tattletale Killer story. Remember that?"

"Who doesn't?"

"Exactly. And that's what worries me. This guy knows how to dig shit up."

"And who's with him?"

"A cop named Milt Smith. He's Winnipeg SWAT. He's also the cop that took down the killer."

McIvor seemed impressed with that. "Do we need to continue surveillance on the cop?"

"Yeah. They're best friends. I think the cop was Spencer's access into CPIC."

"He couldn't be the one with the access code clearance."

"No. That was Cindy Greene." MacDuff pulled a flattering picture of Cindy from the attaché and placed it on the table. "She's an acquisitions clerk for the Bureau of Police Records in the Administration Department of the Winnipeg Police Service."

"A friendship?"

"Too early to tell. But there is one thing. She has Muscular Dystrophy. According to Milt Smith's records, his son also has the disease."

"Okay." McIvor always marvelled at the speed the SSET units could work. "Anything else on this Spencer?"

"He's the same guy who dominated the press conference with the Prime Minister the other day, asking questions about the Coastal Holding mess."

That made Clifton McIvor sigh. "Great. Bet Allison McKay loved that."

"I think she did. She graduated from the University of Manitoba the same year Michael Spencer did." Macduff produced another photo of Michael and Allison together, tossing their graduation caps into the air. "They're friends. She granted his access to the conference."

"Well, that's convenient," McIvor noted. "What about family?"

"He's married with one child. Wife is a nurse at the Victoria Hospital. Daughter is sixteen."

McIvor eyed MacDuff with a degree of caution. "If we send Floyd's team in, what do the probabilities look like?"

"Pretty good. He lives on the Red River with a park across the street, very little traffic and the neighborhood is well shaded. Entry should be relatively easy." MacDuff knew Archie Atkinson lived right across the river. He also knew Archie called Sam Mitchell in San Diego. He decided to omit that from his briefing.

"Anything else?" McIvor asked.

The Deputy Director leaned forward, elbows on his knees, and thumb and forefinger rubbing. "This guy is looking for his father. God help him, this reporter doesn't even know what he's getting himself into. If he finds Larry Hicks, he is going to need our help, Clifton."

"And that's what concerns me here, Braden." McIvor flopped the file back on the coffee table. "I'll give you two days."

"Two days." The eyebrows scrunched. "We might not be able to get into the house in two days."

"You've assigned an SSET unit to an illegal gathering expedition. Now I'm not letting that go on for more than two days so find out what you can while you can. If you convince me that we should take this to TARC and the SIRC, we'll brief the Prime Minister on Monday." McIvor slid the file back across the coffee table to MacDuff. "But, if you find nothing and this turns out to be a goose chase, then we forget Operation Scarlet and leave Larry Hicks dead and forgotten."

CHAPTER 25

The Back Story

>>>PER/REST.'OP'SC-SS-C-DG//<<<

"So what the hell is this?" John Lund growled while choking down a sub when Michael entered his office and dropped the printout on his desk.

"Does any of that mean anything to you?" Michael asked as he closed the door, damping the newsroom clatter.

"I'm eating, Michael."

"Security Service, John, and all that political cloak and dagger stuff you used to cover back in the day. Are you sure you don't know what operation SC means?"

"Security Service..." Lund said, intrigued. He read it. "So what does the rest of this shit mean?" Michael broke down the code. Lund just shook his head in what could almost be construed as disbelief. "It must be Operation Scarlet."

Michael perked up. "Which was..?"

"A botched fuck up." Lund tossed the paper back across the desk as if it was a bad memory and eyed his reporter. "Does this have anything to do with why you're getting Lance to help you with your adoption search, when you're really supposed to be writing your column? And I'm just guessing here, but today's piece looked a lot like something Forbes would write. Back when he was sober of course. What's going on, Michael?"

Michael sat and took the gamble. "I think my birth father was involved in whatever this Operation Scarlet was. I don't know how exactly…yet, but I could use your help me here, John."

"And then you'll get back to doing what we pay you really well to do, right?"

"Absolutely."

Lund leaned back in his creaky chair, considered if he should or not, then said, "Federal Justice Minister Francis Lavelle, remember him?"

Michael did. "Yeah, he was shot to death in his car, right at the Justice Building or something back in '80, right."

"'81 actually."

"What are you saying, John. Did that have something to do with this operation?"

"Well you tell me. He was shot right before he was supposed to testify for a House of Commons Legal Affairs Committee investigating the operation."

"Testify to what exactly?"

"His part in it, I'm guessing. But who knows. He was killed before he could he talk."

Michael's look said *I need more*. "C'mon, John."

Lund sipped his coffee. "It all started with the RCMP in British Columbia screaming at Ottawa because two Security Service undercovers were murdered Christmas eve in '81. Shit was hitting the fan because the Commissioner didn't even know they were there, and that was looking an awful lot like the force was losing control of their Security Service. Anyway, it all came out that the Attorney General of BC had all but bribed Lavelle to green light a rogue operation and transfer three RCMP recruits right out of training camp. They were listed as E-Specials when we were told about their murders, but the reality was, no one at RCMP HQ knew they were there. And the force was damn sensitive about that because they'd been fighting rumours of informants in BC's division."

"So who were they investigating?" Michael asked.

Lund smirked. "Who would you say was the biggest mobster in Vancouver in the '80s?"

Michael didn't have to think that through. It was a name he'd written in his column several times over the past month uncovering the Coastal Holding angle. "Mario Morelatto."

"Yep. One of his Northern Scarlett ships was caught coming out of Cuba, heading for the Panama Canal with a ton of drugs. That really got the CIA interested. I mean really interested since they were knee deep in the Contras business and the drug trade."

"That couldn't have gone over well with the Mounties." Michael said.

"No it did not. And it became a political nightmare for Lavelle's Attorney General buddy in BC, because who wants to be the politician held responsible for the biggest heroine and arms dealer operating right under your nose." Lund stopped, a grin growing. "Do you know who the Attorney General of BC was in '81?"

Michael had to smirk when he said, "Seth Peterson."

"That's right," Lund said.

Michael took a deep breath. "Dangerous people," he said. "Holy shit."

"Yeah, and it gets better," Lund said. "A few years later Morelatto launches SeaCorp and it becomes one of the biggest cargo shipping lines on the west coast, and guess who he puts on the board of Westfor, one of SeaCorps largest conglomerates."

"Seth Petersen," Michael said, the scale of it all starting to make sense.

"And now the Prime Minister is enjoying a majority in the house, and his biggest supporter is still Mario Morelatto. You gotta see the irony." Lund took a bite of the sub, washed it down with some coffee. "But you know what is really fucking ironic here is that ever since the Coastal Holding fiasco broke, the same two names keep making front page that few know were involved in Operation Scarlet all those years ago."

Michael leaned in, every journalist instinct in him tingling. "Who?"

Lund smirked and said, "Premier Roy Graham and that fancy lawyer of his, Coleman Dresher."

CHAPTER 26

The Premier & the Lawyer

Coleman Dresher read over the affidavit while he waited in his plush, Lipton, Jackson, and Mackenzie law office complete with panoramic view of downtown Vancouver at night. He glanced at the Howard Miller grandfather clock across the room. It was 9:00 pm and as usual, it was raining. The affidavit was of paramount importance to Dresher who had to cleverly plot a legal strategy that not only masked his own involvement in the Coast Holding fiasco, but provided a believable defense for his client; the very unpopular Premier Roy Graham. The domino effect Graham's Coastal Holding indictment could have on his business partners - a list that included Dresher - was unsettling to say the least. The whole affair threatened to reveal forty some years of kickbacks, embezzling, political malfeasance, and now maybe even murder. The heat had definitely been on since the story broke, but now with a simple phone call from Ottawa earlier in the afternoon, a new threat had reared up that could truly fry them all.

The door opened and Sasha strolled in, standing before him in a kimono, the front open enough to tease with her perfect breasts. The firm of Lipton, Jackson, and Mackenzie had been vacated for several hours so Dresher demanded she slip into something a secretary wouldn't normally strut around in between nine and five. He was immediately aroused as she knelt down with dreamy eyes and pouting mouth, and performed what she was really hired for. His head tipped back as her warm mouth swallowed him. She was well into the deed when the phone rang and Dresher lunged to answer it, leaving her shocked and dismayed.

"Yeah," Dresher answered.

"It's me," the caller said. His voice deep and unsettled.

"Hang on." Dresher cupped the receiver. "Sasha, why don't you go get some wine out of Glenn's liquor cabinet." He zipped up then dug in his drawer. "Here's the key."

"Excuse me?" she said defiantly.

"This is an important call."

"Important enough to forget I was sucking you off."

Dresher's eyes narrowed. "I pay you a hundred thousand a year for that service, sweetheart. Now move your ass."

Sasha rose off her knees, tightened her kimono, snapped the key out of his hand and marched out. He waited until the door closed behind her.

"Okay," he said into the phone. "Did you find out anymore?"

"Yeah."

"Who is it?"

"A reporter named Michael Spencer."

"Who's Michael Spencer?" Dresher demanded.

~

Sasha heard the name on the other side of the door. She was pissed and decided she had no intention of pilfering senior partner Glenn Ibermann's liquor cabinet. While Dresher took his precious call from Ottawa she breezed into Ibermann's vast office with a new agenda. She wasn't sleeping with a sixty-four year old egomaniac for pleasure anyway; she deserved more than a measly hundred thousand a year, mistress or not. It was time to up the ante and that meant she needed leverage.

She would come to regret the decision but she went straight for Ibermann's phone. A secretary with her bloated salary knew what buttons to push. She held the flash button, then the mute button, knowing they wouldn't hear her. She bit her lip - this was so exciting – and lifted the receiver just when Dresher said, "And who's this cop?"

The deep voice from Ottawa was low and hushed. "Some SWAT guy."

"Is he one of yours?"

"No," the voice said. "Where's Morelatto?"

"He's on the White Knight," Dresher said begrudgingly.

"He left you holding the bag didn't he, Dresher?"

"We pay you remember?" Dresher snarled. If there was a moment when common sense would've ensued for Sasha, that would've been the cue for her to get off the line; but she didn't, this was too good. Dresher's voice more menacing than she'd ever heard before. "Don't fuck with me now. Don't make me push."

"Alright, alright," the caller from Ottawa relented. The deep sigh of a trapped man breathed against Sasha's ears. This is juicy shit! "You don't have to threaten me," the voice said.

"Good." Dresher said, temper easing. "What does this guy want with Operation Scarlet anyway?"

"They were trying to lift Larry Hicks's file."

Sasha could feel Dresher's breathing change over the phone, short gasps and suddenly nervous. "Larry Hicks? Why?"

"Adoption search. Apparently this Spencer guy is looking for his father."

Dresher obviously slapped his desk. "Sonofabitch!"

~

"What do you want me to do?" the voice asked.

Dresher thought a moment, glanced at the closed door before he asked, "Do you have access to the surveillance?"

"I can arrange it."

"Fine, you do that."

"What about the Prime Minister?"

"What about him?"

"He's not exactly an ally."

"Don't worry about him," Dresher said. "Morelatto has him taken care of."

"Right," the voice said, clearly not convinced.

"Just get on with it." Dresher heard Sasha's bare feet puckering across the library hardwood beyond his door. "I'll be in touch." He hung up as she entered his office. He tucked in his shirt and without so much as an explanation, instructed her to get dressed and go home. He wouldn't need her any further tonight.

Sasha was fine with that.

CHAPTER 27

The Drive-By

    A brown Chevy half-ton inched stealthily past the Spencer house at 421 Churchill Drive with the headlights off. A driver and two men were inside, checking out the white brick bungalow that was dark except for a valance light seeping through the kitchen blinds. What they didn't expect was the tourist ship River Rouge, lit up by deck and cabin lights and teeming with party-goers to be lumbering down the Red River, the diesel chug of it's dual engines and taped salsa music echoing in the humid night. The half-ton drove off.

    Five minutes later the Chevy half-ton pulled up and stopped in front of the white bungalow again. The river was quiet this time. The driver played lookout while the two men in black fatigues advanced the front door. Team 2 was tagging the wife who was still on her shift at the Victoria Hospital. Once at the front door, one of them produced a palm held device with LCD revealing a satellite thermal view inside the house. Ghostly white images marked the targets inside, one being Michael Spencer sleeping in his bedroom. The daughter, a teen, was in her room, texting late at night. And the dog was flaked out in the kitchen. Linoleum is cooler, he suspected.

    He pointed the palm held at the door. It was NVD equipped. Night vision digital technology made their intel missions a lot less risky. No flashes, and the images uplinked in real time with 4K resolution and 64 bit encryption. He captured the alarm system keypad just inside the front door with blinking LED to indicate; activated. A CompSec home security sticker was adhered to the top right corner of the front door window. The driver took iPhone pictures of the neighboring houses and park across the street.

    Suddenly the dog's white image on the LCD stirred. He crouched down and signaled to his partner who automatically stepped behind one of the oaks cluttering the yard. They hated pets. It just made their job more difficult. He watched the dog's image stroll into the girl's bedroom.

He waved all clear to the driver then scuttled around and surveyed the back yard and the houses across the back lane for visibility. The row of oaks lining the back fence would cloak their surreptitious activity. The park across the street was desolate and dark. They knew the Spencers had a weekend trip to the wife's parents in Regina planned; something to do with her upcoming birthday – which they knew a party would be held the coming week. Hopefully they'd take the dog, but regardless the team would come prepared.

Satisfied, the two men climbed quietly into the brown Chevy half-ton and pulled away. A 4 x 4 six houses down u-turned and headed in the opposite direction.

CHAPTER 28

The CIA Connection

The man known in intelligence circles as the Chameleon was a man with a lot on his mind. Sam Mitchell, the Deputy Director of Operations for the CIA, had just gotten off the phone with his underling, Sam Cholan, and the news from HQ Langley was not good. The three remaining members of his elite team training in Northern Australia's Red Center just north of Alice Springs were dead; executed in their bunks in safe houses no one was to have known about. And now as a result of the carnage Mitchell would have to provide answers to the oversight committee. He would have to divulge the Javelin's identity, account for funds deposited in numbered accounts in Sydney, and tolerate a tongue lashing from the President's National Security Advisor for requesting the NSA re-task those damn satellites over an abandoned runway no one wanted to know about anymore.

Sam Mitchell was getting too old for the game he had said to his wife when Sam Cholan's cell number popped up on his caller ID. He wanted to enjoy retirement now, spoil his grandchildren, and spend his evenings sitting with his wife on the deck of their nice house overlooking San Diego bay, across from the Silver Strand – a seven mile long tombolo. The US Naval Amphibious Base known for SEAL training could be seen across the bay from their dock. And that was as close as Mitchell wanted to get to any paramilitary covert initiatives anymore. But it was becoming painfully apparent in the last few weeks that all that relaxation was not to be. An inquiry from Winnipeg lit a fire, and the botched joint operation he headed with the Security Service nearly forty years ago just wouldn't go away. He was glad Larry Hicks reconsidered and called him. It was their only hope to put an end to all of it. Larry's birth son up in Winnipeg wouldn't stand a chance without them.

It was a warm Saturday night. Quiet. Calm. It would've been a perfect evening for him and his wife to sit with cocktails and soak up the San Diego skyline glittering off the serene bay, or maybe fire up their small yacht, appropriately named 'Chameleon', and cruise along the Strand or head up to La Jolla. But she was out with the Coronado woman's auxiliary and he was home alone. And alone he would die. It would be the last night of Sam Mitchell's life.

For at that very moment he was so preoccupied he failed to notice the dark figure rising out of the shallow water beside his yacht, aiming a high-powered weapon directly at him. It was the flash of thin red light that startled him. The bullet cleanly penetrated the center of the Chameleon's forehead.

CHAPTER 29

The Tip of the Sword Man

The iPhone rang.

Floyd Webber appreciated his Sundays off; his wife insisted on it. After years in the RCMP's Security Service and CSIS, his wife had earned the sabbatical request. But that all changed when Braden MacDuff came calling mid October 2001; weeks after 9/11 woke up the western world, asking Floyd Webber to head up the new, ultra-covert SSET teams to be cloaked within the Communications Security Establishment (CSE). Sunday's off was only one of Webber's stipulations. The second condition was the ex-Security Service, E Special commander did not want to be strapped to a desk in the nation's capital. The view down Metcalfe Street held no fascination for him and, besides, Floyd Webber had lost his ideological patriotism long before the Security Service's demise in '84. By the time he left to join CSIS, he found the 'old horse' organization fastidious and playing more politics than security. He had his own ideas of how a surveillance team should operate, ideals that clashed with the RCMP's stringent conduct codes that were nearly impossible to comply with while playing the dirty game of espionage. But shortly after he crossed over, the Air India plane exploded over the Atlantic and the disaster all but exhausted Canadian intelligence credibility with reports of tape erasing, asset mishandling, endless malfeasance and side stepping that all but highlighted the dysfunction between the rival agencies charged with the country's security. But when the only remaining witness who could finger the bombers was murdered in his Surrey garage in '98, and all because the Mounties and CSIS couldn't coordinate their efforts, Webber had had enough and left the career, vowing never to return. Then after three tedious years of semi-retirement along came MacDuff and the SSET challenge, promising complete autonomy because Floyd Webber had a reputation for getting results. His third condition was to remain in Winnipeg - Webber's hometown. His wife had earned that much as well.

After a year the first unit proved so deft and stealth that two more teams were commissioned and stationed in Montreal and Vancouver. Thinly veiled mandates were passed and unlimited funds expounded and cleverly hidden within DND and CSE budgets and expense sheets. The SSET had unrestricted jurisdiction over all of Canada and abroad, and if needed, JTF2 command at their beck and call. And while the American congress abandon TIA technology due to privacy violation pressures, the SSET adapted the Total Information Awareness architecture and so won their own satellite configurations to achieve it. Face and gait recognition algorithms were bleeding edge in the new world of surveillance, no matter how many advocacy groups blockaded its use; the technology was there. In recent years the terrorism threats attacking homeland security since 9/11 only fortified Webber and the patriot MacDuff that the SSET would deploy whatever advantage they could get their hands on, and all without political or agency bureaucracy interfering. Even the American's NSA were naive to SSET intrusive power while only a few select CIA had knowledge of Floyd Webber and his elite units; Sam Mitchell had been so privy. This was the world Floyd Webber lived and thrived in, so long as it wasn't on Sundays.

He squeezed out two more bench presses then grabbed the ringing iPhone within arm's reach. Unknown number. He knew it would be Al Garrick calling, as he was ordered, because the team never interfered with the sabbatical. But Braden MacDuff was running out of time in Ottawa and stressed for the hundredth time an hour ago the urgency of the situation. He had to give McIvor something to take to TARC and Hugh Long, the Inspector-General, and quite possibly the Prime Minister first thing Monday morning.

Webber answered. "Yeah?"

"It's me, Chief," Al Garrick said. He sounded too young to be a spymaster.

"Where are we at?"

"I've triangulated their cell phones. Spencer had a few calls about an hour ago. One of them was the cop who was dog sitting for them. He was pissed and told Michael to call him as soon as they get back from Regina. Something about the dog peeing in the raspberry bushes and eating them out of house and home or something."

"Al, I don't want to hear about the damn dog. What else?" Webber reached for a towel.

"A woman named Jessica called Jasmine Spencer's cell."

"Did you trace?"

"Yeah. She's Jessica Ingham, employed at CFS. She works in the big ice cube on Portage. Anyway she said she was curious how the call to a Maggie Gunthier went."

Floyd Webber already knew Maggie Gunthier, but he would have to play this particular mission uncomfortably close to his chest. "Okay. Anything else?"

"Spencer's dad called from Hawaii to wish Mrs. Spencer a happy birthday," Garrick said. It sounded like he was sucking on something; Webber knew it would be a Tootsie Pop. "He didn't use a cell. The number belongs to a bar called The Hula Hut."

Webber grinned. "The what?"

"The Hula Hut."

"Good for him," Webber said, rising off the bench, tossing the towel over the barbell. "Where are the Spencers now?"

"An hour out of Regina."

"Okay, have Gregg pick me up. Tell the team we're a go." There was silence. Webber sensed the question. "What, Al?"

"Why are we tracking this guy, Chief?"

"Because he poses a threat to national security. What do you care?"

"Right, Chief. Mine is not to question why, right." There was always healthy sarcasm with Al Garrick; it was his way.

"Just stay on top of him, Al." Webber clicked off. He ambled upstairs, wondered into the living room and plunked down beside his wife on the couch. She was reading one of those Gina Norris romance novels she was always lost in. He didn't understand what anyone got out of those silly romance novels but it was her Sunday too.

"Take a shower," she said without breaking her read.

"Later."

He went to the fridge, cut up a fresh kiwi and poured himself some OJ, and stared out the window. He couldn't stop thinking about Michael Spencer and his family walking into their home, completely unaware they were being spied on now. But Webber knew it was the right thing to do. It was the least he could do for an old friend.

CHAPTER 30

Meanwhile in the Real World

While Floyd Webber was cutting kiwi in his kitchen, Milt Smith was letting Sabe out the back door of his house on the corner of Kingsway Avenue and Lindsay Street, oblivious to the nondescript sedan parked just off the northeast corner of his backyard fence. Claudette was watching TV and Samantha and Wyatt were safely tucked in. Sabe roamed the yard, panting from the stifling humidity, sniffing in search of a good spot to lift his leg. Raspberry bushes would have to do again.

Meanwhile somewhere east of Regina, Michael's SUV cruised east down the Trans-Canada Highway for home. Katie was sleeping in the back and Jasmine was rambling on about her infuriating mother. Nothing was ever good enough for her. She hated this. She hated that. Nobody was there to help her prepare. She did it all by herself. Rocky, Jasmine's dad, sleeps too much. Who's this Danny Gregory kid? Katie is too young for boys. They're only after one thing; on and on and on.

Michael really wasn't listening. He stared and drove and nodded once in a while, but mostly just thought. He couldn't shake that mysterious call the other night. He wondered what Evelyn Hicks looked like? She sounded so scared and the voice calling out for her in the background sounded concerned, not the hardened tone of a killer or corrupt cop. Somehow Michael just couldn't accept the idea he was the natural son of a traitor, or worse, a murderer. Any thoughts of birth parents eventually brought him around to his dad, Olie Spencer. He was the real father who took him to hockey practices at five in the morning, taught him how to fish and ski, and encouraged him to be a reporter, and who danced with Jasmine at their wedding, and fought back tears when they told him he had a granddaughter. During those Friday catch-up calls, Olie always hinted they should plan another Hawaii visit. It always made Michael smile when he remembered poker nights with his dad and the retired Hula Hut cronies who mercilessly prodded Olie about that pink Hawaiian shirt he was so proud of because Katie picked it out. She truly was the apple of her grandfather's eye. Michael made a mental note to call him when they got home. It felt wrong he didn't know what was happening with the search. Besides, he just missed hearing his voice.

He thought of Nolan Grant while he watched the white lines flick under the fender. He hoped Milt's friend had some light to shed. Lance had emailed earlier in the day telling him he found the articles on Carl Friesen and the murdered Justice Minister, Francis Lavelle. Michael imagined Dr. Friesen mangled in a convertible Corvette and for some reason he couldn't understand, flashed on Archie Atkinson sipping ice tea. He had the nagging feeling he had seen him somewhere before. He recalled Lily Atkinson's warm, infectious smile and Maggie Gunthier's suspicion when she asked his name, that ominous scene from Citizen Kane playing in the background.

A car passed, the glaring headlights hurting his eyes. He remembered a light brown half-ton truck; saw it a few too many times on Friday after they left division D headquarters. Then there was Cindy Greene's computer screen with those two words that summed up the wall Michael had been hitting.

ACCESS DENIED   ACCESS DENIED   ACCESS DENIED
ACCESS DENIED   ACCESS DENIED   ACCESS DENIED

Fuck!!

Jasmine was mumbling somewhere in the distance, then suddenly.

"Michael!" Her green eyes cut like ice. "Are you even listening to me!"

CHAPTER 31

The Invasion Begins

Al Garrick was the product of one too many James Bond movies. As a teenager he devoured books on real life spies and the cloak and dagger world of intelligence gathering and cold war espionage. It was so cool. Now, after being a full-fledged, counter-intelligence agent for CSE for going on five years, the allure of women, adventure, and fast cars with unbelievable gadgets had long since lost its juvenile appeal. The reality of such a career was far less dramatic than anything Ian Fleming dreamed up. That's not to say Al Garrick was disinterested with his work; quite the contrary. After signing up with CSIS at twenty-five, then jumping ship to CSE two years later, he was even more of a spy addict; more so after his appointment with Floyd Webber's SSET unit. The ultra-secret surveillance team was the closest thing to James Bond one could get. The three units were so protected and so secretive Garrick was not even aware of such a team within CSE until he was recruited for his special talent; computers.

His unique skills as a programmer/hacker made him an invaluable asset to the SSET. All three units had at least one satellite communications and tracking technology expert on board; fancy titles to disguise what they really were; hackers extraordinaire. Without them the objectives would not be successful.

Garrick was seated at his surveillance super computer in the unit's covert command center - an office with lead lined curtains shielding the windows and authorized personnel hand-identification cyber-locks securing the one and only entrance. It took him only a few minutes to hack into CompSec's database.

And they call this security?

His rogue program scanned the index, leaving no information tags, and instantly 421 Churchill Drive highlighted. He adjusted the hairline mic to his mouth.

"Chief..."

421 Churchill Drive

"...I got it."

Floyd Webber pressed the dual voice transmitter and aural receiver wedged in his ear when Al Garrick's voice broke over. He was sitting in a new Dodge 4x4 that belonged to his youngest subordinate, Gregg Redekopp; a poster boy for the perfect blend of soldier and agent. They were both dressed in black t-shirts. It was too hot for windbreakers. Redekopp, positioned behind the wheel, kept his eyes on the park across the street. Like Webber, he had the same device wedged in his ear. The entire team had them; sixty-four bit encrypted of course, and virtually impenetrable from outside signals. The SSET had the best microwave and laser tools.

It was 4:00 am. It was dark. It was perfect. 421 Churchill Drive was ten houses up the street from Redekopp's 4x4 and team 2 was waiting in the back lane for the go ahead from Webber. Another of Webber's team, Simon Johnson, was cruising a half-kilometer perimeter around the Spencer residence. Johnson drove a light brown Chevy half-ton.

"Are we clear, Al?" Webber asked.

"We're clear," Garrick responded. "I've overridden their sensors and we have a twenty minute window starting right..."

SSET command

"...Now," Garrick said poking the 'enter' key then rubbing his hands – let the games begin. The highlighted strip of 421 Churchill Drive began flashing on his monitor. "Twenty minutes and counting, Chief."

421

"Are we damn sure, Al?" Webber asked, watching the white brick bungalow up the street.

"We're damn sure, Chief," Garrick said.

Webber grinned at Redekopp, whose face was speckled with shadows of moonlight sifting through overhead oak trees. "We're sure, Rent-A-Cop," he said. Redekopp smiled, he was always ready to go. Webber pressed his ear device again. The damn things never fit properly. "You kids copy that back there?"

"We copy, Chief," one of the members of team 2 replied. They were crouched down between the oaks and the Spencer's backyard fence, cloaked in black fatigues, caps, gloves, and sneakers.

"Move in," Webber ordered and they sprinted across the yard to the back door.

Webber wiped the perspiration from his forehead. "Too damn hot for this isn't it," he said to Redekopp who nodded, keeping a sharp eye.

Webber glanced at his wrist-watch styled LCD mini showing the same satellite intel inside the Spencer house that Garrick was watching on his giant screens back at command. There were no thermal images inside. Seventeen minutes to go. "The Jets aren't going to the playoffs this year," he said.

Redekopp was a diehard hockey fan and took immediate offense. "Yes, they are."

"No they're not."

"Yes they are."

"Redekopp who is your chief and commander."

Redekopp could only sigh and shake his head. "You're gonna jinx the whole season, Chief."

Webber grinned – he loved getting the kid's goat. He pressed the earpiece. "We in yet?"

"Working on it, Chief"

Team 2 crouched a little when the screen door squeaked when opened. The first agent, a woman, worked on the door lock and had it defeated quicker than using the key. Her male partner glanced around, making sure no neighbors had any lights on before they slipped inside. They paused in the landing, careful to not let the screen door cry out again. The kitchen valance light was still on.

"Chief, we're in."

"Okay, one second," Webber said over their earpieces.

They waited for confirmation to proceed. If Garrick's override failed to blind the CompSec sensors, they would have only twenty seconds to vacate the premises. Winnipeg Police would not realize they would be arresting two SSET; no one could ever know that. CSE and CSIS both expected anonymity from SSET operations and would deny any authorization out of Ottawa that condoned the illegal activities of those teams - even if they did have SIRC and TARC approval. The team didn't need the hassle. So they waited.

"Al, confirm Compsec down and neighbors, please," Webber

double-checked. You could never be too cautious.

Redekopp's attention was glued to the side view mirror.

SSET Command

Garrick checked anyway. 421 Churchill Drive was clean and secure. The house next door showed two thermal ghosts prone in their beds. But the white images of a couple two doors over were locked together, a set of arms gripping what was probably a headboard. They won't notice anything. They'd been going at it nightly since Garrick pointed his satellite imagery over 421, and he knew they were good for another hour of humping. He leaned back. God, he was good. "Gotta have faith, Chief."

421

Webber pushed his earpiece. "Go, team 2." He noticed Redekopp locked on his side view mirror. "What?"

"Chief, we got a car coming very slowly with the lights off."

Webber quickly peered over his shoulder as they sank down in the seat when a late model sedan inched past and parked about a hundred feet in front of the Dodge.

"Everything, okay?" It was Garrick over earpieces. He was seeing the sedan as well.

"Not sure," Webber said. They watched the car nuzzle the curb. The instant the brake lights went out the engine went off, a thin stream of exhaust floated from the tailpipe and hung in the humid moonlight. The couple inside met in the middle and by the way their heads bobbed back and forth it was obvious the kissing was rather frenzied.

Redekopp grabbed a pair of pocket sized, night vision binoculars off the seat and smiled.

"I don't believe this," Webber said. "We got a couple necking out here."

SSET Command

Garrick aimed his satellite view over the sedan; a couple thermal necking. "Man, I wanna live on this street."

The computer clock was at nine minutes.

421

Redekopp was still peeping. "Copy that, Al."

"Seen enough yet?" Webber said, sounding more parental than commander.

The young agent answered without looking away from the car. "My season seats at the games aren't this good, Chief."

Webber didn't bother commenting. He pressed his earpiece. "How's it going in there, kids?"

"Almost done," the woman responded. She was in Katie Spencer's bedroom. A couple portraits of what she assumed to be grandparents were on the dresser. She made it a habit not to notice the pictures. Pictures revealed people. Families. Loved ones. This was simply a target's residence and she was simply doing what she was trained to do. So long as she ignored the pictures her conscience ignored her. But who could ignore such a loud, pink Hawaiian shirt. She just had to look. She would not place mics or cameras as Webber did not want the girl's bedroom compromised.

Twelve minutes later team 2 had anchored video acceleration transmitters in the attic and placed wafer mics behind the master bedroom headboard and the bathroom. Next was the kitchen. The man faked a whistle when he drew her attention to the massive dog dish in the corner. It was chewed up pretty good.

"Chief, they've got four minutes," they heard Garrick say over their earpieces.

SSET Command

Garrick had his feet kicked up with a Coke in his hand and his remote keyboard in his lap. "I need a minute to close this window."

421

"Copy that," Webber said, a trained eye on the sedan. Things were getting down right indecent. The couple had flipped themselves into the backseat and the woman's head was out of view. Webber tapped the steering wheel to interrupt Redekopp's spying. "You're going to go blind you know," Webber said.

Redekopp flashed a clever grin, the binoculars still aimed. "Yeah, but what a way to go."

"Three minutes, Candace. You copy that?" Webber said.

Inside the Spencer house Candace Reimer watched Kyle Lenning press another wafer mic behind a family portrait in the living room. "Copy that, Chief," she said, noticing a name and number scribbled on the pad by the phone – *Gunthier*. She twisted her arm to point the face of her LCD wrist watch and snapped a quick shot of the phone pad then followed Kyle to the basement stairs. She pressed another button on her wrist LCD, generating the image of Garrick with his feet kicked up.

SSET Command

"Two and half minutes, Candace," Garrick said when her NVD image opened a separate window. The team's wrist LCD's were dual tasked as micro-digital video camera with real time uplink to Garrick's mainframe super computer humming around him. A compiler program was already tracing the Gunthier number from Candace's picture that was up on one of the monitors.

"Did you get that?" she asked over the speakers.

"System's tracing now," he said, dropping his feet to the floor, pitching the Coke can into the wastebasket, and nudging in to the desk. Al Garrick was preparing to do battle.

421

Webber pressed his earpiece. "Kyle, how you doing in there?"

The woman was straddling her lover, her blouse undone, bouncing up and down with the palms of her hands pressed against the back window for better leverage.

"Wow," Redekopp said. "Is she going."

"Almost done," Kyle Lenning replied from the Spencer's basement rec room. Candace was pressing a micro video camera over the computer desk, lodging it in the smoke alarm in the ceiling. A moment later she pushed the faceplate back in place.

"Chief, we're done."

SSET Command

"A minute thirty seconds, Chief," Garrick said, fixed to the computer clock. It was going to be close, his hands poised above the keyboard, ready to strike.

421

The back window of the sedan was fogged up now.

"You kids clear?" Webber asked. He didn't like when it cut this close.

If the mission was a bust he would be the one answering to Braden MacDuff and Clifton McIvor, and ultimately the Inspector General and the Prime Minister; especially on this one. Larry Hicks's natural son had triggered a storm of panic.

Kyle was conscious how far squeaking hinges carried on a quiet night, and eased the screen door closed till it clicked.
"We're clear," Candace whispered.
They scuttled through the backyard for the cover of the oaks.

"Go, Al," Webber instructed, eyes riveted to his wrist LCD. This was too close.
Redekopp watched the sedan rocking slightly. "I'll bet she's a screamer."
"Gregg," Webber said, eyes on his LCD. "Shut up."

SSET Command

    Thirty-two seconds!
Garrick's fingers nimbly flew around the keyboard. He slapped his hands together as another window generated. He clicked that one down.
    Twenty seconds!
C'mon on, baby!
    Another menu window.
    Fifteen seconds.
    This will conclude your session - do you wish to save this configuration and IP signature on target system?
No! C'mon on. Let's go!
    Ten seconds
    IP signature tracing interface. Track this IP and all data packets?
Yes!
    Trace confirmed. Data mining parameters…please submit.
    All sources. All parms.
Exit!
    Satellite disengaging, mask signature traces?
    Mask confirmed.
C'mon!
    Six seconds.
"Damn, that was close," Garrick sighed and leaned back. Sex wasn't even that good.
"Whoa baby. We're outta there."

421

Redekopp whistled, his grin as wide as ever, still peeping. "This guy is my hero."

Webber was ignoring the sedan now. "Johnson, you got them?" he asked.

Candace and Kyle were already climbing into Simon Johnson's light brown Chevy half ton the moment it approached them in the back lane.

"I got 'em, Chief." Johnson said. He was a big and brawny agent, as he should be since coming from the JTF-2 into Webber's covert world a year ago.

The black caps and gloves were removed and tossed to the floorboards. Candace and Kyle were sweating. It was the heat, not the adrenaline, because this kind of subvert mission was that routine for this team. Johnson high-fived the flaxen haired Candace, then eased the Chevy up the lane.

Redekopp tossed the binoculars to the seat, depressed the clutch, turned the key, slipped the stick shift into first. "The office, Chief?"

But Webber was looking across the Red River at the deck he knew to be Archie and Lily Atkinson's house. "One more stop to make."

"Okay," Redekopp said, knowing full well the instant the headlights lit up the sedan, the couple would be scurrying to cover up. He flicked his eyebrows at Webber.

Webber just shook his head. "I worry about you sometimes, you know that, Redekopp."

Redekopp smiled and hit the switch.

CHAPTER 32

Home Sweet Home

Jasmine and Michael were flaked out on the couch. He stroked her long, flowing black hair while she laid her head on his lap. The blue tooth Bose quietly played smooth jazz. It had been a long, arduous weekend so now began the soothing. Katie was in her room, sure to be texting Danny Gregory. Jasmine rolled over, purred contently, rubbing Michael's lap.

He couldn't relax.

The front window verticals were open. Beyond the oak trees fluttering their leaves in the moonlit wind, he had an unobstructed view of the Atkinson's house across the Red; the nagging thought he'd seen Archie before wouldn't go away.

The front door was ajar, the warm breeze stirring within the foyer ever so pleasantly. Salsa music from afar gradually crept in over the jazz while approaching deck lights gleaned the front window. The River Rouge riverboat lulled lazily behind the trees, its promenade deck loaded with party-goers dancing to the thumping Salsa beat. The ship passed, the carousing dissipated until nothing but smooth jazz soothed the living room. Michael looked down at Jasmine, her eyes closed and beautiful. She sensed his tension.

"You're thinking too much," she said. Her soft green eyes opened, looked up at him. "She'll call again, don't worry."

Then his iPhone rang.

SSET Command

Garrick put down his Coke. He was enjoying the smooth jazz from the Spencer's living room. His super computer finished cloning the caller by the time Michael Spencer picked up his ringing iPhone. Everything from password files to bank accounts, credit cards, internet IP signatures, SMTP and POP email addresses and server logins; virtually the caller's digital fingerprint ripped out of the labyrinthine array of DNS servers the world over in mere seconds. Nothing was private in Garrick's world. A picture of Milt Smith spooled onto his giant monitor, followed by Claudette, Samantha and little Wyatt.

Garrick kicked his feet up with his Coke in hand. And listened.

421

"So, how'd it go?" Milt asked.

Michael glanced down at Jasmine, her eyes closed again. "It was a...good visit." His inflection said something else.

"I heard that," she whispered.

Michael smiled and stroked. "How did the weekend go with Sabe?" he asked Milt.

"Damn this dog can eat. And shit. I've been moving mountains out of the backyard, man."

Michael was chuckling. It felt good.

SSET Command

Garrick nearly choked on a mouthful of Coke and proceeded to laugh himself.

421

"So," Milt said, "anymore phone calls?"

"No." Michael glanced at Maggie Gunthier's scribbled phone number on the pad beside the phone. "Any news from Nolan?" he asked.

"He called me yesterday, said he has a few friends at HQ Ottawa that work in the administration section."

SSET Command

Garrick's feet dropped to the floor, the Coke on the desk.
Here we go.

421

"Get this," Milt said. "His buddy told him the file on Operation Scarlet had been pulled already. Thought it to be odd that someone would physically pull an old Security Service file."

"Curious." The hair stroking halted. "Coincidence?"

"At this point, who knows? I have to admit, man, this little search of yours spooked me on Friday."

"Tell me about it. I haven't thought about anything else."

"I'm a bit concerned we might have put Cindy in a tight spot."

"Yeah, I was too." Michael sat up to Jasmine's slight dismay; the other nagging thought. "We're you getting the feeling we were being followed on Friday." That got a look from Jasmine.

Milt was quiet for a moment then said, "Brown Chevy half-ton right?"

SSET Command

Garrick's mouth dropped open. Webber was going to tear Simon a new asshole for that. He minimized the window and opened another. His trace program was already filtering relevant names from Michael and Milt's conversation, matching from their indexed contacts list, mining the new target's IP signatures and SIN numbers instantaneously. Seconds later two photos popped up on the giant monitor; Nolan Grant - RCMP – Headingley detachment; Cindy Greene – WPS – computer admin.

421

"So you saw it too?" Michael said.

"Yeah, I saw it," Milt said. "What time can I bring Sabe tomorrow?"

Jasmine lifted from the couch and headed for the bedroom. She knew how the boys got when they started, besides her day was over.

"Anytime," Michael said, suggesting he'll be right behind her.

"Good," Milt said, his playful tone back in his voice. "Cause I've gotta go and let that mountain shitter soak Claudette's raspberry bushes again."

Michael quipped that. "I'm going to sleep."

"Fuck you, Spencer."

They chuckled then hung up. Michael killed the jazz, switched the lights off, closed the verticals, locked the front and back doors, set the Compsec security code and nudged one of the stools back in place under the island counter in the kitchen, unaware Al Garrick was watching every move.

Jasmine was under the covers, gone for the night. Michael spooned into her and drifted off. Little did he realize he would wake up in a far different world.

SSET Command

The targets were finally asleep so Garrick was calling it a night as well. The SSET command center had a bed in a back room, appropriately called the Snooze Room, with a sensor alarm that went off if the computer tracers activated. Surveillance meant long hours. He finished another Coke; caffeine the hacker's drug of choice. He popped open the satellite thermal screen for one last check up on the Spencer's white images fast asleep at 421 Churchill Drive. He opened an encrypted chat window; the preferred method of communication for the team and typed a quick message to Webber.

Chief, I think we have enough to get TARC authorization.

Then Al Garrick shuffled into the Snooze Room, plunked into the bed, and drifted off almost the instant his head hit the pillow.

CHAPTER 33

The Freedom Room

The Freedom Room in 24 Sussex Drive had been appropriately named in the Prime Minister's case. He stood under the grand arch leading to the balcony and contently puffed. The sky was cloudy, but rays of sunlight broke through, showering the Gatineau Hills to the northeast and flickering sun diamonds off the Ottawa River churning beyond the estate's backyard precipice. He took a nice, long drag and watched sculler teams practice their symmetrical rowing. He had been a rower himself back in those simple days when he studied law at the University of British Columbia, chased pretty co-eds, and pounded beer kegs; before malfeasance and corruption soured a promising political career. In another month he'd venture to Rideau Hall and bid the Governor General dissolve government, unleashing the election animal. Then it would be fifty-seven days of no sleep, campaigning, hand shaking and speeches. Premier Roy Graham's Coastal Holding committee hearing was in three weeks; July 5th. Once over that hump, and if unscathed from the fallout, the election would be relatively easy for Prime Minister Seth Peterson; at least that's what his inner circle was telling him. He already had a majority in the House of Commons, and contrary to public opinion, he felt the Canadian people would prefer he occupy 24 Sussex Drive rather than his opponent. The Prime Minister did not entertain thoughts of defeat because he had no interest living at Stornoway, the official residence of the Leader of the Opposition; there was no staff to speak of, no RCMP guards, no view of the river, and no chauffeur.

What would be the fucking point to that?

He checked his watch. His private ritual was nearly over. Like a teenager sneaking his first cigarette, he stepped back of the bay window's arch and glanced through the doorway, across the hall to the master bedroom. The bedroom door was open. That meant only one thing. His wife was up. She could have seen him already, probably smelled the smoke; her ovaries and need for sex was all but gone but her olfactory senses were impeccable.

He closed the French doors after flicking the butt over the railing, breezed through the hallway where house staff muttered dutiful good mornings, and descended the spiral staircase that spilled onto the checkerboard tile floor of the main foyer of the Prime Minister's elegant residence. He cordially waved to one of the prettier housemaids dusting off the baby grand piano in the enclosed sunroom as he strolled for the main entrance. An RCMP battalion attended him when he breezed out the heavy wooden door.

Marty, the PM's personal chauffeur, was waiting with the back door of the limousine open for his Prime Minister who marched briskly under the front entrance canopy. "Pushing it kinda close, aren't you sir?" Marty said, glancing at his watch. He knew about the Freedom room ritual. Marty knew alot.

"I'm the goddamn Prime Minister of Canada, Marty, and I'm afraid of my wife catching me smoking," he said.

"We all are, sir," Marty smartly replied as the PM sank into the back while a plain clothes Mountie hopped in front. A row of SUVs proceeded around the circular drive to the wrought iron gate, waiting the Prime Minister's car to accompany the motorcade.

The Prime Minister admired the manicured lawn and immaculately cultivated tulip beds and gave another cordial wave to the gardener as he passed by. The workman was trimming the grass under the row of pine trees that lined the iron fence and afforded Canada's leaders a little more privacy from the prying eyes of summer tourists and nosy press. The motorcade slipped through the gate and overtook Sussex Drive, heading north for Parliament Hill.

Ten minutes later the motorcade sped across the Rideau River where the PM always paid attention to the long, sleek building housing External Affairs; those damn diplomats gave him a pain in the ass. The limo continued onto Wellington, passed the elegant Chateau Laurier Hotel, then Rideau Canal; cluttered with boating enthusiasts as it always is on sunny days. The Gothic blocks of Parliament Hill were just across the bridge.

The Prime Minister buttoned his suit as the limousine pulled onto the cul de sac that circumvented the parliamentary precinct. Tourists were beginning to gather on the vast grounds in anticipation of the Changing of the Guards. The tradition was performed daily during the summer by the Governor General's foot soldiers. In another two weeks the famous RCMP Musical Ride would perform on the front lawns for the Canada Day Celebration. The Prime Minister loved the spectacle. The Peace tower flanked with a gargantuan Canadian flag while a hundred thousand people danced and celebrated with searchlights searing the night sky and fireworks exploding. It was a good time for speeches. One could sway public opinion during such a celebration; he was hoping such a tactic would pay off for the election. Allison would take full advantage of the euphoria on July 1st.

The limousine rested to a gentle stop in front of the center block's sculpted front entrance. The RCMP riding shotgun jumped out and waited by the back door for Marty. As Marty skipped around to fulfill his duty a couple more RCMP scuttled the front steps and gathered around the car. Some early morning tourists were pointing fingers while kids watched intently with little Canadian flags held proudly in clenched fists.

The Prime Minister emerged and looked around the expansive precinct. Green parliamentary shuttle buses were depositing ministers to their appointed offices, while on the grounds, the foot soldiers were preparing to begin their strict and flawless display of service and patronage. A congestion of tour buses parked in front of East and West blocks and spilled tourists with cameras and pamphlets. They converged the lush lawn in droves, some pointing at the motorcade in front of Center Block.

The Prime Minister pushed his way past the RCMP and approached a little girl and her parents. He knelt down to talk to her for a moment. A press photographer quickly framed out the shot and the PM noticed him. He knew before he even walked over to the little girl with her little flag in her little hand that this was a golden opportunity. The PM flaunted his best politician's smile with his hand upon her shoulder. Her face lit up and her eyes twinkled; she was having her picture taken with the Prime Minister of Canada! He urged her parents to get a good view of the foot soldiers beginning their maneuvers. The photographer snapped frames at will and the PM noticed every one. Allison was going to love this.

The RCMP inched around the Prime Minister as the couple descended onto the lawns, waving goodbye as they went, the little girl still flushed from the encounter. You can't buy that kind of publicity, the PM thought as he stepped through the gothic arch of Center Block within his protective huddle.

It was all a brave act for privately the Prime Minister knew what was coming. The storm was upon him and he felt it in the core of his political being. But he could never have predicted just how bad it was going to get.

CHAPTER 34

The Storm from the Past

"I don't know why they all wanted to meet with you this morning," Allison McKay said as she greeted the Prime Minister when he stepped through the door into the outer office of the PMO tucked inside Center Block. She was not pleased. He knew how to gauge her just by the way her hair was spun almost painfully into a ball and her glasses perched on her petite, upturned nose while her head shook vehemently. But this was somehow different. Something was really frazzling Allison McKay and the PM had never seen her this exasperated.

"Who is in there with McIvor?" he asked.

"Commissioner Potts, Inspector-General Long, and Deputy Director MacDuff," she said.

The PM couldn't mask his commingled surprise and concern. "Why Roger Potts?"

"I don't know," she said as if this meeting was unethical without her knowledge.

"Well let's find out," he said, took a breath, then pushed the heavy door to his inner office open.

~

"Good morning gentlemen," the Prime Minister greeted as he walked into his spacious office. The sheer simplicity and Italian Gothic architecture complimented a subtle beige decor that lent character and distinction to the most powerful and prestigious chambers in the country. The Prime Minister stepped behind his vintage desk; the very desk predecessors had the privilege to sit behind and sign their place in history. Behind the desk was an antique, albeit very large table that Diefenbaker's wife had bought with tax payers money for the sole purpose of keeping neat stacks of unresolved bills and Hansard script within her husband's easy reach; why the need for all that paper in the relatively new personal computer age no one could say, but Ottawa was a town substantiated on tradition as much as confederation, so the table had survived every Prime Minister's term since. Four button tuft chairs were precisely set in a semi-circle for the sole purpose of addressing the Prime Minister, but the two confederate portraits of MacDonald and Laurier that clung to the walls dominated the room; their mere presence instilling patronage.

The Prime Minister acknowledged Clifton McIvor and Braden Mac-Duff by first name then threw that politician's smile at Roger Potts as he sat. "Nice to see you, Roger."

"Thank you Mr. Prime Minister," the RCMP Commissioner obliged. Potts was sixty-two years old, and every year showed in his leathery face. He was not an attractive man, but nonetheless an efficient one, and even though the mind was still as sharp as a tack, the thin body revealed wear and fatigue; he was subsequently nicknamed 'The old horse'.

"Hugh," the Prime Minister said, nodding to the Inspector-General.

"Morning, Mr. Prime Minister." Hugh Long tipped the scales at just over two hundred and sixty pounds. But appearances can be deceiving and despite the stereotype attributed to his obesity, Hugh Long, the Inspector-General directly responsible for the actions of the two CSIS Director's to his left, was never to be underestimated. He had built a bulletproof reputation as an equable negotiator and staunch supporter of CSIS's mandates. He also put a lot of stock in MacDuff's gut instincts and more than once lobbied support in the face of relentless SIRC and Privy Council ridicule.

"Well, this is quite a surprise to find all of you gentlemen in my office this morning," the Prime Minister said as matter-a-factly as possible. Allison assumed her supportive stance at his side.

"Well, sir," McIvor began, "this is rather important."

"I already gathered that, Clifton," the PM quipped. "But to have CSIS and the RCMP represented in here at the same time. Well, hell, that must be almost historical wouldn't you think?"

The Directors and the Commissioner exchanged bland glances; the contention was old and accepted as commonplace long ago.

"It just might be at that," Long agreed, the puffy face serious. "But we requested the Commissioner attend. We have a rather sensitive issue that we felt you all should be apprised of."

The Prime Minister noted the seriousness. "What is it then, gentlemen?"

"Sir," MacDuff said as he leaned forward, nodding at Allison. "This is highest clearance."

Allison's countenance fell. She turned to her boss who smiled a thin apology then nodded towards the door. Dejected, she left without a word, her indignant stride hushed by the lavish carpet. The five men waited for the doorknob to click following her exit.

All eyes were on MacDuff. "Sir, on Friday NSID monitored an inquiry via the CPIC system. The inquiry came from the Winnipeg Police Service."

"Winnipeg," the PM said. His brow furled.

"Yes, sir. They informed Deputy Commissioner Klassen who in turn informed myself." Incredulity registered on Pott's leathery face; dissension rumors had been floating around RCMP HQ for some time. MacDuff sensed the old horse's uneasiness and continued, "He sent Chris Kominski to me and asked that CSIS check into the inquiry."

"What was the inquiry, Braden?"

"Personnel information."

The PM turned to Potts. "You didn't know about this, Roger?"

"No," Potts said flatly, his eyes fixed on MacDuff. "Who's records were they after?"

MacDuff checked Long and McIvor. They were bracing themselves. It was all going to change now. The politicians and the RCMP were going to be in the know and the men whose thumbs controlled Canada's intelligence apparatus knew it was going to get ugly. What worried MacDuff most was he couldn't foresee how he was going to control the situation the moment he left the PMO; it really could mean the end of his tenure with CSIS.

"Larry Hicks, sir."

Potts's ire was swift and strong, his fingers clenched the armrests as he sneered at Long. "When did you know about this?"

"This morning," Long countered.

"What about you, McIvor?" Potts seethed.

"Friday. When Braden told me."

"And you?" he scolded MacDuff.

The Deputy Director retaliated with a terse 'shut up' which in turned erupted into a yelling match between the Commissioner and CSIS. The bickering dissipated with the Prime Minister rising out of his lavish chair. It was a tense quiet. "Braden. Go on," the PM said. He was leaning on his vintage desk now.

MacDuff's thumb and forefinger rubbed while he said, "it seems the inquiry went a little deeper than we first thought. Two men were wanting this information for the purpose of an adoption search."

The Prime Minister eyed McIvor. "Larry Hicks's kid?"

"Seems so," the Director concurred. They all knew what that meant.

Potts disgruntlement was summed up with a frustrated sigh and a, "Jesus Christ."

"Mr. Prime Minister," MacDuff said. "We have begun surveillance in the event Hicks does make contact."

The Prime Minister leaned forward and seriously asked, "You know who these men are then?"

"A reporter and a Winnipeg police officer."

"Do you know their names? I am assuming to carry out surveillance you must in turn know who to listen too."

"The policeman's name is Milt Smith. He's SWAT."

"And the reporter?"

"He works for the Winnipeg Free Press. His name is Michael Spencer."

The PM's jaw dropped. The irony hit him squarely. "I don't believe it," he said with a slap of his desk. The four men only watched as the Prime Minister threw his head back and laughed heartily.

"Sir," Long finally spoke up.

"I've met this reporter," the PM finally admitted.

"We know," McIvor said.

"I knew I didn't like him," the PM said.

"Mr. Prime Minister," MacDuff said, still rubbing. "We initiated surveillance on Michael Spencer and Milt Smith on Friday. We are going to require you authorize the investigation."

The Prime Minister tensed, the smile melting to a frown. "What do you mean? You don't have TARC clearance?"

CSIS shook their heads.

"Your endorsement would exacerbate the process, sir," McIvor said.

Potts was on the edge of his seat, gawking past McIvor at the Scotsman. "Boy, you guys are playing with fire." He turned to Long again. "You knew about this as well?"

"This morning," Long said in self-defense.

The Prime Minister eased back into his chair. "So you expect me to give you authorization that you didn't take the time to get. And if you guys get caught with your pants around your ankles, where does that leave me? Do you understand the damage this can do to this office?"

MacDuff and McIvor sat and took the reprimand. Hugh Long simply tolerated it, because that's what one does in the presence of a Prime Minister with the portraits of MacDonald and Laurier watching over his shoulder. Potts just shook his head like so many a commissioner before him when they had to listen to CSIS explain how they mucked it all up; the Mounties still carried the scorn over losing their precious Security Service.

The Prime Minister eyed the men who were supposed to protect Canada's national security; and that meant his office as well. "Jesus, I can just see the headlines. Parliament Hill randomly spying on Canadians, or better yet the Prime Minister condones invading Canadian homes. Canadians looking for their damn parents no less." He pointed at MacDuff. "You better have good reason for violating your protocols, Braden."

MacDuff rose, the eye slits narrowing, the thumb and forefinger rubbing. He tossed a thin file on the desk. "Read this, sir. This guy has made inquiries with contacts at RCMP headquarters here in Ottawa. He made contact with a woman we now believe to be Evelyn Hicks. For all we know this reporter is a helluva lot closer than we think. Now what do you suppose would happen if this reporter meets with Hicks." None of them had to be told what would happen if the reporter and the former Security Service, E Special agent named Hicks actually met. "The integrity of this office is paramount to me so I had to make a decision and I made it."

"Hicks is a traitor," Potts stated as if it was fact.

"We don't know that," MacDuff said.

The Prime Minister hit the desk again, this time with a fist. "I'll be damned if I'm going to take a bath for this twice in one career. You're asking me to accept hands on responsibility in an intelligence surveillance operation. Jesus! I'm about to call an election for christsakes!"

Potts interrupted. "I was posted in K division and I knew Roger McMillan and Murphy Henderson. I also knew Larry Hicks. And it makes me sick to think about how he betrayed the Force. He cost Mounty lives, not to mention the lives of McMillan's children, and as far as I'm concerned he was and is as guilty as hell. An innocent man doesn't run."

MacDuff glanced at McIvor. He was ostensibly looking for some support. The Director's expression conveyed this was not the time to argue Larry Hicks's innocence or guilt. MacDuff slumped back into his seat and cast a quick glance at the silent Hugh Long. The apt negotiator was sitting with his fat ass safely on the sidelines.

The Prime Minister calmed himself and glanced at the file before him. "Who are your operatives in Winnipeg?"

"Floyd Webber," McIvor said. "He's an SSET chief."

"Oh Christ," Potts blurted.

The Prime Minister rubbed his forehead. "How much have they done?"

It was MacDuff's call, so he said, "They're in Spencer's house and are following up with physical surveillance. They're waiting for the go ahead to openly go deep."

The Prime Minister leaned across his desk, pointing between McIvor and MacDuff. "Find the sonofabitch then. Bring him in and we'll put him in front of the Supreme Court. Just get him and don't screw up. You'll have your authorization, but if this hits the public sector you and your

SSET unit take the fall. Understand?"

MacDuff stood like the patriot he was. "Wouldn't have it any other way, Mr. Prime Minister."

"Glad to hear it." The PM pointed at the Commissioner. "The Force has a stake in this as well, Roger."

"We'll be in touch," Potts said then exited through the heavy door.

The Prime Minister sighed and said, "Is there an issue at RCMP HQ we don't know about? Why the hell didn't Deputy Commissioner Klassen inform Potts?" No one had the answer. The Prime Minister handed the file back to MacDuff. "I want daily reports."

~

Minutes later MacDuff, McIvor and Hugh Long marched through the Parliament building. The obese Inspector-General paused for a quick breath when they entered the Center Block's rotunda. While catching precious air he stared up at the architectural lines and ornately sculpted pillars.

"Well," Long said, his voice ricocheting high above. "That seemed to go pretty damn badly."

Part II
and so it begins...

CHAPTER 35

The Past is Here

Michael was going through story leads from his copious sources down in the trenches. His heart wasn't in it and he flipped through them as if it was all just an exercise in tedium; preoccupation with his search permeated everything. He tossed the memos on the desk as Lance ambled by with a fresh coffee for Lund. "You know he could get it himself, Lance."

"Not this morning. He's pissed," Lance countered.

Michael chuckled. *When isn't he?* "So what's the old bull horn so uppity about?"

"The RCMP greeted him in his office this morning."

Shit!

~

Michael barely knocked as he stepped into Lund's office. "What did the RCMP want, John?"

Lund's usual response to barging in was instead a plainly read concern. "They were asking about you," he said, suggesting the door be closed as he leaned back, the poor chair creaking under the strain. "And Larry Hicks." He eyed Michael, the question on his mind obvious – how do they know?

Michael sighed and said, "Milt has a friend at WPS administration. She got the names for us."

"This friend of Milt's…is her name Cindy Greene?"

Michael's stomach tightened.

~

"Here you go, Michael." Lance said, slipping Michael a USB stick.

Michael quickly popped it into his laptop, opened an Archives folder containing digitized versions of newspapers from 1980 and 1981. "Did you find an article on Carl Friesen?"

"Yeah, it's in there."

Michael found the New Year's Eve edition, clicked it with Lance leaning over his shoulder.

"Who are the Mounties?" Lance asked. They were looking at the two pictures of MacMillan and Henderson in their red serge uniforms that dominated the front page.

"I don't know," Michael said while he read.

Slain Officers Honored
Associated Press – December 30, 1980

"We can't believe they're gone," claims an anonymous source when asked about RCMP Corporal Roger MacMillan. The Corporal's body was discovered December 24 in Kitsilano. He died as a result of multiple gunshot wounds. Only a couple miles away Corporal Murphy Henderson's body was also discovered off Jericho Beach by a group of polar bear swim enthusiasts of the Royal Vancouver Yacht Club on December 27. The result of his death was a single gunshot wound to the head.

A spokesperson for the RCMP told the associated press there is no connection between the deaths and any related police work the officers had been involved in.

The RCMP have released nothing further regarding the murders, and will withhold any disclosures until after the holidays out of respect for the families.

Funeral services are to be held in Regina on January 3. A subsequent memorial will also be held January 4 at RCMP headquarters in Ottawa.

"Why are you interested in this?" Lance asked.

"I think my birth father had something to do with those cops' deaths," Michael said as he clicked another article.

"What?" Lance had to sit down now, rolling a free chair in from an empty desk; there were always empty desks because not every reporter can handle the newsroom crunch, let alone Lund.

"It's a long story, Lance." Michael said, clicking another. They read.

JUSTICE MINISTER FOUND MURDERED
Canadian Press - February 12/81

Early this morning Canadian Justice Minister Francis Lavelle was found shot to death in his Cadillac, in a brazen, day light killing.

At present there are no suspects for the shooting, but the nature of the crime indicates a gangland style assassination.

The Justice Minister was currently under fire for the subsequent transfer of Security Service officers from Alberta to British Columbia in an undercover attempt now known as Operation Scarlet. Officers Roger McMillan and Murphy Henderson died in the line of duty, the Mounties have now stated, during their investigation under the auspices of both the Justice Minister and BC Provincial Attorney-General, Seth Peterson, late last year.

Justice Minister Lavelle was scheduled to appear this coming Monday before a House of Commons Justice and Legal Affairs Committee looking into his involvement in the Operation Scarlet scandal.

"Wow," was all Lance could say.

"No kidding," Michael said. "So they were connected." He flipped over to the first article again. The two officers looked so young and proud.

"One of them is your dad?" Lance asked, adjusting his glasses.

"No, my dad is in Hawaii," Michael said. "And no, neither of them is my birth father."

"Is there a difference?"

Michael deadpanned him. "Yeah."

"Okay." Lance knew that look, so he let it go. "So what was Operation Scarlet?"

"That's what I'm trying to find out," Michael said, the dangerous people caveat haunting him.

"Cool," Lance said. "So how was your birth father connected to all this?"

"I'm not sure yet," Michael said. "But he definitely was the third member of that undercover team."

"Was he the one they think was the snitch?" The deadpan look again. "I read some of the articles earlier. Something about they couldn't find him...or something."

Michael considered the possibility as he clicked through more articles. None of this was feeling very good. He tried not to think about Cindy Green and the reprimand Milt was undoubtedly going to suffer.

Lance leaned in over his shoulder. "This is the one on that Friesen guy."

They were looking at a photo of a mangled Corvette with a tattered ragtop, crunched into what looked like the steel girders of the Norwood Bridge. It looked like a wreck that would undoubtedly claim lives. Michael couldn't explain it but as he soaked the photo in he felt sympathy for Maggie Gunthier.

"Was he involved?" Lance asked as he read.

"I don't know. But he was the doctor who delivered me."

"Wow." Lance pushed at his glasses with a slight frown. "Michael have you noticed all these people have died pretty awful deaths. And you're telling me they're all connected to your-"

"Birth father," Michael said. They read the article.

DOCTOR KILLED IN CRASH
Winnipeg Free Press - April 4, 1981

Doctor Carl Allen Friesen, in a single vehicle accident around 8pm yesterday evening, perished as a result of his Corvette sports car running head-on into a support girder along the Norwood Bridge underpass. A faculty member and respected obstetrician at St. Boniface Hospital, he was pronounced dead upon arrival at the very hospital he had left only minutes before the ill-fated crash.

Sources say that Dr. Friesen was on route to Winnipeg's Grace Hospital where he practices in an Out-Reach program for unwed mothers.

The Winnipeg Police report suggested there is a strong possibility brake failure contributed to the crash.

Michael couldn't believe it. It was there in black and white. Carl Friesen worked in an outreach program for unwed mothers. Jesus. Another headline caught Lance's attention. Michael paged down.

SHOOTING DETERMINED AS SUICIDE
Winnipeg Free Press - June 10, 1981

"Where have I seen that name before?" Michael said as he read. The article told the morbid story of a local Realtor committing suicide with the aid of a double barrel shot gun. His young wife had discovered the body in the garage. The true tragedy was their infant daughter had just been born New Year's Eve, 1981.

Lance pointed at the name "Ryan J. Roberts. Is he a part of it?"

"I don't know," Michael said. "But I saw his name in the hospital records. His daughter was born the same day I was."

CHAPTER 36

The Shadows Cometh

"Hello, can I help you?" Jessica asked the man waiting for her in her cubicle when she came back from a mid-day Timmies run. He smiled as he rose. She noticed his eyes immediately because they were dark and melancholy. The hair was trimmed to a brush cut and his face mapped with hard wrinkles; the kind tough men wear. He made her instantly nervous.

"Mrs. or Miss?" he asked, attempting pleasantness.

"Miss."

"My name is Floyd Webber." He flashed a card so fast Jessica barely even registered the maple leaf emblem on it, let alone what department he represented. "I just need a few moments of your time."

Jessica swallowed. "What is this concerning, Mr. Webber?"

"An adoption search you started."

The Smiths

Al Garrick, the telephone system technician, scaled the extendable ladder perched against the telephone poll overlooking Milt Smith's backyard on the corner of Kingsway and Lindsay. Once at the top he pulled a tube like clip from the breast pocket of his telephone repairman's shirt. He snapped it onto the phone line that stretched over the backyard and tethered just above the back door. Thank goodness they still had above ground lines in River Heights, he thought.

He glanced down into the next yard where Milt Smith's neighbor was watering what looked like raspberry bushes along the back fence. The neighbor was watching him and waved. Garrick waved back. Then there was a quick glance into the Smith's kitchen window. He could see Claudette Smith feeding their son Wyatt in a wheelchair.

Garrick slipped what looked like a micro-sized transmitter from his work belt, grabbed a cordless drill out of its holster, and screwed the transmitter in place then fiber connected it to the tubed receiver. It was a thermal sensing, NVD equipped micro video capture unit with camera tracking and gait recognition. Basically, the Smith's carbon signatures were uploaded from the main system to the device; it can recognize them.

He descended the ladder, slipped it on top of the phone company van. It was actually a generic SSET panel van. Inside was a shelve full of phony utility company logos on soft magnetized signage that could be thrown on to mask their covert spying for whatever operation happened to be in play. Garrick, the hacker, drove off like any other telephone repairman for any other job.

421

Jasmine returned home around noon lugging a couple bags of groceries through the back door. She made a mental note to have Michael oil that annoying squeak in the screen door. As usual Sabe was snooping every bag for his Milkbones. He growled when he sniffed the last bag and came up empty.
"No Sabe, not to___."
Her iPhone vibrated in her purse. Sabe bumped her for food before she could answer. "Dammit," Jasmine cursed, smacked his hump and ordered him out. "Hello."
"Jas." It was Jessica. She sounded anxious. "Is Michael home?"
"Hey, Jess. No, he's not. What's up?"
"Are you working this afternoon?"
"Not till tonight. Why?"
"Can you meet me in the Village around two."
"Sure. At Cheezecakes?"
"Yeah."
"We haven't done that in a while. Lydia probably misses us," Jasmine joked but Jessica wasn't laughing, she wasn't herself at all.
"I'll see you later. Bye." And she was abruptly gone.
Jasmine hung up. Something was definitely off. She startled when the iPhone buzzed again. The caller ID read: *Mom*.

SSET Command

The computer was mining the caller and Candace, alone in the office, noticed from her desk. She watched it spew the address and name.

>**11 Dies Bay, Regina Sask - R. Vincent**<

She had no interest to put the headphones on and listen. The computer would transcribe and archive it anyway. Besides she did not relish listening in on conversations, much like she did not allow herself to notice pictures in target's homes. She went back to the file on her desk.

She looked at a photo of Maggie Gunthier among the documents Garrick had hacked from the CFS and CRA databases. She flipped through the file, found a marriage license photocopy. Margret Gunthier. Carl Allen Friesen. It was dated May 10/79. She read the article about the car crash.

Brake failure contributed to the crash?

She had a hunch, typed on her laptop and navigated to a Winnipeg Hospitals website, got a number then made a call. After a few rings a woman answered, identifying herself as the Patient Relations Officer at St. Boniface Hospital.

Cheezecakes

Jessica waited nervously. It was 2:05.
Where is she?
A few minutes later Jasmine sauntered into the restaurant and dug her way through the crowd to their usual table. Cheezecakes was the usual stop after their shopping spree afternoons where they would treat themselves to a slice of Chocolate Swirl or Pecan Rhapsody or Jamaican Rum or whatever the whim. They liked the place. Cheezecakes was like stepping through the classic fifties soda shop. The entire front of the restaurant was a massive window that wrapped wall to wall and floor to ceiling, permitting an unobstructed view of the Village with all the sidewalk shops and cafes. The chrome framed tables and chairs were laminated with cool purples and blues and pinks with big, luminous balloon lamps dangling overhead. The checkerboard tile floor was waxed to an absolute shimmer with a dance space by the fifties style jukebox. Lydia, the mostly Jamaican, partly Canadian owner was the reason the girls loved the place so much. She walked over to their table with her usual big smile and a plate of one of her new creations.

"'ello, Jassman. 'ow are ya doin?"

Jasmine was about to return the greeting with a hug when Lydia raised a finger. The plump hostess set the plate in front of another regular patron sitting at the next table. "'ere ya go Candace. I 'ope ya enjoy it."

"Thanks," the flaxen haired woman named Candace smiled then dug in while browsing the local arts and events paper so common in the village.

Lydia took Jasmine's hug then playfully scorning her Saturday afternoon cheezers for not being around for a spell. She insisted they try a new concoction for her. She stole their menus and left for the soda bar to get them a sample of Bahama Surprise. She was sure they would love it.

Jasmine got comfortable, sipped her water, and asked. "So, what's up?" Every time one of them called an impromptu rendezvous at Cheezecakes that didn't involve shopping it usually meant something was up; Michael did this or that, Katie hates me, Jessica met a new guy, or either of them fretting a diet that didn't take.

Jessica was clearly nervous. "I'm probably over-reacting."

Jasmine leaned across the table, rubbed her hand. "Hey, honey, you okay?"

"It's not me I'm worried about, Jas." Jessica said in a hush as Lydia placed wedges of Bahama Surprise in front of them.

"I'll get ya a couple sodas, girls." Lydia said and waddled off.

~

Candace nibbled slowly and watched Lydia amble back behind the bar. She feigned reading her magazine, nibbling chocolate swirl, and listened to Jessica Ingham tell Jasmine Spencer that someone came to see her this morning, asking about Michael.

~

The girls didn't touch their plates, their forks left properly on their napkins. Jessica was talking very quietly, very quickly. "This guy Webber comes into my office this morning, right. Flashes some card and tells me he is from the Canadian Security Intelligence Service."

"CSIS," Jasmine said.

"Yeah. He asked how long I've known Michael? What is the nature of our relationship? He asked if I knew why Michael was searching for his birth parents and if I knew who they were. I almost screamed when he asked about Maggie Gunthier."

"He knew about Maggie Gunthier?" Jasmine asked in a hushed tone.

Jessica leaned close, whispered, "Jas, he knew about Lily Atkinson."

"This is just getting weird," Jasmine sighed. "What did you tell him?"

"Nothing. I told him I just helped Michael find his birth parents and forwarded a number for Maggie Gunthier. Beyond that I knew nothing. Did I do the right thing?"

Jasmine didn't like this. She had learned over the years to take whatever Michael was working on with a grain of salt. He was a cynic, she was an optimist and they saw the world around them differently, but this was disturbing on a new level. The adoption search was personal and private and should have been a happy moment. Jasmine was there when Michael's mother gave him the letter so she understood. She loved her too and missed her terribly. She missed her father-in-law and privately was more upset than she let on when he decided to move to Hawaii. It was a bit too far away. Katie changed when her grandmother passed and Gramps chose paradise.

"Of course you did," she reassured.

Jessica fidgeted nervously. The big window with complete strangers ambling by wasn't helping. "Jasmine, he knew personal things about me. How did he know that?"

"I don't know," Jasmine said, smiling to diffuse.

Jessica glanced around for eyes that might be staring. "I don't like this, Jas."

~

Candace appeared casual as she slowly enjoyed her Chocolate Swirl and magazine. Someone had plugged the jukebox and The Tragically Hip thumped throughout Cheezecakes at a reasonable volume. She flipped a page.

~

Lydia was back at the girls' table, her pudgy fists pressed to her hips and a frown scrunching up her black face. Their plates were untouched. "'ey, what tis dis, huh? You din't eat anyee? Ah, I save it for you next time," Lydia joked as she gathered up the plates and scooped a twenty dollar bill out of Jasmine Spencer's hand and into her apron.

~

Candace flipped another page as Jasmine Spencer and the CFS woman quickly left. She joined the line of other regulars waiting to pay, said good-bye to Lydia with the promise she'll be back next week – as usual.

Candace stepped out on Osborne like every other shopper on a hot and sticky Monday afternoon.

SSET Command

Garrick glanced up from the RCMP database he was searching through when the ringing flooded his headset. He focused on the monitor screen and waited for the computer to search the caller. Al was not worried about getting a blast from the Spencer's dog, for he had heard Jasmine Spencer put the mutt outside before leaving to meet the CFS woman in the village. It was the sixth ring and Garrick knew voice mail kicked in on ring seven. The greeting ended and the caller and Garrick waited for the message tone.

Beep.

"Hello." Her voice was soft and pleasant, resonating beauty. Garrick was instantly curious. "This is Sandra Langley calling for Jasmine Spencer."

The computer found the location:

```
**CHURCHILL HIGH SCHOOL**
>>main office extension<<
```

Garrick really liked her voice.

"Mrs. Spencer if you could come by the school this afternoon, I would like to talk to you about your daughter and another student named Danny Gregory. If you could call me back to let me know you're coming, that would be great. Thank you very much."

Teenagers, Garrick thought.

CHAPTER 37

The Vancouver Connection

As he stepped off the elevator Premier Roy Graham garnered instant attention. It was his first visit as a client to the distinguished offices of Lipton, Jackson and Mackenzie. Graham was the firm's hottest and most controversial client of late and would undoubtedly attract nationwide press for the firm as July 5th grew near; that kind of notoriety made you worth more than your weight in gold in any law office. The vivacious Sasha Riley stepped from behind her desk to greet him.

"Go right on in," she kindly said.

Graham was in no mood to reciprocate pleasantries. For that reason alone, many in the firm, including Sasha, just dismissed him has arrogant. They were so wrong. He was terrified.

He stepped into the office to find Dresher reclined in his handsome chair and the impressive Vancouver skyline beyond the floor to ceiling windows. One of the most expensive lawyers in town was in the middle of an important call but gestured for Graham to take a seat.

"Yeah," Dresher said into the phone, "he's here now. Okay." He hung up and smiled the way lawyers do when you're fucked. "How you making out?"

"As good as can be expected."

"You want something to drink? I mean something stiff."

"No."

"Okay then," Dresher said. He must have good news for such an optimistic mood, Graham hoped. Or maybe he and Sasha just did breakfast together. Dresher had no scruples whatsoever. It was only 9:00 am and well within character to jump out of his wife's bed, drive to work, and bang his secretary before his first client's appointment. Dresher bragged about Sasha's abilities during their golf games before the besieging summer rains drenched the holes out at the Capilano Country Club. Graham however, was a polar opposite, quite satisfied with marriage to Meredith, a wife who was twenty years his junior. She and their daughter, Rachel, had changed him. And that's what made him a liability now; a politician who suddenly had a conscience was of no use to anybody who had need for political leverage.

But unbeknownst to Graham, Dresher's elevated mood had nothing to do with Sasha. The lawyer had received another call this morning. He had been told an SSET unit was authorized to go deep into Michael Spencer. This was good news but there was a downside. The caller also told him Larry Hicks was alive. Dresher would have preferred him dead, buried, and forgotten, but at least now they knew where he had been hiding and ostensibly could track him. It all meant they were gaining control of the situation, and control and power always invigorated Coleman Dresher.

"Here," he said as he handed Graham his affidavit. "We feel this is our best plan of attack."

The Premier pondered it like it was his last will and testament and death was knocking on the door. But it wasn't death. It was Glenn Ibermann who walked in. He was the last surviving partner and a tall, lanky man towering over six-foot-three, hands like a basketball player and the confident, educated air of a McGill graduate. "Hello, Roy," he greeted with an extended hand and a lawyer's smile. "Would you mind if Coleman and I spoke to you for a moment about your case."

Graham eyed Dresher. He knew it was coming now. The Premier was an ex-foreign diplomatic aide and had earned his doctrine of political sciences at the University of British Columbia - high accolades indeed - so he knew how diplomats and politicians and expensive lawyers ticked. He braced for the betrayal that he had always expected would eventually come from Dresher.

"Look Roy," Dresher began. "We all agree that...well...you should change counsel to Glenn here. To put it simply, Roy, you and I have a history and that doesn't look good. One case of conflicting interest is enough to deal with at one time." Coleman and Ibermann shared a chuckle as if lawyers were the only ones to identify with such legal peril. "If our relationship got out during the trial it would only hamper your defense. I'll still be conferring with Glenn, of course, but he should be representing you. Not to mention this kind of thing really is his ball game, you know. What do you think?"

Graham glanced between the two lawyers. The Premier was tired of being the scapegoat. He had a different plan now and got up and closed the door adjoining the library, returning to his seat with a purpose neither Graham or Ibermann saw coming; there was fight left. "Who the fuck is going to know about our business dealings?" he spat. "They're so secret I barely know about them."

Ibermann's grin dropped. "Roy, take it easy. We're just trying to come up with a strategy to help you better."

"Help me," Graham said. "You don't even know what this is about, Glenn."

"I have read your affidavits, Roy."

Graham's finger pointed at Dresher. "This shit is just about saving their asses."

"What's he talking about?" Ibermann asked Dresher.

Dresher rose out of his seat. "I think I should have a few minutes with Roy, Glenn."

Ibermann looked between lawyer and client suspiciously. "I think that would be a good idea." He vacated as quickly as he entered.

Dresher waited for the door to close then leaned over his desk, his face red with anger. "What the hell is the matter with you?"

"I'm realizing who my friends are."

"You weren't thinking of your friends when you decided to purchase property in Stillwater to line your own pockets, Roy. You got caught with your fucking hand in the cookie jar. What exactly is it that you expect me to do for you?"

Graham rocketed out of his chair, his jaw clenched. "Defend me!"

Dresher relented and sank into his chair. They sat there while the Howard Miller pendulum swung with a hypnotic tic toc.

"You know what I've always wanted to ask..." Dresher said. "Why did you do this? You knew what you were doing, Roy. Why?"

Graham sighed. He was a condemned man because he was Mario Morelatto's patsy and now he was expendable. The Stillwater purchase was a farce but his career and public image would be mutilated in the process and he was sure the set up was staged to snarl bigger political prey than himself. But what did it matter now. Once you accept the game the checkmate will eventually come; and Graham's time had come. All that mattered now was to protect Meredith and Rachel. "I had my reasons," he finally said.

"Roy, I'm trying to keep you politically alive here because we just might have a bigger problem to solve than you."

Graham chuckled the absurdity of that comment. *What could be bigger than my reputation being flushed down the toilet.* "What are you talking about?"

"Larry Hicks."

The name came out of a past long forgotten and hit Graham like a punch to the gut. Subsequently, he had nothing to counter it with other than tugging at his tie. *Fuck!* And then he realized something that now made absolute sense. "Does Mario know? Tell me the truth, Coleman. For shit sake, tell me that much truth."

"I don't know. He's staying on the White Knight trying to avoid any press fallout from your indictment."

Avoid, my ass! Graham thought. "It was never about me. We both know that."

And in that moment something occurred to Premier Roy Graham that had all but eluded him since the scandal broke; a way out. His mind raced with the possibilities and it actually made sense, made complete and lifesaving sense. It was so perfectly ironic that he slowly began to chuckle. The kind of laugh a condemned man laughs when he realizes there's a slim hope.

"Roy..?" Dresher asked like someone does when they finally see a person begin to crack under strain. "You okay?"

Graham smiled. "I could always hope Larry Hicks is alive."

Dresher, on the other hand, couldn't see the irony. All he saw was the threat. "Don't hope too hard, Roy. You just might get what you want."

CHAPTER 38

The Blind Spot

Plausible Deniability is the mission statement that every intelligence organization in continental North America lives and breathes by because no matter how powerful their reign becomes, or how surreptitious their operations are, the bottom line is they are fighting to preserve democracy and that means they answer to the public they are sworn to protect; some politician must be responsible to the voters for the spies. Thereby the Prime Minister appoints two unlucky ministers of parliament to the chairs so commonly joked as the hot seats up on the hill; CSIS answers to the Minister of Public Safety while the CSE is responsible to the Minster of National Defense – which bleeds its way down to Hugh Long in the Inspector-General's quarters and if need be, the Office of the Communications Security Establishment Commissioner (OCSEC). The CSE chair is often regarded as the hotter of the two ministerial seats since CSE is the big boys club when it comes to signal intelligence, and what politician wants to field that press conference. Canadians as much as Americans are pretty sensitive to the idea of having their emails, cell calls, text messages, blogs, Twitter and Facebook profiles yanked out of thin air by a super computer whose sole purpose is to monitor today's online world. And sooner or later that computer would trigger an alarm in the snooze room that is loud enough to jar a deep sleeper like Al Garrick awake.

It was two in the morning when Garrick shuffled to his control seat and those wonderful giant spying screens, the tracing program already logging the Facebook chat between Katie Spencer and Danny Gregory; the logs were backing up to some remote RAID drive humming away in an Ottawa server room just in case the mission went south. The Prime Minister and his band of ministers would shudder at the abuse of power and point fingers with the rest of Canada in the event SIRC and TARC came a calling; so logs were kept.

"What the...", Garrick muttered, rubbing the sleep out of his eyes. He couldn't see Katie Spencer's thermal image in the house. Her bedroom was cold – the satellite term for empty. The dog was laid out on the kitchen floor, just where he always was until Jasmine Spencer got home from her night shift, panting from the heat the air-conditioner couldn't suck out of the humid air. Michael Spencer was on the couch, sleeping, which didn't surprise Garrick. The reporter had been pulling late nights ever since surveillance started, Google searching everything he could find on the Security Service, E-Special, the Lavelle assassination, Mario Morelatto and SeaCorp, Premier Roy Graham and the Coastal Holding mess, and even Larry Hicks; the latter always coming up with no hits. The last website he visited was still up on his laptop – therefore still up on one of Garrick's monitors. It was the SeaCorp home page with a photo of the 69-year-old shipping tycoon Mario Morelatto and his second in command at SeaCorp, Alec Garva. Michael had fallen asleep in the middle of his perusing.

That didn't surprise Garrick either. He had been on Michael from the time he left the Free Press newsroom after reading the archives with that geek, Lance Neuwerth; archives Garrick was reading simultaneously. From there Michael met with the Sun reporter, Ralph Forbes, at Smiley's bar, a local journalism haunt. Around two he picked up Milt Smith from the SWAT station to get the birthday cake for Jasmine's party. They talked about Operation Scarlet and both were worried Cindy Green could lose her CPIC clearance, never mind her job. The team didn't have the Spencer SUV tapped and they didn't need to. Garrick could open any iPhone and turn it into a listening device on a whim. The Apple phones were a Godsend to the signal tracker; they were like transmitters without going through the hassle of planting them, basically wonderful crystal balls of intel gathering that Garrick could manipulate at will.

A perimeter sensor went off along the backyard fence at 421 Churchill Drive. Kyle and Candace had planted several of them while they were waiting for Webber to give the go ahead to enter the house the night the team went deep. Garrick knew it was Jasmine returning home. But where was Katie Spencer chatting?

He lit up another program, home cooked by Garrick to manipulate iPhone GPS. He triggered Katie Spencer's *FindMyiPhoneApp*, from coordinates he robbed from Jasmine Spencer's iPhone – parental controls were another windfall technology for the hacker spies. The iPhone tracker beeped with Katie's location and zeroed in on the satellite imagery on the house, then panned across the backyard until directly over the standalone garage.

Shit! She was in the garage!

The team left a blind spot. Webber was going to tear them a new one for that oversight. Well, at least she was on her iPhone. Garrick sunk into his chair, riveted to the chat feed between Danny and Katie; something about Danny telling her she has to tell her dad what happened today. Danny was freaked out.

Garrick nudged the volume, cracked a fresh coke and got comfortable for a long night just as Jasmine Spencer pressed the garage opener remote lodged in the sun visor of her Miata. And she was not happy finding her daughter hunkered down in the garage.

CHAPTER 39

The Fail Safes

He drove past the light brown Chevy pick-up that was parked about two hundred yards down the street from the white brick bungalow at 421 Churchill Drive. It was the only vehicle along the curb and the truck appeared empty, but he would drive on past and park further up the street, just to be safe. He followed the gentle curve of Churchill Drive until the half-ton was no longer in his rear view mirror. He sat for a moment with the engine off then gently eased the door open. The sleeping houses showed no signs of late night stragglers. Nothing stirred. It was quiet with only the sound of ripples lapping the riverbank. It was so still the oak leaves hung motionless, as if stifled from the humidity.

He grabbed a pair of night vision binoculars from the trunk. It was a well-stocked trunk with a selection of high-powered weapons, surveillance gear and even a MANPADS portable shoulder missile. He eased the trunk closed then like a prowler avoiding moonlight, darted through the park and evaporated within the foliage along the Red River.

A few minutes later he was standing behind a large oak on the edge of the bank, looking across the park at the white bungalow. He observed the Chevy half-ton further down the street again, only now a shadowy figure loomed inside. He knew it was one of Webber's agents. As per his orders he could not risk detection nor could he interfere or hamper the SSET investigation in any way. This was paramount. His orders were simple. At all costs, do not lose the target. Do not fail.

He slipped back into the bushes, out of the moon's reach. He got as comfortable as one could get while squatting in the underbrush. It would be a long night, but he was used to this kind of surveillance shadowing. It was what he was trained for.

Then he spotted Jasmine Spencer's Miata coming up the back lane, the headlights flicking past picket fences. He sunk deeper into the bush when he heard the garage door opener do its work. He could hear the faint arguing between the mother and her teenage daughter echo from the backyard. He knew the squeak was the screen door. The kitchen light came on. Through the living room window he could see Michael Spencer stir awake and join in the heated discussion playing out in view of the kitchen window. The teenager was coming under fire for something. She threw up her hands and stormed off. Jasmine and Michael Spencer continued talking the way parents do when upset with their children. But then it turned into something else. The daughter came back into the kitchen. She seemed exasperated while she talked. The parents listened. Then Jasmine Spencer covered her mouth. What she was just told clearly scared her. Michael Spencer was on his iPhone instantly, checking beyond the big kitchen window, worried they were being watched.

That isn't good.

He saw the shadowy figure in the brown Chevy truck slink below the dash. Then he slipped a secured cell phone out of his pocket, pressed a button. The call was answered but no voice greeted.

"They know," is all he said, tucked the cell away, and got comfortable for a long night.

Kenora, Ontario

At sixty-five Mac Loewen would still be regarded a formidable adversary by any man's standards. He was tall, white haired with noticeable baldness, rugged, tough, smart and like all men his age, had a small paunch. He was the incumbent of the eternal bachelor. Sure there had been some women. He was virile, charming in his day, and enjoyed the opulent life of a self-made man. Not bad for a guy who abandoned his rank in the RCMP almost forty-years-ago and took a chance on a computer startup venture that would change the world. That's how long he had been living on the Lake of the Woods, in his reclusive cabin perched on his own little atoll. That was Mac Loewen, master of his own, servant to none; or at least it appeared that way.

The last six days threatened to change all that. He even cut short his yearly vacation to Baja, California where he escaped the merciless February cold for a few weeks. Now he was back home, his cell phone clipped to his belt, doing odd jobs to keep his mind off the possibility of Larry Hicks coming back from the past.

He had only swung his hammer a couple times when the cell beeped. He cursed and flipped the phone open. "Yeah, Loewen here." It was the call he had been waiting for. He lifted off his knees. "I understand," he simply replied. "What do you need me to do?"

CHAPTER 40

Circle the Horses

Marty was leaning against the front fender of the Prime Minister's limousine, skimming the morning edition of the Ottawa Citizen when another limousine emerged through the wrought iron fence. The car rocked to a stop and the VIP's climbed out and hastily disappeared through the handsome front door of the Prime Minister's residence. It was the fourth limo to wrap it's way around the circular drive in the last half hour.

Marty turned to the sports section and browsed when yet another dignitary's car drove up. This one however was not a limousine but a generic sedan. Two men rose from the back seat. The shorter of the two, with thick, red eyebrows and typical Scottish nose, tipped his head to the chauffeur. Marty returned the gesture to the CSIS Director of Operations with a tap of his hat and watched him stroll under the canopy and disappear inside with Director McIvor.

Marty returned to his paper. He knew why all the limos were dropping dignitaries at 24 Sussex on this fine, clear morning. Marty knew a lot.

~

Clifton McIvor and Braden MacDuff were the last to arrive in the Freedom Room. A team of house staff attended the congregation with coffee and tea while Minister's and their aides milled about the room, enjoying the casualness that simply did not exist on the Hill.

Hugh Long, the Inspector-General, threaded his way through several clusters, shaking hands and smiling. He greeted McIvor and MacDuff with sweat beading his forehead. "Like a goddamned convention, isn't it," he joked.

McIvor managed a smirk while he scanned familiar faces. There was nothing funny about it for MacDuff, his thumb and forefinger rubbing constantly.

"There's been a little change in agendas this morning," Long said over the din. "The Israeli Prime Minister cancelled his visit."

"Why?" McIvor asked.

"Only External really knows that answer. Probably due to the uprisings in the region, but it certainly creates quite bit of a hubbub. We'll have to wait our turn as they say."

"Why weren't we informed?" MacDuff asked poignantly.

"You have been informed," Long said. "I just told you." The Minister turned deadly serious. "Hicks's name does not come up in here until we thin this crowd out. You'll have your turn with the Prime Minister, but there is half a dozen possible leaks in this room right now. Understand?"

They understood.

~

By ten o'clock the Freedom Room had thinned down to only those involved in the covert surveillance undertaken against Michael Spencer. The Prime Minister perused a report while all sat silent. What he was reading seemed to disturb him. He handed the draft back to Braden MacDuff.

MacDuff and McIvor sat on one couch with their RCMP counterparts on another, all in a semi-circle with the Prime Minister facing them from a captain's chair, his back to the clear blue Ottawa sky beyond the grand window.

"So," the PM said. "Have we determined if Hicks was living in Key West?"

"No," MacDuff simply said. The brunt of responsibility seemed to be his baby. And rightly so since his gut instinct spawned the collection of men sitting in the Freedom Room. "The number is listed to a G. Norris, a writer. This person could be a friend, an acquaintance, maybe even an alias? At this time we can't definitely say."

"What does that mean, Braden?," the PM asked. "You're CSIS for Christ's sake."

"We can confirm that for you, Mr. Prime Minister," RCMP Deputy Commissioner Miles Klassen spoke up boldly. "We have a liaison office in Miami."

"We don't want the Mounties digging around down there," MacDuff said. "Hicks would see them coming before they even got off the damn causeway."

"What do you suggest, Braden?" Long said quickly, forever the referee.

MacDuff said directly to the Prime Minister, "We believe he may already be back in Canada. This is not about where he has lived. It's about what he is going to do, because if we found out about his birth son's adoption search, we should assume he has as well. So I suggest CSE. They're best equipped for this level of sensitive signal intelligence and have less committee hurdles to avoid."

"I agree," McIvor endorsed. The Inspector-General and the Solicitor-General concurred with nods of their own. The rest didn't seem so convinced.

Deputy Commissioner Klassen was lukewarm on the idea. "So long as CSE regards us with respect to any valuable information gathered."

"Of course," McIvor said.

MacDuff took the offensive. "Haven't we been forthcoming so far? You've seen all the surveillance reports and been fully apprised of our teams progress." He relented when McIvor touched his forearm. So did Klassen when Hugh Long nodded for the Deputy Commissioner to let it go. This was not the time for turf wars; but the familiar tension was definitely in the room.

The Prime Minister gestured to Paul Young, squashed between the obese Hugh Long and the armrest. "That okay with you Paul? I don't want the Privy Council knocking on my door with the SIRC following."

The Security and Intelligence Coordinator from the Privy Council Office cleared his throat. "Director McIvor briefed me yesterday as to the imperative nature of this investigation. Traitors should be brought to justice. And to that end I will secure the requisite authorizations. That said, Mr. Prime Minister, and as Director MacDuff has stated, CSE, in my opinion, would be the way to go."

The Prime Minister now looked to his Solicitor-General. "What about the Winnipeg Police, Pierre?"

Pierre St. Laurent was a gregarious French-Canadian with the added touch of a rose properly pinned to the lapel. An attire flourish he adopted from his political mentor during proud days serving under Pierre Trudeau. "I talked with Manitoba's Justice Minister this morning before I came. I was assured disciplinary action would be taken and CPIC access for Cindy Greene revoked."

The PM handed the file back to MacDuff. "Now, Braden, what else can you tell us about Michael Spencer?"

MacDuff elaborated from memory, citing Michael Spencer's renowned reporting career and the impressive coverage of the tattletale killer that plagued Winnipeg ten years ago. No one in the Freedom Room asked CSIS how they acquired a synopsis of Michael Spencer's psychological assessment from the psychologist who treated him following the famous case. MacDuff detailed how Michael and Jasmine Vincent met at U of M and that resulted in a child; Katie Spencer. She had apparently suffered a meningitis set back at six months of age and it appeared to be the same time her Dad had entered the psychologist's office. His adoptive father, Olie Spencer, moved to Hawaii shortly after his wife died of breast cancer. Apparently he frequents a bar in Oahu known as 'The Hula Hut.' The SSET unit learned Spencer has contacted a former social worker named Maggie Gunthier in Toronto. This is important. Later the same night is when Spencer received a call from a woman believed to be Evelyn Hicks. And as they all knew, that call originated in Key West, Florida. It turns out to be listed under a G. Norris; a writer of romance novels.

The Prime Minister raised his hand. "I've heard enough, Braden."

MacDuff eyed McIvor, indicating his turn.

"We only have one more point we wish to bring up at this time, Mr. Prime Minister," McIvor said, gesturing the Deputy Commissioner's across from him. "We want your boys in Winnipeg to back off. Tell Commissioner Potts to leave that part of this investigation to us. We don't want them interfering with Webber's team. We'll keep you informed but you have to let us do the gathering. Agreed?"

Deputy Commissioner Klassen eyed the unremarkable MacDuff. "So long as Braden is still in direct contact with me. If Hicks materializes we move."

McIvor and MacDuff agreed. Nods went around the Freedom Room.

At that moment Allison entered, walked right over to the Prime Minister and whispered in his ear. The PM tensed noticeably and stood as did the men around him. "Gentlemen, I'm sorry to cut this short but I have some other matters that need my attention." And with that he left the room with Allison and the RCMP following suit. Paul Young and Pierre St. Laurent bid good day and headed for their limousines, leaving CSIS and their Inspector-General to themselves.

Long and McIvor both noticed MacDuff's scrunched brow. "I'm almost afraid to ask," McIvor said.

"Shit," Long quipped. "Looks like another gut reaction coming on. Every time he has that look my pension is on the line."

MacDuff stood squarely before his Director and Inspector-General. "We have a problem with Mac Loewen in Kenora." Both McIvor and Long tensed, noticing the thumb and forefinger rubbing. They knew Loewen was the fourth member of the Operation Scarlett team that no one had focused on as of yet. "He's been off the grid since yesterday morning."

CHAPTER 41

The Kingpin

The northwest tip of Washington State known as Cape Flattery, jettisons out where the American side of the Juan De Fuca strait spills into the Pacific Ocean, was clearly visible five miles away. From inside his luxurious bridge with classical music serenading, Mario Morelatto was peering through long-range binoculars fixed on another yacht anchored off the southern tip of the cape. He knew it was the 'Chameleon' - port of call San Diego, Ca. She was a meager craft compared to his sleek, hundred-foot vessel aptly named the White Knight. He trained the binoculars on a U.S. Coast Guard cutter advancing the Chameleon, the crew armed and ready to board. "What do we know about this Maggie Gunthier?" he asked with an accent inherited from Greek forefathers.

"Larry Hicks's sister-in-law." Alec Garva's gravelly voice answered from a ship to shore microwave communications intercom.

"Why did we not eliminate her, Alec?"

"I've never heard of this woman before, Mario."

"We didn't know the woman married to the doctor was also Hick's sister-in-law?"

"We just found that out."

Morelatto was displeased. He tightened focus. In the distance the Coast Guard's armed men stormed the *Chameleon*. The Coast Guard commander stood on the aft deck, armed with only a handgun. "The helicopter will rendezvous as planned?" Morelatto asked.

"Yes," Garva answered.

"Good." Morelatto grinned as he peered through the binoculars. He could tell just by the timber of Garva's voice that a question was coming. "What, Alec?"

"What about your crew?"

"What about them?"

"They'll see him."

"They're still sleeping, Alec." Morelatto smiled. "I don't expect the effects to wear off for another hour or so. He'll be gone by then."

"You drugged them?"

"I felt this was a better remedy. A few pretty girls, a few spiked drinks. They'll wake with a hangover, and I'll yell at them for such unbecoming conduct, kick the whores off my boat and no one will ever know the Javelin had come and gone. Not as messy, do you agree?"

"I agree."

Suddenly on the Chameleon the Coast Guard Commander peered through the cabin windows as if he just saw something. He waved frantically for his men to get out of there.

"Anything else?"

"Dresher wants a meet."

"Fine."

Morelatto glanced at his Rolex then pressed the binoculars back to his eyes just as the Coast Guard crew scuttled for the safety of their ship. A cold smile warped his dark pate. "Boom," he whispered.

With explicit synchronicity the *Chameleon* exploded, the blast engulfing both yacht and cutter and splattering debris and bodies high into the blue, morning sky. Burning fiberglass rained down, the calm ocean littering with flaming flotsam. The Commander and a few of his men pierced through the wall of fire consuming the cutter's gunwales just as a second explosion sent burning diesel and oil billowing into a dark mushroom high above the fiery wreckage. Seared victims bobbed in the sea.

Morelatto brimmed with morbid gratification. So far the schedule was precise, right down to the second. He appreciated that kind of attention to detail; two characteristics the Javelin was known for in only the most secret of circles.

"And Alec..."

"Yes."

"This time we kill him," he ordered.

Garva hung up.

~

Forty minutes later and precisely on schedule, compressed air bubbles boiled just off the White Knight's sloped transom. Morelatto watched from the upper deck. A moment later a lean scuba diver surfaced, hoisted himself onto the stern. He shed the gear and proceeded for the upper deck. It was the Javelin. Mario Morelatto welcomed him eagerly. His assassin was an impressive machine.

Twenty-five minutes later a Sikorsky H-76 Eagle helicopter with the SeaCorp logo emblazoned on the fuselage hovered thirty feet above the White Knight, the side payload door slid open. A boom arm had been swung out and an electric winch unwound high tensile wire, descending a lift harness to the upper deck of the yacht below. The Javelin secured the apparatus around his chest and properly ascended. The door sealed, the Sikorsky veered drastically, her white belly gleaming majestically in the morning sun. The pilot would fly across the Juan De Fuca, follow the Pacific Rim coastline of Vancouver Island to Victoria. After landing at Signal hill, the location of SeaCorp's shipyards, it would be a quick transfer onto Morelatto's private jet, then Winnipeg.

~

Aboard the SeaCorp helicopter Alec Garva handed a folder to the Javelin then watched Vancouver Island pass beneath. The Javelin sifted through the photos of Michael Spencer, his wife named Jasmine, but paused when he saw Katie Spencer's photo. He eyed Garva.

"The wife and daughter?"

Alec Garva, the seasoned killer, simply nodded.

CHAPTER 42

The Party

The doorbell rang and Sabe sprang into action, inadvertently knocking the coffee table, leaving both Jessica and Jasmine to dive for their teetering wine glasses.

Sabe!

Jasmine greeted Claudette Smith and the kids stepping into the kitchen. "Happy Birthday!" Claudette sang with a beaming smile and a hug.

"Auntie Jas!" Wyatt screeched, leaning forward in Milt's strong arms.

"Hi, Sweetheart," Jasmine cooed and hugged Wyatt, then young Samantha, looking more and more like her mom. Sabe nudged for some attention. Milt eased Wyatt into a chair and Claudette took off his shoes; always working like a perfectly in sync parental tag team. Milt gave Jasmine the customary peck on the cheek, but something was troubling him.

"You okay?" she asked. She actually knew but feigned an all is good smile regardless for Claudette and the kids.

"That's what I'd like to know," Claudette chimed in while slipping off Wyatt's jacket.

"Michael's in a mood too," Jasmine said. "Wha'd you guys do?"

Both women eyed Milt, but he wasn't in the mood to even play – that in of it self was odd. "I'm fine," he said tersely. Jasmine and Claudette shared a doubtful glance; both were used to dealing with their husband's antics.

"Hi, cutie," Jessica said as she entered the kitchen for more wine and an affectionate pinch of Wyatt's cheeks. She got her customary peck on the cheek from Milt then went straight for the wine decanter on the island. She was pretty tipsy.

"Where's Kat, Auntie Jas?" Samantha asked.

"She's in her room, honey. Go on." Jasmine eyed Sabe. "Take Sabe with you, Sam."

"C'mon Sabe!" Sabe trotted off down the hall after Samantha.

"Where's Michael?" Milt asked once he got Wyatt settled on the couch and the women retreated to the living room with their wine glasses full.

"He's out back, Milt, firing up the barbecue," Jasmine said. The back door squeak told her he was out of earshot before she attempted to dance around the touchy subject with Claudette. Jasmine was more nervous than she let on with the whole adoption affair. She kept a close eye on Jessica downing her wine like a woman on a mission.

~

Milt strolled into the garage to find Michael wiping down the ski boat with a cold beer and Rush's "Limelight" playing from the Bose speaker on the bench. Milt leaned against Jasmine's nice new Miata. "Hey," he said over the music. Michael clicked off the bluetooth app on his iPhone. "Thought you were on barbecue duty?"

"Yeah, right, like nothing is wrong." Michael tossed the cloth at the workbench. He wasn't in the mood for a barbecue, let alone a birthday party. "Was Cindy fired?"

Milt grabbed a beer out of the fridge. "Relieved from duty, pending an investigation and review of her CPIC access to be exact." His expression just hung there - blank.

"What..?" Michael asked.

"Nolan was suspended today."

"Fuck."

"He thinks they've targeted me too. How's Jessica holding up?"

"She's rattled."

"Right now she's getting pretty sloshed."

"She was pretty upset."

"Don't blame her. They had to have been CSIS."

Michael climbed out of the boat. "Yeah well, hang on to your hat...someone approached Kat at school too."

"What someone?"

"I don't know."

Milt cracked the beer. "This is getting intense."

"Yeah." Michael leaned against the bench too. "Said he looked a little like me."

Milt sighed at that. "Like you?"

"Yeah."

"You don't think..?"

"Who knows," Michael said, swigged his beer and let out a deep breath. "But I have a feeling we're going to find out."

SSET Command

Webber stuck his head out of his office. "Candace?"

"Yeah, Chief," she answered, her nose buried in her laptop, perusing the Operation Scarlet files for the past couple of hours.

The Chief touched his ear then pointed at Garrick asleep at his console with the headphones on. Candace snapped up a pen, pitched a bulls-eye off the hacker's head. Garrick startled awake to Candace's mischievous grin and Webber tapping his earlobe. The hacker slid the phones off. "What?" He was grumpy.

"Anything?"

"No, Chief, nothing. They just cut the cake. It's fucking boring."

Webber glanced at the back of the office. The snooze room was vacant. "Where's Kyle?"

"Getting pizza," Garrick said matter-a-factly while checking rooms in the Spencer house.

"Pepperoni and green pepper," Candace offered.

"Uh-huh," Webber dismissed. "Redekopp?"

"421," she said.

"Simon?"

She exchanged a quick glance with Garrick then said, "It's his night off, Chief."

"Uh-huh," Webber bemoaned. "What do I say about personal lives on my team?"

"We don't have any," Garrick and Candice recited with a dry unison; the team hated that motto.

"Make sure you save me a piece." Webber turned for his office. "And Candace, make sure he doesn't fall asleep."

Candace eyed Garrick with a wry grin. "Copy that, Chief." The hacker flipped her the finger. She flipped one back then returned to her laptop. She had found the recruitment photos of a young Larry Hicks, Roger Mac-Millan, Murphy Henderson, and Mac Loewen. She clicked on Loewen's photo and it exploded into a digital profile showing her a log cabin near Kenora, Ontario. The guy was obviously rich. She glanced curiously at Garrick's massive monitor; knew it was a screen scrape from Michael Spencer's Mac book at 421 Churchill Drive. She got up, collected her tossed pen off the floor and leaned over Garrick's shoulder, reading the article on the monitor. "Slain officers honored," she read aloud.

CHAPTER 43

The Drawing of the Pawn

Jasmine sat on the couch, a full glass of wine, her green eyes eyeing Michael's iPhone on the coffee table. "You think they're listening to our phones?"

Michael was at the window, concentrating on the silhouetted oak trees across the street; a viable place to hide and watch his house. The lights were off. "Well that sounds a bit paranoid."

She sipped her wine, rubbed her forehead. This was already too much for her. "Who was at the school, Michael? Who was the stranger that talked to our daughter?"

"I don't know, Jas." Across the river he could see the patio lights illuminating Lily and Archie Atkinson's back porch. The River Rouge was passing beneath the Osborne Street Bridge on its midnight run, the Salsa rhythms beginning to breech the front door.

Jasmine joined him at the window, staring out there where eyes could be watching them. "What if they've been in the house?"

He glanced the wine in her hand. "Maybe you should stop drinking."

"Hey, it's my birthday I'll have you know and -" He noticed something down the street. "What?" she asked, instantly alarmed.

Headlights blinked on, off to the left, about six houses up the street. "Probably nothing."

"Michael!" Jasmine demanded.

"Quiet," he said, his eyes locked on a 4x4 pulling away from the curb. "I've seen that truck before."

Jasmine was looking now. "That one?" It was familiar.

Michael eyed her, reading her. "Have you?"

She stepped back from the window, suddenly vulnerable, suddenly afraid. "Yeah. When I went to Cheezecakes."

They gave each other a look that intimated, are we both getting paranoid.

And then his cell phone buzzed with an unknown caller. He quickly snapped it off the coffee table and answered. "Hello." It was the familiar voice of Maggie Gunthier.

CSIS Headquarters, Ottawa

The unremarkable office was dark.

Braden MacDuff was sitting in his chair, his suit coat draped over the back, staring out his window, and rubbing his thumb and forefinger together. Metcalfe Street was a panoramic glittering at night with the Peace Tower a wash of floodlight. There was something off-putting about the view for the patriot tonight.

MacDuff, the intelligence hard-ass, was having trouble accepting his next move. A transcript of the Maggie Gunthier call to Michael Spencer only two hours ago lay on his desk. That gut instinct of his was stirring – and that wasn't good. If they could pull this one off it would be a damn miracle, he thought. He hoped his man would call soon.

CHAPTER 44

Let the Games Begin

Al Garrick parked his Mazda Z3 just beyond the taxi stand. Candace gawked through the back window while he remained fixed on the rear-view mirror. Several spaces behind them by the south entrance of the James Richardson Airport terminal was Jasmine Spencer's Miata. They watched Michael give his wife a quick kiss then dash through the automatic doors. They knew Spencer's ticket for Air Canada flight 305 was a round trip with only a four-hour stopover in Toronto; just enough time to meet Maggie Gunthier at CN Tower then back home.

Jasmine whizzed by, the top down and her hair tasseling in the slipstream, rounded the corner onto Sargent Avenue, and sped away for the Smith's house. Uncle Milt volunteered to stir up breakfast for Katie; Garrick overheard that at seven this morning, right after he overheard Michael Spencer's flight was to be delayed an hour.

The hacker wasted no time. He dug a silver attaché out of the backseat, laid it across Candace's lap. He popped open the laptop inside and was on-line with Air Canada's reservations website in less time than it took to blink an eye. Candace strained over the top of the open case until she could see the color schematic seating diagram of a Boeing 767; the very plane labeled flight 305, bound for Toronto. She watched Garrick type a flurry of coded commands. The seats on the screen blinked either red or blue. Garrick didn't like what he was seeing. "It's sold out. We're going to have to bump someone to get you on."

"Do it," Candace ordered as she pushed the case onto Garrick's lap, slid out the door, and dashed for the terminal doors.

Normally Garrick would have stung her with a good sarcastic anecdote, but just then he saw an older man step out of the terminal doors ahead, dashing for a cab. He had seen him before, but where? Then it dawned on him. He was older than his RCMP recruit picture, but it was definitely Mac Loewen.

The cab sped off.

Garrick touched his earpiece. "Chief!" he called, watching the cab speed around the exit towards the city. "Chief, pick up!"

The Smiths

Samantha Smith was determined to get her Dad. He was laying on a fold out chair, snoozing under the sun, completely unsuspecting. He'd never see it coming. The rest of her girlfriends egged her on. Claudette had given permission for a sprinkler party; Milt's only condition – no boys.

The skies had cleared and the heat wave hit an all-time high, so the school division took a quick vote, and joyously for Sam and her girlfriends, unanimously declared a day off. Wyatt didn't mind either. He was having great fun sitting in the grass by his mother while she fussed over her raspberry bushes, watching his big sister sneak up on Dad with a loaded water-soaker. With one more mischievous smile at her cadre of girls, all of them goading with whispered 'do it, do it, do it's, she aimed at the shaven head and went for it.

Milt growled. He sprang up and ran for the sprinkler yelling, "You're dog food, girls", bikinis scattering in all directions and giggling uncontrollably. Wyatt pointed and laughed, singing, "Look Dad, look Dad."

"Yeah," Claudette said. "Dad is being goofy."

Milt stalked Sam and her friends with the sprinkler. The giggles and high-pitched screams of twelve year olds caught the attention of the neighbor who made his way to the fence to watch the antics.

After he finally winded himself, Milt reset the sprinkler and the girls resumed running through the cool spray. He gave the water-soaker to Wyatt, gave Claudette a peck on those beautiful lips of hers, then made idle conversation with his neighbor. Be as normal as possible was the plan.

The neighbor seemed to know, probably from past conversations at the fence, that current investigations were off bounds. He did, however, ask if the cable was fixed now because he saw a technician up the pole fiddling with their hook up the other day.

That's when Milt noticed the thin metal tube around the wire overhead. Shit!

SSET Command

Webber huddled around the surveillance computer with some of the team, watching Milt Smith look up the pole in the back corner of his yard, staring right at them through the monitor, then bolt for the house with his son in his arms. Any SWAT cop would know what he saw. "Good idea with the video transponder," Webber sarcastically commended Garrick.

"Yeah, no kidding," Kyle Lenning said.

"We're fucked," Simon Johnson chimed in, hovering over Garrick's shoulder as well. "He's on his cell! He's calling it in."

"Relax," Garrick spat. He was not concerned about his iPhone taps. He set them so they didn't engage until after the target punched the phone number, thereby covering any interface pause that threatened to give them away.

"Hey, check this out," Gregg Redekopp called from the back of the office. Webber led them all into the Conference chamber to Redekopp watching a live CNN broadcast on the big screen. It was the two burning boats fused together at their bows off Cape Flattery. One had US Coast Guard markings still distinguishable on the tattered hull. Both were charred, the upper decks completely gutted and destroyed, the disfigured sterns still smoldering. Uniformed bodies floated face down. Debris littered the sea. It was a sickening sight.

"Turn it up," Webber ordered. Redekopp aimed the remote.

An anchorman narrated over the scene. "According to reports the explosion occurred around 6:30 this morning while the coastguard was boarding the yacht we now know to be named Chameleon out of San Diego. As we reported to you earlier, the owner, Samuel Mitchell, was found murdered two days ago at his San Diego estate. Mr. Mitchell was a former Deputy Director of the Central Intelligence Agency. As of yet there have been no suspects linked to the murder. Whether the two incidents are connected is speculative at this point, but there will be a press conference by CIA Deputy Director Edwin Newhart later today."

"This is nothing to do with us," the Chief dismissed then headed back to his office. But the news was far more concerning than he let his team know. He closed the door, quickly dialed a number he knew by heart. The female voice was familiar to him. "Sheila, get him on the line now." Sheila was a good secretary.

Headingley

Nolan Grant raced his motorcycle into the parking lot and marched straight for the lobby pay phone in the Headingley Bar. He made a quick call then rode for a girlfriend's to spend the night. He knew he couldn't use his cell phone, or the phones at the detachment. It wasn't brain surgery to decipher he could not talk to Milt about what he knew until they were at the club. Hopefully the Mounties weren't aware of their court time. Privately, he was wrestling with gut-wrenching guilt when it came to the simple fact he now had to treat everyone he knew in the Force as an enemy.

~

After a quick shower the following morning Nolan kissed his casual girlfriend good-bye and straddled the Virago and coasted down Trans-Canada Highway #1 East for the city. He checked the mirrors repeatedly for any of those inconspicuous ghost cars.

Unbelievable.

They were now the enemy too.

CHAPTER 45

Maggie and the Adoptee

CN Tower, Toronto

Michael walked gingerly over the glass bridge heading for the elevators. He was nervous, very nervous, and struggling with the impatient mob wasn't helping. After what seemed to be an eternity the doors finally opened and a small horde spilled into the elevator. A flaxen-haired woman pushed her way past a few visitors for the open door. She ended up squishing against Michael, her sandals barely inside the door track.

~

Candace Reimer didn't think she'd make the elevator before the doors closed her off from Michael Spencer. She berated herself for actually bumping against him just to get inside the elevator.

~

The elevator attendant mentioned something about twenty miles-per-hour and the ride taking seventy seconds, but Michael really wasn't listening to her spiel. He was more concerned with what lay ahead of him.

Most riders grabbed their midsections when the elevator lifted off, ascending all the way up the tower's Y shaped shaft. Many of them gasped at the overwhelming view of the Skydome wedged between Ontario Place and the Gardener Expressway. They could see the Toronto Islands to the south and then the vast blue of Lake Ontario stretching to the horizon. For the queasy it could be an unsettling ride, much like a subway train rocking on the rails. Some found handrails more precious while those who felt faint sought solace in a sudden preoccupation with their feet. The further the ground the harder eyelids squeezed. The whole ride was over in seventy seconds. Hopefully Maggie Gunthier was up there already.

Winnipeg International Airport

The Canadair Challenger jet taxied off the runway to a remote section of the airport tarmac where an unoccupied rental car was parked. One hour exactly, Garva and Javelin agreed. Watches were synchronized. The now gray haired, cosmetically aged mercenary disembarked the jet and hopped into the rental car. The keys were concealed in the sun-visor along with airport clearance identification tucked into a clear plastic billfold. The clearance was registered to Coastal Holdings Incorporated, Vancouver, British Columbia; the same company responsible for the rental. The name on the rental contract left on the passenger seat was Larry Hicks. The Javelin sped for the Sargent Avenue security gate.

Winnipeg Racquet Club

"Morning Milt," an attractive front desk receptionist known as Parker greeted.

"Hey, Parker. How ya doin?"

"Good. Usually here on Fridays aren't you?"

"We missed our slot last week," Milt said. "And you know how jumpy I get without my fix." He signed himself in.

"Uh huh." Parker frowned. "Wyatt okay?"

"Oh yeah. Little trooper's fine. Has Nolan gotten here yet?"

"Nope. But someone else is waiting for you."

Milt wasn't expecting anyone else. This was not part of the plan. "Who?"

Parker pointed over Milt's shoulder. "Her."

He spun around to see his blue-eyed friend parked in her wheelchair, watching a couple guys sweat and flop around one of the courts. Milt strolled over to her. "Hi, Cindy." This time, she was not smiling.

CN Tower - Toronto

Height didn't usually bother Michael, but he found himself plagued with a queasiness resembling vertigo. He was bracing himself against the solid glass railing that bordered the circuitous edge of the Space Deck and the slanted observation windows, tilted forty-five degrees for the optimum view of metropolitan Toronto and the creamy blue of Lake Ontario. The

Skypod level dangled several hundred feet below the Space Deck like an airship floating over the parking lot, cars no bigger than ants, people smaller than dots from one thousand, four hundred and sixty-five feet elevation.

The Space Deck was crowded today.

An old woman pointed out Toronto landmarks and buildings to her grandchildren. One of her grandkids extended his small arm over the railing, pointing at the sloped windows and asking if they were bullet proof. Michael smiled along with a few other tourists standing close by.

That's when he noticed Maggie Gunthier looking right at him.

She was a graceful woman, hands cupped together, holding it together as best as she could. Michael saw the wedding ring on her left hand. The crumbled Corvette flashed across his mind. God, what she's been through. Her eyes were tearing as she stared at Michael like he was some ghost who miraculously appeared before her. It was uncanny, Michael thought. This woman didn't even have to ask who he was or tap a few similar looking men on the shoulder. She knew who he was automatically.

People were starting to notice the reunion. Michael couldn't help but wonder which of them was CSIS or the RCMP or whoever the hell else was poking into his adoption by now; the granny with the grandkids even suspect. Michael gently took Maggie's arm and led her for the Skypod elevator.

~

Candace didn't make the Space Deck elevator in time. As she pushed her way through the mob, her outstretched fingers were only a foot shy of the closing door. Michael Spencer and Maggie Gunthier closed off from her. This was bad.

"Shit!" she cursed a little too loud. Some parents frowned such language around their children.

"Candace," a man said behind her. A short guy, wearing an overtly loud shirt, similar shorts and sunglasses, dug his way to her; the typical tourist overdone. She recognized Luke Grogan. He was another SSET from Montreal.

"Are you assigned to Maggie Gunthier?" she asked when he broke through to her.

"Yeah. Where they going?"

"How should I know?"

"Did he make reservations downstairs before he came up here?"

"No. Did she?"

"No," Grogan answered while poking repeatedly at the elevator button. "This is crazy. We're going to lose them."

"Whad'ya mean. There's no sentries down there?"
"No."
"There's no one else?"
Grogan eyed her. "No. They want this kept quiet."
Finally the doors opened. Candace and Grogan piled into the elevator, pressing the Top of Toronto button.
"Why the restaurant?" he asked quietly amid other riders.
"A hunch."

CSIS headquarters-Ottawa

Director McIvor knew today was going to be a stressful one. He was sitting on one of the leather sofas when MacDuff let himself in. The thumb and forefinger were working overtime lately.
"You're not going to believe this," MacDuff said. He flopped onto the opposite couch.
"Today, nothing would surprise me."
"Edwin Newhart won't let us around Sam Mitchell's boat – it's an FBI matter."
McIvor shook his head like he understood the logic. "They're trying to distance themselves from any Operation Scarlet fallout."
"Yeah, or they have a rogue we don't know about. What was Sam Mitchell working on anyway?"
"Mario Morelatto for one," McIvor said.
"Think there's a chance he knew?" MacDuff asked, unbuttoning his suit.
"Possible," McIvor said. "Cholan might whisper in our ear. If Newhart lets him."
MacDuff considered that. "I'll follow that up."
"Sam was a good man," McIvor said. He sighed. The stress was piling up. "Either way, let it go. We don't need another incident in the press. Where's Chester?"
"He's on the target."
"Good. Any luck finding Mac Loewen?"
"We're on it. But right now were working the tower."
"Who did Montreal send?" McIvor asked.
"Luke Grogan."
The director shook his head. "I don't like this Braden. We're tripping over ourselves. Two separate SSET's involved. An NSID agent brought in. I don't know. Maybe we should tell Floyd. We can't afford a loss here."
MacDuff's wincing seemed to suggest his gut instincts disagreed. "I don't want to risk it."

McIvor pondered the deal they had tied themselves too. "Can we trust Newhart and Cholan?"

"Who can ever trust the CIA but we have no choice, Clifton. And let's face it, we need to stop Morelatto now. Especially after Mitchell's murder."

McIvor was getting to old for all of this. "So we're tied to the CIA whether we like it or not."

MacDuff nodded and said, "Cholan is on our side. He wants who ever killed Sam Mitchell"

McIvor turned to his windows and sighed the day. "Spencer at CN Tower now?"

"He and the Gunthier woman are in the restaurant."

CN Tower-Toronto

Maggie managed to settle her nerves with a good stiff drink. Michael surmised the revolving Top of Toronto restaurant was a familiar haunt for her. An easy deduction considering their waitress knew to bring a scotch on the rocks without her even asking. She had two, telling Michael she developed a taste for hard liquor to cope with those brutal winters in Winnipeg. She chuckled; it was awkward and trite, escaping her nervousness with the view facing northeast over the city. In thirty minutes they would be looking out over Lake Ontario. Michael had no interest with downtown Toronto turning below them.

Maggie asked about his stenosis, as if it was a final confirmation that would set her at ease, but Michael wasn't about to lift his shirt in a crowded tourist spot. She deflected the awkwardness with polite questions. How was Lily Atkinson? Lily was pretty feisty, Michael commented. Maggie said she'd have to be to live with Archie all these years. Michael by-passed the small talk with a direct question about her husband's car crash shortly after the Dominion Day Parade weekend. Maggie didn't mince words. She called it what it was; murder.

She asked about children. He produced his wallet and handed her Katie's school picture. Michael was taken aback when some real tears formed. She dug in her purse and produced a photo of her own. He gently took it from her trembling hand. This is what he came for.

"This is my birth mother?" he asked. There she was. After all this he could finally put a face to the name. And Michael understood why Maggie cried upon looking at Katie's snapshot. The resemblance was shocking. "My daughter really looks like her."

"That picture was taken about two years ago."

Evelyn Hicks was smiling on a porch overlooking a beach festered with palm trees. Katie had her smile. "Where?"

Maggie bit her lip and turned away, staring out over the city below. The regret etching her face told Michael she was not permitted to answer.

"It's okay, Maggie."

She glared at Michael, her delicate jaw clenched and her thin face boiled to bright crimson before him. "Is it?" she snapped.

Winnipeg Racket Club

Nolan Grant stepped quickly to the front reception desk, glancing around for anyone who could be paying a little too much attention to him. Parker was all smiles, as she usually was when it came to the dashing RCMP corporal.

"Hi, Nolan," she sung.

"Hi, Parker. Is Milt here yet?"

"Yeah. He's in the cafeteria with a friend of his."

"A friend?" Suspicions abound.

"Yeah, some girl in a wheel chair. I think her name is Cindy."

Cindy? Must be the girl from the WPS Milt had told him about, the one he was worried they compromised during Spencer's search.

Parker smiled flirtatiously. "You know if you're not doing anything for Canada Day, maybe...?"

"Hold that thought."

Parker guffawed that when Nolan bolted for the cafeteria and another customer stepped up to the desk. A customer she had never seen before. He was a tall, older man with harsh black eyes. She liked him.

"Hello," she greeted. "Let me guess. First time, right?"

His smile needed work. "A day-pass please." There was a slight Aussie ascent.

"Sure." She reached below and pulled out a day-pass voucher. "That'll be fifteen dollars."

"Fine."

She smiled – another sale. "And your name?"

"Larry Hicks."

~

Chester slipped his green sedan in the stall beside Milt Smith's black SUV. An athletic bag was on the seat beside him, complete with sneakers and shorts; purchases he made on a quick stop from the airport.

He walked directly to the front desk. The girl with "Parker" on her nametag seemed nice enough. He glanced around. Sitting in the lounge on the other side of the foyer was one of Webber's electronics experts; the

SSET named Lenning. He knew Candace Reimer was in Toronto tag teaming with Luke Grogan. He signed the guest register, paid for his day voucher and proceeded for the cafeteria.

CN Tower-Toronto

The waitress arrived with a couple Caesar salads and another scotch for Maggie then asked if they required anything else. Michael was eager for her to just go away.

"Why did they give me up for adoption, Maggie?" he asked.

She sipped the scotch. Maggie expected this. Questions about murders all those years ago and car accidents that, to this day, she relived in her nightmares. "Don't you want to know about her?" she asked after another long sip.

Michael seemed suddenly uncomfortable. "Maggie, I had a mother. I don't want to replace her."

The scotch was gulped and the waitress summoned. "Well, Evelyn doesn't have another son," she hissed under her breath.

Michael leaned close and whispered as politely as possible, "I didn't make the choice for them, Maggie. They did. I didn't ask that my records be falsified or names faked and phony doctors, you know what I mean."

This time the waitress noticed Maggie's wounded look and that the entrees hadn't been touched. "Is everything okay with your salads, sir?"

"Yes. Everything is fine." Michael said tersely.

"Very well," the waitress replied and carried on. She didn't like him much.

Maggie twisted her glass, the past tearing at her.

Michael sighed, knowing he just pushed too hard. "I'm sorry, Maggie."

"How did you find me?" she asked matter-a-factly. "I thought I had been pretty thorough."

"Death certificate."

"Pardon me."

"Susan Hanis. There was no death certificate."

Maggie hesitated, then said, "There is a death certificate."

"Why couldn't I find it?"

"You weren't looking for the right year. Susan Hanis - 1969. She was Larry's mother," she admitted. "Hanis was her maiden name."

Michael's jaw dropped. "You're kidding."

She sipped, looked at him and smirked. "You look a lot like him." She set her glass down, decided to tell more. "He knew he could hide you in the adoption system and all he had to do was fake the birth name. They could never find you."

"Who are they, Maggie?"
She downed the last of her Scotch, her lips pursed tightly.
"Who are the dangerous people?" Michael persisted.
She suddenly looked uncomfortable and clearly conflicted if she should say more. "I don't know," she finally said. "I've never known."

Winnipeg Raquet Club

Milt did a few lumbering stretches and Nolan secured the acrylic door. Doing normal things was all part of the plan. They couldn't risk talking so they got right to it. Milt delivered the first serve. The heat was on.

~

The Racquet club housed six courts in all, assimilating a horseshoe design with a lounge in the middle. That way everyone could watch the players suffer humiliation in full view of a cynical gallery. The last court had been converted into a make shift weight and exercise room consisting of two pedal machines, three rowing machines, a Nordic Track and a Nautilus machine.

The Javelin decided on the Nordic Track, but not because of the workout preferred. The machine faced the acrylic wall, permitting perfect vantage of Milt Smith and his friend waging war in the court directly across.

A man entered the exercise room wearing a green tee shirt and white shorts and chewing vigorously on a stick of gum. He assumed a rowing machine beside the Nordic Track and introduced himself as Chester.

"Larry Hicks," the older looking Javelin replied. There was no labor to his breathing.

~

Chester didn't flinch. He just rowed as if all was normal. But he'd have to call Ottawa immediately. He knew Larry Hicks was not the elderly man on the treadmill beside him.

CN Tower-Toronto

"I want to meet her, Maggie." Michael had Maggie's dry hand in his.
"I'll call her tonight." She said with a bittersweet smile. "I can't promise anything though, Michael. But I just want you to know that if she decides not to, it's because she's protecting you."

"I understand," Michael said, his attention suddenly drifting to a couple holding hands a few people behind Maggie. They were on the main deck of the Skypod now.

"What is it?" She glanced over her shoulder.

"That couple. I've seen that girl before."

"Funny. I had the same feeling about him."

"You did?"

"Weird, isn't it. Paranoia becomes a way of life."

"Yeah," he said. "Or maybe not." He almost had it. Something was formulating, his thoughts drifting to Jasmine dropping him off at the airport. Picking up his ticket, boarding the plane, then...that's it!

He grabbed Maggie's arm. "She was on my plane this morning."

"She was!" Experience told her not to look again.

"They were in the restaurant too and I think I saw them in the Space Deck."

"What do we do?" Maggie whispered.

"We get the hell out of here."

CHAPTER 46

The First Blood Spilled

Winnipeg Racquet Club

"Michael has to know they tapped you," Milt said. He tucked his chin to his chest, the shower spray massaging the back of his neck. The hot water felt good.

Nolan was rinsing off, washing the sweat off his face. He seemed worried. "They're probably on him in Toronto you know."

Milt stepped out of the spray. "I'm really worried about him."

Nolan punched his shower off. "It takes a lot of pull to do what they're doing, you know that."

Milt eyed Nolan, as if to say *I know*.

An older man with gray hair sauntered in and turned a shower on.

~

Kyle Lenning was beyond bored. He was running out of magazines to flip through. He sat in the lounge, occasionally checking out the front desk receptionist who introduced herself as Parker when she came over to him earlier. She asked if he needed some assistance. He claimed he was waiting for a racquetball partner and it looked like he was going to be stood up. That was when Smith and Grant were fumbling around the court during their last match. The targets had hit the showers so all Lenning had to do was wait and be bored.

Then a man wearing a green tee shirt strutted across the lounge, straight towards him.

~

"Okay, I'm outta here," Nolan said as he tossed his towel in the hamper on the way to the locker room. "Call me the instant Michael gets back."

"You bet." Milt boosted the hot water. It was soothing but not enough to get his mind off Michael.

A few moments later...

"Are you Milt Smith?" a deep voice asked. Milt turned to face the older man with gray hair in the shower with him. He was tall and lean with unusually harsh black eyes. Something was off about him.

"Are you Milt Smith?" he asked again.

Milt leaned forward, out of the water slapping his ears, distorting his hearing a little. Everything felt wrong about this guy. "Yeah. Who are you?"

Suddenly a Browning 9mm with a silencer was aimed.

Milt barely got his hands up. The force of the bullet piercing his heart slammed him into the ceramic wall. He was still alive, cognitive enough to realize he was dying right there in the shower, naked and alone, sliding down the wall. Claudette. Sam. Wyatt. He felt dark and dead and lifeless, vision hazing over white. The world was going away. His last breath echoed in his ears. The gun aimed at his head. A muzzle flash. Everything went black.

~

The second bullet popped between the eyes. Red gushed from both wounds as the large body slumped down the wall. The corpse ending in a sitting position then tipping over, the head banging the floor and resting in a grotesque angle to the body, the arms reaching out twisted and limp. The shower rained, diluting the blood spreading from a crimson puddle under the chest, tracing out the grout grooves in the tile.

The Javelin had no time to waste. He was gone.

~

Kyle Lenning ran full tilt through the change rooms. His sneakers slid across the slick floor where the hall met the shower room. He nearly tumbled like a novice skater, fingers clawing for any handhold to latch onto but managed to anchor himself to the wall mounted hand dryer. Steam from the shower poured into the corridor, saturating the hallway. Then through the mist he saw the body of Milt Smith crumpled against the wall, blood running into the drains.

"Shit!" Lenning cursed then tore off for the lounge.

~

Parker was flirting again. She had one more chance today before Nolan disappeared through the front doors. They were standing just beyond the entrance foyer.

"You know I have tickets to the Canada Day concert, Nolan. How about it?"

"Well___."

"Excuse me," the tall, older man with gray hair and black eyes said as he pushed between them. His hair wet and his shorts damp.

"Yeah, sure." Nolan realized on second glance it was the man in the shower with them.

"Thanks," Parker called after the man. He was already beyond the front doors. "Please come again, Mr. Hicks."

"Who!?" Nolan gasped.

"Mr. Hicks," Parker said.

"His first name?" Nolan had her arms clasped, his abruptness catching Parker by surprise.

"Ah...Len or Lu___."

"Larry! Was his name Larry!" He watched the man climb into a rental car that was parked beside Milt's SUV.

"Yeah," she said. "Larry Hicks. Do you know him?"

"Jesus!" Nolan blurted and went to dive through the front entrance when someone exploded out of the change room door yelling for an ambulance. A few more members ran out screaming someone was shot. In the courts racquet games ceased, balls bouncing to a standstill as patrons curiously approached acrylic walls to witness the pandemonium erupting in their club.

"Oh God," Nolan mumbled.

He knew.

SSET Command

The Chief and his hacker were the only members of the SSET team left to hold down the fort. Webber, leaning on the surveillance desk, was talking to the ceiling mics. Garrick had his feet up. They both seemed a little concerned. Candace was online from the CN Tower.

"Are you sure he made you, Candace?" Webber asked.

"We're sure, Chief. They practically dove into the elevator."

"Where are you now?"

"At the kiosk."

Webber frowned. "You lost them?"

"Sorry, Chief. By the time we got down here we couldn't see them. It's pretty busy here."

"Grogan still with you?" Garrick asked.

"Yeah. He's going back to Gunthier's house. Should I go with him, Chief?"

"No. Spencer's return flight is booked. Just get home."

"I'll need a ticket."

Webber turned to Garrick. The hacker smiled confidently at his boss. Another Comm line blinked.

Webber said, "Check in with me when you get back, Candace."

"Right, Chief," she signed off.

No sooner did the line go dead when Garrick clicked FieldComm3. Panic and commotion echoed from above.

"Al, where's the chief?" Kyle Lenning sounded like he was anything but bored. Alarmed was more like it.

Webber straightened up. "I'm here, Kyle."

"They killed him! They killed Milt Smith."

Garrick and Webber popped out of their chairs. "Jesus Christ!" Garrick said.

"What happened?" Webber demanded.

"Some guy I've never seen before comes over to me. He knows I'm SSET and tells me that someone had just introduced himself as Larry Hicks in the gym. Told me to check the showers. That's when I found Smith. Chief, what the hell's going on?"

"Get outta there," Webber ordered. Another Comm line blinked. It was Braden Macduff's line. "Get outta there now!"

Garrick clicked the blinking comm line. Webber was pinching the bridge of his nose. "I'm a little busy right now, Braden. Something has happened here."

"We know about Milt Smith," Braden said.

Webber and Garrick stared at each other incredulously. The hacker shook his head. The unthinkable was suddenly probable.

"How in the hell do you know?" Webber asked, his mouth gritting.

"It wasn't Larry Hicks, Floyd."

"I don't believe this!" Garrick spat hopelessly.

Webber was pacing now. "Was your man at the Racquet club? Is that who approached Kyle?"

"This is above your team, Floyd," Another voice ordered. It was Director Clifton McIvor.

Garrick groaned that. This was quickly becoming a very bad day. Webber stared at the mics and speakers above him with that calm, controlled authority of his. "How is any clearance above this team,

Clifton?"

"Your computer officer is not cleared for this level," McIvor said. "Understand."

Cheezecakes

Lydia was all smiles, socializing from table to table, squeezing little cheeks and squishing faces. She hadn't seen Katie Spencer for some time. She seemed all grown up and when Lydia asked about boys Katie volunteered Danny Gregory's name.

"And who's dis cutee!" Lydia said to Wyatt Smith sitting on Claudette's lap. "All grown into a fine mon."

"This is our little trooper," Claudette said with a kiss to his forehead.

"Oh, I bet his daddee's proud." Lydia said as she headed for the cash register. People were waiting with wallets out and cards in hand.

Claudette recognized a friend of Milt's approaching their table. He was tall, well built with a brush cut, face abnormally white as he rubbed red eyes and a runny nose. Jasmine didn't know him, but the look on Claudette's face scared her. As he neared, Claudette trembled, as if sensing something dire. Katie and Sam stopped eating when they saw him.

"Uncle Nolan!" Sam said joyously then turned to Katie. "That's my dad's friend."

Nolan just stood there, staring at Sam and Wyatt – especially Wyatt.

Claudette was scared now. "Nolan. Where's Milt?"

Katie and Jasmine were frozen on the stranger, intuition frightening them.

Nolan couldn't say it. He didn't have too.

Lydia came running from the register when Claudette's cry exploded over the mingling crowd. The entire restaurant gawked at the booth by the jukebox.

Claudette fell into Nolan's arms. The girls were crying. Jasmine and Katie were crying. Wyatt didn't really understand. He just cried because his mother's scream scared him.

Smiley's Bar

"Ralph," Jimmy, the devoted bartender, called out from the other side of the bar. He had the wireless phone in his hand.

"Thanks," Forbes mumbled through a mouthful of cheeseburger. "Yeah, Forbes here." The caller talked quickly. Forbes was stunned, the beer lowering. "Milt Smith. Are you sure?" The caller revealed a name. "And this guy was with him?" Forbes was writing the name on a napkin.

Under the name he wrote, *RCMP*.

"Yeah, I know how to find him." He hung up, tossed a ten spot on the bar for Jimmy then dashed for the door.

RCMP-Headingley

"Sir," a constable called out. He was young, barely past being referred to as a recruit, and considering the circumstances of his temporary placement, therefore expected to answer the phone. He didn't know much about the detachment's sudden roster vacancy, but gathered from the rest of the detachment the awkwardness from any questions; it was better to remain ignorant. His new Superintendent hadn't heard him so he called for him again. "Superintendent, sir."

"Yes, constable?" Eastman was chatting with several non-commissioned officers and the detachment secretary.

"Line one, sir."

"Thank you." Eastman reached for the nearest phone. It was quickly apparent the call was very serious. He fell into a chair as if someone had just knocked the wind out of him. He hung up and stared at the curious faces. "That was Nolan." He was shaking his head, as if what he had just heard couldn't be real. It just couldn't. "Milt Smith is dead."

The Free Press

Lance Nuewerth came crashing through Lund's office door. The newsroom clatter flooded in with him. Nuewerth was empty handed.

"Shouldn't there be a coffee in your hand, Lance?" Lund snapped.

Nuewerth caught his breath. "A cop has just been murdered."

"Who?" Lund asked without looking up from his edit copy.

"Milt Smith."

The shock and disbelieve registered on Lund. "Ah, shit." He eyed Lance hard. "When is Spencer back?"

Winnipeg International Airport

Michael was one of the first ones off flight 222. He jogged through the departure lounge, and with the luxury of no luggage to be snatched off the conveyor, was outside a couple minutes later. He checked his watch. It was 4:10 pm. No Miata in sight. He peered beyond the row of cabs uniformly lined up past the taxi stand, immigrant drivers leafing through magazines and paperback novels to ease their sweaty suffering while waiting for fares to summon them.

Michael saw Jasmine's Miata speeding up, veering to the curb erratically. Usually she babied the little car. He knew something was wrong. Her hair covered her face, hands clenched to the wheel, not even a hello. "Jas?" He climbed in, pulled a lock of hair away from her face. Her usually beautiful green eyes were swollen, smeared mascara streaking her cheeks. She was trembling, struggling to hold it together. "Jas, what's wrong?"

Her trembling hand covered her mouth. "It's Milt, Michael," she sputtered, eyes welling up. "He's dead."

Michael Spencer's world just crashed. Painfully.

CHAPTER 47

The Assassin's Wrath

Toronto

The modest house on Silver Aspen Bay in the suburb of Thornhill was much like all the others well after midnight. Relatively quiet with the exception of a living room light flickering off the bay window curtains. The old girl was a late night television watcher. Occasionally the yappy bark of a cranky old poodle echoed from the backyard. That meant one thing. The back door was probably unlocked.

He sat on the passenger side of the government sedan contemplating his task. It would have to be quick. A contract was a contract but he sat there questioning the reasoning for killing the old woman.

He looked at the dead man beside him. That would be an extra five hundred thousand in his Sydney bank account. He reached his gloved hand into the man's breast pocket, thinking 'what an ugly shirt', and retrieved a billfold. He popped it open and slipped out a CSIS ID card. No surprise there. He fully expected his victim to be an agent before he killed him. He replaced the billfold in the pocket then admired his work. The victim felt nothing. One quick and precise clout under the nose and it was over. Blood oozed from the nostrils, jelling between the lips, gobs dripping from the chin and staining the tacky shirt. It was a clean kill.

A dark haired, pony tailed Javelin, dressed in black fatigues, slipped out of the car and left the corpse of Luke Grogan behind.

~

The Grapes of Wrath was on the television but Maggie Gunthier had the volume muted. She was on the phone with the picture of Katie Spencer clasped in her dry, wrinkled hand. She stared at the photo with an overwhelming affection.

"She looks so much like you, Evelyn," Maggie said into the phone. She spent the past half hour talking about her meeting at CN Tower. She decided to omit the CSIS sighting. Evelyn was nervous enough about her estranged son, terrified of the dangerous people she was sure would find out. Apparently Larry was in the dark. Or so they thought.

"What does he look like, Mags?" Evelyn asked. She had been crying.

Maggie gushed. "He's very handsome," she said then frowned mild disappointment. "He's definitely a Hicks though."

"He looks like Larry?"

"I recognized him without asking who he was." Maggie's poodle was yakking up a storm in the back yard. "Hang on, Eve. I have to let Fefe in." The chore took only a minute. Maggie returned, the hardwood creaking under her feet. She ordered Fefe to stop pawing at the pantry door in the kitchen then plunked into her chair, wondering what she was going to do with her pet.

"I don't know what's with her tonight," she said to Evelyn, "she won't shut up."

"When will you see him again?" Evelyn asked. Fefe's yelping was quickly mounting to a fever pitch.

"Just a minute, Eve," Maggie said. She cranked around and gave a holler. "Fefe ! Shut up!" Fefe barked a couple more times. "Fefe!"

Another bark then sudden, almost unnatural quiet.

Maggie grumbled, "What's with her?" She returned to Evelyn. "I don't know when I'll see him again. I'm not so sure that would be a good idea."

"Why?"

She didn't want to talk about CSIS. "Did I tell you he was the reporter who covered that Tattletale Killer. Remember that?"

"Why, Mags?"

What was that?

Maggie hesitated. Where was Fefe ? "Well...its...just that."

"Mags, whats going on?"

"I don't --." A hardwood creak.

Who's here?

The hand was suddenly over her mouth, the taste of glove leather against her tongue. From behind her a forearm thrust across her chest, pinning her against the chair. Maggie writhed with acute terror. The fingers clamped on her jaw, choking the scream, the glove digging into her skin. The phone tumbled to the floor. She went to seize the intruder's grasp, but a force far superior to her own wrenched her head violently to the right. Cracking vertebra thundered her cranium. Consciousness died instantaneously. The jaw fell agape, limp and lifeless. Spittle trickled down her chin.

    The Javelin gently eased the old woman's head to the armrest then wiped his glove on the back of the chair, her saliva leaving a damp spot. He picked up the phone. A woman was yelling on the other end for Mags to answer her. He held the phone an inch from his ear; no intention of leaving hair follicles. He hung up on the frantic woman screaming for Maggie then flipped through Maggie Gunthier's telephone cardex on the end table beside her corpse. He searched the 'P's-nothing, 'L's-nothing, the 'E's-nothing. A picture of a young girl lay beside the phone. He flipped it over and smiled. On the back was written, 'Katie-grade two.' He tucked the photo in his sleeve and backed away, leaving as he had come.

    He moved with perfected stealth through the kitchen and glanced at the pantry. The yappy poodle, affectionately known as Fefe, lay dead in front of the door. Too bad, he thought. He liked dogs. With no time to waste the Javelin, like the shadow of death himself, slipped into the night.

CHAPTER 48

The Trick up Ralph Forbes's Sleeve

Ralph Forbes's battered Ford station wagon was going to need new shocks. The suspension was bottoming out on the washboard gravel road four miles south of the city. The sky was dark and ominous and lightning forked way to the south. He figured he didn't have much time before the rain hit.

Ahead was a vacant, dilapidated farmhouse poised alone on the prairie like the symbol of a by-gone era. A brand new Jeep Cherokee parked beside the house stood out like a neon sign against the threatening black sky.

Forbes veered into the driveway, his low beams glistening off the new truck. The Cherokee's door swung open and a man stepped out. Ralph turned off his engine as the man climbed in beside him.

"No, leave the AC on," the man said. "Humid as shit." He seemed nervous, glancing up and down the gravel road.

"You alright?" Forbes asked.

"I've been waiting twenty minutes?" the man sneered nervously.

"Sorry," Forbes said. "Thanks for meeting me, Hubert."

"Sounds like I didn't have a choice," spat Assistant Commissioner, Officer Commanding Hubert Jefkins. The RCMP looked skyward. "Helluva storm coming." The rumbling echoed. Another flash lit the dark sky to the south. They could smell it coming now. "Let's get this over with."

Forbes lit a smoke and said. "Tell me about Nolan Grant, Hubert."

"Grant? Is that what you want to talk about?"

"Why was he dismissed?"

"Because he asks questions."

"About what?"

Jefkins didn't want to answer. He fidgeted like he wanted to jump in his Jeep and high tail it out of there. Maybe breaking his oath was not so easy this time. He was an Assistant Commissioner now.

Forbes rubbed his head, took a puff. "Michael Spencer doesn't like you much. Said you stonewalled him. Did you that, Hubert?" Jefkins wasn't talking. "Why would you refuse to give him some information about his birth father, Hubert?"

Jefkins bit the inside of his lip; making a decision. "I tell you about this and we are done."

Forbes grin dissolved. "That's a big ante."

"This is as big as it gets," Jefkins said. "Look, I gave you everything you wanted back then about the judge, but I'm done going down the rabbit hole for you or anybody."

"Funny, I got fired for running that story and you got to be Assistant Commissioner," Forbes said. He sounded bitter. "And no one knows it was you who gave him up and you know why, Hubert?"

"I appreciate you keeping my name out of it, Ralph, but this is it."

Forbes thought it through a moment. "Okay. Agreed."

Jefkins took the smoke out of Forbes hand, had a puff. "Ottawa has put a lid on everything. The Commissioner is ready to start chopping heads."

"Why?"

"He's getting pressure."

"From who?"

Jefkins sighed. "Everybody. Jesus. Your friend Spencer has really opened something up here."

"No fucking kidding. Why was Grant dismissed?"

"Because he asked questions about Operation Scarlet and pissed some people off."

"And...?"

Jefkins took another long puff, not sure if he made the right decision. "His name came up on a wiretap between Milt Smith and Michael Spencer."

Forbes stiffened. Michael's worries had just been confirmed. "Whose tap, Hubert?"

"CSIS, CSE, NSID. Who knows? They're all in to him deeper than you can think."

"You know some guy named Floyd Webber?"

"Never heard of him. He CSIS?"

"I don't know. He paid a visit to Michael's friend, the same one who handled his adoption search."

"This fucking search." Jefkins gave the smoke back, suddenly hit with an attack of paranoia, glancing up the road again. "There's a mole in the Force," he finally said. "That's what they're afraid of."

CHAPTER 49

The Time to Turn Back is Over

Michael put the bottle of Jack Daniels to his mouth. He just sat there on the front step, consumed with grief too deep to comprehend. He stared across at the park soaked in moonlight but all he could see was Milt slumped over in the shower, eyes lifeless, blood seeping through the grout to the drain. He was torturing himself with the thought of Claudette and the kids, the guilt and tears would hit again, and he would pull another mouthful, grit as it went down.

He threw the empty bottle into the flowerbed then dug into his pocket for Evelyn's picture. He rubbed it and thought of all the tyranny. It was just an adoption search. Why Milt? Memories were flooding now. He glared at the park across the street, as if he could feel them out there, lurking in the oaks; invading his mourning. He needed to talk to the only person who would help him get through this. The Jack was hitting now. He fished his iPhone out of his pocket as he staggered into the house. Four rings later a comforting, familiar voice answered.

"Hello." The man was groggy.

"Hi, Dad."

"Michael, what is it?" Olie Spencer said, instantly concerned and awake simply by the shakiness of his son's voice. "Are you alright?"

"No, I'm not, Dad. I don't know what to do."

"Michael..."

~

"Are you sure about this," a tired Mac Loewen said to the man crouching beside him behind the oaks bordering the Red River, directly across from 421 Churchill drive. There were no light brown Chevy half-tons or Dodge 4x4's or government sedans spying from the street. There wouldn't be after tonight.

Loewen peered up at the threatening darkness. Stars to the south were obliterated by the swelling storm rolling in over the city. A flash of lightning serrated the black sky, the distant rumble followed.

"It's going to be a wet one tonight," he said. "I may catch my death of pneumonia out here." He moved some foliage aside that obscured Michael Spencer sitting in his living room. He was still talking on his iPhone, still clutching his forehead. Loewen glanced at the man beside him who peered through pocket-sized binoculars. Another crack of thunder permeated. "What's he doing?"

"Crying," the man said, guilt thick in his voice.

Mac Loewen borrowed the binoculars. "Any ideas on how you want to do this without getting him killed?"

The man stared across the river at a two-story home with an impressive deck. "I have an idea," Larry Hicks finally said.

CHAPTER 50

From Dust to Anger

On any other day the rain would've been a welcome relief. But today, the grey overcast only deepened the despair. Michael sat in the back of the lead limousine with Katie tucked into him. She hadn't said a word since leaving the house this morning; that alone was an indication of how scared she was. Claudette's mother, a widow herself, sat across from them with Sam and Wyatt squeezed into her. Wyatt was being remarkably strong this morning. Michael could see the strength of Milt in him. Claudette was sitting behind the driver, sobbing while Jas held her, rubbing and patting her hand.

The cortege motored along with the honorary police motorcycle escort leading the way. It passed under the traffic cloverleaf where Portage Avenue turned into Trans-Canada #1 West, then a half kilometer later turned into the Funeral Gardens just south of the highway. Claudette openly wept when the limousine passed through the Chapel's ornate arches. Samantha clung to her mom. Jasmine soothed both. Katie clung to Michael.

Ten minutes later the mourners stood around the open grave in the rain, umbrellas open, and somberly watched Milt Smith's casket slide out of the hearse. Nolan was among the pallbearers. The odd reporter lurked across the cemetery, snapping shots while the congregation assembled around the suspended coffin, the Canadian flag and a collage of flowers draping over it. The rain pelted through the proceedings.

A tractor started in the distance, an omen to the final preparation of death. The operator would wait until the mourners were on their way down the highway before he filled the grave.

Michael shook hands as people headed back to their cars. John Lund among them, he permitted Michael a few days off then departed with Lance. Cindy Greene's boyfriend pushed her wheelchair over the soft, wet grass. She would hurt for a long time to come. Sam Eastman offered condolences to Claudette then mingled with Nolan Grant by the graveyard road. Jessica stepped away from the gravesite to calm her nerves with a cigarette; something she had not done in years. Nolan lit it for her and had one himself. Claudette wanted to leave immediately, prepare the food and drinks before people came to the house, so Jasmine escorted her to the limousine with the kids and Claudette's mother. Michael wanted a few minutes by himself to say good-bye to his friend.

He wasn't alone for long.

"Hello, Michael."

Floyd Webber stepped up beside him.

Michael couldn't place the man. "I'm sorry. How did you know Milt?"

"I didn't really," Webber simply said.

The tractor operator was negotiating his way from the maintenance shed through the maze of plots to where they were standing. The sputtering motor a sharp contrast to the dull thunder rumbling from the grey overcast above.

"I'm sorry about your friend," Webber said. "But the truth is I'm here for you."

"I'm sorry...who are you?"

"My name is Floyd Webber."

Michael recognized the name. He could see Jessica talking to Jasmine by the limousines, pointing and looking very concerned. "So you're the one who has been spying on me."

"I am," Webber said.

"You've been in my house."

"I have."

"Why?"

"All good questions, Michael," Webber said, glancing around the way spymasters do when they're out in the open. "But we don't have time for me to explain or defend myself." He gestured the coffin. "I think you have an idea of what's coming for you."

Michael couldn't speak. *He just admits it like it doesn't matter?*

Webber could see the look he's seen before when a private citizen tries to find justification for such invasion of personal and private lives. "I realize this may not be the time for this but you and your family are in danger, Michael."

"Stay out of my house," Michael said then turned for the parking lot.

"This is not the only funeral today, Michael."

Michael stopped, looked at the spy man, afraid of what he was about to say. The tractor was only a few rows from the site now.

Webber stepped close to him when he noticed Jasmine Spencer watching them from the limousine. "I know you saw my agent in Toronto."

"Tell her she's not too good at tailing subjects."

Webber peered over at the parking lot, a steady stream of mourner's cars filing onto the Trans-Canada. "Do you remember the man with her at the Tower. Remember him? The guy with the loud Hawaiian shirt that reminded you of your Dad at the Hula Hut."

Michael's ire flared. "Stay away from my family."

Webber took another step in. "That agent had his funeral in Toronto today too. He had two kids just like your friend. And you should know he was keeping an eye on Maggie Gunthier the night someone killed him."

Michael froze, rain droplets dripping from his nose, his sandy hair matted to his forehead. He knew before it was said.

"They killed her, Michael," Webber finally said. "They killed her because they want your birthfather."

Michael hunched over, clutching his knees. Dizziness swirling. He wanted to be sick.

"They want Larry, Michael. They want him bad enough they are going to kill you and your whole family. I have not been spying on you, Michael." Webber leaned to within whispering distance. "I've been protecting you."

Michael looked into the tough face, trying to comprehend a man like Floyd Webber. Then it hit him. "You knew my birthfather. You were part of the operation weren't you?"

Webber, the pro, would never answer that question. He merely glanced at the tractor waiting for them to leave. "Pay your respects, Michael, but don't let your friend die for nothing. I'll know when you're ready to talk." He headed for the parking lot, passing Grant who was coming to check on Michael at Jasmine's insistence.

Michael watched Webber climb into the brown Chevy half-ton and drive through the arches. He couldn't stand the sight of Milt's coffin over the open grave any longer. He was angry now. He asked Nolan to watch Jasmine and Katie, then marched right for a bright yellow VW bug. He climbed in to a surprised Lance Nuewerth behind the wheel.

"Let's go for a drink, Lance."

CHAPTER 51

The Target Takes Charge

It had been a while since Michael had been in Smiley's Bar. He barged in with Lance doggedly following. It was painfully obvious the copy clerk hadn't ventured into a pub all that often, especially a seedy one.

Jimmy the bartender was talking up a couple girls at the bar. He recognized Michael right off.

"Where is he?" Michael demanded.

"I'm right here," Ralph said from a booth before Jimmy could answer. Surprisingly enough he was cold sober. Jimmy went back to his girls as Michael slid into the booth. Lance was about to, but Michael's hand went up.

"Lance, get yourself a beer at the bar." It was an order not a suggestion.

"I don't drink," Lance said quietly. Michael shot the kid a look that said do it. "I'll just get a pop then," Lance offered. "Hi Ralph."

"Hey, Lancy." They waited till Lance was on a bar stool then Ralph got right to it. "You're not hoping I'm going to tell you that you were right are ya, Michael."

"I'm not here to argue." Michael needed a shot.

Ralph could see it. "Hey, Jimmy, we could use a Jack over here."

"Coming up," Jimmy said as he slid a pop to Lance. He walked a couple shots over then quickly got back to his girls.

Michael knocked it back. Ralph pushed his across the table. "You need this more than me." Michael took it. Nothing could numb what he was feeling. Lance even looked like he was concerned about him.

Ralph sipped his coffee. "Sorry about Milt."

Michael rubbed his hand slowly down his face, took a deep breath then admitted, "I'm scared, Ralph."

"I don't blame you." Ralph leaned in. "I think you're in over your head, Michael. I don't know who is killing these people, but they are fucking serious about finding your father." Ralph took another sip. "Either way there's one hell of a story to dig up here."

Michael chuckled, his nervousness showing through. "No shit."

Ralph leaned back, smirked because he had to ask the obvious. "Does Lund know you're here?"

"I don't give a shit about Lund right now," Michael said with a dead serious look. "You let me worry about him. Are you in?"

"Oh, I'm in," Ralph said and finished his coffee. "So, when do we get started?"

"Tonight," Michael said.

CHAPTER 52

The Time to Take Flight

"Jas...Jas," Michael whispered in her ear, gently rocking her awake. It was 4:00 in the morning and he had yet to sleep. He had scoured the house and found wafer mics planted in every room but Katie's. Even micro video transmitters were tucked up in the ceilings.

Jasmine stirred. Michael's hand clamped her mouth before she could gasp, her eyes ripped wide. He touched a finger to his lips, leaned to her ear, whispering almost inaudibly. "We have to go. No talking. Put your slippers on. It'll be quieter."

She climbed out of bed, nervously put on her slippers then made for Katie's room, trying to be as normal as she could. Katie was already up, both mother and daughter haggard and drained from yesterday's funeral. They watched Michael quietly pull a laundry basket out of Katie's closet. He could see how scared they were.

"I made like I was doing laundry last night," he said breathlessly. "We'll get dressed in the truck. Don't speak. I've found some bugs in the house. We have to be quiet. I put Sabe down stairs. He'll be fine. I've made sure to that."

Michael eased open the window, the garage in plain site across the yard. "Trust me," he whispered then helped Katie climb out.

~

Ten minutes later Chester had his night vision binoculars aimed between the Spencer house and the next door neighbors', focusing on the back lane. He observed the Spencer's black SUV coast slowly behind the oaks bordering backyard fences.

"Where's he going?" he muttered to himself while hastily negotiating the riverbank back to his green sedan.

SSET Command

"Rise and shine buddy," Garrick said at the ceiling. He actually took guilty pleasure in calling the team at ungodly hours. The computer clock displayed 6:05 am. He already woke the others. Now it was Simon's turn. A voice answered over the speakers above that Garrick didn't expect.

"He's still sleeping," a sultry feminine voice said.

Garrick quickly draped the headset over his ears, cut the feed to the speakers in case the Chief happened to stumble into the office. He listened to her rouse Simon, then after a few grumbles Johnson's tired breathing filled the hacker's ears.

"What," he said through a yawn.

"Hey, Simon, you dog," Garrick praised. "You're my hero, dude."

Simon cleared his throat. "What's up?"

"Need you at 421."

"Now?"

"Yep. It's double duty time."

"Of course it is," Simon groaned. "I'm on my way."

Garrick's computer pinged with an incoming call to Spencer's.

****A. ATKINSON*****27 KINGSTON ROW******

"Gregg meeting me there?" Simon asked.

"Yeah. Get going?"

Simon disconnected but Garrick had a weird feeling.

The Spencer's bedroom phone was right by their bed, it was the crack of dawn, and they're not picking up? He could see them in the video feed in their bedroom, sleeping under the covers. By four rings he was beginning to wonder if Spencer was going to pick up before voice mail kicked in. He checked the kitchen.

Where is the mutt?

He popped from room to room and couldn't see the dog. Then he found him in the basement, flaked out on the couch. Garrick clicked back to Spencer's bedroom. They hadn't moved. He zoomed in on the bed and realized they weren't breathing. He pushed the lens in as far as he could, leaned close to the monitor and just watched. Then he realized he was looking at dummies stuffed under the sheets and a wig for Jasmine Spencer's long hair.

Fuck!

The voice mail finally kicked in on the ringing phone. It was Lily Atkinson calling to remind Michael not to be late.

Garrick quickly clicked on an icon of Popeye the Sailor Man. A phone ringed in his ears. It picked up and the gruff voice of Floyd Webber answered.

CHAPTER 53

The Moment a Long Time Coming

Michael's SUV zipped across the Osborne Street Bridge then veered onto Kingston Row. This time, however, the tranquility of the lush neighbourhood went unnoticed for Jessica. She was scared by the time they pulled into the Atkinson's driveway. Everything about her life had changed when Michael picked her up this morning. But when he told her Lily Atkinson had requested he visit, and bring Jessica along, they suspected it was to know more about what had happened to Maggie Gunthier. This was going to be a difficult meeting this time. Michael rang the doorbell.

Lily Atkinson was anything but somber when she opened the door. Her infectious smile welcomed them into the cool foyer. Michael and Jessica were a little befuddled. They expected a bereaved Lily greeting them, lamenting Maggie's death, but instead she was elated.

She escorted them through to the back patio overlooking the river. There was a tray of lemonade and frosted glasses already set out. Michael couldn't help feel something was up. This was just weird.

"I thought some lemonade would be nice," Lily said, passing out glasses.

Jessica wondered why there were six. "Lily, why so many glasses?"

Lily didn't answer. She sat down and looked directly at Michael, embraced his hand. "Maybe some good can come of all this."

Michael tensed and said, "Lily, what's going on?"

"Your search is over, Michael dear," she proclaimed, rose from the table, opened the patio doors, and said, "You can come out now," to someone lurking in the living room. Her mysterious visitor stepped out into the sunlight.

He was an elderly man, bearing no resemblance whatsoever to Michael, strolled across the porch with his hand reaching out. "You really are his son," he observed. "My name's Mac Loewen. Nice to meet ya, Michael."

Michael shook his hand bewildered and confused. Then another man filed onto the porch with Archie directly behind. He was in good shape for a man his age and well tanned. The eyes were steel blue. The jaw line set a little firmer yet the nose so exact to Michael's the two men could share it. The hair was peppered with grey, but noticeably sandy colored in youth. Baldness did not appear to be inherited. He was casually dressed with a white and blue polo shirt, light slacks and loafers. Larry Hicks was as nervous as Michael.

Michael stood in awe. It was like studying himself years from now. Whether he looked good or not didn't enter the equation. There he was, the mysterious man himself.

"You must be Jessica Ingham," Larry said kindly. He smiled Michael's smile. Jessica couldn't help it. A tear formed and dripped down her cheek.

"Yes," she managed.

After another glance at his son he sincerely said, "Thank you."

"You're welcome, Mr. Hicks."

Michael and Larry just stood there, natural father and son, not sure how to proceed.

"If you don't mind," Larry said to everyone. "I'd like a moment with Michael."

Mac Loewen was the first through the doors, followed by Archie who clearly wasn't sure any of this was a good idea. He urged Lily and Jessica to follow them into the house, the old girl a tad miffed at being removed from what should have been a joyous reuniting.

Jessica hesitated leaving Michael. He nodded he'd be fine. Archie closed the patio doors as she step inside.

Father and son were alone on the deck now, the awkwardness normal and expected. "Funny," Larry began. "I actually imagined this being quite different."

Michael wasn't in the mood for casual conversation. Milt's casket haunted him. His family was on the run now because of this man.

Larry reclined into one of the patio chairs and gazed at the river below where a pontoon boat was trolling against the current. "Please sit, Michael."

Finally Michael cleared his throat to speak. "I need some answers. I deserve that."

"I know," Larry said. "I will get to that in good time."

"You'll get to that right now. Do you know what has happened to me since I tried to find you?"

"Yes, I do. And hiding your family at your in-laws in Regina won't protect them," Larry said. There was a sedateness to his voice; the calm of a man who has been under the gun before. He looked out over the river again. "If I know then they'll know. We don't have much time."

Michael shook his head. He was tired of strangers insinuating they knew more about his private life than he did. "They want you, not me. Do the right thing, surrender yourself so I can get my life back." He marched for the patio door.

"It's not that simple, Michael." Larry said as he rose out of the chair with a grunt - the first visible sign of his age - a deliberate tone to him now.

"Yes it is," Michael shot back.

"You came home last Sunday night from your in-laws," Larry said a little too matter-of-factly. "You talked with Milt Smith. He told you that Nolan Grant told him the Operation Scarlet file had been re-opened. That got Mr. Grant suspended. You both worried about Cindi Greene. I understand she's on forced leave and her CPIC access is revoked." Larry pointed towards the living room. "Your friend in there, Jessica, had called asking about Maggie. So they know about her now as well. Maggie called you. That got her killed." Larry choked up, cleared his throat and continued. "Milt Smith was SWAT, helluva a sniper from what I'm told, and a good friend who was going to help you with this search, maybe even find out who the dangerous people were. That got him killed."

Larry took a step in, his tone regretful now. "I've spent my life trying to protect you from all this, Michael. Whether you believe that or not doesn't matter. There is only one reality now and they will not stop. More lives will be in danger." He gestured inside. "Miss Ingham in there. Archie and Lily. And if they've lost your family for even the briefest of moments, Michael, they might even go after Danny Gregory or your daughter's schoolteacher, or your boss at the paper, John Lund, or your reporter friend with the drinking problem, Ralph Forbes, or Lance Nuewerth who seems a little too technical for his own good. They already know about the Hula Hut in Oahu."

Michael sunk into a chair, the fight draining out of him. Larry was decidedly pained, watching Michael struggle the unimaginable with a grimace.

"You don't even know who you'd be running from," Larry continued. He pointed down at the river. "And what makes you think you can hide from someone like Floyd Webber."

Michael sprang for the porch railing and peered down at the river below. He felt his knees give out. His thought he was going to vomit right there on Archie Atkinson's patio. The pontoon boat was sloshing against the current. Floyd Webber was standing on the bow. Michael recognized the driver as the agent who drove the light brown Chevy half-ton at the graveyard. He turned to Larry, completely trapped and out of his depth.

"Webber is SSET," Larry explained. "Trust me when I tell you very few people even know what that is." He stepped to the railing. "The first thing we have to do is lose him." He looked right at Michael and said, "You can hate me later. But right now, we have no time."

~

Webber was amused when Spencer and Hicks bolted from the porch. "I don't believe it," he said to Simon Johnson at the helm. "He's gonna run for it." Webber pressed his earpiece. "Al."
"Yeah, Chief," came the quick response.
"He's running. And Hicks is with him. Get me a helicopter."
"Done," Garrick replied.
"Gregg..?"

~

"Here, Chief," Redekopp responded from inside his Dodge 4x4 parked six houses down from 421. He was looking across Churchill Park, watching the pontoon boat pick up speed.
"Stay with him until I'm in the air," his chief said over everyone's ears.
"Copy that," Redekkop said, cranked his 4x4 around but failed to notice the green sedan parked a hundred yards past the Spencer house.

~

Chester watched his laptop mounted on the dash of his government green sedan. A southern quadrant map of Winnipeg popped up at the touch of a key, with a red dot bleeping over the blue squiggly line labeled Red River. Chester wrenched his head around in time to catch Spencer's SUV speed across the Osborne Street Bridge. He had no reason to pay attention to the Ford Explorer riding Spencer's bumper. Tires squealed when Chester accelerated after the Dodge 4x4.

~

"Kyle. Candace," Webber said as Johnson guided the waterbus under the very bridge Spencer's SUV had just passed over.

~

"We're on him, Chief," Candace said as Kyle Lenning spun his Mustang around after passing Spencer's SUV on Osborne. She pressed her earpiece. "They're heading north, towards the Village, guys". Spencer's

SUV swerved from lane to lane about twenty car lengths ahead, weaving through the Saturday morning traffic that always clogged Osborne.

"They're really moving," she said as Kyle sped past a Ford Explorer.

~

The waterbus cleared the bridge and Webber once again was squinting into the sun. "Don't lose him. Al, I don't have a helicopter yet!"

"It's on its way, Chief."

~

Michael saw the Mustang fly by from the passenger seat of Mac Loewen's Explorer. And right after was a Dodge 4x4. He recognized the driver.

"It's Webber's team alright," Larry said from behind the wheel. Jessica was in the back seat, really scared now.

Michael watched his SUV dart erratically in and out of traffic way ahead. "He scratches it, he pays for it."

"Mac knows what he is doing." Larry said. "He's the one person I completely trust."

Michael dug his iPhone out of his pocket.

"Now who you calling?" Jessica asked.

"Someone I can trust," Michael said, eyeing Larry until Lance Neuwerth picked up. "Lance, where's Lund? Whad'ya mean he's not there? Look, I don't have time, Lance. Meet me at the airport in ten minutes. Bring that laptop with you. I'm really counting on you. I'll explain when you get there. Move!" Michael hung up.

Larry's driving skills were a little clumsy, suggesting he hadn't had to deal with big city traffic in quite some time.

"When's the last time you drove?" Michael asked, grabbing the passenger handle over his door.

"How old are you?" Larry said with a chuckle. Neither Michael nor Jessica found that funny.

~

Spencer's SUV slowed to the posted speed limit in the curb lane. Kyle goosed his Mustang and pulled along side. Candace peered at the driver. He was old, balding and robust. He smiled and waved.

"Shit!" she cursed, "it's Loewen." She pressed her earpiece. "We've lost him! We've lost him!" She searched out the back window. No sign of another similar truck.

"Chief..!"

~

"...Candace, where are you?" Webber asked, pacing on the pontoon boat's bow, his frustration evident to Johnson.
"Coming up to the Village," Candace said.
"Get your ass to the airport. Now!" He looked skyward as the pontoon glided around another bend in the river. "Al, where is my damn helicopter?"
"You should see it," Garrick replied.
"Chief," Johnson said, pointing over Webber's shoulder. A Robinson Mariner light duty helicopter listing on its amphibious flotation came into view as they cruised out of the bend. The aircraft was in the middle of the river. The pilot opened the door as the pontoon boat pulled alongside. Webber quickly buckled himself in.
"Where to, sir?" the pilot asked as his bird lifted off.
"Get me over the Village."
The helicopter tipped drastically to the right and headed north.

Winnipeg International Airport

Larry and Michael walked Jessica to the American Airlines counter. The attendant smiled politely and inquired of tickets.
"One ticket, please, for the lady here," Larry said. "Nassau, Bahamas."
"And her name?" the attendant asked, pecking her keyboard.

SSET Command

Garrick was scanning the American Airlines passenger database, searching for non-advance ticket purchases. He watched 'Nassau, Bahamas' being typed in. Curious, he thought. Not far from Key West. The passenger's name was Susan Hanis; a dead end.
"Damn," he muttered then bounced himself out of the program to hack his way back into the Air Canada mainframe.

Winnipeg International Airport

"...Passport?" the attendant asked pleasantly.
Larry gestured at Jessica's purse. She dug out a passport and nervously handed it over. The name beside Jessica's picture was Susan Hanis.
"Luggage, Miss Hanis?" the attendant asked.

Jessica nodded 'no' and the attendant handed her a one-way ticket. Jessica took it then stepped back and asked Larry, "How will I know how to find her? How will she know me?"

Michael produced a picture from his wallet. It was the photo Maggie had given him of Evelyn on a tropical porch, which he now assumed to be the Bahamas. "This might help."

Everything had culminated for Jessica at that very moment and she wrapped her arms around Michael and cried softly. Behind her back Larry nodded to Michael for the departure gates. Michael knew without being told there was no time for sentiments.

"Jessica," he said gently. He eased her out of the hug. "You have to go. Jasmine will find you."

A few minutes later he embraced her again at the boarding gate and told her he would be in the Bahamas as soon as he could. Reluctantly, she volunteered her ticket to the stewardess and disappeared onto the American Airlines jet.

~

Chester watched the Spencer's SUV pull into a metered stall near the airport terminal. He was caught totally off guard when an elderly man slid out from behind the wheel. This was bad, very bad. He popped open the glove compartment and retrieved his Glock then hopped out of the sedan and ran for the SUV.

~

Kyle, Candace and Redekopp stormed the airport's main entrance with earpieces in, passing by Lance Nuewerth on his way out.

The three split up to cover more ground with Kyle and Redekopp scurrying up the escalators to check the departure gates. Candace hustled past the long bank of airline ticket kiosks on the main level, searching faces and hoping for a miracle. She overheard Garrick in her ear say Bahamas and the name Hanis. She stopped when she heard the name. Susan Hanis? She knew that name. She pressed her earpiece. "Al," she said, cutting off Webber demanding the airport be closed down. "Did you say, Susan Hanis?"

"Yeah. Why?" Garrick responded.

"What is it, Candace?" Webber demanded.

She bolted for the American Airlines kiosk. "Chief! That's her! That's Ingham!" She jumped to the front of the American Airlines counter. Several irritated grunts bellowed from waiting passengers.

The young attendant frowned. "I'm sorry, miss, but you'll have to wait your turn."

"Did a redheaded woman with two gentlemen - one young with sandy blonde hair and the other older - board the plane?"

The attendant eyed Candace with a petty smugness. "I'm sorry, I can't just give out that information." A CSIS card was quickly in her face.

"Get me your supervisor now," Candace demanded.

"Ma'am, I have___," she attempted to say but Candace cut her off.

"Now!"

~

While the airline attendant returned to the American Airlines counter with her supervisor, Mac Loewen was in the parking lot reading the instructions on the parking meter.

"I hate the city," he mumbled to himself when he realized he had to pay for his stall inside the terminal. He hadn't figured on walking that far. He was just supposed to leave Spencer's keys under the floor mat and pick up his Explorer on the opposite side of the parking lot. That was far enough in this muggy heat. But he felt the blunt poke of a Glock gouging a sensitive spot around his kidneys. "Hey," he blurted as his assailant spun him around and tossed him against the hood of Michael Spencer's SUV.

"Fuck," Chester cursed, retreating the weapon to his side.

"Military intelligence? JTF-2?" Mac speculated.

"Sir," Chester responded.

"You know who I am?" Mac asked as if he was talking to a subordinate.

"Yes, sir," the military agent replied. The old man's finger was nearly touching his nose.

"You're Braden's gofer, aren't ya. You tell your people they made a deal and they had better stick to it if they want to see Morelatto behind bars. Understand?"

"Yes, sir," Chester complied with a tight lip. His target had eluded him. For a professional that was hard to take.

Loewen pointed at Spencer's SUV. "Take your homing device with you, too."

"Yes, sir."

~

Mac climbed into his Explorer across the parking lot, slipped an old flip phone cell out of his pocket. He pressed the "1" key that auto-dialed a frequent number, the same number that had called him when he was hammering nails on his dock back in Kenora. The line picked up on the other end. There was never a hello or friendly greeting.

"They're coming to you," he simply said and hung up. Mac Loewen squeezed his eyes and cursed himself. That Christmas Eve in Vancouver back in '81 was never going to go away for the driver.

~

Nolan had been busy since Michael called him right after they put his friend on a plane for the Bahamas. Michael was with his birth father, Larry Hicks. That was already too much information over a phone. CSIS was chasing them. With Milt murdered it didn't have to be said that Nolan was the logical loose end. The RCMP were still camped out on his doorstep. It was difficult to gauge just how violated Nolan felt. He lost his career, his dignity, his friend, and now had to run for his life, all in the space of three days.

So after bidding Michael good luck, he hopped onto the Virago and arrived at the airport twenty minutes after Michael's Airbus flight to Vancouver departed. Nolan's primary concern was avoiding the Force. Guaranteed airport security would have a full profile on him by now. He went to the information booth as Michael had instructed and asked if a letter had been left for him. The girl in the kiosk was the daughter of one of Michael's fellow reporters at the Free Press. He read it, tossed it in the trash, and hustled over to the American Airlines counter to purchase his ticket for Nassau, Bahamas. While standing in line he overheard a flaxen-haired women ask about first class seats for Oahu, Hawaii. There were two guys with her. Nolan wouldn't have thought anything of it, but one of the two was the guy who burst out of the Racquet Club change rooms yelling for an ambulance when Milt was found shot.

Jesus, they're CSIS!

Nolan bought his ticket for the first outbound flight using an alias and wondered if the Bahamas was far enough.

CHAPTER 54

The Hula Hut

The Hula Hut was exactly what one would expect. An over-sized thatch shanty on the beach to accommodate a retirement village situated two miles south of Waikiki. Beyond the open air patio a reddish orange sun was melting into the aqua blue where breakers rumbled the sandy beach. The sweet smell of salt and seashells perfumed the air. This was the life.

Candace and Redekopp were sitting at the bar. So far the bartender, a native islander, couldn't recall the name Olie Spencer.

"Are you sure?" Candace persisted.

"Yes, I'm sure," he stated most categorically then excused himself and ventured out from behind the bar with a tray of fresh beers. His clientele of Hawaiian shirted retirees were thirsty over at the checkers table. The same place they were every day around the same time.

Gregg ambled over. The retirees ignored the young agent, concentrating on the only priorities that pertained to them anymore; beer and checkers. "How 'bout you guys," he asked.

One of the old guys interrupted his checker move to point at the native islander now back behind the bar. "Just like Kino said, young man. Never heard of him." His opponent jumped his king. "How in the hell--."

"You're not paying attention, Fred," the opponent scorned.

"You're cheating again," Fred accused. He chided his buddies. "You boys watching him?"

The opponent was appalled. "I don't need to cheat. You're the worst player out of all of us for Christ's sake."

"Make your move, Fred," another player said. It all seemed like an everyday scenario.

Before Fred could touch his checker, Gregg threw a twenty spot onto the board. Fred, for the first time, looked up at him.

Gregg sported a wry grin. "I'll play. You win you get the twenty. I win you tell me where Olie Spencer is."

"Are you deaf?" Fred turned to one of his buddies. "Harold, give the kid your hearing aid." That roused hearty laughter. "We don't know an Olie Spencer, son." Fred picked up the twenty. "Do you know what the exchange rate is these days? Hell, down here this paper is worth about-," he faced his crew, "what do you think fellas?"

"Ten bucks," quipped one of them. They all laughed again, clinked their beers together.

Candace had heard enough. She marched over and threw down the photograph of Milt Smith's assassin. The laughing quickly stopped.

Fred looked up at her. "He's cute. Your boyfriend?"

"No," she said. "The guy who just might show up here looking for Olie Spencer. He's already killed a Winnipeg cop named Milt Smith. Maybe you could pass that along."

Heads around the table hung low. Fred handed the picture back. "We don't know an Olie Spencer, young lady," he said.

Candace took the photo then glanced at Gregg. "Let's go."

Gregg plunked his CSIS card down on the table. "Maybe he'll come in here or something. If he does you might want to get him to call us. Thanks guys." And with that Gregg followed Candace onto the beach.

The retired gang watched until the two CSIS agents were out of earshot then Fred picked up the card and handed it to his opponent wearing the pink Hawaiian shirt his granddaughter had bought him last Christmas.

"Is that cop your son's friend?" Fred asked.

Olie Spencer couldn't answer. He liked Milt an awful lot.

"We're here for ya, buddy." Fred said with concurring nods around the table.

Olie appreciated their support. Michael had phoned from Vancouver only a half hour before the agents showed up. Olie had asked Michael why Jasmine and Katie weren't sent to stay with him. But sitting there with the CSIS card in his hand, and an assassin on the loose, he knew Michael was right. They wouldn't have been safe in Hawaii.

Olie Spencer reached for his beer, hoping the dire consequences threatening his family could be stopped in time.

~

"Oh well," Gregg said as he and Candace climbed into a rented Land Rover parked on the edge of the beach. "At least we're in Hawaii."

"He got the message," Candace said.

"Yeah, I think they we're lying too."

Candace looked directly at Gregg. "He was playing checkers."

Gregg looked across to the thatch bar. "You mean Fred?"

"The other one."

"How do you know?"

"His picture is in Katie Spencer's bedroom."

Gregg started the truck. "Thought you didn't look at pictures, Candace."

"Usually I don't, but it's pretty hard to ignore a pink shirt like that."

CHAPTER 55

The Kingpin & his Pawns

Vancouver

Coleman Dresher gunned his silver Porsche 924 over the Lion's Gate Bridge under a twilight sky. The annoying drizzle finally relented by the time he got off the green at the Capillano Golf and Country Club. He was putting his clubs in the front trunk when his cell buzzed. The message was simple.

The top of the Seacorp building in one hour.

Dresher pulled up to Roy Graham's limousine waiting in the underground parkade beneath the Seacorp building. The elevator was passing the fifth floor before Graham spoke. He seemed more nervous than usual. "Why did he call a meeting?"

"How should I know?" Dresher simply said.

Graham watched the floor numbers light up over the doors, growing more anxious as they sped for the roof. "He's going to kill us, Cole."

"What!"

"I think he's going to kill the Prime Minister too."

Dresher lashed out with a hard slap to Graham's shoulder. "Shut your fucking mouth. Christ, Roy, have you lost your fucking mind?"

"You said yourself, we're going to have to watch out for ourselves."

"Yeah, and you're going to get us both fucking killed talking like that."

"It makes sense, Coleman. They've got Seth Peterson in their pockets. The merger deal could go through and the only obstacle for Mario is the Prime Minister."

"Fuck, you're not listening to me!"

"And you're not listening to me! They don't need us and we know too much!"

Dresher pinned Graham against the wall, his forearm pushing into the

Premier's throat. "You're the liability, Roy! But those assholes still need me! Do you know why?"

"Coleman," Graham pleaded under the arm forcing him to the floor now.

"Because the bastards don't know who their mole is. They kill me and they're dead. Fucking dead! You hear me!"

Graham's eyes were bulging, gasping for air that couldn't come. Then Dresher hoisted him up and brushed the wrinkles out of his suit.

"Not another word about it, Roy," Dresher said with an eerie calm. "Not another word."

The elevator reached the observation level and the doors opened to reveal SeaCorp's Sikorsky helicopter awaiting them. Dresher stepped out onto the roof and scaled the ladder up to the helipad, the landing lights illuminating his suit a phosphorous white. He stood on the platform, looking down at a frightened Graham, and waved for him to get a move on.

Graham knew his fall from grace was nearly complete.

He climbed to the helipad, his face as white as the lights shining up at the twilight sky. He stepped wearily through the boarding door and forty-five minutes later the Sikorsky was hovering over the White Knight drifting in the Strait of Georgia somewhere between Vancouver Island and the mainland. Morelatto and Garva were waiting on the upper deck, watching their descent. Roy Graham was convinced that within the hour he would be dead, his body sinking to the bottom of the strait. Just one more liability rectified.

The White Knight

"How 'bout a drink, Roy?" Morelatto asked. "Alec, get the Premier a drink."

Drinks in hand, Morelatto led them to the upper aft deck and reclined on the white leather couch. It wrapped around the full girth of the deck overlooking the cockpit and transom. The other man already seated with beer in hand was all too familiar to Dresher and Graham.

Jake Munroe nodded diffidently. He had aged rather well since '81 and still wasn't one for lawyers. He studied the Premier; the weak link in their corrupt little group. "Buying anymore land, Roy?" Munroe asked with a cocky smirk.

Graham ignored him - he always distanced himself from a psychotic like Munroe – and eased himself onto the sofa, intentionally across from Morelatto; the further the better.

"No crew on board tonight?" Dresher asked, as if he just realized they were alone on the bridge.

"A night off," Morelatto informed. "They escorted some lady friends back to Victoria." He leaned over and whacked Dresher playfully on the knee. "Shame you missed it, Coleman. You would've liked them."

"Enough of this," Munroe said impatiently. "We want to know what's going on with his trial." The question was aimed at Dresher while a finger pointed at Graham.

"It's set for July 5th," Dresher responded confidently.

"Are you still representing him?" Munroe asked; it sounded more like a threat.

Dresher smiled. "All under control, Jake."

"Uh huh. And how is that?"

"We had a meeting this week at my office and new counsel had been appointed to Roy's case."

"Who?"

"Glenn Ibermann."

The burly Munroe looked to Morelatto. "Is he with us?"

"No," Morelatto said.

"Good," Munroe said with a sneer at the lawyer and politician. "I like the idea of a lawyer knowing nothing."

Dresher ignored the dig. "I'm sure this whole affair will blow over without a hitch."

"It better," Munroe said, eyes locked on the Premier. "It better."

"Ah," Morelatto said. "I'm sure Roy will be fine."

Dresher asked for another drink; a scotch this time. "So, what about Larry Hicks coming back to life. How we going to take care of this?"

Munroe leaned forward. His directness was intimidating. "You don't worry yourself about that. We're already taking care of it."

Dresher glanced at Graham. The Premier knew, as did everyone else, just how vulnerable Coleman felt now. They didn't need the lawyer either. Their mole was obviously doing a better job. Or Dresher, which would be highly probable, had been double-crossed.

"So what do Roy and I do now? Hicks is a problem for us too you know." Dresher gulped his scotch.

"You do nothing, Coleman," Morelatto said. "All we need from you is to get Graham's trial under control." Morelatto stood. The meeting was over. "Jake will escort you back to Vancouver. We have to be careful right now, gentlemen."

Dresher was speechless. Graham mute.

Twenty minutes later, Morelatto and Garva watched the helicopter fly across the Strait for the distant lights of Vancouver.

"Have they gone?" a sexy voice asked from the cabin door.

"Ah, Sasha, my dear. Yes, yes. He is gone."

Dresher's very expensive secretary joined the nefarious men on the aft deck.

"Alec, a drink for the lovely lady."

"Sure, boss," Garva obeyed and stepped behind the bar.

"You'll have to excuse Alec, my dear. He is not one to appreciate such beauty. But I, on the other hand, I do. You are very beautiful." Morelatto touched her cheek and Sasha in turn smiled seductively. It was what she did.

Unfortunately for her she did not see Garva advance behind her with black leather gloves on and a switchblade in his right hand. Before she comprehended why her head had been tugged violently up, her throat was slit in one quick stroke. Alec pushed her overboard before she started gagging on her blood. They watched the beautiful woman drown and eventually evaporate from view into the cold, murky depths.

Garva tossed the blade and gloves over the side.

Morelatto sipped his drink. "Find Larry Hicks. I want him and his son dead, Alec." He drank the last drop and headed for his stateroom. "Don't mess it up this time."

Alec Garva nodded the way an old and loyal soldier would. "Yes, Mario."

CHAPTER 56

Down on Granville Street

Michael climbed out of bed and, with sleepy eyes and a veil of five o'clock shadow, pulled Lance's laptop and an old flip phone from his overnight bag, connected to the net via the cell phone and hooked the laptop in. It was the primitive way to do it, yet so archaic Lance was sure Michael could log in undetected.

Michael navigated his way into the Free Press's secured email server. It was slow as hell but eventually he opened one unread email from Lance. Apparently the RCMP had a nationwide hunt going on for Larry Hicks and his birth son. Lund wasn't too excited having Forbes working with the Free Press on the story, but made nice anyway. Lance hoped everything was okay in Vancouver.

Larry knocked and stepped into the room. "We should go."

Minutes later Michael and Larry stood in the foyer waiting for a cab. It was drizzling. A hooker and her paying customer staggered between them. Larry and Michael watched them push through the front doors.

Only on Granville Street

"Can't we just pay cash for a rental?" Michael didn't like waiting.

Larry watched the street beyond the door with the trained eye of a former spymaster. "Even if you use cash, rental companies have to draw up contracts. Webber would be watching for that."

Michael sighed. "So, I guess we take a cab all the way to White Rock then?"

"We take a cab," Larry replied then pushed through the front entrance.

~

Alec Garva couldn't remember the last time he found himself lurking along Granville Street. His urge to seek out young lovers from the seedy world of the sex traders had all but died since his diagnosis two years ago. Now Garva existed day by day, waiting for the HIV virus infecting his body to explode into full-blown AIDS. Life wasn't fair for the seasoned killer.

He stood under a black umbrella and waited for the hooker. As she approached him from across the street, darting between the traffic and beckoning horns, he found himself wondering what it was about fishnet stockings and high heels that was so appealing. This one in particular was especially trashy, just another bimbo spreading her wares. And maybe a deadly virus, he seethed. Alec Garva never much cared for women anyway, least of all a desperate junkie willing to sell whatever was needed. In this case it was simply information on the old man and the reporter. She overheard they were heading to White Rock – taking a cab apparently. Her john was across the street, impatiently waiting with a paper-bagged bottle and her company.

Garva gave her a fifty, told her to keep her mouth shut, then sent her off. He slipped out of the alley between a confectionery store and a Blues club. Before he climbed into his Lincoln Town car he glanced up at the Seacorp Building hovering in the distance - the tallest skyscraper in Vancouver looming over Coal Harbor. What the hooker told him would go no further than his ears. He was not following Larry Hicks for the boss. Alec Garva had one play left to bring down Morelatto and his empire before the end. But he needed Larry Hicks to do it.

CHAPTER 57

The Missing Piece

White Rock, BC

    Rita Halbern was not the slim, vivacious beauty she had been in '81. The past year had not been gentle on her once fine features, and she fretted over her unsightly wrinkles and matted grey hair in the mirror. An old friend of her brother's had called earlier and was stopping by; someone she had never expected to see again. Regardless, she couldn't deny some company would be a nice change. Her mornings were, as most widowed seniors complain, boring and mundane since her husband Phillip past on. His death, a year ago now, had firmly planted a void in her life. Phillip had been sick for a long time, emaciated from emphysema and completely dependent on Rita's unwavering care. The last year consisted of prednisone and Ventolin, hooking up oxygen, and lifting a dying husband five or six times a day for the short journey between the living room and the bedroom. Watching her once virile man wither to a skeleton was torturous. And then it all took a fatal turn. Two weeks before Phillip's death their physician diagnosed him with cancer of the liver. He went into the hospital that afternoon and spent his final ten days waiting for death to claim him. Morphine made the passing painless, but it also robbed Rita of her final good-bye. She kissed his forehead, as she had every night, then left for the last time.
    The funeral was as pleasant an affair as one could expect, but considering the circumstances all who attended knew Phillip was in a better place. Old friends who still lived in Nanaimo, BC - Phillips hometown and final resting place on Vancouver Island - showed up to pay their respects. Phillip's closest cousin, Frank Lehman, a retired lawyer whose daughter now maintained his hometown practice, told story upon story of those rowdy days of their youth together. Everyone laughed, and maybe Phillip did too,

Frank suggested. They all knew Phillip Halbern had lived a good life.

The Lehman's had managed to talk Rita into spending the night. Since the funeral had been their first visit in as many years as any of them could remember, Rita opted for the comfort of family rather than her secluded trailer in White Rock. Frank and his lovely wife, Gloria, sat with her on the front porch overlooking Departure Bay. They reminisced and drank tea. It wasn't too long before Frank's whiskey was spicing the evening up pretty nicely, all things considered. It was too soon to miss Phillip even though she felt she should. After all, she had been a good wife.

Sometime during the night Frank asked if she ever thought about the killings that Christmas Eve back in '81. The question came out of left field and seemed to catch Rita by surprise. There hasn't been a day since that she has not been haunted by what happened. She still had her brother's wedding picture hanging on the wall. Her niece and nephew's last school pictures have never been moved off the stereo. She cringed when remembering the multiple funeral; the kid's coffins were so small. Looking back she couldn't understand how she got through all that tragedy.

"Christmas was definitely not the same, that's for sure," she pronounced as Frank's wife, Gloria, refilled her tea.

Frank added the splash of whiskey and revealed a secret about the killings that he and Phillip had been keeping all these years. Rita was speechless – secret? Even Gloria was hearing about this for the first time.

Apparently a package had been delivered to Frank's law office hours before the killings by an RCMP agent named Murphy Henderson. It came with the stern warning to tell no one. The Mountie gave Frank a number for some guy named Sam Mitchell in San Diego that he was supposed to call if anything was to go wrong. It was all very cloak and dagger. Frank found out after the killings it was all setup by his cousin, Phillip, who was asked by Roger, his brother-in-law, to hide the package for safekeeping. Not even Phillip knew what was in the package or what Roger was involved in; they knew not to ask.

Rita was cannonballed. How could she have not known her brother had made such a pact with her husband? After the murders Frank was tempted to call the Mitchell fellow, but Phillip forbade him; pledging him to secrecy all these years. Frank admitted that the news of the killings scared him to death. But when there was barely any mention of the kids being murdered gangland style on Christmas Eve, he was truly terrified and tossed the package in a safety deposit box in the bank across the street from his office. And tried to forget about it.

They finished the whiskey bottle off that night.

And now a year later Rita Halbern stood at her kitchen window looking out over Semiahmoo Bay, nervously waiting for Larry Hicks to arrive on the doorstep of her double wide trailer in White Rock. The bay was calm this morning. The sky was clearing to a warm blue. Lots of sun poured into the kitchen. She curbed her anxiousness with little tasks; vacuumed, dusted, watered the spider plant suspended in a homemade hanger in the window. An hour later the knock finally came and she took a deep breath before opening the door.

"Hello, Rita."

~

If there was one distinct feature that froze Larry Hicks's image in her mind over the years, it was the eyes. The smile was still as warm as she remembered, and Larry had the sincerest voice; commanding yet friendly, but the blue eyes caught one's attention right off.

Rita eased the screen door open. "It's nice to see you again, Larry." She wished she had taken time out of her mundane morning to apply some make-up. Larry and another man she didn't know, stepped inside.

Larry took her hand in both of his. "You're looking great. How's everything?"

"Fine, fine," she lied, smiling at Michael, the stranger in her house. "And who is this?"

Larry was about to put his hand on Michael's shoulder, but averted at the last moment. It was still awkward. "This is Michael Spencer, Rita. He's...ah...helping me with the investigation. Michael is a reporter from Winnipeg."

"A reporter?" The last thing Rita Halbern wanted was her name in the paper. Killers read papers.

What if they found me?

Larry could see the fear surge. "I'm sorry, Rita. I should have introduced him as my son. I didn't mean to alarm you."

Michael fixed on Larry with wide surprise. Son!

"Your son," she said, utterly taken aback, glancing between them a couple of times before she figured out this was the child Larry Hicks and his wife had so eagerly anticipated all those years ago.

"How is your mother?" she asked Michael.

Michael eyed Larry. "I'm adopted, Mrs. Halbern."

Rita saw the pain in Larry the instant adopted was uttered. She knew exactly what it all meant. "I'm so sorry."

"Not your apology to make, Rita," Larry said. "May we sit down and talk?"

Later, fitted around her kitchen table, Michael could smell the coffee brewing while Rita talked about Phillip's cancer, the funeral, the tea and whiskey binge with Frank and Gloria last year, and then the killings. But the coffee aroma reminded Michael of home and he couldn't help think of Jas and Katie on a beach somewhere in the Bahamas, living with a fear they've never known before. He was feeling responsible. As Rita went on about the murders, he glanced at the pictures of the MacMillan children on her stereo; murdered children gunned down on Christmas Eve; little coffins lowering into graves. What kind of people could do such crimes? The guilt he inflicted on himself over Milt's murder twisted like a dagger while he watched this sweet lady sob. She snapped a few Kleenex from the box on the fridge beside a tin of Slim Fast, and remained there till she calmed herself down.

"Rita," Larry said, knowing he had to be sensitive now. "I need to ask you something."

She eased herself back into her chair. Another sniffle. Another blow. She finally said, "Frank lives just outside of Nanaimo."

~

The phone call was quick and terse and judging from Frank Lehman's surprise, one he never figured on receiving. He reluctantly agreed to meet them at the ferry terminal and take them to his old law practice downtown. It was obvious Frank Lehman didn't want Larry Hicks and whatever criminal element might be stalking him to invade his front porch.

Rita said they'd be on the three o'clock ferry then hung up, offering to refill coffee cups.

"No thank you," Michael said graciously.

Larry pushed his away. "We should get going. I'm sure you understand."

"Of course," Rita replied. "I'll get my keys."

Keys? Both Larry and Michael looked at each other.

"I'm going with you," Rita said as she reached into the broom closet and snatched her car keys from a hook on the inside of the door. "How else are you going to meet Frank?"

"A picture would be fine," Michael said.

"If I had one, Michael, you'd be welcome to one, but..."

Larry shrugged. "Maybe a ride would be a good idea. It would take forever to get to Horseshoe Bay," he said to Michael.

"Of course it would," Rita said.

CHAPTER 58

The Spies & Assassins Cometh

White Rock, BC

Chester was on his cell, chewing gum and watching the RCMP spy on Spencer and Hicks exiting the trailer accompanied by the older woman. Chester's sedan was parked about five trailers back of the Mounties who were in turn about four units from the woman's home. He watched the targets climb into a yellow Ford Pinto. A real time scan of the license plate with his iPhone when he first arrived told him the car was registered to a Rita Halbern.

"What do you want me to do?" he asked the caller on speaker as the Pinto backed out of the driveway.

"I don't want the horsemen on their tail. We can't risk anything right now." Braden MacDuff said. "Stop them."

"Yes, sir."

Horseshoe Bay, West Vancouver

The Javelin strolled along the government pier, passing the outriggers shop on the end of the wharf. He looked out over the scenic Horseshoe Bay with its bordering hills and mountains of jagged, snow-capped peaks beyond the north ridge. Across the bay two BC Government ferries were loading cars and passengers at the docking terminal, tires clanking over the ferry's steel ramp echoed over the water. Seawell's Marina to the left of the pier was full of boats and yachts tethered in countless slips, all protected by a massive cement breakwater.

The Javelin descended the gangplanks halfway along the quay to the executive boat docks, checking slip numbers as he walked. After passing three impressive crafts, he found her. He noted the slip number - 4B - then quickly dashed back up the gangplank, eyeing each yacht much like any other boating enthusiast. He quickened his pace once on the pier, heading for his rental car parked just off the dock. A rental he secured with his Coastal Holding employee card. He glanced out over the marina one more time; committing the layout to memory. He would waste away the rest of the afternoon in his hotel, maybe squeeze in a little surveillance on his second target, or hire some female companionship to kill a few hours before returning to Horseshoe Bay. He knew the Graham's yacht, Rachel's Dream, would be departing her slip shortly after six.

CSIS headquarters

MacDuff was on the phone when Sheila escorted Chris Kominski through the door. For someone who looked so cool and arrogant all the time, the stress was visible on this visit.

"What can I do for you, Kominski?" MacDuff asked as if he had no time for political hand holding this morning.

Kominski said, "I just got a call from our Assistant Commissioner in Vancouver. Seems he had a team staked out at the residence of a Rita Halbern in White Rock. Do you know who she is?"

"Yes," MacDuff replied as if all members of the intelligence community should know the name.

"They found Hicks and Spencer with her. Did you know that?"

"No. I didn't," he lied.

"Have you any idea where they are now?"

"None. Do you?"

"I did. These officers followed them to some house in Kitsilano. A house right on the corner of 1st street and Yew." Kominski took a brave step into the desk. "That's the house right? Where Roger McMillan was murdered, right?"

"Is it?"

"Yeah, I've done my homework here, Braden." First name basis was a dangerous presumption for someone the likes of Kominski, but he was too scattered to notice the eye slits tightening. "I've read the Scarlet files."

"Really? I thought your secretary had given them all to me. You have photocopies of top secret files?"

"Yeah, yeah, whatever." Kominski snapped. "Where the hell are they?"

MacDuff leaned back, gave the brownnoser his undivided attention. "What do you mean, Kominski? We were waiting for the Mounties to do that for us."

"Cut the shit!"

MacDuff lifted out of his unremarkable chair. Insolence was something he couldn't stomach from Kominski. "You better get your slick ass out of my office."

Kominski dug in. "You're fucking with me. Someone took out that surveillance team. Shot the tires out for Christ's sake. I say it was one of yours."

"Say what you like."

"Where are they?"

MacDuff smirked; he was going to enjoy this. "The last time you got information from us an old lady and her dog died and I had to bury a damn good agent. Maybe there's something you should be telling me."

Kominski was stunned. "Jesus," he finally said. "You think it's me. Don't you?"

MacDuff didn't answer. His scowl said everything.

Kominski shook off the accusation and turned for the door, but before leaving he looked back at the face of unblinking stone and said, "You're wrong, Braden. I know what you think of me. I feel it every time I come in this office. But you're wrong." And with that a dejected Chris Kominski left the unremarkable man in his unremarkable office.

Sheila stuck her head in the door after Kominski disappeared into the elevator. "You alright, Braden?"

"Yeah," he replied, not entirely comfortable with what just happened. "I'm fine."

Sheila dismissed herself and Braden MacDuff found himself standing by his window, wrestling the unsettling feeling that he may very well be exactly what Kominski purported him to be; wrong.

CHAPTER 59

The Present Collides with the Past

Nanaimo, BC

Like clockwork the ferry coasted into Departure Bay and nestled into the terminal dock at three o'clock. The ship shuddered from the dock moorings hugging it into place. Cars and trucks and passengers filed off as casually as crossing a bridge, and it was easy to tell the regular commuters from the awe-struck expressions of the novice tourist.

Larry sat on the upper deck, torturing himself with thoughts of Murphy Henderson riding the exact same ferry that cold Christmas Eve in '81. He worried about Jasmine and Katie and hoped they had made it safely to Evelyn and their beachfront villa on Eleuthera Island. He couldn't risk calling yet. And as long as Evelyn kept them offline, they should be well hidden from the evil hunting them from the shadows.

Michael came up the stairs to the upper deck with Rita following. Larry watched Michael help her – her knees weren't what they were. That gesture alone said everything to Larry about what kind of man Olie Spencer's son was; the man his son had become.

"Larry, are you ready to go?" Michael asked.

Larry got up, hoping that they would find what he needed in Nanaimo, because he had no plan B to save anybody.

Lipton, Jackson, and Mackenzie

"Did you want to interview secretaries next week, Cole?" Ibermann asked. The Howard Miller clock struck chimes. It was 3:00 pm. Dresher just wanted to go home, pack and get the hell out of the country before Morelatto targeted him. Graham's paranoia was infectious and Dresher was about as paranoid as one could get now.

He and Ibermann were waiting for a call from the Premier's office. Sasha's murder and her association to the law office representing the Premier only served to stoke the media. And, needless to say, it didn't require a lot of fanning to ignite the scandal embers. Subsequent headlines would dominate the front page on a daily basis with July 5th drawing closer. One could only guess the proverbial kettle could boil over before then. Graham was teetering already. They were going to suggest a week away for the Premier. Load the family in his yacht and get away from it all for a while. But the day was rapidly sinking to dusk and Graham had yet to call. Dresher figured he probably skipped out of sight once he heard the news of Sasha's death. It was easy to ascertain she was probably on the White Knight, somewhere below decks, while they were enduring Jake Munroe's threats. But one thing was blatantly obvious. Sasha sold him out - the bitch!

"Coleman?" Ibermann said again.

"No," Dresher replied. "Let's get another secretary in here. I need somebody now."

"I could take your caseload if you want. You and Anita can get away yourselves for a few days."

Before Dresher could respond the phone rang. He answered. It was Graham. The conversation was short then Dresher hung up. He was looking more scared than stressed. Ibermann had a pretty good idea as to why. His sister had phoned the other night when her husband jumped in the Porsche after receiving a phone call. The name Morelatto came up. Ibermann didn't want to hear anymore, considering of course, the conflict that presented to their prominent client at the moment.

"Well, that was Roy," Dresher said. "He'll be in to see us first thing in the morning. He's taking his family out for a cruise this evening."

"The press will be all over Horseshoe Bay."

"I know."

Ibermann rose, buttoned up his expensive suit. "I hope he keeps his mouth shut."

Dresher rubbed his throbbing temples and said, "Me too, Glenn. Me too."

CHAPTER 60

The Path to Redemption Begins

Nanaimo, BC

There wasn't much one could say about Frank Lehman, Michael concluded. He was your typical small town, retired lawyer with too much time on his hands. They were at the old office - as Lehman referred to it - right in the heart of downtown Nanaimo. Lehman's daughter who reminded Michael a little of Claudette, took over the firm when Lehman decided to retire. She was clearly put out having to take time from whatever case she was preparing to rummage through their quaint little law office for some illusive key her father had never talked about before. Michael steadied the library ladder that swerved around on a rail while Lehman's daughter teetered on the top rung, groping for file boxes on the top shelves; an impressive feat in black pumps and a skirt.

Larry and Frank were searching old case files in the back room. Frank had loosened up a little since turning white as ghost when Larry first stepped off the ferry. So now, two hours later and a few cups of coffee spiced with free poured whiskey, every other file held a story that needed telling. Larry was growing impatient and emerged on two separate occasions with a look that told Michael how frustrated he was.

Time is ticking dammit!

Michael opened the door to the back room, interrupting one of Frank's recollections. Larry was happy for the reprieve.

"I want to call them now," Michael said. He was beyond worried about Jas and Katie and was ready to climb the walls of Frank Lehman's quaint little law office.

Larry reluctantly conceded with a sigh. "Use a pay phone and use coins."

USS Intrepid

The moon was full over the calm and silky Caribbean some fifty miles southeast of Nassau, Bahamas. The frigate had laid anchor a mile off the pearl white beaches that lined the western shores of Eleuthera island two miles south of Governor's Harbor township.

A very uncomfortable Sam Cholan acknowledged the ensign who had just stuck his head through the galley door.

"You're wanted in the room, sir."

That's how they referred to the signal intelligence control chamber set up on the surveillance frigate commissioned solely for those top-secret missions of the Central Intelligence Agency. They simply called it *The Room*.

"Thank you, ensign."

Sam Cholan hated boats. If he could save face in front of the crew and get away with it, he would be wearing a life preserver in his sleep. It was definitely a phobia. Then there was the unsettling and sometimes embarrassing bouts of seasickness. It was simple. Cholan, former field operative then Station Chief in Tel Aviv back when it was a hell on earth, and then promoted to Assistant Deputy Director of Operations two years ago, was not cut out for life at sea. But he would endure any hardship to find the bastards responsible for Sam Mitchell being gunned down on the porch of his San Diego home; Mitchell was the reason Sam Cholan had a career at all.

He followed the ensign through the narrow corridors and down two decks. They stepped past the ready room; a briefing chamber where the navy SEAL team dispatched to Cholan's command was receiving background on Operation Scarlet. Drone surveillance photos of Mario Morelatto and the Javelin aboard a super yacht somewhere in the Juan De Fuca strait were tacked to one side of a cork board, alongside pics of Larry and Evelyn Hicks, Michael and Jasmine Spencer and their teenage daughter Katie. As Cholan passed, Director of Operations Edwin Newhart and the Seal commander were pinning a few more snapshots to the board; Jessica Ingham and Nolan Grant had arrived at the Hicks beachfront home late last night.

A few paces further down the corridor the ensign swung open the bulkhead door to The Room. A lone seaman snapped to attention the instant Cholan stepped inside. He looked young enough to still be dealing with pimples and puberty.

"At ease, Berger." Cholan said. "What's up?"

"You might be interested in this, sir," Seaman Berger suggested, punching his keyboard, tightening on the frequency he was currently invading.

"What do you have?" Cholan assumed a seat beside the SIGINT officer. This was child's play for someone of Berger's training.

"A call, sir, originating in Nanaimo, British Columbia. I believe its target one, sir."

"Play it back for me?"

"Yes, sir."

Cholan glanced at the impressive hardware all integrated into one overwhelming control panel. Above was a video screen revealing white thermal images walking around a room, or more accurately a kitchen. There was a swirling heat bloom contained within a small box; the oven. Thermal images of two women were kneeling down to the bloom. It was suppertime in the Hick's villa overlooking Bonefish bay.

"Who was on the phone with him?" Cholan asked.

"The woman, sir. Jasmine Spencer."

"Anyone else from the house?"

"Their daughter."

Berger hit a button. Minute hiss from the speaker above, a ringing phone, then a pick up. "Hello?" It was the teenager.

"Katie," a man's voice replied.

It was a noisy connection to put it lightly. Cholan pointed at the speaker. "Can you clean that up?" The seaman tweaked a few knobs and Cholan nodded approval.

"Dad!" the teenager boomed. She sounded worried. "Where are you?"

"I can't tell you that right now." He sounded covert. "How's Mom?"

"What do you think? She's pretty upset. We both are, Dad."

"Okay. Listen Kat, we can't talk too long."

"I'm not five, Dad. I know what's going on."

A pause. You could feel a tension between father and daughter just by her change of tone. Cholan and Berger glanced each other, the seaman shrugging.

"Put Mom on."

"Fine." The teenager sounded annoyed again. The phone was passed over.

"Michael?" The woman's voice was shaky.

"Hey, babe."

"Where are you?"

"I can't tell you...just in case. But we're okay."

Her tone was terse, anxious. "We've been worried, Michael."

"I know. I know. Please, don't worry. Did Jessica make it there alright?"

"Yeah, she's here. So is Nolan."

"I'll be there as soon as I can. Promise."

A man's voice spoke up in the background.

"Nolan wants to talk," the woman said. The phone was passed again. Masculine breathing closed in on the line.

"Michael, you making any progress there?" It was the Mountie they knew to be Nolan.

"I'm not sure yet. Look, we should be there in a couple of days, no more, okay."

"Don't worry. Everyone will be fine."

"Nolan, if anything happens to___."

"It won't, Mike. I promise. I won't let anything happen to them."

Another pause, a heavy sigh.

"Thanks, Nolan."

"Keep your head down, Mike."

Hiss filled the chamber. Berger turned off the feed. Cholan lifted off the metal chair. "Anything else?"

"Nothing, sir. Since they came back from the market it's been pretty quiet."

"Call me if there's anything alright, anything at all. If they leave the house I want to know about it."

"Copy that, sir."

Nanaimo

"I found it!" Frank Lehman's daughter said from the top of the ladder. Larry and Frank stepped out of the back room just in time to see her pull the key from the pages of an old Canadian Tax Law text.

"Goddammit, that's where I put it," Frank cursed his poor memory. "Well, hand it over, Corina."

Corina stepped down the ladder, placed the key in her father's hand.

That only took two hours! Michael and Larry both thought with a quick glance at each other.

"The bank is right across the street," Frank said, leading Larry and Michael out the door. Corina bid them good-bye and returned to the business of practicing law. She was glad to see them go.

Horseshoe Bay

Capilano Marine and Sport Sales, Ltd., the placard screwed to the side of a white panel van read. In smaller print underneath the heading was; *sales-service-rentals-repairs*. The Javelin, donning blue slacks and a company shirt climbed from behind the wheel after pulling up to the very spot he had vacated earlier in the afternoon. He whistled merrily while strolling around to the side cargo door. He swung it open, grabbed a Snap-On toolbox and a lunch container and set off down the government pier; just another working stiff on a sunny afternoon.

An incoming ferry sounded its horn as it lumbered into the bay. Seagulls glided through the air while pleasure boaters populated Seawell's marina, readying themselves for a leisurely cruise. The bay was a commotion of summer activity in the early evening. All that was about to change.

~

Parked to the east of the government pier, looking directly out over the bay was a BCTV Mobility News van. The cameraman and the anchorperson had spent the past hour staking out Premier Graham's yacht, *Rachel's Dream*.

"Why did he name it Rachel's Dream ya think?"

The reporter frowned at her cameraman while she checked her hair in the sun visor mirror. "That's his daughter's name. You didn't know that?"

"Should I?" he replied smartly. He wore a *BCTV Crew* tee shirt with khaki shorts and, of course, all season hiking boots. "I'm the tech, remember."

"He's our Premier, Nick."

Nick grinned at the sheer feebleness of that argument. "The guy's crooked, Tabs."

Tabs was short for Tabitha - Tabitha Reynolds to be exact, the very reporter who flew home directly from covering the federal/provincial conference in Winnipeg and sold her producer on the probability of the Prime Minister's involvement with Premier Graham's illegal purchase. The probing into the stock affiliations linking Graham and Petersen through Westfor, International was done. Now her producer just required confirmation and that had to come from the mouth of Premier Graham himself. Tabitha was after the anchor desk and this story was going to get it for her. She'd have to thank Michael Spencer for that the next time she heard from him.

Nick was looking through binoculars, adjusting the focus on slip 4B and the repairman approaching the yacht's stern.

"Find me a politician who isn't," Tabitha continued, touching up her lipstick.

"Hey, check this out."

"What?" The visor was quickly popped up and she peered through the sunset glared windshield. "Who is that?"

They watched the repairman glance up and down the finger dock then casually board Rachel's Dream. He set his Snap On toolbox down in the cockpit and appeared to be studying a work order.

"You better get this," Tabitha said.

"No kidding." Nick was already reaching for his camera rig unaware he was about to shoot the most crucial tape of his career.

Nanaimo

Rita had opted to wait in her yellow Pinto while Larry and Michael followed Lehman across the street to the bank. She had no desire to see what was in a safety deposit box responsible for so much death and tragedy. Lehman shared her trepidation and excused himself once the bank manager showed up at the customer service counter.

The manager introduced them to a safety deposit box supervisor who led them downstairs and produced the matching bank key. She plugged it into the box then left Michael and Larry alone in the chamber with the typical, "Take all the time you need, gentlemen."

Larry waited till the supervisor was up the stairs then opened the box. Inside was a series of yellow manila envelopes. One had reel-to-reel tapes, bound and dated with felt marker. Another had scads of photos of ships and tankers coming and going. Several more were choked with documents, reports and manifests with black striped margins.

Michael had no idea if what Larry was hoping to find was actually among the contents and Larry wasn't explaining. That suited Michael just fine. He was anxious as hell and wanted to get to the airport so he could be with Jas and Katie in the Bahamas as soon as possible. That's all that mattered anymore.

Larry grabbed the garbage bag out of the wastebasket, rifled the envelopes into it then they were back in the Pinto and heading for the ferry docks.

CHAPTER 61

The Telling of the Lie

"Aren't they wonderful," Rita sang to everybody on the upper deck. She was overjoyed seeing a pod of killer whales frolicking off the ferry's port bow. Tourists and, oddly enough, regular commuters gathered to observe. Fingers pointed, cameras clicked, and excited children screeched with amazement. Rita was glad to be out of her little trailer, forgetting about the past for a while.

Michael and Larry went below soon after they departed Nanaimo. She understood. She saw the curiosity in Michael's face, read the time alone they needed to get to know each other. So Rita enjoyed the glee of children watching black flukes slapping calm swells.

~

Larry and Michael watched the whales from their windowed booth on the main deck, the dorsal fins jutting above the water like majestic black masts in a regatta, the spray from their blowholes misting rainbows against the summer dusk.

It reminded Michael of the west coast vacation they had taken when Katie was seven, her innocent face pasted to the very same window the entire trip across to the island. That was before Danny Gregory and iPhones and attitude; back when she was still his little girl. He was missing her and doing his best to curb the panic he was feeling. But stating that out loud would just be idle conversation when he really wanted Larry to tell him what he had been dying to know since Jessica Ingham showed him that grimy adoption case file.

Larry sensed it. "I know you want to ask me, 'why'?"

"You heard them die, didn't you?" Michael asked. "You called Roger MacMillan that night, and heard it. That's why you gave me up." Michael could only sigh when Larry nodded and returned to the whales, the pain of it all close to the surface. "I just wanted to find my birthmother. Just give her…" Just saying it was hard for Michael. "…a note. My mom wanted her to know that she gave her a gift, that you both did, Larry. And me, I just wanted to be able to tell her – tell Evelyn – she made the right choice for me. But I didn't expect all this."

Larry drew a deep breath. "I know. And I'm sorry. But you are going to have your moment to tell her. I promise. She needs to hear that from you." He looked directly at Michael, a hatred seething behind those blue eyes. "And those bastards are going to pay."

Michael leaned in, lowered his voice when he asked, "What was Operation Scarlett, Larry? Off the record?"

A little girl a few booths down screamed with delight at the whales. Larry glanced around the deck. It was crowded with families and tourists; too crowded. He slid out of the booth. "I think we need a bit more privacy."

~

Passengers were not permitted on the car-decks while the ferry was steaming across the channel, but Larry and Michael ignored that rule. The Pinto was parked one row back from daylight flooding through the raised ferry gate. The stench of oil, gas and salt was overpowering. Larry opened the door, reached inside and grabbed the garbage bag from the back seat. He plopped it on the Pinto's hood, pulled out papers and manifests with Northern Scarlet letterhead, RCMP memos with black striped margins, and an assortment of pictures.

"It started out as a shadow op," Larry began. "We were supposed to collect the surveillance on Morelatto's shipping activity out of Vancouver while the CIA did their number on him."

"Their number on him?"

Larry fingered through the photos, found what he was looking for and handed it to Michael. It was a black and white snap shot of three men on what appeared to be a pier. Michael recognized the younger Mario Morelatto but the other two were strangers.

"Who are these two guys?" Michael asked.

"Alec Garva. He was and still is Morelatto's top commander. He's also the one who helped frame Lavelle."

"As in Francis Lavelle?"

"Yeah."

"How?"

"Homosexuality."

"Lavelle was gay?"

"So is Garva. They were lovers."

Michael's jaw dropped. "Holly shit. I had no idea Morelatto was that powerful. I mean, corrupt, yes, but this…"

"You have no idea," Larry said, indicating they should be inside the car when they heard voices coming from the stairwell.

~

They were sitting in the Pinto now, the windows rolled up, and Larry well into the briefing. "The stage was already set for Morelatto to take over the drug trade. He had the ships and could get the product through the Panama Canal right into Vancouver, giving him a direct tie with the Medellin and Cali cartels. Hence, the CIA's interest in him because drug money funded the guerrillas they were combating in Nicaragua."

"The Iran-Contra scandal," Michael said, shaking his head. "Incredible."

"Yeah. By the time the Contras hit the news the CIA wanted our help to put Morelatto out of business. The last thing they needed in the Gulf region was another drug kingpin. Of course we find out later it was because he was cutting into their drug money. Anyway we were brought in, ordered to go in dark, which meant we had no backup, no way to get out if it went bad." He eyed Michael. "It was a suicide mission from the start."

Michael had one of the reel tapes dated Nov '81 in his hand. "So you guys were taping all this?"

"We were tapping everything, even our own conversations, making sure we were covering our own tails, in case of…political tap dancing." The thought of it still left Larry feeling betrayed.

"So he was after these tapes?"

"Yes."

"What was so bad he'd have children killed over?"

Larry took a deep breath. "We stumbled onto them planning to assassinate the Prime Minister."

"Wow," Michael said, his mouth dropping open. "And that's on these tapes?"

"Yeah," was all Larry could say - the whole affair still seemed unbelievable.

"So that's why he had Francis Lavelle killed, your partners killed, the doctor killed, and everyone killed." Michael pinched the bridge of his nose and said, "And you and Evelyn were safely hidden from all this until I…Jesus!"

"Partly," Larry said. "Sam Mitchell, the CIA liaison for the operation, was murdered a couple weeks ago in San Diego. He's the one who helped hide us, helped to protect you. When they killed Sam, I knew they'd find you and then they'd be coming for us all over again." Larry glanced past the loading ramp at the BC Coast in the distance, remembering a friend. "You know the funny thing is he had been asking me for years to come out of hiding. But I couldn't. I just couldn't risk it," Larry said with a long, regretful sigh. "Maybe if I had he would still be alive." Larry wiped his eye. "They'd all still be alive."

"So he knew where you were all this time?" Michael said, commingled confusion and anger stirring. "Why didn't you do it, Larry?"

Larry sighed heavily. "I still had someone to protect."

"Evelyn?"

"I could protect Evelyn. She was with me."

Michael's frustration swelled. "Who then? A chance to clear your name and everything, they just needed what you could prove." Michael held up the tape. "They just needed all of this. I don't understand. The CIA offered you help and you didn't take it - why?"

Larry eyed him hard. "Because Lavelle couldn't have known where the safe house was back in '81, any more than he could have known that Sam Mitchell lived in San Diego. He wasn't the mole. Whoever betrayed us was still in the force, and who knows how high up the chain of command now. If I gave Sam what he needed to stop Morelatto that meant exposing myself and then I couldn't protect the one thing I vowed to Evelyn I would always protect."

"My friend was killed, Larry!" Michael snapped.

"I know that," Larry shot back.

"There's no one left to protect!"

"Yes there is."

"Who?!"

Larry leaned back, his shoulders sagging. He stared at Michael like a father to a son. "You, Michael" he said. "I couldn't risk them ever finding you." Larry's eyes were wet from the pain of it twisting out of him. "This is not about clearing my name. This is about finding that sonofabitch that keeps selling us out so I can get our lives back," Larry's voice choked. "I don't want you suffering for this. I know I gave you up, I know what I did. But you're still my son, and I couldn't do it. I just couldn't."

Michael could only sit there, helpless and overwhelmed, as Larry fell against the wheel and wept.

~

They were topside again, perched against the railing, looking out over the coastal rim of Bowen Island bordering the mouth to Queen Charlotte Channel. Horseshoe Bay was a little under half an hour away.

Michael was rubbing his hands to keep grief at bay. "He was like a brother to me." He slammed the railing. "Milt died because of me! Because of a fucking letter."

"No," Larry said, clasping Michael's forearm. "It was not your fault. Don't lose sight of that, Michael. It was them. They killed him to force me out in the open. They played us."

Michael spotted Rita further up the railing, the broken woman tossing bread at seagulls with a group of commuters. He cleared his throat and eyed Larry hard. "Does that help you, Larry? Does that help you deal with the murders?"

Larry couldn't speak. He felt the loathing dead on.

"How about Roger and Murphy?"

Blue eyes glared at blue eyes. But Larry stood firm. His son needed this.

Michael leaned close. "The name Ryan J. Roberts mean anything to you, Larry?" Larry locked on Michael, fear of what he was going to hear flushing his face. "He had a daughter born just a couple of hours before me. You remember him, don't you? They found him around the same time Dr. Friesen's Corvette became part of a bridge. His head shot off. Imagine that, a suicide with a long barrel shotgun."

Larry remembered the realtor in the plaid pants and wing tip shoes who kissed the nurse and chanted *it's a girl* on New Year's Eve, 1981.

He had been dead all this time!

Larry still had the *It's a Boy* cigars Ryan Roberts jammed into his hand in the maternity waiting room that night. They were tucked into the bookshelf beside the purple beanbag chair in the villa back on Bonefish Bay.

"My god," Larry muttered. "They were closer than I thought."

Vancouver

Alec Garva's town car was parked with the front wheels turned into the curb. Point Grey Road was a few blocks ahead, at the bottom of the hill. It looked like a bandstand was being set up on Kitsilano beach for the outdoor Canada Day concert. Garva remembered the last time he was at this particular location in the dead of winter, sitting in the back seat of a Lincoln. He glanced at the quaint little house on the corner, at the very window where the children's shadows had danced around the Christmas tree nearly forty years ago.

Then his cell vibrated.

"Yes?"

"Alec." It was Morelatto.

"Yeah, boss?"

"Are you at Vancouver Center yet?"

"Yeah. I'm here. Dresher hasn't moved." Two young teenagers jumped off the steps of the house on 1st and Yew in bathing suits, one clutching a Frisbee. They strolled off down the hill, arm in arm for the beach.

"Good. Jake is taking care of things in Winnipeg. I need this to be over once and for all."

"Right, boss." He hung up.

Alec Garva slipped his cell into his pocket. It would be the last time he would ever talk to Mario Morelatto. He popped open the glove compartment, slipped out a reel to reel tape – similar to the ones Larry and Michael had found in the safety deposit box.

"It will be over soon," he pledged to himself.

Part III
the end game...

CHAPTER 62

The Time for more Death has Come

Horseshoe Bay

"Think he's gonna show?" Tabitha Reynolds asked. They were still camped out in their BCTV News van overlooking Horseshoe Bay. She put her feet on the dash and watched Rachel's Dream lull in slip 4B. It was too boring for words. The tranquil orange sun to the west was practically slipping behind the coastal mountains now. Soon it would be dark. *So much for making the six o'clock news flash*, she grumbled to herself. Nick was reading to pass the time.

"Anything else to read?" she asked, searching through his camera bag between the two captain's chairs.

"Yeah," he said.

She pulled out another magazine. It was a *Penthouse Forum*.

Nick shot her a sly grin. "Yeah, that's the one."

And that's when they saw Premier Graham's SUV pull up at the gangplanks leading down to the docks, a scrum of eager reporters dashing for him.

Tabitha and Nick were out of the truck like a shot.

~

Roy Graham was not the only victim, if one could call him that, since the Coastal Holding story broke. Needless to say the controversy surrounding his purchase of a federally run salmon hatchery station a few miles south of Stillwater, BC had mushroomed into more than he bargained. No matter what his attempts to quell the scandal and shield his wife and daughter, the headlines continued to hammer them.

On the surface it looked like Graham stood to reap nothing but money from the deal. The station was to be converted into a major lumber shipping port, a distribution center if you will for Westfor International with only SeaCorp ships laying way for ports the world over. Since Coastal Holding received a proportional fee for brokering the deal, it was blatant conflict of interest and a scandal was born. But one thing was all too clear to the press and to the voters; at the hub of Coastal Holdings and Westfor International and SeaCorp was none other than the Premier himself. He had stock in all three subsidiaries. He was guilty as hell.

But now the scandal had taken a morbid turn.

A passing ferry discovered Sasha Riley floating in the Juan de Fuca strait. To make matters even worse, she was murdered, her throat slit right to the spine. It was ghastly. The Premier's office was inundated with calls since the identity of the woman was linked to his lawyer, Coleman Dresher.

Just one more knot in the noose, Graham thought nervously when reading the paper over morning croissants. His wife, Meredith, had asked if he knew the young woman. Roy didn't know what to say. What could he say? She played both ends to her own death and screwed Dresher too - and rightly so. He was going to go down with Graham just as hard because Mario Morelatto needed his Prime Minister to suffer the harsh lesson of loyalty and obedience.

Graham was so tempted to just spill his guts right there on the pier when Tabitha Reynolds from BCTV jammed her microphone under his nose. He was holding Meredith's hand who in turn clutched her teenage daughter, Rachel, as they dug their way through the scrum for the safety of their yacht, Rachel's Dream.

"Excuse me," the Premier yelled over reporters clamoring around them. It was no use. The scrum tightened on the Premier at the gangplank, choking his escape, his grip on his wife and daughter lost. Young Rachel looked scared and overwhelmed. Regardless of what he did, or whom he hurt, he was her Dad and she cried out for him as the scrum pushed Meredith and daughter further from the Premier.

Graham squinted against the harsh glare of lights and television cameras pointed at him. It was apparent there would be no dodging the media this time. He sighed and singled out Tabitha who had masterly maneuvered herself directly in front of him. As Tabitha rallied her question about Miss Riley at him, Graham found himself hoping Larry Hicks was close at hand. Ironically, Graham had no idea Hicks was actually aboard the Maid of Vancouver ferry entering Horseshoe Bay with air-horns blaring.

Premier Roy Graham had finally come to the moment where he reconciled himself to his fate. "What was the question, Tabitha?"

~

"What's going on over there?" Rita and her new friend wondered.
"I'm not sure," Michael said.
Under them the engines were humming in reverse, the ferry slowing to dock at the Horseshoe Bay terminal. Larry turned to the tourist beside him. He pointed at the man's binoculars; used earlier for whale watching.
"May I?" Larry asked.
"Sure." The man obliged, pointing across the small bay at the government pier. "I think that's Premier Graham."
Michael looked quickly to Larry. "Is it?"
Larry could see Graham in the middle of the reporter's scrum. He veered the binoculars to Graham's yacht. The Premier's wife and teenage daughter were clutching each other. The girl was crying.
Larry handed the binoculars back. "Thanks."
"No problem." The man said and moved on.
"It's Graham alright," Larry said to Michael. The coincidence was not lost on either of them.

~

Chester was a bit further down the railing on the ferry, watching the man who had lent Larry Hicks his binoculars stroll by with the rush of passengers heading for their autos. His attention shifted to the press mercilessly hounding Premier Graham and his family when just short of the government pier a silver Porsche 924 came to an abrupt stop. He wished he had not left his own binoculars sitting on the front seat of his car, parked below, about two rows behind the rusty Pinto.

~

The Javelin couldn't believe his luck when the silver Porsche 924 pulled up in front of him with tires screeching. The lawyer climbed out. Coleman Dresher seemed panicked, peering down at the gaggle of reporters gathered by slip 4B.
Perfect!
The Javelin's second target had just presented himself.

~

"That's Dresher," Larry said.
They watched Coleman Dresher jog along the pier, racing for the

gangplank.

"Something is going on," Larry said to Michael.

"C'mon, boys," Rita beckoned. She was nervous, the past haunting her again. "We should get to the car."

"In a minute," Larry said. "In a minute."

~

Roy Graham finally dug through the reporters to join his wife and daughter already aboard their yacht, camera lights and boom-arm microphones invading. Meredith Graham held her husband's hand. But a question halted him.

Almost made it!

"If resignation was demanded," Tabitha asked, "would your seat on the boards be terminated, Premier Graham?"

It was the question that provided his opportunity. It was now or never. Spill your guts or take it with you to your grave. His family pleaded with him to come aboard and escape the madness. But, instead, Roy Graham turned into the glare of camera lights.

"Excuse me," a voice beckoned from behind the scrum. "Perhaps I could answer that question for my client." The lights and cameras swung around to Coleman Dresher. He smiled with the confidence of a trial lawyer as the reporters pushed in around him. Through the microphone booms Graham and Dresher's gaze met. The Premier knew exactly what the lawyer had just done. There would be no confession today, no bleeding of sins. Dresher had just seen to that.

Graham turned away from the feeding reporters to look upon the bay, the ferry, the mountains; his escape. He climbed aboard, up to the helm, and turned the key. The twin MerCruiser sterndrives came to life, exhaust gurgling while young Rachel tossed the lines off.

Graham eased the yacht out of the slip, glancing back at Dresher deflecting fatal questions on the dock. He was their victim now. He defended Morelatto till the end but he would eventually be sold out too. No doubt Morelatto leaked Dresher's affair with the departed Sasha Riley to boil the lawyer in his own hot water. Anita would clean him out, his brother-in-law, Glenn Ibermann, would banish Dresher from his posh office at Vancouver Center. There was no fighting it. The best you could hope for would be to escape with your life. And Roy Graham almost made it.

~

Michael watched Premier Roy Graham's cabin cruiser idle out of the marina, fleeing the media. "There's going to be no justice, is there?" he said to Larry, who was also watching the yacht coast by the cement brake water, a soft thrush cresting off her chines as she propelled towards the small rock atoll with an unmanned lighthouse situated on the farthest most reach into the bay.

"Define justice," Larry said. The diesel hum beneath their feet died. The whining of hydraulic ramps nesting in place permeated the seagull's begging for tossed treats. Soon they'd hear motors starting below and the clanking of cars crossing onto dry land and accelerating up the terminal embankment.

~

Rachel's Dream cleared the lighthouse, listed starboard for the inlet. Before throttling up Graham checked to make sure Rachel was seated down in the cockpit below, her life preserver on.

Meredith wrapped her arm around her husband, kissed him and told him it would all blow over soon enough. He didn't need to be in public office anymore. It was time now for family. Meredith knew little of her husband's dark closets. She would never know.

Roy Graham clasped the throttle firmly in hand then gunned the Mer-Cruisers wide open. The tachometer needle wound past four thousand RPM and it was over in a flash of light.

They felt nothing.

~

"Jesus Christ!" Michael yelled as the explosion rocked them with a whump of scorched air burning their faces. Commuters hugging the railing were knocked over from the shock wave. Graham's yacht instantaneously reduced to a fireball floating on the water, hull splinters and shrapnel raining down.

Michael felt Larry's hand under his armpit and with surprising agility for his age, hoisted him to his feet.

"C'mon, Michael!" Larry yelled over the pandemonium. "Quickly!"

Rita and her new friend were clutching each other, mouths agape as they stared with horrified shock. She didn't even notice Michael and Larry dashing for the bow.

~

The Javelin had just replaced his Snap-On toolbox in the trunk when the explosion slapped the bay. He glanced at the Porsche. The second would be soon enough. He closed the trunk and slid behind the wheel gingerly. He cranked his rental sedan around and left the wharf and pandemonium behind. He would wait for the Porsche somewhere along the highway, then in a few hours he would be airborne again. The burning yacht spewing black smoke against the orange sunset reflected in his rear view mirror. Now his account would be well over a million.

~

Chester was fast to react. For an old man, Larry Hicks impressed him. He followed father and son off the ferry and ran up the embankment. They were heading for the government pier through the melee of stunned onlookers. Commercial and pleasure boats were already approaching the burning yacht.

~

"Nick! Nick! Did you get that?"

"Yeah, Tabs, I'm on it," Nick yelled back, fumbling his rig to his shoulder, framing the fiery wreckage. A barrage of media raced past him, some already off the gangplank and crowding the end of the pier. On the breakwater, onlookers watched the boats circle for survivors. Sirens blared when a Coast Guard cutter near the bay on routine patrol in Queen Charlotte Channel responded to distress calls sent out only seconds after the explosion. Nick panned to get the oncoming rescue in frame.

And then there was Coleman Dresher. Tabitha poked Nick on the shoulder.

"I'm getting it, dammit!" he said.

"Look," she said, pointing up over his shoulder at the pier. Nick cranked around in time to see a terrified Dresher jump into his very expensive sports car. He tore away, tires spitting gravel.

Nick and Tabitha quickly ran for the end of the wharf. She could see her career blossoming already. And they got the mysterious man who had boarded the yacht on tape.

Jesus, what a story!

~

"Larry, let's get outta here!" Michael said. The smell of burning fiberglass stung the nose. Beyond the hills shaping the south shore of Horseshoe Bay, helicopter blades pounded the air. More Coast Guard, Michael suspected. Then he noticed the media around them. Anonymity was still a crucial element to their plan. Larry was mesmerized, the burning boat a reminder of the dangerous people he had been forced to spend his life running from.

Michael spotted Tabitha among the reporters on the pier. He grabbed Larry's arm. "Too many cameras. Let's go."

~

Motherfuckers!
They got him! Jesus, they got him!
For the second time today, Dresher was thoroughly scared.
Oh fuck!
His hands were shaking so badly he could barely pilot the Porsche onto the exit ramp heading out of Horseshoe Bay and onto the Trans-Canada back to Vancouver.
Where do I go? Can't go home! Can't go to the office! Oh fuck! I'm dead!
In his panic Dresher's driving skills were suffering. As he merged recklessly with oncoming traffic a lumber transport carrier swerved to miss him, the air horn roaring.

"Shit!" He veered wildly, the Porsche's rear wheel spitting dirt and grass as it spun over the shoulder. The car, more than driver, corrected and Dresher raced along the shoulder, suicide passing the evening traffic.

But not even a Porsche 924 can out run death.

~

The Javelin tried to stay on the Porsche's tail. He merged onto the Trans-Canada but dropped back when a lumber transport swerved to make room for the silver Porsche now five cars ahead of him. The Javelin assumed the second lane and accelerated.

He could not wait too long. If the lawyer put more than a few kilometers between them, the remote would not ignite the charge. He had the perfect opportunity when the lawyer nearly spun out of control off the shoulder. The detonation would have catapulted the vehicle right into the ditch. He would not miss a second opportunity. He stomped the gas, catching up to the Porsche drifting erratically between lanes and shoulder. Cars were dropping back in order to avoid colliding.

The Javelin was nearly caught up again when the lumber truck moved in behind the Porsche, obstructing his view of his target. A GMC with a fifth wheel camper was riding alongside the Javelin, boxing him in behind the transport. He couldn't let Dresher get out of range. He reached for the remote on the front seat and dropped back several car lengths behind the semi.

~

"What are you doing, asshole," the trucker driving the Peterbilt cursed with his head shaking. The rig was loaded just outside of Brackendale around noon; late as usual. He scoffed down a quick midday breakfast, then later in the afternoon a fast, greasy lunch at the gas station in Britannia Beach, his last stop on the ride home down highway 99 that threaded along the southern shore of Montagu Channel and eventually tagged up with the Trans-Canada at Horseshoe Bay. He was finally on the homeward stretch. Garth Brooks was spilling out of the stereo, singing about how the world would not change him when suddenly the lunatic in the Porsche merged without so much as a shoulder check. The trucker hated guys like that, their fancy cars and their high-to-do attitudes, driving like they own the road. *What an asshole!* He needed a little scare.

The trucker slipped his rig in behind the Porsche, close enough that he hoped to provoke with a little tailgating. It had been a long day behind the wheel.

"Holly shit!" the trucker screamed when the Porsche suddenly exploded only two car lengths in front of him. The rear bumper from the European sports car impaled into the Peterbilt's grill and the back spoiler smashed the windshield. The trucker had no choice but to abandon the wheel and dive down across the cab to avoid the impact. Shards rained on him. He could feel the shifting weight that meant tons of lumber was pushing a jackknifed tractor ahead. Tires screeching. Gears grinding. Metal Twisting. Tie down chains snapping. Lumber spilling. Garth singing Ain't going down.

Jesus Christ!

He hung on, waiting for the crash that was sure to come.

Then gravity tugged his chest, the dash pushing against him. The truck was going over.

~

The Javelin dropped back behind the fifth wheel camper, which was also jackknifing into the ditch when the semi tipped, spilling its load over the Trans-Canada.

He accelerated into the ditch with the mastery of a NASCAR driver and passed the havoc he created. And at the forefront of the pile up, the lawyer's fine Porsche, burning in the middle of the Trans-Canada Highway East, tattered parts strewn to where it eventually coasted to a stop after the explosion gutted it.

The Javelin lunged his sedan back onto the highway then gunned for Vancouver. He figured it would take the better part of an hour or more to make Sea Island, and with any luck Morelatto's private jet would touch-down in Winnipeg in a couple of hours.

He glanced the mayhem in the rear view mirror. The gutted Porsche, the over-tuned semi, the camper in the ditch, it was a masterpiece. Things were going to plan. Now his account would be over two million.

And the night wasn't over.

CHAPTER 63

Lance & Ralph

Smiley's Bar

"Have you heard?" Lance asked as he slipped his skinny butt into Ralph Forbes's booth.

"Heard what?" Ralph was drunk. The five o'clock shadow was thickening into quite the straggled beard. A shot of Barcardi found it's mark and Jimmy was waved over for another.

"You're drunk," Lance said with marked disappointment.

"You're gonna make a helluva reporter, kid." The words were slurred. Another shot was downed.

"He's dead," Lance spat. Ralph's scrunched scowl told the kid he needed more. "Premier Graham is dead!" Lance said with a toss of his hands. "God, what's wrong with you?"

Ralph cleared the stupor. "Dead? Graham?"

"And Coleman Dresher."

It was as sobering as a strong cup of coffee. Ralph had to think it through a moment then he eyeballed the kid, trying to focus. "Both of them? Are you sure?"

"Graham on his boat. And Dresher was car bombed right on the Trans-Canada."

Jimmy walked over another shot but Forbes pushed the glass away. "Better give me some coffee, Jimmy." He leaned to Lance, who in turn leaned away from the stench of alcohol. "Where's Michael?"

"He was there."

"Shit," Ralph muttered. "Put it on my tab, Jimmy," he shouted across the bar. Jimmy wasn't surprised.

"Michael needs us, Mr. Forbes?" Lance said.

"Right after I have a few cups of coffee, we're on it."

CHAPTER 64

The Driver must Pay

Kenora

Mac Loewen was in the dark.

He just sat there with a bottle of Russia's finest distilled perched on the arm of a big wooden chair with tacky blue cushions. He hadn't moved much the last couple of days except to take a piss, but other than that, he just stared out the big windows of his expensive log cabin, and let himself get lost in the view of Lake of the Woods. The moon was full over the lake. The tiny ripples weaved over the serene water like an artist's brush.

It was too soon for the media to call the explosions that killed Premier Roy Graham and Coleman Dresher what they really were; assassinations. Loewen would laugh if not for the fact that he was drinking himself into a Vodka stupor. The irony was blatant. He was going die. And it was going to be bloody.

It had been a long time coming. There were moments since '81 that he actually thought it was getting easier, that the nightmare of Murphy Henderson with his brains blown all over the slushy beach, or Roger MacMillan's kids dancing around the tree that Christmas Eve, would fade into some compartment of his brain that would spare him the torture of his relentless guilt.

He poured another.

Over the last couple of days he even considered writing it all down, but a confession now would serve no purpose. He would be thought of as he would be thought of. If they figured out how and why he fell prey to Morelatto, why he accepted the money, why he went through with it, even after the murders, what would it change? What pain would it ease? Nothing. He could tell the country what really happened to Justice Minister Francis Lavelle, how Loewen had set up the young politician with the rapacious appetite for lewd oral sex underneath the bridges of the Rideau Canal.

But the money was too much. He had grown up poor, wanted to be the man he had become, albeit by more honest means, but nonetheless, he wanted the power that came with money. No one ever inquired as to where his investment monies for all that Apple stock came from; the pockets of Mario Morelatto.

He poured another down.

He deserved what was coming. And not even his final act to help Larry could repay the pain he had caused. You can't out run your crime. It's that simple.

He swigged the last of the Vodka. It burned. He pitched the glass at the stone fireplace. The bottle followed.

And that's when he heard the creak behind him in the dark. There was a stealth to the way the air moved – a precision that existed in his presence. The trained hands of whom Loewen knew to be the Javelin clamped his neck, forcing him to the floor.

Mac Loewen closed his eyes. He was finally going to be free.

The Javelin's slash was quick and precise, the blade cutting clean through the neck to the vertebra.

The driver was no more.

Kingston Row

Two hours later, Jake Munroe and the Javelin eased a rented SUV along Kingston Row till they came to the house in the crook of the street they knew to be the home of Lily and Archie Atkinson. If only Archie had not made that call to Sam Mitchell in San Diego, they may never have known how to find the former Mountie and his retired CFS wife.

The SUV stopped. The Javelin disappeared around the back of the house while Munroe made a call on his cellphone. Morelatto insisted on updates, especially since they could not find Alec Garva anywhere since Graham and Dresher had been dealt with at Horseshoe Bay.

Two silenced flashes flicked inside the Atkinson house. The Javelin was back in the SUV and they were aboard the private jet, flying thirty-five thousand feet over Chicago within the hour. They would be in Fort Lauderdale, Florida before sunrise.

CHAPTER 65

Meanwhile Back in the Bahamas

USS Intrepid

Sam Cholan had just gotten off the satellite phone with Edwin Newhart, who was back at CIA headquaters in Langley, Virginia. Braden MacDuff in Ottawa had reported SeaCorp's Canadair Challenger jet departed Winnipeg International bound for Chicago. Cholan was sure Floyd Webber wasn't going to sit back for long. But ultimately it really didn't matter because regardless of what games played out, Michael Spencer and the elusive Mr. Hicks had yet to show themselves since the Graham explosion in British Columbia. So until then, the CIA had their end of the deal to carry out and the Canadians had theirs.

Cholan found himself once again being summoned to The Room. He stuck his head through the bulkhead door. "Whad'ya we got, Berger?"

Seaman Berger removed his headset. "Call just coming now, sir."

Cholan sat. "Put it on speaker."

"Yes, sir."

They listened while the phone in the villa rang.

Villa - Governor's Harbor

The phone rang. Nolan picked it up. "Michael?"

"Hi, Nolan," Michael said. "How are they doing?"

"We're okay," Nolan said, glancing at Jessica, Jasmine with Katie, and the always calm and reassuring Evelyn seated around the living room. "When are you getting down here?"

"Don't want to say over the phone. Can you put Evelyn on? Larry wants to talk to her."

Nolan passed the phone to Evelyn then told a relieved Jasmine and

Katie that Michael would be joining them soon.

Evelyn talked a moment, bid Larry good-bye and hung up. She excused herself and strolled through the patio doors. She walked quickly around the side of the house and down the Palm tree choked driveway before she allowed herself to cry. After all these years, her son was finally coming.

CHAPTER 66

The Past closing In

Bloedel Conservatory - Vancouver

The cell phone hadn't rung for the past hour. Alec Garva chose not to think about it. If Morelatto had discovered what he was about to do, it wouldn't matter anyway. Besides AIDS was going to claim him soon enough.

A typical drizzle sprinkled the windscreen and in the quiet the delicate droplets drummed, almost soothingly, on the vinyl roof of the car. The radio was still off. He had heard enough about Graham and Dresher and talk of bombs. He reached into his breast pocket and pulled out a cassette tape just as a rusty Pinto pulled into the conservatory parking lot.

It would all be over soon now.

USS Intrepid

"Sir," Berger said as he stepped onto the bridge at 0100 hours.
Sam Cholan and the SEAL commander were discussing their surveillance of the villa in Bonefish Bay. "What is it, Berger?"
"Two people from the house, sir. They've taken a walk on the beach."
"Who?"
"Grant and Ingham."
"Sir?" the SEAL commander cut in. "This could mean a change in strategy."
Cholan didn't have time to consider the variables. He glanced to the east, where a half mile off starboard the nocturnal lights of Governor's Harbor glittered. He couldn't move until he received the go ahead from Edwin Newhart. The latest intel from Langley was they suspected the assassin known as The Javelin was definitely aboard the private jet heading south. That information came from Floyd Webber's team in Winnipeg.

According to Newhart, Webber was getting tired of the waiting game. But until Larry Hicks and Michael Spencer touch down in the Bahamas, Webber was handcuffed.

"We just observe, gentlemen," he said to the men on the bridge.

24 Sussex Drive - Ottawa

It was as perfect a time as any for the Freedom Room ritual, the Prime Minister surmised.

Why not the middle of the night?

He stood at the window, puffing and contemplating the fall out that would naturally ensue such a ruthless attack on a Canadian politician. It was all out of his control now.

The Prime Minister had met Rachel Graham once when she was only eight years old. She mirrored her mother.

He puffed.

How much longer his secret would be safe was anybody's guess. But one thing was for sure. Allison McKay would have to mastermind well beyond the call of duty now.

Then there was the heightened security besieging 24 Sussex. It seemed like only moments after the explosion in Horseshoe Bay the JTF-2 clandestine unit descended on the residence with unbridled enthusiasm. Sniffer dogs fettered out the possibility of incendiary devices. Security clearances were rechecked, including Allison McKay's and even Marty's. Staff were issued new itineraries and restricted to the main floor. No one was permitted past the spiral staircase to the Prime Minister's living quarters unless summoned directly and accompanied by a JTF-2. The house and grounds were electronically swept. Properties bordering the Prime Minister's residence were fleeced for any chance of weaponry; an annoyance to some foreign dignitaries living in the neighborhood. Luckily for the boys and girls from External Affairs, those very diplomats were unaware of CSE's heightened cellular tapping while they were ushered along in their plush limousines as a result of the Graham assassination. Of course Paul Young and the rest of the Privy Council's Security Intelligence Review Committee were none the wiser as well; nor would they want to be.

The Prime Minister should have been grateful with all the attention, but he wasn't. The JTF commander cautioned him to avoid the Freedom Room balcony during the smoking ritual. The window would have to do.

The Prime Minister puffed nervously.

CHAPTER 67

The Final Act of Alec Garva

Bloedel Conservatory – Vancouver

Alec Garva stood in the rain. He was wearing a fedora and long coat over his suit. He was an opposing figure standing at the far end of the courtyard promontory overlooking the lush park beyond the precipice. By day the conservatory tucked in Queen Elizabeth Park would attract tourists and gardening enthusiasts. Inside the massive dome of diamond shaped glass panels and metal framework was an indoor tropical jungle of exotic birds. But at night the lights shimmering from inside licked the cement courtyard wrapping around the dome, turning the grassy knolls and streams and sculpted lawns into a foreboding weave of shadows.

At least that's how it felt for Michael when Larry and he climbed out of the Pinto, their eyelids fluttering from the rain. They were soaked by the time they made the courtyard. Larry instinctively checked for probable snipers lurking beyond the promontory wall bordering the conservatory's courtyard as Alec Garva stepped out of the shadows.

Without a word Garva led them around the domed conservatory, past the water fountains to a wood deck with slat overhang to shelter them from the rain. He sat down on the bench and admired the light cascading from inside the conservatory. Within this surreal park in the heart of Vancouver the air was fresh and clean and tingled when breathed deeply. "It's nice here, no?"

"Yeah, whatever," Michael dismissed. "Why are we here?"

"Michael," Larry cautioned with a gentle hand on his forearm.

Garva ignored it. He eased his hand into his trench coat pocket and offered the cassette tape to Larry. "Here, Mr. Hicks."

"What's on this tape?" Larry asked.

"Everything you need to get your life back."

USS Intrepid

Cholan tightened the focus on his night vision binoculars. It was a clear night. He watched Evelyn Hicks lug a pale of water to the fire pit on the beach and douse the flames. Their targets were turning in for the night. Cholan panned further up the beach. No sign of Nolan Grant and Jessica Ingham.

Stupid, he thought. The Canadair jet had touched down somewhere north of Fort Lauderdale, the pilots detained. No one else was aboard, so essentially the best spy agencies of the free world had lost their assassins. The threat level jumped a few notches. If Ingham and Grant did not return before sunrise, he would send in the SEALS.

The sun would be peaking over the island within the next few hours.

Bloedel Conservatory – Vancouver

"What makes you think I need this?" Larry asked.

Michael eyed the cassette Larry now held in his hand while rain dripped through the overhead slats. The sound of water droplets slapping pavement echoed around them.

Garva spoke evenly, with no emotion or regret. "I know you got the tapes from your safe house, but you won't find the one you need among them."

"And which one is that?" Larry pressed furtively.

"The one when you recorded us planning to kill the Prime Minister during your operation. The lawyer kept that one in his safe."

"You mean the lawyer you blew up," Michael snapped.

Garva only smiled. "Yes, Mr. Spencer, that one." He pointed at the cassette. "But there's more on there."

"Such as..?" Larry asked.

"Morelatto ordered the hits on your Sam Mitchell in San Diego and on Graham and Dresher." He looked at Michael with what could almost be construed as regret. "And your friend too, I'm sorry to say."

Michael couldn't believe what he just heard; they actually planned to kill Milt like he was a pawn in some game.

"Why?" Michael demanded. "I want to know why you're giving this to us now? After all these years you suddenly have a conscience?"

Garva ignored him, focused on Larry. "I'm sorry."

Larry's eyes narrowed. "I'm not here for that."

Garva glanced between them. "Then we are done here, yes."

"This is not done," Michael seethed. "You killed my friend you sonofabitch!"

Suddenly the distant sound of a helicopter hammering the night air reached them through the rain. Garva lifted off the bench and stepped between father and son. He could make out faint flashing red lights beyond the conservatory's aurora. The hammering was coming quickly.

"Did you set us up?" Michael scowled.

Garva turned to them, a gun eased out of his pocket, yet oddly calm. "You need to go now."

Suddenly the helicopter's search beacon switched on, its beam swathing to find prey lurking in the park.

"Run!" Larry yelled.

As they turned to flea a pistol shot rang out. They saw Garva's body collapse, splattered sinew dripping from the slats over the spot where the trigger was pulled. The gun clutched in the lifeless hand smoking from the barrel.

"Let's go!" Larry grabbed Michael. The rapport of an automatic weapon from above cut through the helicopter clangour. Bullets chewed up slats and deck, debris flying. The helicopter pivoted, the search beam slicing through darkness and rain, bullets spitting from the bird.

"Run! Run!" Michael yelled. They bolted along the edge of the waist high wall and hopped a small flight of stairs with bullets tattering cement behind them.

"The conservatory, Michael!"

The beam circled to find them. They crouched, gauged the distance across the open courtyard to the conservatory doors, and bolted. The beam found them. Round after round punching holes in the cement wall. Then the helicopter banked for a clear shot.

"Go!" Larry yelled.

They ran for the main doors and prayed to God they weren't locked. If they were they would be trapped.

~

Chester was sitting in his green sedan when the helicopter passed over the Bloedel Conservatory's parking lot. The Sikorsky H-76 Eagle hung in the conservatory's aurora long enough for Chester to make out the logo emblazoned behind the loading door.

SeaCorp.

He didn't have the moment it would take to watch the helicopter's fusillade. He dove out of the car and threw open the trunk, snapping the Stinger MANPADS launcher to his shoulder. He hit a button, the Stinger beeped, homing in on the helicopter.

"C'mon," Chester yelled, tightening his aim as the helicopter spun around, hovering in the aurora directly over the conservatory, the search beam hunting for its prey.

A long, unbroken tone sounded in his ear and Chester fired, the launcher kicking against him. The Stinger rocketed an exhaust trail through the heavy drizzle, right into the Sikorsky's engine shroud, the explosion blowing the windows and doors out. The fireball wreckage seemed to hang there for a moment, the rotor blades whirling pathetically, before plummeting like a rock for the glass dome.

~

The loading door from the helicopter hit the courtyard, smoldering only a few feet from them. "Jesus Christ!!" Michael yelled.

"Run!" Larry screamed.

They hurdled themselves over the cement wall as the flaming helicopter crashed through the conservatory dome, diamond shaped glass panels exploding as the twisting structure collapsed into itself. Lethal fragments of rotor blades jettisoned in all directions, hacking the horticultural beauty. The rare exotic birds instantly overcome from toxic smoke bleeding from the Sikorsky.

Larry hit at an awkward angle, catapulted forward into a painful somersault, moaning in agony.

"Are you okay?" Michael shouted over the deafening roar. Suddenly a hand shoved him out of the way.

"Let me help," the man insisted.

Michael recovered, ready to strike.

"Michael!" Larry yelled over the fire. "He's with us."

"Who is this guy?" Michael asked, the merry-go-round spinning wildly behind scared blue eyes.

"Chester Caron," Larry said. "Meet my son."

"Mr. Spencer," Chester said with a terse handshake. "It's nice to meet you and everything, but right now I think we should get the hell outta here before the troops roll in."

"Michael," Larry ordered. "Help me up and let's get outta here."

"But who are you?" Michael asked as he helped Chester lift Larry.

Chester slung Larry's arm over his shoulder. "I don't exist, Mr. Spencer. I'd like to keep it that way."

Michael propped his shoulder under Larry's opposite arm, shaking his head. "I hate this shit."

They carried Larry down the path, away from the burning carnage.

They staggered along the path that spilled into the parking lot to find the rusty old Pinto with a jagged fragment of helicopter blade embedded in the grill, coolant draining profusely under the front end.

Chester and Michael got Larry into the front seat of the government sedan. Michael was about to jump in the back when he remembered Lance's laptop. It was in the Pinto. He ran for it with Chester and Larry yelling at him to move. In a flash he was in the sedan, the car squealing away, leaving the burning promontory overlooking Queen Elizabeth Park to light up the night sky.

CHAPTER 68

It Is Far from Over

SSET Command

Webber bounded through the cyber-locking door and walked directly to the computer desk. "Did you get him?" he asked Garrick.

"Yeah."

Webber pointed at the ceiling, indicating he wanted the line open. "Braden?"

"Floyd," the Deputy Director responded from above, a controlled timber to his voice.

"Where is Spencer's family?"

"The Bahamas."

"Where exactly?"

"Floyd, we agreed."

"I don't give a shit about Cholan and Newhart and the goddamned CIA right now. I want to know Michael Spencer's family is safe and I'm going down there to do that. Get me one of those jets you guys love to put me in."

"Spencer's family is taken care of, Floyd. We have the SEAL team ready to move."

That wasn't good enough for Webber. "They just want their rogue assassin, Braden. You know it, and I know it. Now where are Larry and Michael?"

"In Vancouver."

"Is your man on him?"

"Yes."

"Imagine that." The sarcasm was thick. "Mac Loewen is dead, Braden. Did you know that?"

A pause above. "No."

"I'm guessing he was Morelatto's mole. Oh and by the way my team just found Lily and Archie Atkinson executed in their damn house. Archie, Braden! One of us! And you and I both know why that happened. Bodies are piling up. Gut instinct isn't turning the trick now."

"Careful, Floyd."

Webber stared at the ceiling as if God himself had appeared. "You owe me more than this, Goddammit!"

Braden was silent for a long moment. Webber could just see the thumb and forefinger rubbing, thinking. "Braden," he pushed.

"Understand, Floyd, we still don't know how deep this goes."

Webber slammed the computer desk, veins budging out of his neck. "Get me a fucking plane, Braden. Now!!"

"I'll get back to you, Floyd." MacDuff hung up.

Webber pitched a chair across the office. Garrick dared to say nothing.

CSIS headquarters - Ottawa

Braden hung up from Webber and immediately punched another blinking line. "Yeah, MacDuff here." The thumb and forefinger were really rubbing.

"It's me," Chester Caron answered.

"What's happening out there, Chester?"

"Well, sir..."

Vancouver

"...I got him," Chester said to the Deputy Director of Operations in Ottawa over the satellite phone his sedan came equipped with. The phone was on intercom mode.

"Hello, Braden," Larry said.

"Jesus," MacDuff said, relieved. "Larry, are you okay?"

"Yeah."

"Did you get the tape?"

"We got it," Larry said, looking at the auspicious cassette that would be responsible for his life back. He would deal with the regrets later.

"And Garva?" MacDuff asked.

Chester stopped at the red light on the corner of Cambie Street and Marine Drive. A municipal black and white skidded through the wet intersection with sirens blaring and lights flashing. A stream of fire trucks followed in exactly the same fashion.

"You'll know all about it soon enough, Braden," Larry said while they watched the emergency vehicles head for the fire in Queen Elizabeth Park.

Larry glanced regretfully at his son then said to the phone, "Some hired contractor named Javelin killed Maggie and Milt Smith."

"We know. I'm sorry about Maggie, Larry," MacDuff said.

"How long have you known?" Michael snapped from the backseat.

"We lost one of our own at the hands of this man as well, Mr. Spencer. I do, however, regret your loss."

Michael was biting his lip, withdrawn to watching the wiper blades work tirelessly, justice or even a reason was not going to come now. "Just get me to my family."

Larry agreed and said, "Were going to need a plane, Braden."

"Understood."

"And the rest of our deal?" Larry asked.

Michael glanced between Chester and Larry. "Deal?"

Larry eyed Michael. "Braden?"

MacDuff said, "I contacted Sam Cholan right after you phoned, Larry. They're all fine. They were having a bonfire on the beach."

Larry explained to Michael, "Sam Cholan is one my contacts with the CIA. They've been keeping an eye on Evelyn and your family down there for us." Michael didn't know what to say.

Braden's voice turned serious. "We have a problem though."

The three of them exchanged a nervous glance. "What is it, Braden?" Larry asked.

"We lost the private jet somewhere around Fort Lauderdale."

"They probably have cloaking?" Chester offered.

"Jesus." Larry rubbed his forehead. "They found out. How did they know?"

MacDuff sighed from the speaker. "We think it was Mac Loewen, Larry. I'm sorry."

Chester and Larry exchanged a shocked look.

"Mac...," Larry blurted, the possibility too unreal, too unbelievable. "All this time." Then came betrayal, his jaw grit. "Do you have him?"

"He's dead," MacDuff said. "We believe it was the Javelin according to Webber. They also killed Lily and Archie, Larry."

Larry felt that in his gut. He turned to the window to hide his wet eyes, his mind rifling through the past, something not adding up. "Someone else had to have been feeding him from HQ. There still has to be a mole, Braden."

"We know," MacDuff admitted.

Larry checked Michael decidedly worried in the back seat. "Get us down there, Braden."

"I'll have a plane ready for you. Chester, you get back here a sap."

"Right, sir," Chester said, punching the gas and weaving through traffic congestion. The sedan was coming up on the Arthur Laing Bridge that crossed the Fraser Delta onto Sea Island. The lights of Vancouver International blurred through the heavy drizzle.

"I'll have Sam Cholan move now," MacDuff said. "They'll pull them if you want, Larry."

"Do it!" Larry ordered. The director hung up.

Michael reached over the seat, grabbing the satellite phone and holding it inches from his birth father's face. "Call them! Now!"

Larry dialed, held the phone to his ear. It was ringing.

Suddenly Larry's face went white. "What the___."

There was no dial tone.

SSET Command

"Okay, you've got your plane," MacDuff said from above.

"About damn time," Webber sneered, marched for his office.

"Chief," Simon Johnson called from the conference chamber. "You need to see this."

Webber stepped through the glass doors to his team watching a CBC news flash. The banner read: *Live from Vancouver's Bloedel Conservatory.*

News footage told the whole story. The conservatory decimated with a destroyed helicopter crashed in it. The scene was still thick with smoke. A brigade of fire fighters and police scurried about.

"How much more is Vancouver supposed to endure in one week," the anchorperson remarked. The body discovered on the conservatory courtyard was identified as one Alec Garva, an executive with SeaCorp who died of a single gunshot to the head. Upon closing the anchorperson stated that Mr. Morelatto was not available for comment when Premier Graham's boat exploded. The Premier's attorney, Coleman Dresher also died in a separate car bombing. Mr. Dresher's personal secretary was found in the Juan de Fuca strait earlier this week, also murdered. They all have ties to SeaCorp.

"Braden," Webber said, fearful of what he didn't know. "Was Larry there?"

"Yes. But they're alive. They're with our man. I'm putting them on a plane now."

Webber turned for the door. "I'll be in the air in ten."

CHAPTER 69

The Newsroom Two-Step

"I don't believe this!" The old bullhorn was pacing through a tantrum and it would be Nuewerth's first as a full-fledged reporter. The office door was wide open. "Two murders in this city last night and one in Kenora and we have nothing. Nada! Zip!" Lund dropped into his squeaky chair. "Has Michael checked in with you?"

"No," Lance said timidly.

"Christ. He was probably involved in that shit that went down in Vancouver last night. That was a SeaCorp helicopter they said, right?"

"Yeah."

"And Garva. Goddammit! Morelatto's top dog too." His big fist smacked the desk. "Michael was supposed to keep us in the loop all the way along."

"I'm sure he will," Nuewerth said, eyeing the door - escape.

"Yeah. Wouldn't that be considerate?" The chair groaned. "Well, he's on his own now."

Ralph strolled through the open door. He looked even worse than he did when Nuewerth sobered him up at Smiley's last night. "Jesus," Lund said. "You look like shit."

"Thanks. I didn't sleep much last night." Ralph flopped into a chair, slipped a notepad from his sport coat, and got right to it. "Wanna hear this?"

Lund sighed, leaned back; he knew what Ralph was after and it wasn't just the story of the decade. "Is this worth me hiring you back?"

Ralph's smile stretched from ear to ear. "Michael had me do a back ground on this guy in San Diego named Sam Mitchell when he first found out about his birth parents. He was high level CIA, real black ops stuff. Anyway, he turns up dead on his dock down there a few days later, but guess who called his house that night."

Lund scrunched his face into his palm, his patience going fast. "Who?"

"Archie Atkinson."

Nuewerth and Lund shot each other a surprised look. The ole bullhorn felt an excitement he hadn't felt for a long time. "Run it under Michael's column." Lund was out of his chair now. "Need your source, Ralph."

Ralph groaned. "You're an asshole you know that."

"I won't use your source, Ralph, if Michael's snitch in Ottawa comes through...I promise. But I still need it."

Ralph considered it a moment. "Am I hired?"

"I can't print without the source, Ralph. Don't do this a second time."

Ralph ran his hand through his thinned hair with a long sigh. Somehow the decision wasn't as burdensome as he would've thought. "Assistant Commissioner Hubert Jefkins. He's the Officer Commanding of 'D' division."

"Wow," Lance said, impressed.

"Lance," Lund said, reaching over his desk for Ralph's notepad. "You write up the Atkinson murders." He eyed Ralph with renewed respect. "We'll discuss salary later. You won't be disappointed. Get on a plane to Ottawa. You've got Coastal Holding."

Lance was nearly through the door, eager to start building a career, when Lund said, "Lance. Check your e-mail. Michael might have sent more notes."

CHAPTER 70

Nippy & the Ride Home

Governor's Harbor - Elethuera, Bahamas

Below the wing the thin strip of Eluethera Island rose out of the aqua blue Caribbean as the jet descended. It reminded Michael of their honeymoon in Cancun. He craved Jasmine's kiss more than ever.

Larry tried repeatedly to reach the villa before they landed. Cell service on the island was sketchy at best most of the time. They both needed to know Ev and Jas and Katie, along with Jessica and Nolan, were safe. As much as Sam Cholan and Edwin Newhart promised to keep an eye on the villa, Larry knew Michael needed to hear his family's voices. "Evelyn probably took them to Hatchet Bay or the Glass Window Bridge," he offered. The smile was thin; Larry was worried.

They touched down, hurried through the tiny island terminal – thanks to immigration officers happy to see Mr. Norris back home – and ran for the one and only taxi.

"How far is it?" Michael asked as they climbed into a battered, old white '60 Meteor converted into a private cab with Nippy's taxi brush painted on either side.

"Depends," Larry said. He was rubbing his leg, still a little tender from the tumble over the promontory wall.

"On what," Michael said, looking around the empty parking lot. "Can't be gridlock."

"On who's driving." Larry winced as he climbed in the back. He rolled his eyes at the aged cabbie behind the wheel; tattered dreadlocks and a tired blue shirt. "It'll take a bit longer," he said to Michael then greeted the cabbie. "Hi, Nippy."

Nippy tossed his newspaper to the floorboards. "Hey d'here, Mr. Norris," he sang pleasantly when he saw the familiar face in his rear view mirror. "It's good to see you, mon."

"Thanks. Get me home. And hurry. There's an extra twenty in it for you."

Nippy liked his tips, but twenty bucks was worth turning around and smiling for. "Twenty bucks?"

"Yes. And hurry."

"Well," Nippy said, gripping the wheel and banging the transmission into drive. "You'd better be hanging on, mon." He tromped the gas and with tires squealing, Nippy's battered old Meteor sped away for Bonefish Bay. All three of them were unaware of the man standing just outside the entrance to the airport, dressed in a black tee shirt and shorts and eating a kiwi to counter the Caribbean heat.

Floyd Webber watched the cab leave. There was no other taxi to be had. He wasn't happy.

USS Intrepid

"They're in a cab, sir," Berger informed Cholan who had just stepped into the room, checking the live drone feed playing on the monitor above.

"That's a cab?" Cholan asked, pointing, skeptical. "How old is that car?"

"It's the Bahamas, sir." Seaman Berger simply replied, tweaking knobs.

"That's not an answer."

"But it is, sir."

Cholan had bigger concerns at the moment. "Fine. Anything else?"

"No, sir."

"What about the Mountie and the woman?"

"They're down the beach at Ronnie's bar, sir."

"Well, at least we know where they are," Cholan said and turned for the hatch, paused. "But the Javelin is still out there. Do you understand that?"

Berger looked at his superior, realizing he offended when he didn't mean to. "I understand, sir."

Villa

The driveway was narrow and choked with overhanging Palms. Nippy negotiated his old cab with all the subtlety of a grandmother on the freeway during rush hour. Larry tossed the twenty over the front seat as Michael climbed out of the Meteor before Nippy even managed to find the brake pedal with his lazy foot. The old car rocked from the back doors slamming one after the other, Michael and Larry dashing for the villa.

"Hey, mon!" Nippy yelled out his open window. "She's classic y'know."

"Jasmine!" Michael called as they hustled through the patio doors. They were slightly ajar. "Katie!" No responses.

Larry went directly to the phone sitting on the wicker end table beside the purple beanbag chair. The dial tone was buzzing with a pre-recorded operator instructing to hang up and try your call again. That wasn't normal. He replaced the phone then climbed the spiral staircase to the loft. Michael watched him check each of the three bedrooms with anxiousness growing.

"Tell me this is a good sign," he begged Larry who descended the staircase with a purse in hand. He handed it to Michael. "This is Jessica's." He eyed Larry hard. "This can't be right."

"This is the Bahamas." Larry limped past him for the patio doors.

"What is that supposed to mean?" Michael tossed the purse on the beanbag chair and followed Larry onto the beach. The gentle cadence of breakers was everywhere.

Larry spotted something. "It means it's the Bahamas. We don't lock doors, we don't set alarm clocks, we drink at noon, and we don't always take our purses and wallets." It was an imprint in the sand, the kind the keel of a boat cuts upon skirting the shore. A platoon of footprints tracked from the water to the villa.

Michael saw what Larry saw. "Tell me this is good."

Larry peered out over the bay, straining to see anything lurking along the western horizon of the Caribbean; nothing but water and sky.

"I hope so, Michael." He turned for the villa. "I hope so."

CHAPTER 71

The Two Left Behind

Ronnie's Bar

    A Marlboro was all Jessica could get her hands on. The local islander at the next table said she could buy a pack of du Mauriers at the gas station if she wanted. But Jessica was far too shaken to venture far from Nolan's side, least of all to satisfy her cravings. She took the cigarette. She was anything but calm. They had taken a walk through Governor's Harbor; just a reason to get out of the villa and relax a bit, but what they found when they returned was more than a little upsetting; Evelyn, Jasmine and Katie were gone. Jessica's panic was spinning wildly out of control and not even the nicotine was subduing her.

    Nolan on the other hand had a different response. He saw the invasion imprinted in the beach in front of the villa and abruptly whisked Jessica away from the possible threat. He was tiring of sitting like a duck in a pond. That was not his nature and it was time to start thinking like an RCMP officer again; it was time to stop being a victim.

    He returned from the bar with a couple beers. He noticed the cigarette burning in her hand and glanced at the smiling islander. He offered Nolan one from the pack. Nolan declined and sat in close to Jessica. He could feel her tremble as his arm wrapped around her back. He kissed her cheek. She was cold with fear. He rubbed her hand soothingly, telling her he ordered up some conch fritters for them. He could smell the beach from the sand caked in her thick red hair. Last night would be one of those memories he would remember for the rest of his life.

    "Listen," he said.

    She blew a stream of smoke at the ceiling then let her weary eyes lock on him. "What?"

    "The bartender said he'd call a cab for us. We could get you some place safe on the island. Maybe a resort or some public place, somewhere with a lot of people around."

"What about you?" She was disturbed with the idea of being left alone.

"I have to find out what happened to them, Jessica. I promised Michael."

Villa

"Larry," Michael called through the open patio doors. He was kneeling in the sand, about five paces from the dormant fire pit.

Larry was inside on the phone, trying to get through to Edwin Newhart's private line at CIA headquarters in Langley, Virginia. Newhart's secretary simply said the director was not available. He slammed the phone; something was wrong. He could feel it. He joined Michael on the beach, staring out at the aqua blue Caribbean, trying to see the ship that should have been there.

"Maybe your friends didn't make it in time, Larry," Michael said, his worry read easily.

Larry didn't know what to say. Michael could very well be right. The only consolation was Morelatto needed the manifests and pictures, but most of all, he'd want Hicks in the flesh. For that reason, Larry had to believe Morelatto would need hostages, not corpses. But Larry had no cards left to play, no tricks up his sleeve, only a growing fear that he ultimately let Evelyn down again. He had to get a hold of Newhart or Sam Cholan. And the ship had to be somewhere off shore, drifting out there, watching and listening. They swore it on Sam Mitchel's memory.

"Let's not panic," he urged.

CHAPTER 72

The Last Hands of the Game

Juan De Fuca Strait, BC

Within hours of leaving his unremarkable third floor office in the CSIS building on Metcalfe Street, Braden MacDuff found himself sharing the front compartment of an EH 101 naval transport helicopter. The Scottish eye slits tightened against the morning glare burning through the windows. Two hundred feet below the churning Juan De Fuca stretched to the rocky shores of Vancouver Island to the west.

Across from him sat Chester Caron, dressed for a JTF-2 full assault, and five commandos ready to do their duty. The White Knight lay two miles to the southwest, moving at roughly thirty knots, running like hell for the American border.

"About two minutes, men" Chester looked to MacDuff. "He'll have a crew on board."

MacDuff's look said everything. It had only been ten hours since he listened to the tape Alec Garva had willingly given Larry Hicks and Michael Spencer at Bloedel Conservatory; the same tape the beautiful secretary Sasha had stolen out of Coleman Dresher's office safe, and willing turned over to Morelatto only to have her throat slit and dumped into the Juan de Fuca. But what was most sobering for MacDuff was that after all these years of suspecting his sitting Prime Minister was crooked, the tape was the final blow to his unwavering patriotism. Listening to Seth Petersen and Mario Morelatto conspire an assassination plot on then Prime Minister Pierre Trudeau back in 1980 was bad enough. But hearing them orchestrate the fate of Murphy Henderson on Jericho beach, Roger Mac-Millan and his family in the safe house on 1st and Yew, and Francis Lavelle moments before his Senate Committee hearing in Ottawa, made his blood boil. The murders of Premier Roy Graham and Coleman Dresher were expected if nothing else. As far as MacDuff was concerned, they deserved what they got; albeit Graham's wife and daughter were tragic. But now came the real damage control that director Clifton McIvor and Inspector-General Hugh Long insisted be surreptitiously carried out because it would be best for the country, the agency, and the idea of democracy and civil rights. The real malfeasance would never reach the people, never taint the PMO, and never besmirch Canada.

He turned to his window, stared hard and long at the coastline to the west, the radiant sunlight bleaching his stone face white. "You get this sonofabitch one way or the other, Chester," he ordered. Chester understood.

24 Sussex Drive - Ottawa

It would be an understatement to suggest Allison McKay's professional world exploded simultaneously with the tragedy in Horseshoe Bay. Her precious time had been dominated with relentless bids for exclusive interviews with her Prime Minister since the bombings. There wasn't a paper or news agency anywhere in the world that didn't have graphic, disturbing scenes of the Rachel's Dream explosion. An in lieu of the incident and the impending July 5th arraignment, the media aftermath was anything but routine and expected.

But there was one particular call that set Allison more on edge than any other. A reporter named Lance Nuewerth had contacted her, implying he had reliable information pertaining to a conversation she had had with Premier Roy Graham shortly before the Coastal Holding purchase. Within minutes, she left the PMO in the Langevin building, directly across from Parliament Hill, hailed a cab on Wellington and raced for the elegant residence on Sussex.

But, alas, with all the heightened security and JTF-2 sentries she could not discuss her situation with the Prime Minister until they were comfortably tucked into his plush limousine. Even then privacy was not guaranteed. The limo proceeded along Sussex in the middle of an overbearing procession of motorcycles and security vans; virtually a mobile enclave. How the Prime Minister convinced the officer in charge to have the RCMP sentry, who usually rode shotgun in the front seat, to stand down was only a testament to his power. He simply said 'no'. Of course they had no choice, regardless of what orders were handed down from HQ. It was bad enough CSE probably had infiltrated his digital profile from top to bottom; all for his own good they would claim. The limo was all he seemed to have left.

The PM asked Marty to turn up Oscar Peterson a little louder than usual today.

"How did they find out?" Allison asked, more than a little rattled.

"I don't know," the Prime Minister simply said, watching the External Affairs building pass by. The career was crumbling quickly now. They had the tape. The fact it was the Free Press, Michael Spencer's paper, only added insult to injury. There was no question in his mind whose career would have to be sacrificed. He patted Allison's hand with a sympathetic grin. "It will be fine."

"No it won't," she snapped.

He ignored her tone. "Now's the time to be calm and rational."

"What am I supposed to do?" she asked, her usually controlled voice strained. Allison, for all her talents, lacked the experience to deflect accusations of impropriety that would surely come now. And the Prime Minister was counting on it.

"You do nothing," he offered. "They wouldn't dare run this story without a confirmation. If they want this one they're going to have to dig it out themselves." The Prime Minister leaned forward, resting one hand over the front seat in order to pull himself up to Marty's ear.

"Let's drop Miss McKay at home, Marty."

"Yes, sir."

Marty knew a lot. And no one was the wiser.

CHAPTER 73

The Reckoning

Villa

Nippy made good time from Ronnie's Bar to the villa. He turned around with his best smile and an open palm extended for his well-deserved tip.

"Wait right here," Nolan said as he pulled Jessica out of the backseat with him. "We'll be right back."

"Sure ting, mon," Nippy said out his open window after them as they hurried up the drive. "I jus 'ope it's worth my time," the islander grumbled to himself when they disappeared around the front of the villa. He fiddled with the radio. He hated waiting. Especially for fares he knew were not tippers. Then someone else climbed into the back and Nippy felt the pressure of a gun barrel against his temple.

Jessica could hear Michael talking to someone inside the house. Her pace quickened. The instant she sprinted through the patio doors, Michael hugged her tight, the phone still clutched in his hand, Jasmine's voice bleeding from it, demanding to know what was going on.

"Where are they?" Jessica begged. Before Michael could answer Nolan tumbled violently through the patio doors.

Jessica screamed as Nolan somersaulted into the wicker table, grunting with the wind knocked out of him. His head came to rest on the beanbag chair, his eyes wide while trying to suck air back into his aching lungs.

Michael held onto Jessica as the Javelin stepped through the doors, pushing his semi-automatic pistol into Michael's face.

USS Intrepid

"What's happening!" Jasmine screamed, shaking the phone at Sam Cholan and the SEAL commander to do something. "What's happening!"

Katie and Evelyn watched Jasmine's tantrum with horror. She was scaring them. Cholan grabbed the phone and listened.

Villa

"On your feet," the Javelin ordered. He was calm, exuding a complete sense of control and confidence in his ability to make one suffer if his order not heeded.

Michael stared at the gun. He knew the man pressing the automatic to his forehead was the one responsible for Milt's death. But all he could think about was dying. He rose to his feet, his knees nearly giving out from under him. The assassin grabbed Jessica out of his arms and sent her reeling to the sectional, her scream ricocheting around the vaulted living room. Jake Munroe casually stepped inside, toe to toe with Michael. "You," he said slowly, barely above a whisper, "should tell me where he is." Munroe could see Michael's commingled anger and fear, enjoyed it. "Where is he, Michael?"

"Hello, Jake," Larry answered for Michael from the loft above.

Munroe smiled up at the former E-Special, Security Service officer. "Hello, Larry." He pressed his .45 at Michael's forehead. "It must be what, over forty years. But I finally got you, you sonofabitch. Now get down here."

USS Intrepid

Katie clung to Evelyn. "Mom!"

Jasmine was in a fit, pushing against Sam Cholan. He got her into a chair, told her to calm down. Katie dove for her mother's side. Cholan ordered the first mate to summon the chief medical officer – he needed order on the bridge - then he grabbed the phone off the deck. He recognized the voice he heard ordering Grant to keep his ass on the floor; a voice he conversed with from his Langley office through undocumented calls to the Red Center of Australia's Northern Territory. He snapped his fingers at the SEAL commander. "The Javelin's in the house." He turned to the Captain at the helm. "Get us within range. Now!"

"Bring us about 2-4-5 degrees," the Captain ordered and his crew responded with military quickness. "Get the rubbers in the water."

"Yes, sir."

The chief medical officer stepped onto the bridge. It would be the second time Jasmine had swallowed pills since being brought aboard.

CHAPTER 74

The Place where Karma Kills You

Villa

Jake Munroe glared at Michael. "So, I'll take that tape now."

"We don't have it," Michael said.

Munroe flashed a wicked smile and nodded at the Javelin. The assassin produced a wallet sized photograph. Michael swallowed hard. It was Katie; the same picture he gave Maggie back at the CN Tower the day she died.

"So you kill old women, too," Michael said. The Javelin had no response. Munroe took the picture out of his assassin's hand.

"Pretty girl," he said. "You should be proud. And maybe a little more fucking cooperative, Mr. Spencer."

"We don't have the tape, Munroe," Larry said. "Garva died before we could get it."

"Oh, okay," Munroe sneered then nodded at Jessica. "Kill her."

The Javelin put his gun to Jessica's head. Nolan instantly reacted, lunging to tackle the assassin, but the Javelin careened around easily, driving Nolan to the floor, followed by a quick and sure fist to the face.

Munroe staggered back, his reaction slowed by age, just enough for Michael to seize him around the neck. Munroe collapsed backwards, falling on top of Michael, his .45 still in hand. Reflex squeezed the trigger and a misfired round shot into the vaulted ceiling.

Jessica screamed as Nolan recovered, kicking the Javelin's gun from his hand. Larry jumped from the couch and kicked it away, sending it spinning under the beanbag chair, then went to save his son.

But Munroe saw him coming and the .45 discharged again. Only this time the bullet caught Larry in the upper chest, knocking him backward over the Javelin, justly knocking him off Nolan, who with unsurpassed agility, sprang to his feet.

Larry fell head first into that stupid beanbag chair, his right hand inadvertently slipping underneath. He felt the gun brush his fingertips and instinctively went to seize it, but the wound in his shoulder burned as if a soldering iron had penetrated. He cursed, helpless to watch Michael and Munroe scuffle in a life or death battle. The Javelin roundhouse kicked Nolan into the wall. Jessica screamed again, tucking herself into the corner, wishing it would stop.

"Michael!" Larry yelled as Munroe rolled over and with one properly placed pistol whip, rendering Michael unconscious. Munroe was out of breath, but gratified seeing Nolan was no match against the experienced mercenary. A snap punch to the nose and the blood was thick and red and ran down the Mountie's chin like spilled paint. Jessica screamed again.

"Finish him!" Munroe ordered. Nolan was barely standing when the final roundhouse connected, catapulting him into the patio doors with enough force to shatter the glass and send him spiralling outside.

Jessica was utterly terrified that she had just witnessed Nolan's death. The Javelin went to step through the smashed doors and finish off his opponent when he remembered his weapon under the beanbag chair. As he turned, Jessica bolted with everything she had for the beach, for her life.

"Get that bitch," Munroe commanded.

The assassin hustled after her.

Munroe struggled and groaned to his feet and eyed Larry splayed out against the beanbag chair, the man he had waited a lifetime to kill. He picked his .45 off the floor, cocked the hammer back. Michael came too, moaned on the floor behind him. Just beyond the beachfront entrance Nolan Grant laid motionless, the sand around him polluted with glass shards and blood. There was no one to stop Munroe now.

Larry winced from his burning shoulder, yet managed to move his hand slightly, the motion hidden under the beanbag chair.

"I've waited a long time for this," Munroe snickered, raising the .45 till the barrel aimed right at Larry's eyes. "Time to finally fucking die, Hicks."

Larry smiled. "Bye asshole."

A shot rang out.

USS Intrepid

"Who fired the shot!" Cholan shouted at Seaman Berger.

Berger was wearing his headsets, his concentration locked on the thermal images on the screen above. The two of them watched a white figure stagger and drop to the floor of the villa. The figure was dying.

Cholan snapped the radio handset from the control panel. "Base to

Alpha! Base to Alpha!"

"This is Alpha, over," the SEAL commander responded over the speaker system.

"Take the target!"

Villa

Michael was shocked and horrified. He had thought he had just witnessed his birth father being murdered right in front of him. But Larry's cold gaze remained fixed on Jake Munroe. There was no report ringing between the wood floor and high ceiling. The silencer in addition to the muffling only permitted a pop to be heard as the bullet exploded out of the purple beanbag chair.

Munroe gasped, coughed gobs of blood. The .45 slipped out of his dying fingers and dropped to the floor. He seemed utterly surprised to be hit. In his disbelief he glanced at the bloody hole over his heart then slumped to his knees with a thud. How ironic that Hicks would be the last person he would see. He clutched his chest, gasped a final breath, and crumpled to the floor.

Larry could only stare at Munroe dead. It was finally over.

"Larry?" Michael pushed himself up. There was genuine worry and relief until they heard Jessica's guttural scream beyond the shattered patio doors.

"It's not over," Larry said, reaching for help up. Michael got him to his feet. They heard Jessica scream for help this time. Michael went to run, but Larry grabbed him with his good arm, pointing at Munroe's .45 on the floor.

Michael snapped it up and ran through the broken doors, running full out till he was on the beach. The Caribbean horizon was broken by the outline of a military ship, cruising in about a mile beyond the bay.

Another scream in the distance! He saw Jessica desperately kicking at the Javelin way down the beach, the assassin easily backhanding her to the sand.

"Jessica!" Michael yelled. She was too far away. He wouldn't get to her in time.

~

Jessica's cheekbone felt like it exploded inside her face. "Please," she begged.

The Javelin knelt to finish her off but stopped, looked beyond the surf and saw the black Zodiacs skipping over the waves for the beach. Time had run out. He clutched her hair, ripped a large commando knife from its sheath, the serrated blade refracting sunlight as he raised it high over his head.

Then he hesitated. He heard Michael Spencer yelling over the breakers, running full out towards them. He had a gun in his hand. The Javelin eyed the woman, tightened on the blade. But then out of nowhere he saw the cop diving at him at the last minute. In a movement quicker than a blink, he tucked and twisted to effectively flip him over, leaving Nolan gasping for air knocked out of him yet again.

Jessica screamed when the Javelin gripped the knife with both hands to plunge it deep into the cop's heart.

"Stop!" Michael yelled, the .45 aimed. The Javelin stopped, slowly rose like a menacing killer unaffected by a gun in a trembling hand. "I swear I'll kill you, you sonofabitch."

The Javelin lunged and swiped the blade at Michael's neck. Jessica screamed. Michael squeezed the trigger. The gun only clicked. It was empty!!

"Michael!" Nolan yelled, went to roll over.

A slash barely missed Michael's midsection. Another. He tried to back away but couldn't back-peddle fast enough. The Javelin rushed him, the blade raised to kill. Nolan sprang to his feet, going for the tackle but then...

A volley shattered the air. Everyone froze.

The assassin was hit. He staggered around to see the shooter standing under the coconut palms that lined the beach.

"Where did you come from?" he muttered with a typical Midwest accent then dropped to his knees.

Michael couldn't believe it. Floyd Webber kept his gun trained on the assassin bleeding in the sand. He saw the Zodiac's approaching two hundred yards off the beach, automatic rifles hoisted to sharpshooter's shoulders. Webber knew Sam Cholan and his SEALs would harbor no intentions of taking their contracted mercenary alive.

The Javelin saw them too. The Zodiacs slowed. The shooters tightened their aim.

"Down," Nolan yelled, pushing Jessica to the sand, covering her. Michael dropped, arms over his head as the salvo from the Zodiacs gunned down the assassin. Jessica screamed under Nolan hiding her face from the execution.

The Javelin convulsed from bullets riddling his chest. Blood exploded out of him in a crimson spray and the assassin was dead before his corpse hit the surf.

When the shooting stopped Jessica's screams turned to crying, burying her face into Nolan's chest.

Michael and Nolan checked each other. They were okay.

Webber stood over the body. He smirked at Michael who was sitting on his butt in the sand with a nasty gash across his face and forehead. "You okay?"

"I'm okay."

If Michael was surprised with Webber suddenly popping out of the palm trees a few thousand miles from their home, he said nothing about it. Jessica was still crying. The three men simply watched the Zodiacs slide up onto the beach.

~

Like a well-oiled covert ops unit, the SEALS went to work cleaning the scene, stuffing the dead assassin into a black bag. Nolan and Michael looked on as only they could knowing that regardless of how bloody the end was for the killer they now knew to be called the Javelin, nothing would bring back Milt. He was gone forever and now, after it was all over, it would hit them; they would mourn and it would be long and painful and never quite heal.

The SEAL commander introduced himself to the SSET chief, congratulating him on stopping the piece of shit that was now zipped in the body bag and out of sight.

And just like that it was as if it had never happened. The assassin's identity would be erased, reports and top secret files detailing his deadly work for the agency would find the incinerator, probably before the Zodiacs even hit the water back to their ship.

"Where's the other one?" the commander asked them all. "The one the Mountie's want?"

Michael pointed to the villa where a second SEAL team with the black bag carrying Jake Munroe's body just stepped through the shattered patio window. Another SEAL stepped out into the warm, Caribbean sun, waving frantically for medical help inside.

"Larry!" Michael ran for the villa.

CHAPTER 75

The One Who Knew Everything

Ottawa

It had been several hours since he made the last call. And to kill time and contemplate his fate, he blended in with midday shoppers milling around Rideau Center, browsing the men's section in Eaton's for casual clothes and changing right in the retailer's fitting rooms, depositing his uniform in the garbage on his way to the transit turnaround on Elgin. He changed buses two or three times as he zigzagged all over downtown Ottawa in an attempt to elude the Mounties he was sure had tailed him this morning. Since the explosion in BC there was not one member of the Prime Minister's personal staff exonerated of suspicion. But he didn't deserve scrutiny. He deserved sympathy for he was an unwilling participant, simply a witness because of the boss he piously served.

He stood by a phone booth in Castle Heights along McArthur Avenue, a few blocks from a casual girlfriend's, and stared at the phone number he had scribbled on the back of an envelope. The envelope had the House of Commons seal on the back flap. There were always a few in the glove compartment of the Prime Minister's limousine.

He watched the traffic and the pedestrians proceed by the phone booth. To him they were the naive status quo unaware he was about to bring down their Prime Minister; the candidate they voted to run their country; the crooked politician who would not be running in the federal election after today.

His eyes swept over the newspaper dispenser beside the phone booth. The front page of the Ottawa Citizen mesmerized him just like it did when he stared at it back in his girlfriend's apartment. A portrait of Roy Graham, his lovely wife Meredith and their daughter Rachel with the banner headline 'Murdered'. He felt responsible. A young girl died because he kept secrets. And for his loyalty he received money and benefits and more holidays. None of it mattered now. Once he spilled what he knew to the reporter, not even the Prime Minister himself could control the outcome. Graham's assassination changed everything; and it would definitely change Ottawa in the coming months.

Marty knew a lot. And now it was time to hand over what he knew.

He punched the number for the Ottawa Sheraton Hotel. The call was answered as if the person on the other end had been hovering in anticipation of his call.

"Hello," an eager voice answered.

"It's me."

"I was beginning to think you weren't going to call," Lance Nuewerth said.

CHAPTER 76

The Nice & Neat

Villa

"I've never been shot before," Larry mumbled. He was on the floor in the villa, grimacing from the pressure Michael was applying to his shoulder. The SEAL commander radioed the Intrepid for the chief medical officer stat. Five minutes later Sam Cholan and the MO were aboard a Zodiac, skipping wave tops for the beach, passing the two SEAL skiffs racing back to the Intrepid with their black body bags.

Michael kept pressure on Larry's wound until the MO arrived and took over. Jessica had been given a healthy dose of Valium, thanking Cholan and the SEAL commander for rescuing them in the nick of time.

Michael joined Nolan on the couch while he was getting his nose bandaged. They both were thinking about Milt. "He would've said something stupid right about now," Nolan said with a quip. "Something to make us laugh."

"Nah," Michael said, his steel blues welling up. "He'd wanna eat."

Sam Cholan ordered an ensign to check on the ETA of the air ambulance to transport Larry to St. Margret's Hospital in Nassau. They couldn't treat Larry's wounds aboard the Intrepid – something to do with the fact that Cholan and the Seals would have to post haste their asses but fast the hell out of the area to avoid any awkward Senate Subcommittee questions; what happened on the beach never actually happened on the beach. Cholan knelt to Larry with a sympathetic hand on his good shoulder. "Sorry we can't do more, Larry."

"That's okay, Sam. I understand."

Cholan looked to Michael. "He's one tough SOB this one." He rose, stopped before the shattered patio window. "By the way Braden got Morelatto, Larry. Thought you'd want to know."

"Hey!" an ensign said urgently, sticking his head just inside the broken glass doors. "There's a local down out here. I think he's a cabbie."

Cholan turned to the MO with a look that gave the order for him to check on the islander. The medical officer promptly left with the ensign.

"My family?" Michael asked Cholan who pointed beyond the beach at a loaded Zodiac racing towards the villa. Michael wasn't sure why he said it, but he did. "Thank you."

Sam Cholan smiled. "You're the one who needs to be thanked, Mr. Spencer. I'm just glad we were able to help." Before Cholan left, he nodded to Floyd Webber – the kind of acknowledgement one spy gives to another for a job well done. The Chief was sitting in the purple beanbag chair. A nod was all that was returned.

Webber stepped to Michael with a Gina Norris novel in his hands and pointed at the arriving Zodiac with a literary celebrity aboard. "I'm hoping she'll autograph it," he said to Michael. "Whad'ya think? My wife reads this damn stuff like it's going out of style."

Michael was amused. It was something he didn't want to admit too, but on some level he liked Webber. Wasn't sure why, just did. Maybe because he knew it came back to him.

Webber pointed at the gash. "How's the face?"

"Okay."

"Good. Good. Well, don't sit on your ass in the sand too long." The grin spread across the tough face. "It'll make you soft." He looked down at Larry, could see he was in pain, the gauze a glowing crimson. "Stay out of trouble, you old dog." Larry extended his good hand. Floyd clamped it in his; years of brotherhood between them. "Don't get all mushy now, Larry."

Larry smiled. "Not a chance you hard ass." They both laughed. "Thanks, Floyd."

"No need to thank me..,Mr. Norris." They all smiled and the intrepid Floyd Webber bid his last good-bye and sauntered across the beach to the Zodiac that had just deposited Michael's family. He hugged Evelyn like an old friend then climbed into the Zodiac and sped off for the ship in the distance. Michael was frozen where he stood – there was his birth mother! He was suddenly overcome.

"Just tell her what you told me, Michael," Larry said. His eyes were wet. "That's all you need to say."

Michael felt his palms sweat, took a deep breath, and walked across the sand to meet the woman who gave him life.

CHAPTER 77

The Full Circle

    Evelyn Hicks had grown up like any other little girl during the '60s and '70s. She and Maggie were inseparable sisters who'd comb each other's hair and dream of the strapping men they would marry and the children they would have. But, alas, life could be cruel. It was a sad parody to realize the future would only present one child between them, and that child would be regrettably surrendered. Gone were diaper changes, baby's first steps, smiles and words. The temper tantrums, the first foray into running away, when the child only made it around the block when they realized they strayed too far from safety. All part of the periodic episodes of rebellion and insolence parents lament. Sports, fights, mud from head to toe in spring and fall and frozen toes from skating on the outdoor rinks too long in February. That first love along with the dates, dances, and tip toeing in the house drunk and way past curfew. The day dad and son head out to buy that first car. Long hair and rock music thumping from the bedroom with enough thunder to shake pictures from the wall and drive parents mad. A wedding day and the opportunity to tell a bride as enchanting as Jasmine how proud she felt to finally have a daughter-in-law. Rejoicing when Jasmine would've handed her Katie, a granddaughter.
    These were all the moments Evelyn Hicks had bestowed to the Spencers. And now, as her son walked across the beach towards her, all she could think about was that cold night New Year's Eve 1981, her beautiful baby boy swaddled in wraps, crying to be nursed by his mother. He was without a doubt the most beautiful thing she had ever seen. It had all been wrong. Fate had been brutally unfair.
    But now nothing mattered. She let it all go and took a bold step towards a reunion. They stood there a moment, on the beach bordering the Caribbean, warm breeze tingling every pore and nerve. She studied every feature on his perfect face, regardless of the nasty gash that deepened

her guilt and remorse for all he had been forced to endure. Nonetheless, he was Larry all those years ago. Her son. Her baby. The instant he touched her shoulder and smiled, tears dripped down her cheeks.

Evelyn Hicks held her son and for the second time in his life, kissed his forehead and told him she loved him.

They hugged then laughed, virtual strangers with this inseparable bond.

"So," Michael said between sniffles. "Got any plans for New Years'?"

Evelyn's face flushed, her eyes floating with a plethora of emotion. She clasped his hand tightly and said, "I do now."

She embraced him again and soaked in every hug she had ever surrendered.

CSIS headquarters

"Thanks, Edwin," MacDuff said quietly and hung up. He turned for his patriotic view, more tainted than he cared to admit tonight.

"So..?" McIvor asked, seated in the chair with his tie loosened. It had been a long day.

"Larry is at St. Margret's Hospital in Nassau," MacDuff said. "He's fine." He sank into his unremarkable chair.

"And Webber?"

"He'll be back home in a few hours."

McIvor sighed. There was a more pressing question. "And the Bahamas? How much mess?"

The red eyebrows scrunched. "The area was swept. No one even knows we were there."

McIvor rose out of his chair, stepped to the window and that patriot's view. "A reporter does."

CHAPTER 78

The Call Home

The view overlooking Nassau at night and the liquid moon that trickled over the Caribbean like fresh cream was soothing. Michael wasn't sure what time it was. The wee hours of the morning, three maybe four o'clock, it really didn't matter. He sat there in the chair, looking out the hospital window painted with the early etchings of a tropical twilight, feeling good about being alive.

Alive.

He had placed a call to John Lund earlier. The story was on the front-page, tantamount to every other newspaper and six o'clock broadcast throughout the country they figured. He hoped that would give Claudette and the kids some peace – yet that seemed unlikely.

Yet, despite everything that had happened since Jessica gave him his adoption file back at the ice cube on Portage Avenue, there was a calm now. It happened the moment he met Evelyn on the beach. After forty years, for reasons that would probably never make complete sense or reason, he knew unequivocally who he was the moment he met his birth mother. Or perhaps he always had. Yet maybe there was something to be said for predisposition, and even though he had been raised, and was in every sense Olie Spencer's son, he had noticed similarities in Larry and himself over the time they had been together - despite his wanting to ignore such inherent characteristics - that could not be dismissed.

He looked at Evelyn. She had fallen into a deep sleep in a cot that had been sequestered for her at Jasmine's insistence. Then Jasmine and Katie, Nolan and Jessica had been whisked off to a nearby hotel ten miles down the coastline; a gratuity extended to them on behalf of Edwin Newhart and the CIA with the assurance a private jet would fly them home in the morning. But Michael chose to stay.

Larry had yet to stir after being wheeled out of the operating room but in that time Michael and Evelyn talked and got to know each other. She wanted to know everything. He rambled through adolescence, journalism and marriage. They talked of Milt and Maggie and the Atkinsons. She talked of her first romance novel, coping with self-imposed exile, and how the Gina Norris novels kept them from going broke. Eventually she got around to asking about his mom. Katie spoke of her often, missed her terribly, she had said. "Jasmine told me about her cancer," Evelyn said gently. "I would have liked to have met her."

Michael reached into his pocket as he rose out of his chair. Evelyn was awestruck when he placed the letter from his mom in her hand. "This is for you," he said – his promise fulfilled. She opened it, her hand easing over her mouth as she read.

~

An hour later, Michael slipped out of the austere room on the fourth floor of St. Margret's Hospital atop the hill overlooking Nassau Harbor and found the payphones in a waiting room at the end of the hall. He sat down on the old couch. It, like everything else about St. Margret's, was old and weathered by time. The LCD TV hanging on the wall seemed out of place. Michael had the phone in his hand when he saw the Prime Minister on CNN Live, being led out of 24 Sussex Drive by an RCMP brigade, press crushing in on him asking about his part in the assassination of Premier Roy Graham. And then the newscast showed the PM's chauffeur, some guy named Marty, talking to the microphones. Michael grabbed the remote on the couch, clicked the TV off. He'd had enough of all that. He plugged his finger in the rotary dial. It took a minute for the connection to complete. While he waited his eyes swept over the assorted issues of Pride, Time, and Life magazines strewn over the coffee table. The phone rang. "The Hula Hut," a man answered. Mingling voices and rumbling ocean surf drowned ukulele guitar in the background. Michael rubbed his sore eyes. He had truly come full circle. But nothing ever seemed real or complete somehow until he sat down and talked to his dad about it.

"Olie Spencer, please." Michael said, smiled when he heard the bartender call his Dad. His fingers tightened around the phone. The swell was rising in his eyes. He couldn't remember the last time he had missed him as much as he did right at that moment. Hawaii seemed too far away. He could hear the phone being passed from one hand to the next, his Dad asking the bartender if it was his son. Michael wiped a tear.

"Michael!" the voice that comforted him his whole life washed through him like a wave.

"Hi, Dad."

Manufactured by Amazon.ca
Bolton, ON